D0962430

Lisa Jackson is a #1 *New York Times* bestselling author of more than eighty-five books, including romantic suspense, thrillers, and contemporary and historical romances. She is a recipient of the *RT Book Reviews* Reviewers' Choice Award and has also been honored with their Career Achievement Award for Romantic Suspense. Born in Oregon, she continues to make her home among family, friends and dogs in the Pacific Northwest. Visit her at lisajackson.com.

Delores Fossen, a *USA TODAY* bestselling author, has sold over seventy-five novels, with millions of copies of her books in print worldwide. She's received a Booksellers' Best Award and an RT Reviewers' Choice Best Book Award. She was also a finalist for a prestigious RITA® Award. You can contact the author through her website at deloresfossen.com.

#1 *New York Times* Bestselling Author

LISA JACKSON

STRANGER ON THE ISLAND

Previously published as *Mystery Man*

**HARLEQUIN
BESTSELLING
AUTHOR
COLLECTION**

**HARLEQUIN®
BESTSELLING
AUTHOR
COLLECTION**

Recycling programs
for this product may
not exist in your area.

ISBN-13: 978-1-335-49834-2

Stranger on the Island
First published as Mystery Man in 1991. This edition published in 2022.
Copyright © 1991 by Lisa Jackson

Secret Delivery
First published in 2009. This edition published in 2022.
Copyright © 2009 by Delores Fossen

For questions and comments about the quality of this book, please contact us at CustomerService@Harlequin.com.

Harlequin Enterprises ULC
22 Adelaide St. West, 41st Floor
Toronto, Ontario M5H 4E3, Canada
www.Harlequin.com

Printed in U.S.A.

CONTENTS

STRANGER ON THE ISLAND

Lisa Jackson

Chapter 1

"I think I've found your man."

Chelsea Reed froze. She glanced up sharply from the jewelry counter where she'd been taking inventory. "Devlin?" she asked, focusing on the short man with unremarkable features and small eyes. Adrenaline surged through her. "He's alive?"

Ned Jenkins tapped the countertop with his blunt fingers and a smug smile played on his lips. He was one of the best private investigators in the Bay Area, and Chelsea had hired him three months before to find Devlin McVey. Now, surrounded by silk dresses, brilliant scarves and designer handbags in the boutique, Jenkins looked like the proverbial fish out of water.

"I'd bet money on it," he said, seeming satisfied with himself.

"Where is he?"

Jenkins snorted. "The Caribbean. Looks like he wanted to disappear, but good."

"The Caribbean..." Chelsea swallowed against a suddenly dry throat. Her fingers gripped the counter. So Devlin, damn him, had run away, leaving her alone to deal with her grief.

Memories—some wonderful, some filled with pain—swam before her eyes. Her heart began to knock in her chest. She glanced quickly around the three connecting rooms of the old converted row house. A few customers browsed lazily through the racks and Melissa, a salesgirl for the boutique, was standing in the front window display case, pinning a bright pink belt around the slim waist of a mannequin.

"Melissa—can you hold down the fort a few minutes?" Chelsea asked unsteadily. She could barely concentrate on anything other than the fact that Devlin McVey was alive. Now he had a lot to answer for.

"Will do," Melissa said around a mouthful of pins.

"Sally will be back shortly and Carrie will be in at four. If you need me, I'll be in the kitchen." Her knees threatened to buckle though she'd waited for this day for over a year.

"Got it," Melissa replied, making an "okay" sign with her fingers and thumb.

Chelsea turned back to the small investigator. "Let's go into the back room where we'll have a little more privacy."

He shrugged. "Wherever you want."

He followed her through a door behind the counter and down a short hall to the kitchen of the old house. To keep her hands occupied Chelsea poured them each a cup of lukewarm coffee, then motioned for Jenkins to sit at a chipped formica-topped table.

"Okay," she said, finding her voice. "Let's start over. Where exactly is he?"

"On an obscure island called Paradis. Believe me, this place is off the beaten path."

Her fingers clamped around her cup. "And you've seen him—you're sure it's Devlin?"

For an answer he snapped open a battered old briefcase, pulled out a manila envelope and dumped the contents of the packet onto the table. There were several snapshots and a large, glossy eight-by-ten color photo which he slid across the table. "Unless I miss my guess, this man is McVey."

Chelsea picked up the photograph, heart racing at the sight of a handsome, roguish-looking man with tanned skin, bladed cheekbones and unruly black hair that brushed across the collar of his faded denim jacket. His eyes were hidden by mirrored aviator sunglasses, his jaw disguised by a dark beard. He was grimacing and he looked tough and hard. "I don't know," she said quietly, remembering Devlin as he had been—dark and sensual, with a hard edge that hinted of danger. This man could be him, but then again…

"Well, he's changed his looks, of course. People usually do when they want to get lost," Jenkins said, leaning forward and tossing another picture, a photograph of Devlin taken six months before the accident, onto the table. "But check out his cheekbones—hmm? And the way his hair parts a little off-center? And his nose—" he pointed to the larger photograph, then to the small snapshot "—compare them. Identical. Looks as if that nose was broken somewhere along the line—maybe more than once."

"Several times," she thought aloud. There was a similarity in the two pictures; she too, could see it. Her pulse started to pick up speed but she willed herself to remain calm. Even if this man did prove to be Devlin, there were still so many unanswered questions. She studied the photograph as the minutes ticked by. Yes, the man could be Devlin, but she wasn't sure… "I'd feel better about this if I could see his eyes."

"I know." Jenkins gave a snort of disgust, as if he wasn't used to being outfoxed by his quarry. "The only time he took off those damned glasses was in the café and it was too dark to get a shot."

"What color?"

"Pardon?" Jenkins's reddish brows inched upward.

"His eyes. What color?"

"Oh. Blue—intense—piercing," the investigator replied with a frown of dislike. "Kind of creepy, the way he stares at you. His eyes are the first thing you notice about him."

"Yes," she agreed, remembering the force of Devlin's gaze. "Did you speak with him?"

Jenkins shook his head. "Nope. Didn't want to tip my hand." His mouth drew into a defensive frown. "You did say you wanted him located but not confronted."

"Yes, that's right," she assured him. "But I want to know everything there is to know about this man."

"Mitch Russell. That's the name he goes by." Jenkins sipped from his cup and scowled. "I did a little poking around and found out that he claims to be from Chicago, just one more disillusioned American looking for the good life in a tropical paradise. It's crazy, if you ask me. Why would anyone want to leave the U.S. of A?"

Good question, Chelsea thought, but kept her face noncommittal. Why indeed? Unless he was hiding something. Her heart wrenched a little. "Tell me about—what did you call the island? Paradise?"

"Paradis. It's French for paradise, located about thirty miles southwest of St. Jean in the Caribbean. The only way to get to it is by boat or hydroplane." He waved impatiently. "There was a landing strip once, but it's overgrown and no one uses it anymore."

Narrowing her eyes, she examined the photograph again and the more she studied it, the more she was certain Jenkins was right. The man in the picture was Devlin! She'd found him, at last! She couldn't help but smile as she envisioned confronting him. What would he say? What *could* he?

"Did you find out anything else?" she asked, and Ned Jenkins grinned, a wide, toothy smile that made her uncomfortable.

"Here's the report." He reached into his shabby briefcase again and tossed a buff-colored file onto the table. "Not a whole lot in it. I didn't ask too many questions because I didn't want Russell to know I was on to him." He gave her a wink. "You said to keep this low-key and I always aim to please."

"Good." She skimmed the report and frowned. The typed pages didn't give her much more information than Jenkins had already told her. Seeing the bill tacked onto the last page, she reached into her purse, withdrew her wallet and wrote Ned Jenkins a check for services rendered. "Just tell me one more thing," she said, handing him payment.

"Shoot." Jenkins eyed the figures she'd written, nodded to himself and tucked the check into the inside pocket of his jacket.

"How did you find Devlin?"

Jenkins's blue eyes sparked. "I hate to admit it, but I got lucky. That happens sometimes. No one around here knew from nothing and even my friends down at the San Francisco Police Department weren't any help. Everyone acted like he really did bite it in the boat accident. But I checked back with the airlines and flashed his picture around. Eventually a stewardess on a cross-country flight recognized him—or thought she did. Even then, he looked a little different from the pictures I had, he was starting to grow a beard, but she was sure it was our guy. There seems to be something about Mr. McVey that the ladies remember."

Chelsea didn't comment—she didn't want to think about the raw sexuality that was as much a part of Devlin McVey as the badge he wore, or had worn, for the SFPD. Nor did she want to think of the string of beautiful women who had fallen in love with him in the past few years. After all, she wasn't interested in his love life, or his sexual charms, she told herself. She only wanted to find out why he had disappeared and what had happened in the accident—the accident from which Devlin had disappeared and that had taken her fiancé's life. Her heart wrenched a little at the thought of John. If only she knew why Devlin had been so insistent that John meet with him that day. What was so all-fired important that they had to talk privately on Devlin's boat in the middle of a storm?

Jenkins scraped back his chair. "Is there anything else I can do for you?"

"Yes," she said impulsively. "I'm going to have to go to Paradis. While I'm gone, I want you to keep poking around. See if anything surfaces around here."

"It hasn't for over a year," he speculated.

"I know, but it's always possible."

"Okay, I'll nose around. Maybe I can find someone at SFPD who's willing to talk. And if you change your mind, and want your friend back on American soil, just let me know. McVey wouldn't be the first man I tracked down and brought back home."

"No, thanks. I think I'll handle this my way."

Jenkins paused, his brow furrowing. "There's something I don't understand about this. You were planning to marry McVey's best friend, the guy who drowned in the accident, right?"

Chelsea swallowed hard. Grief stole into her heart. John Stern's death was still hard to accept. "Yes."

"So why all the interest in McVey?"

Chelsea had a ready answer for a question she'd asked herself a million times. "Because Devlin was John's best friend and he was supposedly killed, as well. I never believed it. And this—" she tapped on the large photo of Devlin "—proves I'm right. I think he might know something about John's death—something that hasn't come out in the police reports."

"Stern's death was ruled an accident."

"I know, but I'm not convinced."

Jenkins eyed her and rubbed the back of his neck thoughtfully. "Listen, I'm going to give you some free advice."

As if she hadn't heard enough from everyone on the planet, she thought.

Jenkins rambled on. "Drop this thing. If your fiancé died in an accident, it's over. If there was something else involved, let the police handle it."

"I just want to know why Devlin disappeared," Chelsea replied. And why John died.

"He might have his reasons. Some people who vanish like it that way."

Too bad, Chelsea thought, catching a glimpse of the bearded man in the picture. If this man were truly Devlin—and she had begun to believe he was—he had a lot to answer for.

Jenkins reached for the door handle just as Chelsea's partner, Sally Bedford, flew into the room, nearly running him over.

"Sorry," she said automatically, then spied Chelsea in the chair. "Oh, God, Chels, I didn't mean to interrupt." Sally was immediately contrite. Her kinky blond hair glistened with raindrops and the shoulders of her raincoat were damp. "It's a downpour out there! I'm soaked to the skin." She shook some of the rain from her hair. "Can you believe it—it's nearly June and we're having a rainstorm that won't quit!"

"It's okay, we're through here."

"Good, because I just dashed through the shop and the floor's crawling—and I mean crawling—with customers." Her boots squished as she walked to a small closet and hung up her coat.

"I'll take care of the customers," Chelsea replied with a quick grin. "You dry off."

"Hey—what's this?" Sally looked at the photographs scattered across the table and her perky face fell. "Oh, no, Chelsea, you're not still trying to find Devlin, are you? Can't you face the fact that he's gone? He and John both?"

Chelsea didn't bother to respond. She gathered up the photographs and stuffed them into Jenkins's manila envelope. "We'll talk about this later," she said over her shoulder as she tucked the envelope into her oversized bag, then shepherded Ned Jenkins back through the store.

Sally was right on one count. The floor was a madhouse. Melissa was busy with two women vying for the latest creation by Marcel De Vasia. Three teenage girls fingered the hand-painted jewelry. A harried young woman was trying on hats and another woman in her twenties was eyeing a fuchsia jumpsuit.

Chelsea helped three customers choose accessories to go with the dresses they'd picked out while Carrie manned the shoe department. Melissa sold two De Vasia originals and managed to keep both women happy.

Two more customers strolled in and Sally, revived, emerged from the back room with a ready smile. She sold the jumpsuit and two raincoats within fifteen minutes.

As the afternoon wore on the crowd thinned.

It was well after seven when the last customer, laden with a package containing a silver belt, peach scarf and two pairs of slacks, finally walked out the front door of the store. Sally turned the bolt, lowered a Closed sign, and, sagging against the door, whispered, "Another day at the zoo!"

"Amen." Chelsea straightened the racks while Sally headed for the till to balance out for the day.

Carrie and Melissa had already taken off and the shop, aside from the soft notes of jazz drifting from hidden speakers, was quiet. Chelsea slid out of her pumps.

As Sally added the checks and cash, she grinned, showing off deep dimples. "Well, at least it was a profitable day at the zoo."

"That's good."

"No, that's great," Sally said, slamming the till shut.

Sally and Chelsea had been friends since college and had opened this shop four years before. Located near Ghirardelli Square, the boutique had grown and flourished, become chic and popular enough to expand until it now filled the entire first floor of the old remodeled house. Sally was talking of opening another store, either in Union Square or out of the city entirely in Sonoma, but Chelsea hadn't been able to work up the necessary enthusiasm.

In fact, she could hardly think past the accident that had taken her fiancé's life.

"I don't suppose this is a good time to tell you that I'm going to need a few weeks off," Chelsea said as she snapped out the lights.

Sally sighed. "Come on—let's talk." Stuffing the receipts for the day into the bank bag she would drop into the night depository on the way home, she added, "I'll buy you a cup of coffee."

"You're on."

The kitchen had grown dark with the evening. Chelsea flipped on the overhead fixture and Sally grabbed the handle of the glass coffeepot.

Wrinkling her little nose, she swished the dregs of brown liquid down the drain. As she started a fresh pot, she glanced over her shoulder at Chelsea. "Okay," she said, "so now it's later. Out with it. You think you've found Devlin, is that it?"

"I'm not sure," Chelsea admitted, dropping into a chair and retrieving the envelope with Jenkins's photographs from her purse. "But I have to find out."

"Why?"

"Because there are so many questions that don't have any answers," she replied quickly.

Shaking her head, Sally scrounged in a cupboard for sugar substitute, then waited as coffee began to drizzle into the pot. "Devlin and John are dead," she said quietly, "we both know that."

Chelsea whispered, "Devlin's body never washed up."

"That's not unusual. San Francisco Bay is a major piece of water, you know. And there was a storm that day. They were crazy to be out there. Anyway, Devlin's body could have been washed out to sea."

"I don't believe it. I won't." Chelsea looked at her friend as Sally poured them each a cup of fresh coffee. "Devlin was a cop—he always landed on his feet. I just can't believe he's dead."

"Can't believe it—or won't believe it?" Her lips drawing into a thoughtful frown, Sally dropped into the chair across from Chelsea. "It does happen, you know."

Chelsea didn't answer, just swallowed a mouthful of hot coffee.

But Sally didn't give up. She propped her chin on one hand, and studied the pictures spread across the table. "This guy—he's supposed to be Devlin?" she asked, pointing to the image of the man with the heavy beard.

"Yes."

"How can you tell?"

"I just feel it."

Sally's lips pursed. "He could be anyone with that beard." Her blond brows pulled into a tight knot as she glanced up at Chelsea. "Look, I know how you feel—"

"Do you?" Chelsea flung out, her frustration of the past year surfacing. "I don't think so. I don't know if anyone does."

"Maybe not, but you've been through a terrible loss."

Chelsea's throat closed. The boating accident and storm had been unexpected. John and Devlin had left her at the docks. She could still remember John, squeezing her, whispering that he loved her. She'd clung to him, her dark hair blowing across her face, her gaze, as she looked past John's shoulder, landing squarely in Devlin's mocking blue eyes. The air was heavy and gusty and filled with the tangy salt-sea scent. She'd felt a premonition then—a tiny trickle of fear that had dripped into her heart.

"It's not easy to lose someone you love," Sally was saying, adding sweetener to her cup and stirring slowly.

Chelsea thrust up her chin. "I know you and the rest of the world don't approve. I also know you think I'm on some wild goose chase. But believe me, finding Devlin is something I have to do. I have to find out what happened to John."

"Or what happened to Devlin?"

"Both!"

"What if this man isn't Devlin?" Sally asked, holding up the eight-by-ten and staring at the print. "Will you give up? Or will you go on searching—clinging to a dream that Devlin's alive somewhere and, once you find him, will give you all the answers you're looking for?"

"I don't know."

"John's gone, Chelsea. So is Devlin. Accept it."

"I can't. Not until I'm sure."

Sally shook her head and threw up her hands in exasperation. "Well, do what you have to do, heaven knows you're going to anyway. And don't worry about anything here, I can handle the store."

"I don't know how long I'll be gone. It may be longer than a couple of weeks."

Sally stared at her friend. "I said I can handle it. Do what you have to—be gone as long as you need. Just take care of yourself, okay?"

"I will," Chelsea promised, but she wondered what would happen when she ran into Devlin again.

"I wish there was some way to talk you out of this," Chelsea's older sister, Felicia, said the next afternoon. Felicia had stopped by her apartment when she'd learned from their mother that Chelsea was planning to leave for Paradis. And, as usual, Felicia was fit to be tied.

Pacing in front of the couch, her long plum-colored skirt swirling around her calves, Felicia sighed theatrically and rolled her eyes in typical exasperated big sister fashion. "Why don't you just give it a rest, Chels? Get on with your life. Sally said you were thinking of expanding the shop and I think it's a good idea—so much healthier than this—" She pursed her lips and motioned to the photographs neatly stacked across the coffee table "—this morbid obsession you have with Devlin McVey!"

Chelsea bristled. "I'm not obsessed."

"Sure."

"You know I have to check it out."

"Oh, so now you have a mission—a quest, right?" Felicia said sarcastically. She rubbed her temples, as if she felt a headache coming on. "God, Chelsea, why don't you grow up?"

"I just want to know the truth."

"Oh, do you?" Felicia lifted a skeptical dark brow. "Well, the truth is that you keep hanging onto a dream, Chels, and somehow that ridiculous dream is wrapped up in Devlin McVey. For the past year—no, thirteen months—you've thought of nothing else."

Chelsea didn't argue, just let her older sister rant on. When Felicia was on a roll, there was no stopping her. Chelsea glanced at Felicia over her shoulder, as if she were listening, but she kept tossing clothes from the small closet of her studio loft onto the couch. Blouses, dresses, tank tops and shorts were draped over the back of the sofa-sleeper and her two beat-up pieces of luggage stood ready near the kitchen alcove.

When Felicia paused to take a breath, Chelsea cut in, "I don't need another lecture, you know."

Felicia tossed her straight red-brown hair over her shoulder and her eyes narrowed. "You know your problem, don't you?" Felicia demanded, crossing her arms over her chest. "You're too much like Dad."

Chelsea froze, a beige blouse dropping from her fingers. "I'm not—"

"You two are cut from the same cloth—always searching for something more, something dangerous, something…a little wild. And you don't fool me. I know that you've tried to look like you've been playing it straight, but it's an act, Chelsea. Mom has probably forgotten, but I remember you as a kid. You were always the one getting into trouble in school."

"And you were always ready to run and tell Mom and Dad."

Felicia colored a little but added, "It was a good thing we were never in one place long enough for your reputation to catch up with you!"

"My reputation?" Chelsea repeated, stung.

"Of taking dares, you know, that sort of thing. I was always bailing you out! Remember when you talked three kids into skipping school with you and sneaking into the country club pool in the middle of December—"

"Enough already," Chelsea cut in, quickly. "What does how I behaved in grade school have to do with this?"

"It's all the same thing. You were never satisfied, just like Dad."

"Dad has nothing to do with this!"

Felicia lifted a shoulder. "You even had Mom convinced that you'd finally settled down—not that I ever believed it, mind you. But I live with Mom, I saw the change in her when you started dating John. And then, when you and Sally started your business, Mom was proud, I mean really proud."

Chelsea felt her shoulders droop a little.

"And then there was John." She sighed. "He was too good for you, you know. Too straight and narrow. An architect, for God's sake! But, he wasn't enough, was he? Oh, no, not for you," Felicia added with an envious glint in her eye. "You had to get involved with Devlin!"

"I wasn't—"

"Sure you were." Felicia slid her younger sister a knowing glance. "It was obvious. I'm surprised John didn't catch on. You were different around Devlin. I could tell. I could almost feel the energy between you two. All this charged sexual attraction just simmering under the surface. It was downright disgusting!"

"That's nonsense!" Chelsea argued, but felt a telltale blush creep steadily up the back of her neck. Guilt prickled at her mind.

"And I know what appealed to you. Devlin was sexy—damned sexy—in an earthy kind of way." Felicia colored and added quickly, "But he was all wrong for you—in so many ways. He was a cop, for crying out loud! Like Dad! Can't you remember the hell we all went through with Dad's jobs? And think about how hard it was on Mom. Why you'd want to involve yourself with a man—"

"I don't want to get involved with Devlin, Felicia," Chelsea said through tight lips. Why did she and Felicia always fight? "I just want to locate him and find out what happened to John!"

"Devlin's dead," Felicia said flatly.

"I don't think so." Chelsea snatched the snapshot of Mitch Russell from the tabletop and stormed across the room. "This man looks too much like him for me to give up now," she said, shoving the photograph under Felicia's disapproving nose. "There's a reason John died, Felicia, and a reason Devlin's hiding down in some God-forsaken island in the Caribbean, and, no matter what, I'm going to find out what it is!"

"So now it's an adventure!" The lines around the corners of Felicia's mouth turned bitter. "Dad thought it was an adventure, too—remember? But he was never satisfied, was he? Hauling us from town to town all across the country didn't do it, becoming a cop didn't do it, divorcing Mom didn't do it, and taking up with that…well, that girl half his age didn't do it, either! Think about it. John didn't make you happy and Devlin, even if he were alive, wouldn't, either!"

"I don't remember asking for your advice," Chelsea said tartly. She stripped a pair of white slacks from a hanger and tossed them into her suitcase. "You're saying I'll never be content."

"I'm saying you're wasting your time and chasing a dream that doesn't exist." She eyed her sister speculatively. "You know, I think you *like* following in Dad's footsteps."

"That's crazy! I'm just trying to get to the bottom of John's death."

"Yeah, sure." Felicia rolled her eyes, then studied her nails.

"I am."

"And this has nothing to do with any hidden feelings you might have had for Devlin?" Felicia taunted.

Chelsea's shoulders tightened at Felicia's tone. She whirled on her sister. "The only feelings I have for Devlin McVey are friendship. Period."

"Uh-huh. Right. And that's why you can't believe he's dead."

Chelsea held up her palms. "There's no reason to

argue, Felicia," she said through clenched teeth. "This is just something I have to do, okay?"

Felicia's mouth drew into an unforgiving line. "I'll tell Mom why you're going."

"I already did. Now, all I want from you is your assurance that you'll come in here once a week and water the plants. If that's not too much to ask! And if it is, I'm sure Mrs. Murphy across the hall—"

"I'm just trying to spare you some heartache, that's all," Felicia insisted, her brows lifting in feigned innocence. "Someone's got to look after you."

"I can take care of myself."

"Can you?" Felicia mused. "I wonder." With a long-suffering sigh, she tucked her tiny purse under her arm. "Well, if you want to throw away your money and waste your time and set yourself up for a major— and I'm talking major, here—fall, that's certainly your prerogative."

"Thanks." Chelsea wanted to say more, to snap back an equally hot retort, but she held her tongue. Felicia had, after all, remained at home, staying with their mother after their parents' divorce, trying to help her pick up the shattered pieces of her life. Though now she could move out and find a place of her own, Felicia preferred to stay with Mom and play the part of the martyred older sister, and Chelsea tried her best to keep her temper in check.

"Just think about one thing," Felicia suggested cattily as she grabbed her umbrella, snagged her raincoat from the hall tree near the door, and glancing back over her shoulder, lifted a lofty brow.

Chelsea hated to ask, but couldn't help saying, "What's that?"

Felicia skewered her younger sister with a knowing glare. "If and when you run into Devlin McVey again, take a good long look in the mirror and ask yourself why you've been so hell-bent to find a man who's trying his damnedest to remain dead!"

Chapter 2

The plane, a small prop, touched down with a jarring thud that pushed Chelsea's already queasy stomach right up her throat.

She gripped the arms of the seat and sighed in relief as the pilot taxied to the tiny airport—if that's what you'd call it. Little more than a few landing strips, several hangars and a low, flat building that served as terminal, the tiny airport of St. Jean left a lot to be desired.

As she climbed off the plane, the tropical heat of the island hit her full force. Beams of sunlight reflected off the whitewashed buildings. A whisper of a breeze brushed Chelsea's cheeks. The gentle gust caused the fronds of palm trees to sway high overhead. Shifting shadows danced gracefully on the tarmac.

Chelsea picked up her luggage in the terminal and

checked through customs. Once she was outside again, she approached a cab driver who was leaning on the front fender of his Chevrolet while perusing a magazine written in French.

"I need a ride to the docks to catch a boat to Paradis," she said. "Can you get me there?"

"No problem," the driver, a heavyset Creole man with graying hair and a thick accent, promised. He tossed the magazine into the open window of his beat-up old Chevy and stuffed her bags into the trunk. He held the door for Chelsea, then slid behind the wheel. Flashing her a blinding smile in the rearview mirror, he said, "Twenty minutes to the docks."

The cab bounced along rutted, winding roads, past grand hotels with red tile roofs and wide verandas guarded by lush vegetation. They traveled to the heart of the lazy, sun-washed city of Lagune where only a few high-rises competed for the view of a pristine bay.

The docks were a madhouse. Fishing boats, cabin cruisers, sailboats and yachts filled the crescent-shaped harbor.

Sunlight shimmered on the aquamarine water and sailboats skimmed across the sea. Chelsea's throat grew tight as she watched a sloop slice across the bay. The small boat wasn't unlike Devlin's. Once again, she remembered the last time she'd seen John and Devlin, just before their fateful outing, and shoved the unhappy thought aside.

Shivering a little, she found her sunglasses, slid them onto the bridge of her nose and stepped onto a small cruiser named the *Anna Marie*. It would, the round-bellied captain assured her, take her on the final leg of her journey, from St. Jean to Paradis.

Other people crowded aboard, their different voices and dialects rising over the soft lapping of the water and the thrum of the boat's idling engines. Chelsea surveyed the group heading for Paradis, but she kept to herself, her thoughts racing ahead of the small craft as it chugged into the open sea.

Why would Devlin, who had grown up in California, hide here on a remote tropical island, letting everyone he'd known think him dead? What had happened during the storm that had taken John's life?

John.

A hot pain knifed through her heart and, as she stood against the rail, she glanced down at her left hand where once she'd worn his engagement ring. Swallowing hard, she remembered John's athletic good looks, wavy blond hair and easy smile. He'd been her friend for years and falling in love with him had seemed natural and right, the easiest path for her life. And safe. John had been safe. As far removed from her father as any man she'd known.

Felicia had been right in one respect, she admitted grimly to herself. Their father, Paul Reed, had been a man who had sought danger, a man whose professional as well as personal life had been lived on the edge, a man, in the end, who had disappointed and hurt his family.

She'd vowed never to fall for a man like her father, and John Stern had been Paul Reed's antithesis. Her chest grew tight as she thought of the man she'd chosen to marry, a kind, gentle, fun-loving man who was as rock-solid as he was handsome.

Only one person had challenged her love for John,

and she frowned as she remembered the night John had told Devlin they were getting married.

"Can you believe it?" John had cried, grabbing Chelsea around the waist and swinging her, laughing, from her feet as they stood near the Christmas tree which glittered by the balcony of John's bay-front condominium. "She's finally said 'yes.'"

"Imagine that," Devlin drawled, the lines around his mouth showing white against his tanned skin.

"I've been asking her for months!"

"Well," Devlin's inky gaze had moved slowly from John to Chelsea's flushed face and lingered a second too long before he'd held up his bottle of beer. "Congratulations. I hope you're both happy."

His gaze left her as he drank slowly from the long neck of his bottle and Chelsea remembered studying his Adam's apple as he swallowed and noticing the way his black hair brushed the back of his neck. She'd wondered what she felt for him then. Anger? Disgust? Or unwilling attraction...

"Stop it," she told herself now, refusing to continue a memory that had burned in her mind for over a year, a memory that had made her question everything she'd ever believed in, a memory that had eclipsed all her memories of John.

She squeezed her eyes shut for just a second, willing away the sardonic look in Devlin's features, the mockery in his gaze. He'd always set her on edge, and yet she had to find him, had to know the truth about the accident.

Shoving her hair from her face, she stared at the blue-green water, feeling its spray as she leaned over the rail. Far ahead in the distance, a small island rose from the sea—a tiny emerald-green cone poking out of the ocean.

Soon they would be docking. Her heart began to race. What if the man wasn't Devlin? What would she say to him? How would she deal with the disappointment? Or, conversely, what if Mitch Russell *was* Devlin McVey? There must be a reason he was hiding down here, and he might not take kindly to her bulldozing her way back into his life.

Too bad.

She'd come this far—she wasn't about to turn back now. Besides, he deserved it. If he had left his friends and relatives to think him dead, then he deserved to have his life thrown out of kilter, and she had the right to some answers about what had happened on that windy day in April in San Francisco Bay.

As the captain guided the *Anna Marie* into harbor, Chelsea strained to see the port, a tiny town named Emeraude sprawled around several weathered docks that jutted into the shimmering water. Fishing boats, canoes and sailboats, rocking gently with the tide, were lashed to the moorings. A plank boardwalk curved over a sandy stretch of beach and led to the town, which was little more than a few sunbaked buildings lining the waterfront.

This village seemed so remote, so unlikely a spot for a big-city cop to end up. Unless he were running from something. But that was ridiculous. To Chelsea's knowledge, Devlin McVey had never run from anything in his life. Until now.

"There's a first time for everything," she told herself.

The captain tossed ropes that looped over moorings on the docks as the *Anna Marie* settled into port.

It's now or never, Chelsea thought, grabbing her bags and climbing onto the bleached wooden pier. Her stomach was in knots, her jaw set. Within hours, she could come face-to-face with Devlin again.

She shared a taxi, a decrepit gray station wagon, with an older couple, the Vaughns, from Miami. The apricot-haired woman, Emily, chatted nonstop while her husband, Jeff, suffered in silence, only interjecting a grunt or two when Emily would pause and ask, "Isn't that right, dear?"

Chelsea couldn't wait to get out of the cab. Her nerves were already strung tight and Emily's senseless chatter only set her more on edge as the old wagon snaked up the winding, rutted road to the one resort on the island. Lush green vegetation encroached on the dusty road and provided a leafy canopy high overhead, but the inside of the cab was hot and stifling.

"…so we decided to try something more secluded, a little less touristy, if you know what I mean," Emily went blithely on, "and Paradis seemed perfect. We heard all about the Villa from a friend. It was originally built in the twenties by some rich oil baron who wanted a private spot where he could get away from it all, probably to keep a mistress or two. Isn't that right, dear?"

"Right," Jeff said on cue as the driver pulled into the circular drive of what, years ago, must have been a glorious resort. A two-storied Mediterranean-style mansion with once-white stucco walls, wide verandas and a sloping tile roof stood shabbily behind an overgrown courtyard. The roof of the hotel had been patched over the years and the dingy walls were in sad need of paint.

Grass poked through the cracks in the pavement and the gardens rambled untrimmed. A fountain, rusted and no longer operational, stood in the middle of an empty wading pool and unkempt vines crawled across the ornate grillwork on the balcony surrounding the second story.

"Welcome to the Villa," the cab driver said, as he collected their fares.

"Isn't it spectacular?" Emily gushed, eagerly climbing out of the cab.

Spectacular wasn't the word Chelsea had in mind. Run-down maybe, or once-grand, but definitely not spectacular. The sun was beginning to set and shadows stole over the main courtyard as if trying to hide the tired building's most obvious flaws.

A porter carried her bags into the main lobby and Chelsea felt a stab of regret for the old resort. Inside, the floors were tile, the staircase hand-rubbed walnut and the carpet running to the second story wine-red and worn. Circular fans moved lazily overhead and fading sunlight drifted through tall paned windows.

But the condition of the hotel didn't matter, she reminded herself. She was here with a purpose: to find Devlin.

To that end, she checked into her room on the second floor, and spying her reflection in the mirror over the vanity, cringed. She'd been traveling since dawn and she looked rumpled and tired. Her slacks and blouse were wrinkled, and her unruly red-brown hair was springing out from her ponytail in wild clumps.

She quickly showered and changed into white slacks and a red tank top, then brushed her wayward hair and wound it into a knot at the base of her skull.

A dab of makeup and a shot of eyedrops, and she was as ready as she'd ever be to meet Devlin.

She headed for the door, but stopped dead in her tracks. What if he'd left? Jenkins had been gone four days. What if, in that time, Devlin had taken off? Or what if he's really not Devlin McVey and you've traveled all this way for nothing? Her heart nosedived.

"Think positive," she told herself, squaring her shoulders as she marched through the door and turned the key.

According to Jenkins, Mitch Russell, as he called himself, spent some of his evenings in the bar at the Villa. Otherwise, he frequented several other watering holes in town.

Chelsea decided to start downstairs.

The bar was at the back of the hotel and in no better shape than the rest of the Villa. A single bartender served drinks and waited the few tables scattered around the dark room. Candles flickered and the windows had been cracked open, allowing the sound of insects to infiltrate the whispered conversations, clinking glasses and occasional burst of laughter. Paddle fans fought a losing battle with smoke and the hint of a breeze brought with it the scent of the sea.

Chelsea sat in a corner of the room, ignoring the curious glances local patrons cast in her direction. She sipped from a glass of wine and nibbled on the salted nuts, but her eyes were trained on the door from the lobby.

Within a few minutes a lanky man in his early thirties settled onto a stool at her table. His wheat-blond hair was long, tickling his ears, and he had a lean face with a narrow nose, teeth that overlapped just a little and eyes that stared straight into hers. "Mind if I join you?" he asked.

"I'm waiting for someone."

He scanned the bar and apparently seeing no one who was any competition, he shrugged. "It wouldn't hurt if I bought you a drink."

Chelsea didn't want anything to do with this man or any other man—aside from Devlin. Her stomach was already in knots and she didn't need to try and make small talk with this stranger. "I don't think so," she said, offering him a cool smile.

"Well, I'll just wait until your friend shows up."

Chelsea bristled a little. "I'd rather wait alone."

He arched a skeptical blond brow. "You're sure?"

"Positive."

"Okay." Lifting a shoulder, he added, "I can take a hint, especially when it's hurled at me." He offered her a confident smile. "The name's Chris Landeen if you change your mind or if your friend doesn't show up."

"Thanks," she said, feeling suddenly foolish. What if Devlin didn't show up? Well, she hadn't come all this way only to stop now. She sipped her wine again and settled in for a long wait, her gaze once again on the door.

She didn't have to wait long. She felt a prickle of apprehension as a gust of wind caused the candle on her table to flicker and dance.

At that moment, a tall, broad-shouldered man in snug-fitting jeans entered the room.

Her heart kicked into double time as she stared at him. Dressed in faded jeans, a black T-shirt, and a well-worn denim jacket, he crossed the room in an easy, fluid gait. A full, black beard covered his chin and his gaze, a deep, calculating blue, swung lazily around the room, landing full force on Chelsea.

She swallowed hard and rose, smiling, thanking God that he was safe—for when she gazed into his electric blue eyes, she knew for certain she'd found Devlin McVey. Now, at last, she could put together the missing pieces of the puzzle of John's death and get on with her life.

"I can't believe it," she whispered, crossing the room, her heart pumping furiously.

One dark brow lifted curiously. "Believe what?"

"That you're here—I mean, oh, God, Devlin, why?"

"Excuse me?" he drawled, his expression blank.

"What're you doing down here? What happened on the boat?"

He glanced from her to the eyes of several men at the bar, then his gaze came crashing back to hers. "Did I miss something?" he asked slowly. "Do you think you know me?"

"Of course I do. Devlin—"

"The name's Russell. Mitch Russell." A trace of irritation edged his words.

"But—" She was about to touch him, but stopped and let her hand drop to her side. "You're telling me that you're not Devlin McVey?"

"Lady, I think you've made yourself a big mistake."

"But…your voice, your walk…" The world spun crazily for a second. This couldn't be happening. He *was* Devlin. He had to be! "Devlin—"

He stared at her as if she'd gone mad. "Look, I don't know who this Devlin character is, but you've got the wrong guy!" Turning toward the bar, he motioned to the barkeep. "The usual."

Chelsea stood in the middle of the room, caught between the present and the past. Was her mind playing tricks on her, or was Devlin playing a cruel game?

Mitch glanced over his shoulder. "You want a drink? You look like you could use one."

"No… I don't think so." She licked suddenly dry lips and tried not to feel like a fool. She'd come all this way, spent all this money, wasted all her time for what? To confront a total stranger and act like an idiot?

She noticed the way people let their glances slide away, the manner in which their lips curved in amusement. Well, the show was over. Drawing on her courage, she walked to the bar and slid onto the empty stool next to Mitch's. "I, uh, didn't mean to—"

"Don't worry about it." He shook his head and she stared at his profile—identical to Devlin's. Her breath caught in her throat.

"But, it's just that you look so much like a…a friend of mine who's missing."

"Look," he said, turning toward her, "I told you to forget it." He lifted his shoulders easily. "It was an honest mistake."

"But—" she paused, confused. "You really do look like—"

"It happens."

"No, you don't understand," she said in a rush, wanting to shake him, to make him listen. "Devlin was supposed to have drowned but his body was never found and—"

"Are you coming on to me?" he asked suddenly.

"W-what?"

"I asked you if you were coming on to me. Either

you're trying to get me interested or you're a nut case. Now, which is it?"

Chelsea's jaw dropped open in shock. "It's just that you bear this incredible resemblance—"

"Yeah, sure." He took a swallow of his drink, then looked her slowly up and down, his gaze nearly burning through her clothes as it rested on the stretch of fabric across her breasts.

Chelsea's heart thumped crazily.

"So what's it going to be?" he demanded, his eyes centering on her lips. "You and me? Upstairs?" He glanced through the open lobby door to the curved staircase and Chelsea's temper skyrocketed. "Your room?"

"Not on your life!"

His expression turned cynical and cold. "Then leave me alone. Okay? I'm not your friend Devin."

"Devlin—Devlin McVey."

"Whatever." He turned his attention back to his drink.

Mortified and furious, Chelsea slid off her bar stool. How could she have made such a disastrous mistake? She glanced back at the man at the bar, his profile hard-edged and rough, his features carved and angular, his black, unkempt hair curving over the frayed collar of his jacket. He had to be Devlin. He just had to be!

She walked quickly out of the bar, ran upstairs and once in her room, sluiced water over her burning cheeks. As she stared at her reflection in the mirror, she gritted her teeth. She hadn't come this far to give up so easily. No matter how insufferable he planned to be!

She intended to confront Mr. Mitchell Russell again, but the next time, she'd meet him in a more secluded spot—away from the interested eyes of the other guests at the Villa.

She had pictures of Devlin with her, and pictures of John. She'd wave those photos under his nose and watch for his reaction. He couldn't be that immune.

Or could he?

It had been over a year since she'd seen him, a year since he'd disappeared from San Francisco.

She closed her eyes. Why had Devlin disappeared? Why? She couldn't stop the questions from pounding against the back of her mind.

There had to be a reason Devlin was pretending to be Mitch Russell, but what was it?

Opening the window of her room, she stared out at the moonlit night and let the sea-laden breeze cool her face. The scent of jasmine and lemon filtered in, ruffling her hair and cooling her burning cheeks.

Her fists clenched in renewed determination as she watched the moon slowly rise over the ocean. If Mitch Russell wanted a fight, he'd get it, but she wasn't giving up until she was convinced that he wasn't Devlin.

And what then?

Chelsea cringed at the thought. The man in the bar, the cruel man with the hot blue eyes, was Devlin. She could feel it. All she had to do was prove it.

Chapter 3

What if he skips out?

The thought struck Chelsea like a thunderbolt as she dropped to the corner of her hotel room bed.

Now that she'd come face to face with Devlin, how could she be sure that he wouldn't leave? He'd already avoided the police and any friends or family he had back in San Francisco. Since she'd tipped her hand in the bar, he would now realize that he was found out in Paradis. What was to prevent him from sailing to St. Jean and taking the next plane to God-only-knew-where?

"You've bungled this, Reed," she growled at herself as she yanked off her clothes and tossed them onto the bed. She couldn't let him slip through her fingers! Not after she'd spent so much time and effort and come so far to locate him. No, she thought, changing into a pair of black slacks and a black pullover, she had to make sure that he would stay put and find out where he lived.

And you're going to do that by spying on him? the rational side of her mind questioned.

"You bet I am!" She pulled her hair from the neck of the pullover, donned running shoes, then headed quickly downstairs. Feeling a little foolish in her cat burglar outfit, she dashed through the side door not far from the bar, then lingered in the shadows by the empty wading pool, her eyes trained on the entrance.

Nerves strung tight as bowstrings, she spent the next forty minutes checking her watch, drumming her fingers impatiently on the wall and telling herself that she was acting like a certifiable lunatic.

And what if Devlin waltzed out of the bar and climbed into his vehicle? There were several trucks and cars parked in a side lot and if Devlin climbed into one of them, she'd be stuck with nothing more than a license plate number.

She considered calling a taxi, and asking the driver to wait until she needed him, but discarded the idea. On the deserted island roads, Devlin would spot a tail instantly. After all, he had been a cop, an undercover detective no less, and her amateur sleuthing skills were no match against him.

Despite her arguments with herself, she stuck it out and eventually he emerged, alone, hands plunged deep in his pockets, walking with the same quick, athletic stride she remembered. She held her breath and crossed her fingers, smiling to herself when, instead of heading toward the parking lot, he walked around the corner of the hotel.

Chelsea didn't waste any time. She took off after

him. The glow from the windows of the Villa and the moonlight filtering through the dense foliage gave her some illumination, but she had to hurry to keep pace with Devlin's swift steps.

She rounded the corner of the hotel and followed a flagstone path which skirted the swimming pool, then flanked the edge of the forest. Her quarry, a mere hundred feet ahead of her, never once glanced over his shoulder.

That worried her. If this man were indeed Devlin, he would surely remember her and he'd know that she wouldn't give up easily. He'd *expect* her to follow him.

So, what if Mitch Russell wasn't Devlin?

The thought struck her cold and she shoved it angrily from her mind as she half ran to keep up with him, staying in the shadows, careful that her shoes didn't scrape against the stones. Mitch Russell was Devlin—he had to be! No one person could look and sound that much like another! No, her every instinct told her that this man was not only Devlin, but that he had something to hide.

He disappeared at the edge of the hotel grounds and vanished into the trees edging the east side of the resort. Great, Chelsea thought as she followed. The flagstones gave way to a sandy path. Chelsea slogged on, hearing the sound of the sea, the rush of water and feeling the air grow cooler as she squinted against the darkness to stay on the trail.

She hadn't thought to bring a flashlight, but wouldn't have used one if she had. A single beam would only alert Devlin to the fact that he was being followed. So she walked on, clenching her teeth and biting her tongue when her toes stubbed the root of a tree and she almost yelped. Hang in there, Chels, she mentally encouraged, squinting against the darkness and wishing she could quiet the hammering of her heart.

Where was he going?

Eventually the path widened and the trees gave way to a stretch of beach that glimmered silver in the pale light from the moon. She took one step onto the beach and glanced north and south, sweeping the water line in both directions. Her heart plummeted. The sand was deserted. Devlin was nowhere in sight.

How had she lost him? She was sure she'd followed him. There had been no fork in the path, no trail angling in another direction—at least none that she'd seen.

She swung her gaze left and right again, but the beach was empty. Deserted. Desperately, she narrowed her gaze on the sea, but the shimmering water stretching from the sand to the night-black horizon was unbroken. No solitary swimmer appeared and no shadow lurked near the water's edge.

"Damn! Damn! And double damn!" she swore. How had he eluded her?

Tossing her hands into the air, she stepped farther out onto the beach and kicked at the sand. Some detective she'd proved herself to be! She couldn't even follow one man less than a mile. Pathetic, that's what this entire scenario was—downright pathetic! Nancy Drew had nothing to worry about in the competition department.

Furious, Chelsea thrust her chin forward in determination. Well, she wasn't about to give up. So he'd lost her tonight. Tomorrow was another day. And to-

morrow, things would be different. Unless he decided
to take off in the middle of the night! In frustration,
she shoved her hands through her hair. He wouldn't
be able to pack up and disappear in just a few hours,
would he?

Since she'd blown tailing him, her only other option
was to find out about him from some of the regulars
in the hotel. They would know where he lived, what
he did for a living, maybe some detail from his past...

Muttering under her breath she turned and started
back along the path.

"Giving up so soon?" a male voice boomed.

Chelsea froze. Her heart slammed in her chest. She
whipped around, facing the edge of the forest of the
northerly side of the path and saw him.

Devlin, damn him, was leaning insolently against
the trunk of a large palm tree. His hands were plunged
in his pockets and his shoulders rested against the
bark. His face was shadowed but she didn't doubt that
he'd been hiding there since she'd emerged from the
thicket of trees. He probably watched her scour the
beach for him while he silently laughed at her.

"You nearly scared the life out of me!" she flung
out, her pulse jackhammering.

"You deserved it." He shoved himself upright and
closed the short distance between them. If he'd been
smiling, his expression had changed. Now his face
was dark and dangerous, his bearded chin rock hard.

"I was just..."

"Out for a midnight stroll?" he mocked. "Sure."

There was no use lying, so she didn't. Instead she
stood her ground, inches from him, tilting her chin de-
fiantly upward, her shoulders automatically stiffening.

"I guess I didn't get through to you in the bar," he said evenly, his teeth flashing white against his beard. "I don't like people spying on me."

"I wasn't—"

"You weren't following me?" he asked, towering over her.

She'd already decided she couldn't lie and, truth to tell, she had always been a lousy liar. "Okay, I was following you," she admitted.

"Why?"

"I told you why in the bar."

"Because I look like your boyfriend."

"My friend," she corrected.

The moonlight cast a silver sheen to his eyes. "Okay, lady, what's your game? Who set you up to this?"

"No one. And the game's simple. I'm here looking for—"

"Yeah, I know. Well, you haven't found him so you can just leave me alone!"

She couldn't let him go that easily. "Don't you remember me?"

"I already told you. I've never laid eyes on you before. Now, if this is your idea of a joke—"

"No joke, Devlin."

Quick as a striking snake he grabbed both her upper arms in a hard, viselike grip. His fingers closed over her skin. "The name's Russell. Mitch Russell." His face looked nearly sinister. "I suggest you remember that." Frowning, he loosened his grasp a little. "And just who are you?"

"You don't remember me—?"

"Hell, no!"

"Chelsea," she replied, shaken to her roots. She'd been so sure. He even smelled like Devlin and his earthy scent brought back memories she was better off forgetting.

"Chelsea what?"

"Reed. You know—"

"I *don't* know. Not a damn thing! Except that you're down here, making up some wild stories that just don't make any sense." His lips tightened and he sucked in a short, angry breath. His gaze, rigid and calculating, skated down her front. "Why did this Devlin character leave you?"

"He didn't leave me—not exactly."

"Oh, yeah, he was supposed to have died…right? But somehow he's resurrected down here."

"Devlin disappeared in a boating accident. His friend died. John Stern. My fiancé." Was it her imagination, or did his eyes flicker a little? Or was it just the shadow of a passing cloud scudding across the moon?

"Let me get this straight. You were engaged—to another guy?" he asked incredulously. "But you're down here looking for the one who was just a friend."

"Yes."

"Geez, woman, this just gets better and better!"

"Please, just listen, Dev—er, Mitch." The name stuck in her throat and she had to force it over her tongue. "I just want to talk to you. Show you some pictures."

His mouth lifted at the corner and his eyes darkened seductively, but he didn't let go as he studied the contours of her face. "So this *is* a come on."

"No!"

"Then I'm not interested!" His grip relaxed, his

arms dropped to his sides and he let out an exasperated breath. "Just leave me alone, okay? I don't like women who try and mess with my head."

"I need to talk to you—"

"You need to talk to a shrink!"

"But—"

His smile slashed coldly in the darkness. "I'm not interested in anything you're peddling. If you've been set up for this and someone's paying you to play some kind of sick joke on me, tell him the last laugh's on him. Or, if you're just looking for a little fun," he added suggestively, "I'm only interested in one thing. Got it?"

The bastard! Her skin crawled at his suggestion. Who was this guy? "In your dreams," she said.

"No, lady. In yours." With that he shoved his hands into his pockets, turned, and strode quickly up the beach.

Chelsea was left furious, insulted and downright angry. "Of all the insufferable, egotistical, revolting..." She bit her tongue to keep from swearing soundly.

What did you expect? she asked herself as she turned and headed back to the hotel. Anger burned up her cheeks, but she forced it back. She'd have to hang on to her patience in order to deal with Mitch Russell.

Don't give up, she told herself. Remember John. Remember Devlin!

She spotted the lights surrounding the hotel and started running, through the forest and along the flagstones flanking the pool. She walked into the main lobby and climbed the stairs, slowly counting to ten and calming herself. If this was the way Devlin planned on playing the game, fine. Two could play.

In her room, she kicked off her running shoes and headed for the shower. She'd had enough for one day, but tomorrow, watch out—round two! If Mr. Russell thought she would back down so easily, he damn well had another think coming!

The next morning, Chelsea wrapped herself in a yellow sundress, stepped into white leather thongs and decided to explore Emeraude. Maybe if she poked around, she could find out more about the mysterious Mitchell Russell without having to square off with him again.

There had to be more to his character than the fact that he insulted women for a hobby, she thought ruefully. At least she hoped so.

Swinging a straw bag over her shoulder and plopping a matching hat on her head, she marched downstairs. Outside, the sun was hot, the temperature already soaring, the moist earth steamy as the ground began to bake.

Chelsea asked a dark-skinned taxi driver to drop her off near the docks in town, then she stared out the window, seeing flashes of silvery-blue water through the trees as a glimpse of ocean appeared through the dense greenery.

Within twenty minutes, the taxi was grinding to a halt. Chelsea paid her fare and then set about exploring the town where Mitch Russell lived.

Emeraude was little more than a sleepy fishing village—a tourist town that had faded in popularity over the years as the larger, more commercial islands had gained favor with trendy vacationers. But the dusty streets were lined with a few shops—boutiques, bakeries, bookstores, craft shops and an art gallery or two. Two blocks from the waterfront, a shaded, open-air market was laden with fresh fish, produce, island art and jewelry.

Several cafés were strung along the docks, and a block inland, a jumble of brick and concrete buildings housed apartments, the local government, a bank, a real estate firm and a few miscellaneous business offices.

The mood of the town was slow and lazy, and Chelsea didn't mind. In fact, if her head hadn't been filled with Devlin or Mitch or whoever the devil that arrogant man was, she might enjoy the lazy, sun-drenched pace of Paradis.

Her stomach rumbled, reminding her that she hadn't stopped for breakfast. She strolled into a small café overlooking the waterfront and slid into an empty booth upholstered in worn yellow vinyl. The menu was written in French and Chelsea's high-school fluency stopped on the second item.

A slim, dark-skinned girl, with an easy smile and sleek black hair braided past her waist, sauntered over to her table and helped Chelsea choose a breakfast of shrimp creole, eggs and island bread, whatever that was.

"You'll love it," the waitress assured her in a French accent. "Everyone does."

Chelsea wasn't convinced, but within minutes the pretty girl returned with a large, steaming platter.

The shrimp was so spicy it nearly brought tears to Chelsea's eyes, but it tasted divine and the chewy island bread, spread with honey and butter, melted in her mouth.

"Hot, *non?*" the waitress asked, refilling Chelsea's iced tea glass as Chelsea took a bite of shrimp.

"Hot, yes!" Chelsea replied with a smile. She sipped the cool tea and thought about Devlin as the waitress, whose name tag read Simone, poured coffee at nearby tables.

Why was Devlin eluding her, lying to her, and worse yet, mortifying her? Devlin had always earned a reputation with women, but Chelsea had suspected that his exploits were vastly overestimated by John. She, herself, had never seen any indication that Devlin was into fast women and one-night stands. In fact, in the few double dates she and John had shared with him, the women, never the same one twice, had seemed far more interested in Devlin than he had been in them.

And then there had been Devlin's wife, Holly, who had died long before Chelsea had met him. He'd never spoken of her, but John had mentioned that Devlin had been destroyed by her death. Chelsea had never learned how Devlin's wife had died. "It's something he never discusses," John had warned her.

As for the other women—those ladies who found Devlin's cool aloofness so attractive—Chelsea had never become friends with any of them. Some women went for the distant, disinterested type, a male who presented a challenge. Chelsea didn't.

She stared out the window and sighed. Mitch Russell was far from cool and aloof. He was frank about his intentions; in fact, he was rude to the point that no sane woman would want him. But maybe that was the point. Maybe his challenge of offering to take her to bed was just a bluff. There was the possibility that he was just trying to scare her off.

But why?

The question rattled around in her mind for the next fifteen minutes while she finished her tea. She still didn't have an answer as she walked to the front desk and dug into her purse for some cash to pay her bill.

As Chelsea opened her wallet, a petite woman with short red hair and a burst of freckles across her nose bustled through the door and hurried up to the counter.

"The usual, Simone," she said as the waitress tallied Chelsea's bill. "Two coffees, a tea and whatever pastry you've got—preferably something with marmalade." She fanned herself with her hand, "Can you believe this heat?" she asked no one in general, as she looked in Chelsea's direction.

"Aren't you used to it?" Chelsea asked.

"Me?" The redhead laughed. "Heavens no! I doubt I'll ever be used to the temperature. And the *humidity!*"

"But you came in here ordering 'the usual.'"

The petite woman laughed, crinkling her freckled, upturned nose. "Well, it's the usual down at the shop where I work, but I've only been here a couple of years." Her brown eyes twinkled. "I know that sounds like a long time, but I'm far from a native. I'm from Idaho, about fifty miles from Boise, and sometimes I miss winter—I mean real winter with snow and ice and frostbite!"

Chelsea was intrigued. "Do you?"

"Oh, don't get me wrong, I came here for the sun and sand, but once in a while the heat gets to me, really makes me swelter, and I'd just about kill for subzero temperatures. Oh, by the way, I'm Terri. Terri Peyton.

I'm the manager of the Boutique Exotique just down the street." She extended her hand.

"Chelsea Reed," Chelsea replied.

Terri's handshake was as enthusiastic as she was. "Here for a visit?"

"Mmm." Chelsea nodded, finding the right amount of cash and leaving it next to an ancient cash register.

"How long are you staying?" Terri asked.

"I'm not sure yet—probably a couple of weeks."

Simone returned with Terri's order.

"Paradis is a great place," Terri enthused, obviously forgetting the charms of winter in Boise. "So romantic, you know."

So far, Chelsea hadn't noticed.

Terri handed Simone some bills. "Keep the change," she said, then turned back to Chelsea. "If you're interested in shopping for something out of the ordinary— jewelry, scarves, clothes, gifts or island art, we've got it at the B. E.—that's what we call the boutique." She fluttered a wave with her fingers, and carrying two white sacks, opened the door with her backside and left.

"Terri, she knows everyone on the island," Simone commented as she picked up Chelsea's tab and cash.

"I thought she said she's only been on Paradis a couple of years."

Nodding, Simone grinned widely. "This is true, but Terri, she makes it her business to know everyone. Come back again."

"I will," Chelsea promised. She shoved open the door, adjusted her hat and thought about the pert little redhead. Terry was friendly and warm. Obviously she met people easily. No doubt she'd come across

Mr. Russell. The wheels turned in Chelsea's mind. Perhaps Terri would like to help Chelsea fit together some of the pieces of the intriguing puzzle that was Mitch Russell.

Chelsea spent the afternoon exploring the town. She picked out a hand-knit sweater for her mother and even found some straw place mats dyed a raspberry shade for Felicia. After all, Felicia wasn't so bad, Chelsea thought with more than a little twinge of guilt for the fight they'd had at her apartment. Felicia, in her own perverse way, was only looking out for her younger sister's best interests—or so she thought.

At four-thirty Chelsea's feet were killing her. Aching from walking in thongs along the hot cobblestones, she rested on the corner and spied the hand-painted wooden sign for Terri's shop.

With a weary smile, she yanked open the screen door of the Boutique Exotique. And exotic it was. A blue-and-green parrot whistled loudly from a huge aviary near the window and a cockatoo plumped his feathers in a large wire cage in the opposite corner of the room. Artwork and crafts decorated the walls and tables. Bright clothing hung from spiraled racks. Straw, canvas and leather bags swung from pegs planted in the ceiling near the walls.

"Chelsea!" Terri called, glancing over her shoulder. She stood at a counter, draping shell necklaces over a rack.

"I thought I'd come in and look around," Chelsea explained. "My partner and I own a boutique in San Francisco."

"Do you!" Terri cried. "Well, come on, let me show

you everything." And she did. While another sales-clerk dealt with the few other customers who drifted in, Terri gave Chelsea the grand tour.

Chelsea bought two pairs of wild earrings, a pair of hand-painted sunglasses, another hat and a white sun dress with a pink-and-green belt.

"You didn't have to buy out the store," Terri said, grinning as she rang up the sale.

Chelsea laughed. "I think I left a few things for your other customers."

The parrot cawed and Terri rolled her eyes.

Chelsea said, "My partner calls our shop a zoo. If she only knew…"

"This bird, too, can be yours," Terri teased, motion-ing to the parrot. "For a nominal fee—"

The parrot ruffled his wings loudly and repeated, "Nominal fee."

Handing Chelsea her bag, Terri leaned across the counter and stage-whispered, "Don't let him know, but he's a real pain sometimes."

"But the customers adore him, I bet."

"They don't have to clean his cage," Terry said with a sour look, then added, "If you wait a few minutes, I'll close up and we can go somewhere for a drink."

"I'll wait." Chelsea dug in her bag, shoved her new pair of sunglasses onto her nose and strolled outside.

Twenty minutes later, the two women were seated at an outdoor café overlooking the docks. A striped umbrella shaded their table as they sipped iced tea and lime. Terri was explaining her life story—how she ended up in Paradis after a painful divorce. "I just wanted to get away—escape, I guess you'd call it—from Rob. So I found a spot as far away as I could from Boise and the rest is history!"

"That's when you started working at the shop?"

"Mmm, actually, I'm part owner." She swirled her drink. "Believe it or not, I'm actually a kindergarten teacher, but when I left Idaho, I wanted to start all over. You know, new location, new career, new man— only trouble is, I haven't found the new man yet."

"You will," Chelsea predicted.

"I hope so."

Chelsea eyed her new friend. "Is that how a lot of people end up here? Because they're leaving something or someone behind?"

Terri lifted a tanned shoulder. "You mean the Americans?" At Chelsea's nod, she added, "I suppose."

It was now or never. Chelsea plunged on. "Simone said you know most of the people on the island."

"Not most, but some."

"Have you ever met Mitch Russell?"

Nodding, Terri smiled dreamily. "Of course. He showed up in Emeraude about eight or nine months ago, I think. And he was definitely the most interesting man to walk off the boat in a long time."

An arguable point, in Chelsea's estimation. "What do you know about him?"

"Not much," Terri admitted. A small crease formed between her brows. "He's a mystery man of sorts. You know the type—doesn't get too close to anyone, hangs out at the bars some nights."

"No wife?" Chelsea asked.

Terri shook her head. "Well, no wife down here. Who knows what he left behind."

What indeed?

"So—you already met him?" Terri asked.

"Mmm. Last night in the bar at the hotel," Chelsea said, then gambled. Reaching into her purse, she yanked out her wallet and flipped it open to a page with a picture of John, Devlin, and herself on Devlin's sailboat. She slipped the photo from the wallet and handed it to Terri. "That's a picture of my fiancé, John, his best friend, Devlin McVey, and me. It was taken over a year ago."

Terri set down her drink and pushed her sunglasses into her hair. "You're engaged?" she asked.

"Was. My fiancé was killed in a boating accident and I'm looking for his friend."

"This guy—right?" she pointed to the picture of Devlin.

"Yes. He disappeared after the accident."

Terri didn't react, just studied the photograph. "What do you mean 'disappeared'?"

"He left San Francisco, didn't tell anyone where he was," she explained, not mentioning Devlin's deception of letting everyone think he was dead. "I think Mitch Russell might be Devlin."

"You're kidding!" Terri's reddish eyebrows skyrocketed. She stared at the photograph with new interest.

"I'm dead serious. Take a long look—" she encouraged, mentally crossing her fingers that Terri would agree with her. She needed reinforcement.

"I don't know…"

"Picture Devlin with a beard like Mitch's."

Terri's face pulled into a knot of concentration. "It's possible, I suppose, but why would he change his name?"

"I wish I knew. Obviously, he doesn't want to be recognized."

"And you saw him last night? Talked with him?" Terri asked, her eyes rounding. "What happened?"

"He claimed he didn't know me, but…"

"But, what? You think he's lying?"

"I wish I knew," Chelsea admitted, blowing her bangs out of her eyes and staring at the ice cubes melting in her drink. "Somehow, I have to find out."

"Is there a reason he'd want to hide?"

"That's the million-dollar question," Chelsea said. She decided to keep the fact that Devlin had been involved in the boating accident a secret. At least until she confronted Devlin or Mitch or whoever he was.

"Well, I don't know much about Mitch Russell." Terri dropped her sunglasses back onto the bridge of her nose. "No one does. As I said, he showed up here several months ago and he keeps pretty much to himself—lives in a cabin about two miles up the beach from the Villa, just around the northern point. Oh, he hangs out with a few locals occasionally—usually at the bar in the Villa or at the Dauphin Bleu, or someplace like that, but he doesn't have a lot of friends."

"What about women?" Chelsea asked impulsively, despising the question. Mitch Russell's interest in the female population wasn't really any of her concern. Chelsea was only in Paradis to find out the truth.

Terri's lips pulled down at the corners. "I've never seen him with a woman—not like on a date or anything. And his name hasn't been linked with anyone in particular. Sometimes he hangs out with a couple of guys who live somewhere else and there's usually a girl—well, woman really, she must be twenty-one or two—with them."

For an unfathomable reason Chelsea's heart dropped.

"And, of course, he's around women, but as for anything serious—" she lifted her palms toward the sky "—I haven't heard about it—not that I would, necessarily." Terri slid her sunglasses back onto her nose. "Believe me, he's gotten his share of attention from the women tourists."

"I'll bet," Chelsea said dryly. Just like Devlin.

"He comes from somewhere in the midwest—Chicago, I think."

"What does he do for a living?"

"Nothing that I can tell," Terri said thoughtfully. "Though I heard he was working on some book."

"A book?" Chelsea repeated with a twist of her lips. Oh, sure. Devlin—writing a book? Restless, ever-moving Devlin sitting down at a computer or typewriter for hours on end? No way!

"That's the rumor."

"Do you know anything else about him?"

"Not much. Once in a while he goes over to St. Jean, but I don't know why."

"Regularly?" Chelsea asked, interested.

"Fairly—maybe once every week or two. But that's not so unusual. Paradis is pretty small, especially if you're used to a big city." Terri finished her drink and studied the picture again. "This man—" she tapped a peach-colored nail on the photograph "—if he had a beard, I suppose, could be Mitch, but it's pretty hard to tell."

"I know," Chelsea agreed, in frustration. "I guess the only way I'll find out is by talking to him again."

"That shouldn't be such a hardship," Terri teased.

If you only knew, Chelsea thought.

That night, she waited in the bar again. Self-consciously, she sipped her wine and ignored the curious looks sent over the shoulders of several men—men she recognized from the night before. She heard a few of the whispers and laughs, caught more than one smirk or interested eyebrow lifted in her direction, and she knew the knowing smiles were at her expense.

Still, she sat alone at a tall table, absently twirling the stem of her wineglass, nibbling on pretzels, and pretending not to notice the speculative glances cast her way. Three different men tried to occupy the other chair at her table and one asked her to dance, but she made it clear she was waiting for someone and acted as if she didn't see the mockery in each man's eyes.

Staring through the haze of cigarette smoke, she lingered for nearly three hours.

Mitch didn't show up.

She'd probably scared him off, she realized fatalistically. Great. So what was the next step? She'd already wasted a day on the island—well, perhaps not wasted. Terri had been helpful and she'd enjoyed the petite redhead's company. However, as for Devlin, she didn't know much more than she did when she arrived in Emeraude yesterday.

She left her second glass of wine half-full, tossed some change on the bar, and walked through French doors to a patio outside, away from the noise and the smoke.

Fresh, salty air blew in from the sea, snatching at her hair and cooling her face. The moon, three-quarters and shining brightly, hung low in the sky. Thousands of stars winked overhead.

Shoving her hands into the pockets of her new sundress, Chelsea shoved on a rusted wrought-iron gate that squeaked in protest as it opened. She followed an overgrown sandy path that skirted the old Villa and forked into the same flagstone trail she'd followed the night before. Without thinking twice, she hurried past the swimming pool and started down the path that led through the woods to the beach.

Terri had said that Mitch lived past the north point on the beach, and Chelsea intended to check it out and wait for him if need be.

The path widened and unconsciously, Chelsea glanced at the trunk of the tree where Mitch had waited for her the night before. But tonight, she was alone. The strip of white sand was deserted and the sea lapped lazily at the shore. A ribbon of moonlight rippled on the shadowy water.

On a lark, Chelsea kicked off her sandals and waded in the warm sea, wondering at the rashness of her plan to wait for Devlin at his house.

If he hadn't already left Paradis.

She plucked her sandals from the ground and gathering her courage, started north along the beach, cool sand squishing between her toes. She'd wasted enough time trying to learn something about him. It was time for a showdown.

Trying to convince herself that she wasn't about to make the biggest mistake of her life, she followed the deserted stretch of sand around a curve and past a few cabins with lights burning brightly in their windows.

The beach narrowed to a path that twisted around a rocky jetty. Chelsea followed the overgrown trail along the edge of the ocean until it widened again for a short distance.

Only one house occupied this tiny northerly beach, a small cabin with a tile roof and a broad front porch that faced the sea. A beat-up vehicle—a truck or rig of some sort—was parked in a rutted lane and a couple of chairs occupied the porch. A hammock stretched between two trees. Further away, at the ocean's edge, a long, sun-bleached dock stretched into the dark ocean. Against the pier, a sailboat was lashed to the moorings and rocked gently with the tide.

Chelsea's teeth bit into her lip. Obviously Devlin's love of sailing hadn't been destroyed in the accident. Her heart hammered loudly as she approached the house.

What if this were the wrong place?

Just because Terri had given her general directions didn't mean that this little cabin belonged to Mitch Russell. The windows were open, no shades drawn, and lamplight glowed in the darkness.

Closer to the cabin, her hands beginning to sweat, Chelsea craned her neck to peer cautiously into the living room.

The inside of the cabin was sparse, furnished with a worn couch, coffee table and chair. The walls were stucco, the floor, weathered boards covered by an old rag rug.

"It's now or never," she whispered to herself as she

walked stiffly up the two rickety steps to the front door and knocked loudly.

Her stomach twisted.

The seconds ticked by.

Sweat gathered between her shoulders.

No one answered.

What now? she wondered, but even as she did, she reached forward, her fingers wrapped around the doorknob. She pushed and the door creaked open on rusty hinges.

Her heart thundered. She shouldn't be doing this. She was trespassing, for God's sake! And she didn't know anything about Mitch Russell. He could be on the run. Maybe he owned a gun. She glanced around, but couldn't see anything.

Swallowing against a suddenly dry throat, Chelsea took a step forward, but couldn't cross the threshold. Even though the door hadn't been locked, this seemed a little like breaking and entering—well, entering at least—and she didn't want to have to try to talk her way out of a complaint lodged by Mitch.

But then, she'd come this far, hadn't she?

"Mitch?" she called, and her voice sounded little more than a whisper. This place was giving her the creeps! "Mitch?"

Behind her, the breeze picked up, tickling her neck. She felt someone's gaze upon her back and froze. The deep male voice, hard-edged and sounding so much like Devlin, stopped her cold. "Take one step inside and I'll call the authorities."

His voice was like an electric shock. Chelsea nearly jumped out of her skin. Heart thudding, she whirled around.

"What the hell are you doing here?" he demanded, glaring angrily at her. Standing near the curved trunk of a palm tree, his silhouette was just visible against a backdrop of moon-dappled water. He wiped a hand over his face and shoved wet hair from his eyes. He wore cutoff jeans and nothing else. His hair shimmered in the moonlight and his wet shorts clung to him, hanging low on his hips. His chest was bare and dark hair stretched across the broad expanse only to narrow into a thin trail that disappeared beneath his exposed navel and nearly indecent low-slung cutoffs.

Chelsea's mouth turned to cotton at the sight of him half-naked. His abdomen was flat and hard and his chest rose and fell, as he breathed raggedly from his swim.

"I called for you but no one answered," she said lamely.

His expression murderous, Mitch ground out, "You sure don't know how to take a hint, do you?"

"I just wanted to talk to you."

"Yeah, right," he said with a disbelieving snort.

"I did. Really."

"So talk."

"I have pictures—pictures of Devlin. I'd like to show them to you."

"I'm not interested."

The man was absolutely maddening! "What would it hurt?"

He didn't answer for a long moment. His eyes regarded her with sultry appraisal.

Chelsea could barely breathe. She felt his hot gaze, so much like Devlin's, and it caused her blood to quicken through her veins.

Scowling, he crossed the sand that separated them, then climbed the two steps of the porch, stopping only inches from her. She had to tilt her head up to look into his eyes and it was all she could do to meet his gaze— hooded and darkly sensual. He smelled of salt, sea and musk, and droplets of water still clung to his beard.

He was too close and she wanted to back up a step, to put some distance between her body and his, but she held her ground, rather than retreat into his house.

"Will you leave me alone if I trip down memory lane with you?" he asked, his breath hot as it whispered across her hair.

"I—I don't know."

"What will it take to convince you that I'm not your boyfriend?"

"I told you, he wasn't my…" She swallowed hard as he crooked one lofty brow. "Just look at the pictures—hear me out."

"And then you'll be on your way?"

"Yes."

"And you won't bother me again?"

She hesitated. She'd always been an awful liar, but she knew if she told him the truth, he'd shut her out and that would be the end of it. "I—I'll try not to."

His jaw slid to the side. Leaning one shoulder against the rough walls of the house, he reached forward and touched the tip of her chin with one long finger. "Maybe we can work a deal," he said silkily.

Chelsea shuddered. "A deal?"

"Yeah. I listen to you and you—" he cocked his head toward the interior of the house "—you spend the night with me."

She hesitated just a heartbeat. "No way."

"No?" His fingers slid easily along her chin and down her throat. Chelsea quivered inside but didn't move. Staunchly, she held her ground.

"I'm not here to bargain sexual favors," she said tightly.

His gaze slid downward to the swell of her breasts. "I wonder."

To her horror, her traitorous pulse leaped. "Well, you can wonder and rot in hell while you do it!" she snapped, though the constriction in her lungs was nearly painful.

He clucked his tongue and his eyes glinted mischievously. "Strong words for a woman who wants something so badly."

"All I want is information—nothing else."

Mitch's lips twisted beneath his beard and his finger moved lower, to the circle of bones at her throat. "This guy—Devlin—he must've meant a lot to you."

That was a tough one. "He did."

"You were friends?"

"Yes," she whispered, trying to concentrate on the conversation while Mitch's fingers slid lower still, closer to her breast.

"Lovers?"

"No!"

"No?" he asked, disbelieving and she stepped back and flung his hand away.

"No!" she repeated, her voice sounding torn even to her own ears. "I—I was in love with his best friend."

Mitch's blue eyes darkened to midnight.

"If you'll just listen to me, I'll explain everything."

Eyeing her thoughtfully, he shoved his hands into

the back pockets of his cutoffs. "Okay, lady, I'll listen. But on one condition."

"And what's that?"

His eyes glinted like blue fire. "After you spin your little tale and I look at your scrapbook, you either leave me alone for good or spend the rest of the night in my bed."

Chapter 4

Chelsea tossed her hair over her shoulders and angled her chin upward rebelliously. "Get this straight, Russell. I'm *not* interested in sleeping with you—"

"Even if I turned out to be this Devlin guy?"

Her heart pummeled against her ribs. "Even then."

He crooked a dark, disbelieving brow.

"And as for leaving you alone, I can't do that. At least not yet!"

"Then I guess we don't have anything to talk about." He leaned down, as if the consequences of their conversation meant nothing to him, and brushed the sand from his still-wet legs.

She couldn't believe he was turning her away. After practically undressing her with his eyes, he didn't have the decency to hear her out! Narrowing her eyes, she asked, "Don't you even want to see the pictures?"

"I couldn't care less."

"But—"

"Look, lady, I already told you I don't know you and I don't give a damn about your boyfriend."

"I thought I told you, Devlin *wasn't* my boyfriend."

"You've told me all right, but you seem pretty interested in him. How far have you traveled, hmm? How much money have you wasted to get here? From where I stand, you seem to have more than a passing interest in your lover's friend."

That did it. Her temper went through the roof. It was all she could do to keep from slapping him. "If you'd just hear me out," she said through clenched teeth. "You'd understand—"

"Why don't you just leave me the hell alone?"

"Because I can't!"

"Give it up, lady!" He flicked an angry glance at her, eyeing her dress with disdain. "Paradis isn't a place for a wealthy woman, or haven't you figured that out yet? Why don't you go chase your petty fantasies in Martinique or Bermuda or the Bahamas? I'm sure you can find someone willing to go along with your fairy tale—"

"Because you're here," she interrupted.

He didn't move a muscle. His blue eyes turned as dark as the night sky as he silently appraised her.

Chelsea's breath caught in her throat. Her pulse leaped crazily and she had to battle the emotions that tore at her soul.

"Not me, Chelsea," he said quietly. "You're looking for someone else."

"I don't think so," she whispered, her gaze locking into the inky depths of his.

"You think I'm lying?"

"Yes."

"Why?" he demanded, his face a knot of consternation.

"Because you know something that you'd rather keep secret."

He shook his head slowly. "You really expect me to believe this?" he said, nearly laughing. "Lady, if you could only hear yourself. If you ask me, you've watched one too many TV movies."

Refusing to be ridiculed into submission, she crossed her arms over her chest. "Why won't you just admit that you're Devlin?"

"Because I'm not, dammit." He plowed stiff fingers through his wet hair and the brackets surrounding his mouth turned white. "What does it take to get through to you?"

"Just listen to me. Let me show you the pictures…"

He tensed suddenly, every muscle turning rigid.

When she opened her mouth to continue, he whispered a soft, "Shh." He placed a staying finger against her lips and gave a curt shake of his head.

She got the message. Chelsea's words died on her lips. And his apprehension infected her. She strained to listen but only heard the sounds of the night.

Mitch squinted, eyes narrowed against the shadows. His gaze darted quickly across the isolated terrain, searching the darkness of the tropical woods and sweeping across the ocean. Lips tight, he muttered, "Get inside." When she didn't immediately obey, his jaw hardened and without another word he wrapped a strong arm around her waist.

"Hey!"

Hauling her quickly over the threshold, he kicked the door shut behind them.

Chelsea struggled against his tight hold. "What do you think you're doing?"

"Shh!" he hissed. He dropped her unceremoniously onto the couch, then locked and bolted the door, closed the windows and snapped the shades shut.

Frightened by his bizarre behavior, she quickly scrambled to her feet and started for the front door. But he grabbed her hand roughly and spun her around. "Who followed you?" he demanded.

"W-what?" Her stomach slammed against her diaphragm.

"Did you bring someone with you?" He wasn't playing games. His face was hard and set. His fingers tightened over her arm, biting into her flesh.

Chelsea's blood ran cold. "No—I don't know anyone on the island. No one but you."

"Look, lady, for the last time, you *don't* know me!" He gave her arm a shake.

"No one followed me!"

"Are you sure?"

"Yes—I think." Sighing, she threw up her hands, casting his fingers off her. "I didn't really pay attention, but the beach was deserted."

"Not good enough." His back teeth ground together as he snapped off the lights. The cabin was suddenly black as pitch.

"Hey—what're you doing?"

"Just making sure you were alone."

"Why?" she demanded, squinting, trying to get her bearings in case he was playing some trick on her.

"Just shut up for a second, will you?" he asked, peering through the blinds.

The house grew silent except for the island breeze that soughed against the roof and the dull, distant roar of the ocean. Chelsea's nerves stretched tight. Here she was, alone with a man who was either a virtual stranger or a man who couldn't—or wouldn't—remember her—a man who had played havoc with her emotions in the past. Either way, she was in an impossible situation.

A cold sweat ran down Chelsea's back. Had she inadvertently lured someone to Mitch—someone dangerous? Or was this just another of his ploys to get rid of her? Maybe he was trying to scare her off. She wouldn't put it past him.

Slowly, her eyes adjusted to the darkness and she told herself she should be afraid—locked in this unknown house with a stranger. Even if this man proved to be Devlin, he'd changed to the point that she didn't feel at ease with him—not that she'd ever been completely at ease with Devlin. There had been an ominous and rough side to him—a side that had intrigued, yet frightened her. But Devlin had shown a depth of character, a sense of humor, cynical though it might be, and a certain warmth, loyalty and charm that Mitch Russell was sorely lacking.

Yes, there had been times when Devlin had been cold and calculating, when as a detective for the San Francisco Police Department he had been forced to be so. But there had been a human side to him as well—an honorable side. Chelsea wasn't sure that Mitch Russell had any honor. In fact, she decided that he probably had ice water running through his veins.

Her skin prickled as she watched him. He stood at a side window, peering through the slits between the blinds, the corded muscles of his chest stiff and tense.

The minutes dragged out. Chelsea fidgeted apprehensively on the couch. Was he trying to scare her? Well, dammit, he was. She was frightened, but she really didn't understand why. What could be so threatening that he would drag her in here and lock the door? Nothing, she decided. He was just into melodrama, hoping to frighten her away. Well, she'd surprise him.

The silence became deafening. Finally, when she thought she couldn't stand the tension straining in the room a moment longer, he flipped on a small table lamp. But he didn't open the blinds.

"Satisfied?" she asked.

"No." He glared at her as if she were some kind of Jezebel. His gaze raked down the scoop neck of her dress, the full white skirt. "You couldn't have worn anything that would have stood out anymore than that, could you?"

"What are you afraid of?"

"Not afraid. Just cautious."

"Or paranoid?" she baited.

To her surprise he actually grinned—a cynical smile that didn't quite touch his eyes. "Probably."

"You really thought someone followed me? Why?"

He lifted a shoulder.

"And why all this secrecy—this cloak and dagger stuff? What are you, some kind of spy?"

He snorted. "Hardly."

"No?" She lifted a mocking brow. "Then what? Running away from the law? Or maybe the I.R.S.? Or are you hiding here with a new identity, Devlin?"

In a split second his smile faded and he clenched a fist, raising it as if to crash it against a wall, then, abruptly straightened his fingers. "For the last time," he muttered, his voice strained by his rapidly escaping patience, "I'm not your precious Devlin."

"He wasn't *my* anything."

"Yeah, right. You do a lot of denying but not much convincing."

She ignored that jab. "So who do you think followed me?"

"I don't know." Motioning impatiently with his hand, he said abruptly, "You said you had some pictures. Why don't you show them to me and be on your merry way?"

"Nothing I'd like better," she replied curtly. Quickly, she opened her purse and retrieved the envelope of photographs. She dumped the contents onto a scarred coffee table and watched Mitch's reaction. He crossed the room, but barely glanced at the pictures.

Chelsea's heart constricted. How could Devlin act so callously disinterested when he and John had been so close? Desperately, she handed him a picture of John and a part of her died when not the least bit of emotion crossed his face. Oh, Lord, had she been so terribly wrong about him?

"I don't look like this guy," he finally said, his eyes returning to hers. "Not at all. I don't get this—"

"That's not Devlin," she cut in hastily. "It's John, my fiancé," she said, her throat suddenly hot and dry when she thought of John and all their plans. Why did it seem so long ago—so far away?

Mitch glanced at the photograph, then let it drop back to the table. "If this guy's the one you were supposed to marry, why all the interest in his friend? Or did you have a thing going with him, too?"

Chelsea had to grit her teeth to keep from flinging back a hot retort. "No, I just need to talk to him—to you. I—I need to know what happened."

Mitch's jaw hardened. He kicked the table out of his way, grabbed her by the forearms and hauled her to her feet.

"Hey—stop—"

"I'm only going to say this one more time, lady," he ground out, his breath hot against her face, the tips of her breasts brushing his chest. "I'm not, never was, never will be Devlin McVey! And I pity the poor bastard who is, because you're obviously going to chase him to the ends of the earth—or some poor slob who looks like him." His gaze raked over her face. "Why do you care?"

"Because I need answers," she said, her eyes beseeching his. "I want to know why Devlin insisted John go out on the boat that day—what they had to discuss. And I want to know why he faked his death, what happened on that boat, and why he ran away."

Something deadly flickered in Mitch's eyes and he released his viselike grip on her arm. The hard line of his mouth gentled. "Has it ever occurred to you that McVey might be dead?"

She closed her eyes against that horrid truth. "I can't believe Devlin's gone."

Mitch's head snapped up and his eyes narrowed on hers. "Why not? Just because his body didn't wash up?"

"It's—it's just a feeling I've got. That's all."

"Where did this happen?"

"San Francisco Bay."

"Lord, woman, that's one helluva stretch of water. Couldn't McVey's body have washed out to sea?"

No! "It's possible."

"What do the police have to say about it?"

"They seem to think that Devlin and John got caught in a storm, they had engine trouble of some kind, maybe a leak in the gas line, which caused an explosion, and a swell capsized the boat, smashing it into some rocks and both men drowned." Chelsea gazed steadily into his blue, blue eyes. "But I find it hard to believe that could have happened. Both Devlin and John were expert sailors."

"They wouldn't be the first ones to lose out to the forces of nature," he said cynically. Raking his fingers through his hair, he picked up another snapshot that had fallen to the floor when he'd kicked the table. In the picture Devlin stood on one side of her, John the other. Ironic, she thought, how she'd always felt torn between these two friends.

Frowning, he rifled through the remaining photographs, one after another, eyeing them with maddening calm, not showing the least bit of emotion—as if he really didn't know the men in the pictures—as if he had no memory of Devlin McVey's past.

An overwhelming wave of disappointment flooded through her. She almost believed that this man wasn't Devlin, but she remembered that Devlin had been an actor, and a convincing one at that. He'd been a man comfortable with lying and assuming roles as an undercover detective for the police force. Perhaps "Mitch Russell" was feigning indifference just to get her out of his life.

"This, I assume, is Devlin," he said finally as he pointed at one small photograph of Devlin. In the picture, Devlin's blue eyes were filled with mischief and a crooked smile slashed across his clean-shaven jaw.

Chelsea's insides clenched. Even in a still photograph, some of Devlin's rakish charm came through. "Yes," she said, aware of the catch in her voice.

"There's some resemblance," he reluctantly conceded, his lower lip protruding thoughtfully, "but I'm not your guy." His eyes met hers again and they were filled with questions. "San Francisco is a long way from here. How'd you find me?"

"A private investigator named Jenkins."

"And he just happened to pick Paradis?" Mitch asked skeptically.

She quickly sketched out how Jenkins had discovered Mitch Russell and returned with the news. As she explained about her hasty trip, she watched Mitch carefully. His expression didn't alter—he still stared at her as if she were a certifiable lunatic. Nonetheless, she continued on with her story, including the events of the past two nights. "...so that's how I ended up here and that's why I know that you're Devlin."

"What do you want me to say? That I'm this guy?" he asked, sounding incredulous. Lifting one hand he added, "Okay, let's just pretend I'm Devlin McVey— oh, do I have a middle name?" he mocked.

"Andrew."

"Okay. I'm Devlin Andrew McVey. Now what?"

The muscles between Chelsea's shoulder blades tightened. "Now I ask you what happened on the boat that afternoon."

"I don't know." Not a glimmer of regret crossed his face. In fact, he seemed almost bored with the game.

"It was this day," she gritted out, frustrated beyond belief. She shoved a picture across the table, a picture of John, Devlin and her, arms flung around each other, the sailboat tethered to the side of the dock. The sky was gray and overcast, the sea slate-colored. Wayward strands of her dark brown hair whipped across John's laughing face. "You remember the day—April twenty-sixth of last year! The day the boat went down, the day John lost his life, the day Devlin McVey disappeared!"

"You're crazy!"

"Don't you remember John? Your best friend!" Dear Lord, why was he playing this game with her? Why? Hadn't she suffered enough? Shaking, her throat hot with unshed tears, she took in a long breath. How many times had she relived that fateful gusty day? How many nightmares had caused her to wake up to her own screams, to feel the sheets soaked with sweat as she saw over and over again in her mind's eye, how John had drowned.

Mitch's voice, when he finally spoke, was soft. "I've known a lot of men named John in my life," he admitted frowning, "but I don't recognize this man." He let out a long, whistling sigh and his hard-edged features gentled. "I'm sorry for all the pain you've gone through, really I am. But I'm not your missing friend. You have to believe me. I know it might be hard to accept, but you'll have to look elsewhere or deal with the fact that McVey obviously drowned along with your fiancé."

"I can't!" she cried, pounding an impotent fist into the worn cushions of the couch.

"Why not?"

She shook her head, wishing she had more than intuition to go on. "If…if Devlin were dead, I think I'd know it. Feel it."

"You cared for him that much?"

The question stopped her cold. Coming from this man, whose gaze was so intense—so damned piercing, she found the words difficult. "No—yes—oh, I don't know." Realizing she sounded as crazy as he obviously thought she was, Chelsea rubbed her arms as if from a sudden chill. "He was—no, *is* my friend and he's not dead. He's not!"

"You certainly are a stubborn thing," he observed.

"When I know I'm right."

He rubbed a hand around the back of his neck and Chelsea tried to ignore the innate sexuality of his muscles moving effortlessly under his skin. "I wish things were different, Chelsea," he finally said, sounding as if he meant it, "but I can't help you."

"I think you're lying to me," she said with difficulty.

"I'm not—"

"Devlin, please!"

"Dammit, woman, give it a rest!" Angry all over again, Mitch shoved the pictures aside. Several slid onto the beaten plank floor. "I hope you didn't already pay this clown of a private detective of yours, 'cause if you did, you just lost yourself a pile of money!"

He'd hit a raw nerve, but Chelsea didn't flinch. "My deal with Jenkins is none of your business."

"Exactly! None of this—" he motioned toward the pictures scattered on the floor and table "—is my business! And I'm none of yours. So why don't you pick up your photographs, stuff them into your purse, waltz out of here and leave me the hell alone?"

"Can you prove to me that you're *not* Devlin?"

His eyes narrowed a fraction. "I shouldn't have to. But if it'll make you feel any better, okay."

He strode stiffly through the kitchen to another doorway, which she assumed led to his bedroom. Within seconds he was back, opening a beat-up wallet. He unfolded the leather and stared at the contents, then dropped an outdated Illinois driver's license onto the table along with three major credit cards issued to Mitchell P. Russell.

"The P is for Palmer—which, by the way, was my mother's maiden name. She was Marian Adair Palmer Russell, my father was Brian Joseph Russell. They're both gone now and I had no brothers or sisters or cousins who I was close to. As for pictures, I have a few of my own." He handed her a wallet-sized snapshot of himself and a beautiful blond woman with laughing blue eyes and a mischievous smile. Tiny dimples graced her cheeks and her arms were thrown around the neck of a black shepherd. "That's Angie," Mitch said quietly. "My wife."

Chelsea's heart dropped. "You're married?" she whispered, hardly believing her ears.

"I was," he replied softly, his lips flattening over his teeth. "We were in an accident." He glanced away. "I was injured—broke my hip and a couple of ribs, got cut up a little, but Angie didn't make it. Neither did the dog."

"Oh." Chelsea felt like a fool. Obviously this man still grieved for the beautiful, smiling woman with the impish blue eyes, easy smile and silken blond hair. "I—I'm sorry."

He shrugged, as if her empathy were of no consequence. "You need any more proof?"

Chelsea swallowed. The suspicious side of her nature required more than one photograph and a few credit cards, yet, there was a ring of truth to his story that she couldn't dispute. "Devlin had a wife, too," she said woodenly. "She died a few years ago."

"Then I feel sorry for him," Mitch said quietly. "It's hell." He rammed the photo back into his wallet. "Satisfied?"

She nodded mutely, wishing she could argue with him. But the pain shadowing his eyes was real and the evidence he'd shown her held up his claim.

"I don't like giving people my life history and I sure as hell don't need to prove myself to you. So, unless you have an ulterior motive for coming here, I think you'd better leave."

Her throat was suddenly desert dry. Nervously, Chelsea licked her lips. She didn't want to leave and yet she knew that staying would be to invite danger. "I don't have an ulterior motive."

One side of his mouth lifted cynically. "No? Well, if you really do think I'm your friend McVey, I sure would like to know what was going on between the two of you. Anytime you want to give me a demonstration, I'll be ready."

All the empathy she'd felt for him disappeared. Fury shot through her, but she quickly counted to ten. She wasn't going to let him goad her. Though her stomach was in knots, Chelsea calmly gathered her pictures from the table and floor. "Would you? I wonder. You know, Mr. Russell, I don't believe you. I think you're just trying to scare me into running off."

He didn't bother to hide the mockery in his eyes. "Try me," he invited lazily.

"No thanks."

His lips twitched. "No?" He crossed the room, reaching the door and throwing the bolt.

"Not if you were the last man on this island."

He laughed then. "Don't challenge me, Miss Reed," he warned. "You'll lose."

She shook her head and wished she was anywhere else on earth. "You've got an ego that just won't quit."

"You're here, aren't you? And I don't remember issuing an invitation."

Was he laughing at her? What she wouldn't do to wipe that smug smile off his lips! "Don't flatter yourself," she remarked, heading for the door, but as she reached for the knob, he sprang, grabbing her arm and spinning her around sharply. She landed against him with a thud.

She gasped and as she did, his lips captured hers in a kiss that tore the breath from her lungs. Unexpectedly his mouth covered hers and his tongue, wet and sensual, slid between her teeth to touch and explore.

She tried to pull free of his grasp, but his arms tightened around her.

"Stop it!" she cried when he lifted his head, but she was trembling from head to foot.

"It's what you really wanted, wasn't it?" he growled, shoving her against the door, her bare back pressed hard against the painted wood.

"No!"

"Come on, Chelsea, admit it. This cock-and-bull

story about dead fiancés and best friends is just for kicks. You're down here—some wealthy woman who's probably tired of her husband or lover—and you're looking for a little adventure. Sure, you found me and I look like the guy in the photos, but that's not what this is all about, is it?" With one long finger, he slowly traced the line of her jaw, causing her skin to tremble expectantly. "That's not why you're so damned persistent when you know I'm not Devlin."

Furious with herself, she shoved his hand aside. "You're despicable!"

"No, just willing," he teased, shifting so that his hips pressed intimately against hers, his thighs hard and demanding, his wet cutoffs creating a damp impression upon her cotton skirt.

"I already told you I don't want to go to bed with you," she said, her voice hoarser than usual.

"And I say you're a liar." He kissed her again and this time his lips were less punishing, his mouth molding gently over hers.

She turned liquid inside and hot spasms pulsed through her blood. Desire, unwanted and long buried, surfaced, yawning and stretching within. As his body trapped hers against the door, he placed both hands on the sides of her face, his tongue rimming her lips, tickling the inside of her mouth and sliding sensitively along her teeth.

"Don't!" she cried, jerking her head to the side, but the sound that issued from her lips sounded like a moan. She reached behind her, found the knob, and jerked open the door. "You're the most insufferable man I've ever met!"

"And you just keep coming back for more."

"And you just keep flattering yourself!"

Mitch stepped backward into the house and Chelsea nearly stumbled across the porch. Her breathing was tight and hard. Embarrassment washed up her cheeks and burned in her mind as she glared back at him. Good Lord, the man was actually smiling!

How could she let him touch her so intimately? She'd let him *kiss* her, for God's sake!

"Good night, Miss Reed," he taunted. "Come back when you want to show me more—"

Chelsea straightened and glared across the porch at him. "I won't give up, you know. If you're Devlin, I swear—"

"Don't waste any more of my time. The next time you come to me, think about your reasons and don't think I'll pretend to be some ghost or fantasy. When you show up here again—and I have a feeling you will—I'll assume it's for me."

"Your ego is incredible!" Her jaw dropped.

"At least I don't delude myself."

"Go to hell!"

His smile fell from his face. "I think I've already been."

Chelsea turned on her heel and, forcing her legs not to run, marched stiffly back to the path. Disgusted with herself and her purely physical reactions to a man she couldn't stand, she trudged along the moon-washed shore and told herself that she wouldn't give up, she couldn't! And if Devlin wanted a fight, damn it, he'd get one!

Get a grip on yourself, Chels, she thought, stumbling along the path through the trees. Angry that she'd let him goad her into so vulnerable a position, she seethed all the way back to the hotel. When he couldn't get her to leave by conventional methods, he'd used his masculinity as a weapon and she'd fallen into the easy trap. All he had to do was pretend to be interested in her and she had turned tail and run.

But what other option did she have? Return his passion—real or construed—with her own? Where would that lead? Right into Mitch Russell's bed—or Devlin's bed. That thought sent unwelcome anticipation through her mind.

"Never!" she spat, but knew she was more susceptible than she was willing to admit. Devlin had proved that once before.

She climbed up the stairs to her room, more determined than ever to find out the truth about one Mr. Mitchell P. Russell. There were ways to check out his story. As she opened the door, she wondered about the beautiful blond woman—his wife—in his photograph.

How did she know that the blonde wasn't still very much alive? Or that she was his wife?

"You don't," she reprimanded herself as she stepped into her room and locked the door behind her. When it came right down to it, she didn't know much about Mitch Russell.

What if he's really who he says he is? He had the identification and story to prove it. And what did she have to go on? The fact that he looked like Devlin, that he sounded like Devlin, that he smelled like Devlin? What else? What hard evidence?

Dropping her head into her hands, she squeezed her eyes shut and more doubts assailed her. If he were really Mitch, she looked like a fool. It's a wonder he didn't call the police or the mental hospital! And she'd kissed him so passionately.

Because you thought he was Devlin. What if he isn't? She froze inside, mortified beyond words.

She couldn't think about that, not now, not until she was sure. Willing her eyes open, she noticed that the red light on her telephone was flashing, signaling that someone had left her a message.

"Now what?" she wondered, dropping onto the bed and blowing her bangs out of her eyes. She dialed the operator and was told that Felicia Reed had called her.

"Great," she mumbled, hanging up and punching out her mother's number. Just what she needed—big sister lecture number seven, which repeated just about every other week.

It took several tries before the long distance, overseas connection finally went through.

Felicia answered on the fifth ring.

"Hi," Chelsea said, pretending she didn't have a care in the world.

"About time you called!" Felicia replied, her voice faint through the poor connection. "Where were you? It must be past midnight there!"

"It is," Chelsea agreed.

"Well, did you find this man—this Mitch Russell?" Felicia asked, worry edging her voice.

"Yes."

"And?"

"He swears he isn't Devlin."

"Good. So you'll be home in a couple of days," Felicia decided for herself. "I'll tell Mom—"

"No!"

"What?"

"Don't tell Mom anything. Just because the man says he's not Devlin, doesn't mean a thing."

"But can't you tell?" Felicia demanded.

"No." And that was the truth. "One minute I believe him, the next, I'm not so sure."

"Oh, great. Now, you're not even sure." Felicia sighed impatiently. "And what does he have to say for himself?"

"He thinks I'm a nut case."

"I like him better already," Felicia observed dryly.

"Thanks a lot."

"Well, you have to admit it, Chels, this is really reaching. I mean *really* reaching. Even for you."

"I don't think so," Chelsea replied, squirming a little. She did have doubts herself. If Mitch were really Devlin, he was pulling off the acting job of his life!

"Well, I just hope you smarten up and give up in a few days. This is really taking a toll on Mom. She worries, you know."

"Let me talk to her."

"I can't. She's in the tub. But I'll tell her you called."

"Do that," Chelsea said, just to get Felicia off her back.

"And when can I tell her you'll be home?"

"I don't know yet," Chelsea admitted.

"A week maybe?" Felicia prodded.

"I'm not sure."

There was a tired, long-suffering sigh from Felicia's end of the conversation. "You can't take off indefinitely, you know. You have responsibilities—we all do."

"I'll call Mom later," Chelsea said, adding a quick goodbye and hanging up. She lay back on the bed and flung one arm across her eyes. Some of Felicia's points, she admitted grudgingly, had merit. Maybe this was just a wild goose chase. And maybe, though she hated to admit it, she had come to Paradis for more than answers about John's death.

Frowning, she rolled over on her stomach and propped her chin on her hands. Thinking of John was difficult. Thinking of Devlin was confusing. Thinking about both of them together was downright scary. She'd been pulled and pushed between them for over a year and a half, caring about them both, but denying any feelings other than friendship for Devlin. Well, most of the time, she thought guiltily, not letting her mind wander too far into that forbidden territory that was reserved for Devlin McVey.

If only it weren't so complicated! If only she could turn back time to the first night she'd met Devlin— the first night she'd come face to face with his rakish good looks, confident smile and biting sense of humor.

Life had been simpler before she'd met Devlin, before he'd caused the first of her doubts to surface, before she'd questioned her love for John. She grabbed a pillow and clenched it to her chest, wishing that John were still alive and that they could go back to the easy life they'd shared before Devlin.

Devlin—always Devlin! Why couldn't she just accept that he was gone and forget him?

Because he was unforgettable.

Meeting Devlin had been a turning point in her life and even now, in this lush tropical paradise, she could remember that cold September night when Devlin McVey had caught her so unawares and from that moment on, her life had been turned inside out...

Chapter 5

Winter had come early to northern California that year. Even in the early evening the sky was the color of slate, the cold waters of the bay reflecting the same somber shade.

Chelsea didn't mind. She was young and in love and she smiled to herself as she locked her car and, carrying her purse and a bottle of wine, walked up the five short steps to John's condominium. There were still lingering traces of summer in the courtyard, straggling red and white impatiens and dried yellow-headed marigolds splashed worn color in the greenery and added to Chelsea's lighthearted mood.

Shaking the rain from her umbrella, Chelsea rang the doorbell. She and John were going to share an evening alone and she'd been looking forward to it all week.

The door swung open and John, a chef's apron tied over his slacks, his oxford shirtsleeves rolled over his forearms, grinned broadly. "You're in for the treat of your life," he predicted.

"Uh-oh, you've been experimenting in the kitchen again," she charged, eyeing his apron.

"Nope, it's better than that."

She walked inside and his brown eyes flashed devilishly. "So what's the surprise?"

"Fantastic news!" He wrapped his arms possessively around Chelsea's waist. "You're finally going to meet Devlin!"

She'd heard of Devlin McVey, of course. "Ah, so the mysterious friend suddenly appears," Chelsea teased, kissing John lightly on the forehead. Still bundled in her raincoat, she shook the drops of water from her hair. "About time."

"He's been busy." John waited as she handed him the sack with the bottle of chardonnay. He eyed the bottle and wrinkled his nose.

Chelsea untied the belt of her coat. "Too busy to visit a good friend?"

"Come on, Chelsea, you understand about Devlin."

Oh, she understood all right. Devlin McVey, whoever he was, just happened, in John's opinion, to be right up there with the Almighty himself. Tough competition, in Chelsea's estimation. John hung up her coat in the closet near the door and Chelsea rubbed her arms.

John's condominium was warm and cozy. A fire crackled in the tiled hearth and classical music filtered through the rooms from hidden speakers. A huge drafting table occupied a space near the floor-to-ceiling windows and cream-colored leather couches were arranged between teak-and-glass tables. Brass lamps glowed in the corners, and high over the bedroom loft, rain peppered the skylights.

She followed John into his kitchen where the scents of garlic, onions and tomatoes mingled together in John's special primavera sauce. "This must really be a special occasion," she remarked, eyeing the simmering sauce. She hated to cook, but John was as comfortable in the kitchen as he was in his architectural office in Oakland.

"It is. You remember me telling you about Devlin," John said, uncorking a bottle of zinfandel, ignoring the wine she'd spent all of five minutes selecting. She wasn't surprised. According to John, she wasn't a wine connoisseur, nor a gourmet, nor even had an eye for interior decorating, but she didn't let his prejudices bother her. All in all, he was probably right, she thought ruefully.

"Hard not to remember Devlin." John spoke of Devlin often, not that she really cared. In fact, she was intrigued that he was actually going to show up. "Devlin McVey, cop extraordinaire," she said dryly.

"There are worse things in life than being a cop."

"Not in my family," she replied, remembering the horrid nights she'd lain awake worrying about her father. There had been times he hadn't returned home for days and she'd caught her mother crying and praying that he was alive. Paul Reed had survived, though he'd been shot and hospitalized more than once in his career as an undercover detective. No, thank you very much, she didn't need any more reminders of how hard the life as a policeman's wife or daughter could be.

"You'll like Devlin. Trust me," John told her.

"Can I reserve judgment?" she asked winking at him as he handed her a glass.

John laughed. "Don't I have good taste in friends? I chose you, remember?"

"How could I forget?" She and John had met in college and he'd shamelessly pursued her. They'd studied together, gone to football games and parties and always gotten along well. "The perfect couple," their mutual friends had called them. Practical. Predictable. Fun-loving but levelheaded. Loving John had been safe and comfortable—like wearing a favorite old bathrobe. And everyone, her sister and mother included, had told Chelsea to count her blessings that such an even-tempered, successful man loved her.

"Time you settled down with one good man," her mother had told her during her senior year in college.

"John's perfect," Felicia had cooed. "And an architect! Oh, just think, Chels, when you get married he could build you a house—I mean a real house—something contemporary that hangs out over the ocean or maybe a traditional in the Heights. I'm so glad you found someone to keep you sane!"

Chelsea hadn't been all that comfortable with Felicia's attitude, but as she'd long since given up her wilder tendencies, she didn't let Felicia's comments get under her skin. Because Felicia had been right. Chelsea *had* been wild in high school and her first couple of years in college. But, during her senior year at Berkeley, she'd settled into a comfortable life-style with John. He was a great friend and a wonderful companion. Good-looking, athletic, witty, John was every girl's fantasy.

So why had she resisted the natural step of moving in with him? It wasn't that she was holding out for marriage, but, if she delved deep into her heart, she knew there was a small piece missing in their lives—what, she couldn't really say, because, as everyone agreed, John was the greatest.

She picked up a piece of carrot from the counter and munched on it, for which she was rewarded with one of John's mock dark looks. "So why haven't I met Devlin before?"

"My fault," John admitted. "He's a lady-killer." His lips tugged upward at the corners. "I didn't want you to drop me and fall for him."

"You thought I would?" she teased, giggling.

"It's happened before."

"Not with me."

"You haven't met him yet."

"Oh, ye of little faith," she intoned, laughing at John's consternation. She loved him, she did! He was perfect. She'd be crazy not to love him.

"I'm not kidding, Chels, he's got a reputation a mile long. Women drop like flies for him. It must be that birthmark he has," John added slyly. "It's right about here—" he pointed a finger high on his hip, very close to his crotch "—and it looks like a crescent moon—"

"Give me a break," Chelsea said, laughing and punching him on the arm.

"I'm not kidding."

"And *I'm* not interested. Come on, back to your story."

"Okay, okay. Anyway, Devlin and I met a long time ago." John was furiously stirring his sauce. "We were freshmen in college in L.A., before I transferred up to Berkeley."

"Where you met me," she put in.

"Right. Best decision I've ever made." He shot her a knowing glance. "Anyway, back in L.A., Devlin and I ended up in the same dorm and we hung out together, even though we didn't have any of the same classes. We just hit it off."

"So what happened?"

"All hell broke loose. Come spring term, there was some theft going on in the dorm and one of the guys—his name was... Sean... Sean Lavery. Sean insisted that he'd caught Devlin going through his room."

Chelsea was interested. She sipped her wine. "Go on."

"There'd been some thefts on campus. Well, it turned out Devlin *had been* in Sean's room, but not for the reason everyone thought. Devlin was sure the guy was involved in some drug deals on campus and he wanted to prove it."

"He was a policeman—even then?" she asked skeptically.

"Nope. And that's how he got into trouble. There was a big scandal, the story was written up in the school paper. Both Devlin and Sean were kicked out of school."

"That's not fair!"

"Devlin *was* trespassing."

"But—"

"I know, but Sean's parents were big school alumni. Each year, they gave megabucks to the school athletic program—you know the type—Mr. and Mrs. Joe College. They came unglued and started legal proceedings, the whole bit, against the school and Devlin."

"How could they?" Chelsea asked.

John lifted a shoulder. "Anyone can sue anyone—all you need is enough money to pay an attorney's fees."

"So Devlin quit school?"

"He transferred. And, really, it was probably best that Devlin left, because most of the guys didn't like the fact that he was playing the part of a narc. Even though Sean was into pretty heavy stuff. The irony of it was that when Devlin and Sean left, the thieving stopped."

"Sean was the culprit."

"Yep. Can you beat that? The kid was rich and had everything money could buy." John frowned as he tasted his sauce. He reached into the cupboard and scrounged until he found the spice he wanted, which he added generously to the copper-bottomed kettle.

"Anyway, I was the only guy on the floor who believed Devlin. I let him bunk with me when no one else would talk to him. I figured he got a bum deal. After the year was over, I transferred up to Berkeley." He glanced at her and smiled. "And then, eventually, I met you and the fairy tale began." He kissed her lightly on her lips.

"You lucky devil," she said with a laugh. "So what happened to Devlin?"

"He went out of state, finished school and became a cop in Cincinnati. He was married for about a year, but his wife died."

"Died?" she repeated, stunned.

"Yeah, she was killed in a car accident. Devlin always blamed himself for not being able to drive her where she wanted to go that night." He frowned. "Anyway, losing his wife really tore Devlin up and he never talks about it—so don't bring it up," John warned.

"I won't." She felt a pang of pity for John's friend.

"Anyway, since Holly died, Devlin's been in several different cities in the midwest. And he's dated at least a million girls."

"Didn't grieve long," Chelsea remarked.

"People have different ways of dealing with grief and Holly's been gone quite a while." He stuffed a lid back on the saucepan and wiped his hands. "So, about two months ago, he landed a job with the SFPD. He's some sort of detective, I think."

One more strike against him, Chelsea thought, though it didn't really matter. What John's lady-killer friend did with his life wasn't her concern, unless, of course, it involved John.

The doorbell pealed and John asked, "Would you get it?"

"No problem." Chelsea was already on her way. At the entry hall she yanked open the door and stared face-to-face with one of the most darkly sensual men she'd ever seen in her life. He wore a white T-shirt, leather jacket and tight, faded jeans. His hair, a little longer than fashionable, was jet black, his face tanned, his jaw strong and blunt, and his eyes a piercing shade of crystal blue. One side of his mouth lifted into a sardonic smile.

"Don't tell me," he said, his gaze warming, "you must be Chelsea."

She extended her hand and felt his fingers clamp around her palm. "And you're the infamous Detective

McVey," she replied, forcing a cool smile as she withdrew her hand. Oh, she could see how this man had earned his reputation, but, fortunately, he wasn't her type—not her type at all. In one glance she could tell he was much too rough around the edges for her—much too stuck on himself. "Come on in," she said, remembering that he'd had his share of pain and trying to sound friendly. "John's doing his best Julia Child impersonation."

"I heard that," John warned, his voice ringing from the kitchen. "Just remember he who criticizes the cook, leaves this place hungry!"

"What's going on?" Devlin asked, "John, are you really *cooking?*"

"Someone has to," John replied and Devlin cocked a dark eyebrow at Chelsea.

"Don't look at me," she replied. "I'm not into domesticity."

At that, his lips twisted into an interested smile and his blue eyes sparked with reserved insolence. "A feminist?"

"At the very least."

"And you're involved with John?" he mocked, causing the hackles on the back of her neck to rise a little.

So what if John was a little on the traditional side? At least he wasn't asking *her* to cook for his irreverent friend.

More agitated than she had any right to be, Chelsea followed Devlin into the kitchen. She noticed his easy, athletic gait and the way his jeans hugged his hips. She forced her eyes upward. The man was obviously aware of his innate sexuality and he didn't even bother concealing it.

John poured Devlin a glass of wine and handed it to his friend. "Salut!" he said, touching his glass to Devlin's.

Devlin smiled—the first real grin Chelsea had witnessed—and took a long swallow of the wine.

"So what do you think of my girl?" John asked, wrapping an arm around Chelsea's waist.

Devlin's gaze returned to Chelsea's face and to her mortification, she felt a blush creeping up her neck. "She'll do," he said.

"She'll more than do," John said boldly. "Whether she knows it or not, she's going to marry me." He squeezed Chelsea then and kissed her cheek and she ignored the uncomfortable urge to wriggle out of his arms. She'd prefer to keep their future out of the conversation for the time being. Besides, what she and John planned was private.

"Is that so?" Devlin asked.

"Well, it's not written in stone, but just you wait, once she gets that business of hers off the ground, she'll run out of excuses for putting me off. And you'll get a chance to be best man."

"I can hardly wait," Devlin drawled sarcastically.

Chelsea wanted to kick John in the shins, but instead, she turned back to Devlin and changed the course of the conversation in a more conventional matter. "So what brought you to San Francisco?"

"The right job at the right time," he replied evasively and fortunately John, seemingly unaware of any friction between Devlin and Chelsea, brought up the Forty-Niners football season.

For the rest of the evening, through the appetizers, wine, salad, main course and dessert, conversation was light. Chelsea relaxed a little. Devlin wasn't all that bad—just a little on the cynical side. And John liked him. That much was obvious as they talked and laughed and eventually moved to the couch in front of a television where they watched a football game already in progress.

Chelsea sat between the two men. John's arm was comfortably slung across her shoulders and now and again he squeezed her, but she couldn't keep her mind on the game or John. Instead, she glanced at Devlin furtively from the corner of her eye. Though she was nestled next to John, it was Devlin's presence she noticed, the way his scuffed Nike was braced against the edge of the coffee table, the bend of his knee, the stretch of denim over his thighs. She wondered what his wife had been like and why he had never remarried.

With effort, she pried her gaze away from him and mentally kicked herself for being one of "those" women who found him attractive.

When the evening wound down, she was relieved. As Devlin walked out the door of John's condominium, she let out a long sigh. The ordeal was over. She'd never have to see him again. Now, she and John could go back to their idyllic existence again.

Of course she'd been wrong. Devlin was back in John's life and in a big way. Friends for life, they began sailing together and Chelsea was always asked to go along. Often she did, ignoring Devlin's masculinity and telling herself that the reason he bothered her was because he was a cop—a detective, no less—in the same line of employment as her father had been. Though, when she thought about it much later, she realized that she'd been deluding herself. Despite her hard lessons growing up, she felt a deep-seated admiration for anyone who was willing to lay down his life for the law and that included a grudging respect for Devlin.

And therefore, in an unconventional way, she admired Devlin.

In late November, John announced they were going to Lake Tahoe for the weekend, with Devlin, of course, and, Chelsea assumed, his latest woman. In the past two months, she'd been introduced to five different women whom Devlin had dated.

"I don't even know how to ski," she argued in the confines of her own apartment, wanting to bag out of yet another uncomfortable situation with Devlin. And a weekend, for crying out loud! How would she survive being caught with him for two days and nights? It would be pure hell! "Besides, I—"

"Don't tell me you have to work. Sally already told me she could handle the shop."

Chelsea clamped her mouth shut. "Fine! Just fine!" She dropped onto the soft pillows of her couch. "Well, what about Devlin? The way I remember it, cops work round the clock. How'd he manage a weekend off? Isn't he low man on the pole?"

"I don't know, but it worked out."

"Great!" Chelsea grumbled, then heard herself and sighed loudly.

"What is it you've got against him?" John asked quietly. He flung one leg over the arm of the couch and leaning forward, touched the crease between Chelsea's eyes.

"I don't have—"

"He hasn't done anything to you."

"I know, I know, it's just that he rubs me the wrong way, I guess," Chelsea tried to explain. "Before he came here, you and I, we never fought and now—" she shrugged, finding the words hard to say "—now we argue a lot."

"About Devlin," he said.

"Yes!"

Frowning, John smoothed the wrinkle from her brow. "I think it's your problem, Chels."

"He doesn't like me," she replied, then cringed a little inside. It sounded so petty.

"Maybe that's because you never gave him a chance. You had your mind made up to dislike him the minute you heard he was a detective."

Chelsea couldn't argue with that, though she wanted to. Damn it, she didn't want to like Devlin and she didn't know why. Maybe it was because he seemed dangerous and reckless somehow—reminding her of the wild days of her youth. Whatever the reason, she didn't want anything to do with him.

"Come on, Chels, give the guy a break. The only crime he's committed is being my friend."

John did have a point, she decided ruefully. And it wasn't like her to judge someone so critically or act so childish. "Okay," she finally agreed with a smile. "Lake Tahoe, here I come."

"That's my girl!" John gave her a bear hug and she mentally crossed her fingers that she could get along with Devlin and his girlfriend.

However, things didn't go as planned. John called the afternoon they were to take off and explained that he had to work late, to finish a project for a big client who wanted some last-minute changes on the design of his waterfront home.

"Ride up with Devlin and I'll catch up with you later at the cabin," John said.

"Without you? Are you crazy?" Chelsea's fingers tightened around the receiver.

"Oh, come on, Chels. I thought you were going to try and get along with Devlin."

"I was—I mean, I will, but I'd just be more comfortable with you."

"And so would I," he said, his voice tight. "But I really don't know when I'll be finished."

"I'd be glad to wait."

"Go up with Devlin and Mary, Chels. He won't bite."

She wanted to argue further, but decided against it. John was already in a bad mood and no doubt Devlin was in a worse one. So, for once, she'd try not to make any waves. "Okay, I'll see you later," she said.

"That's a good girl. Love ya," John said and clicked off.

Chelsea tried not to be bothered by his little endearment. It was just John's way. Every once in a while, he had to assert his male authority, and when he did, she usually bristled, but this weekend, come hell or high water, she was going to make the supreme effort to get along with everyone. Including Devlin and his date.

Except that Mary canceled. Her seven-year-old had come down with chicken pox.

Devlin explained all this as he was loading her suitcase and two bags of groceries into the back of his Bronco.

Chelsea could hardly believe her ears. Standing in

the pale glow of the streetlight, her breath misting in the air, she realized that for the next few hours she'd be trapped alone with Devlin.

Fog had crept into the city and the night was dark and close. She shivered, but not from the cold. A little frightened at the prospect of being alone with him for hours, she hiked the collar of her ski jacket against the mist and told herself she was being a fool. She wasn't scared of him—well, maybe a little intimidated, but that wasn't so bad, was it? She could handle the situation as well as Devlin McVey. At this point, she had no choice.

Devlin slammed the back door of the Bronco.

"I guess it's just you and me," he quipped, flashing her a crooked smile that touched a forbidden part of her heart.

"For the time being." More than a little on edge, she climbed into the rig. He sat beside her and he shoved the four-wheel drive into gear. The Bronco lurched forward. Without a word, Devlin steered them toward the freeway heading east.

As they drove through the clog of Friday evening traffic, she tried not to notice the length of his leg, so close to hers, or the way his long fingers curled over the gear shift, or the earthy scent of his cologne.

This is all wrong, her mind screamed at her, but she pretended that being alone with him and driving to a remote cabin in the mountains was an everyday occurrence.

Chelsea never had been very good at small talk, and from the long stretches in their conversation, she guessed Devlin was even less adept at talking about nothing than she was.

Licking her lips, she tried to concentrate on the night-shrouded foothills and the forests of the Sierra Nevada mountain range.

Devlin turned on the radio, which eased the need for conversation, but Chelsea felt tense as a springboard.

"Do you have any idea where we're going?" he asked, glancing at her as the road wound through thick stands of pine.

"Mmm, if I can remember," she said, nodding. "John and I were here a couple of years ago. The cabin belongs to a friend of his. But I was here in the daylight."

"Well, I'll have to count on you," he admitted. "All I've got is an address."

"It's near Heavenly Valley Ski Resort."

Devlin laughed and the deep sound echoed through the rig. "That really narrows it down."

"Okay, okay, you just drive and I'll give directions."

He sighed dramatically. "Just like a woman," he muttered, but, for once, she wasn't irritated. In fact, she smiled to herself. Maybe spending some time alone with Devlin wasn't going to end up being a nightmare. There was a chance that they could learn to like each other, at least for John's sake.

Snowflakes began to fall from the dark sky, collecting on the windshield and sprinkling the ground with a fine white powder.

"If you're interested, there's a thermos of coffee and an extra cup in the backseat," Devlin said, shifting down when the Bronco started to climb a particularly steep grade.

"Sounds great. You want some?"

"Absolutely."

Twisting, she rummaged around until she found the thermos, then carefully poured them each a cup. Fragrant steam filtered to her nostrils as she settled back in her seat and started to enjoy the ride. The snow glistened like diamonds in the illumination from the headlights. Chelsea felt an unlikely contentment as she sipped the strong coffee.

If nothing else, she decided, this weekend with Devlin would be an adventure.

It took another hour before they finally located the small cabin tucked in the snow-dusted pines. Built of rough cedar, with a pitched roof and paned windows, it stood alone in a clearing, looking empty and cold.

"Shangri-la?" Devlin asked skeptically.

"Close enough. John would like to buy it someday," Chelsea replied. "He thinks Heavenly Valley is appropriately named."

"And you?"

Chelsea lifted a shoulder as she climbed out of the Bronco. "It's beautiful up here," she admitted, "and I love the snow, but I don't ski."

"And you're engaged to John?" he asked, hauling the bags from the back of the rig. "That's a situation that will have to be rectified."

"We're not engaged yet," she said, her boots crunching on the new snow.

"John acts like it's only a matter of time."

Chelsea didn't reply as she fumbled with the key John had given her. The lock finally clicked and she shoved open the door, snapping on the lights with her free hand.

The cabin smelled musty and unused. Chelsea

threw open the windows and Devlin went to work on the fire. Kneeling in front of a river-rock hearth, his head angled up to check the flue, he lit a match, mumbled something under his breath, then headed outside for firewood.

Chelsea went to work in the kitchen, which was separated from the living room by a long butcher block counter. Unpacking the groceries, she furtively watched Devlin as he returned, crumpled yellowed newspaper and stacked dry chunks of oak in the grate. She noticed how snowflakes had melted in his dark hair, causing it to glimmer. She studied the movements of his hands, quick and sure, as he prodded the logs with a poker, and she felt her breath tighten in her lungs as he leaned forward and blew on the flames, fanning them expertly as his breath whistled through his thin lips.

Quickly, she diverted her gaze, pretending interest in making dinner. "I hope beef stew is okay," she said, rattling noisily in the kitchen as she looked through the cupboards for the right size of pan.

"I'll eat anything."

"I'm not the greatest cook," she replied, surprised when she looked up and he was standing next to her. Her stupid heart fluttered a second.

"So you've said," he drawled lazily, eyeing her. "John doesn't seem to mind."

"No, uh, he accepts me the way I am."

Devlin didn't respond, just cocked an interested dark brow.

"You don't believe me."

"I've just thought John was the button-down-collar type."

"Meaning?"

"That he wants the traditional things in life."

"Such as?"

"A house in the city, a mountain cabin for vacations, a station wagon and a Porsche, two point three children, and a wife who can entertain, cook and…" He let the rest of the sentence slide and she knew he'd nearly mentioned something about bedroom prowess.

"Maybe you don't know John as well as you think you do," she said, stung.

"Maybe you don't."

She wanted to argue with him, to tell him that John loved her and nothing else mattered, but she knew she was wading in dangerous waters. Her relationship with John was something private and she meant to keep it that way.

While she worked on the meal—adding the finishing touches to the stew she'd started the night before, and baking cornbread—Devlin turned on the water and carried her bags upstairs to the loft bedroom. She thought about sleeping under the sloping roof, lying in John's arms while Devlin was bunked downstairs in the other bedroom. The thought made her uncomfortable and she regretted ever agreeing to this trip. She and John had been lovers since college, yet now, with Devlin in the same cabin, she was as flustered as a schoolgirl and for the first time she felt guilty and a little ashamed.

"Ridiculous," she muttered to herself. John wanted to marry her. It was she who was holding out. And for what?

She didn't want to think about all the reasons and excuses she'd come up with for putting off the engagement. She glanced at the phone, hoping John would call.

"It doesn't work," Devlin said.

"Why not?"

"I guess John's friend doesn't want to pay for service when he isn't here."

"But—what if John gets held up? Or his car breaks down? Or—"

"John can take care of himself," Devlin said quickly. "He'll be here when he gets here."

There was no arguing with that deeply intellectual logic, Chelsea thought sarcastically. She scooped steaming, thick stew into two bowls, then cut squares of the cornbread.

Devlin poured her a glass of wine and opened a bottle of beer for himself. "You don't like wine?" she asked as they sat in front of the fire.

"Nope."

"Why not?"

He lifted a shoulder. "Not my style."

"You drank it at John's—the first night I met you."

He slid her a sensual glance. "Well, I didn't want to be rude," he said. "I did have to toast the bride-to-be."

"I'm not—" she dropped the subject. If he wanted to mock her, so be it. She just wouldn't rise to the bait.

They ate in silence and he even took seconds. "You've got hidden skills," he remarked when he'd finally finished.

"Meaning?"

"You *can* cook."

"Don't tell John. It's my secret."

With firelight playing over his features, he leaned back on one elbow, and nudged off one battered Nike with the toe of his other shoe. Then, warming his feet, he eyed her. "So what is it with you and John?" he asked, sipping from his second bottle of beer.

"What do you mean?"

"Seems to me John's a helluva catch."

"So I've been told."

His eyes slitted. "But you don't believe it."

"Of course I do."

"But you don't want to marry him."

"Yes, I do. But not…yet…"

"Most women would lick their chops if a man like John wanted to marry them."

"And you know so much about women?"

He smiled lazily. "I know enough. Women like John. He's good-looking, takes care of himself and makes a pile of money."

"You left out kind, generous and intelligent."

His lower lip protruded in a thoughtful frown. "Because those attributes aren't high on the list for most women."

"Depends on whose list you're reading," she threw back at him. He had some nerve!

"Okay," he said, drinking a long swallow. "Tell me about your list, Ms. Reed. What is it that makes you want—or in this case—not want—John Stern."

"I do want him!"

"Then marry the bastard and put him out of his misery!"

"I don't know what you're talking about."

"Sure you do. He's hung up on you—has been for a few years. And you keep sidestepping him. Why?"

"I don't think it's any of your business."

"He's my friend," Devlin said flatly, as if that explained everything.

"Then you'll understand that he would want our private life kept that way."

He slowly set his bottle aside. Eyeing her, he moved closer. "Privacy is one thing and I'm all for that. But I don't like anyone stringing someone else along."

"And that's what I'm doing?"

"I don't know. Is it?"

"What is this—the third degree? Well, *Detective* McVey, this isn't a police interrogation room and I don't have to answer any of your questions!"

His mouth quirked a bit, lifting into a wicked little smile that she found incredibly sexy.

"I love John," she said simply, hoping that one statement would end the conversation.

His eyes darkened. "How much?"

"What?"

"I asked, 'how much' do you love him? Not enough to marry him."

"The time just hasn't been right."

He slid her a disbelieving glance. "As I pointed out, most women would jump at the chance—"

"I'm *not* most women."

"Amen." He was so close to her that only a hair's breadth separated them, yet they weren't touching.

Chelsea held her ground and pretended that her heart wasn't slamming against her ribs, that her mouth hadn't turned to cotton, that her palms hadn't begun to sweat. She clung to her wineglass in a death grip and realized that her knuckles were showing white.

"What makes you tick, Ms. Reed?" he asked, his breath fanning her cheeks, his eyes searching her face as if she were some intricate puzzle. "You know what I think it is?"

"I couldn't begin to guess and I don't really care—"

"Pride and independence. You can't give up your freedom—at least not to a man like John."

"John's wonderful and—"

"And you don't love him," Devlin said flatly, studying his nails and rubbing his thumb on his forefinger. "At least not enough to marry him."

"I do," she replied quickly. She swallowed hard, unconsciously licking her lips at the lie. Devlin was partially right, of course, but she couldn't admit it, not even to herself. She loved John, but all along she'd known there was something missing in their relationship, something vital, something passionate and wild that she suspected existed between some couples.

She didn't scoot away when Devlin's fingertips touched hers and though she knew she should jump to her feet when he leaned forward, she couldn't move.

"Don't," she whispered, but he only shifted closer and his mouth closed over hers so quickly the breath was trapped in her lungs. His lips were warm and hard and sensual, and it took all her willpower not to respond. Good Lord, she couldn't be kissing John's best friend!

His arms wrapped around her and he lifted his head, his eyes burning with a secret blue flame that caused her blood to race like quicksilver through her veins. "Admit it, Chelsea, what you want is someone more exciting, someone who'll set you on fire."

"This is insane," she whispered, struggling, but his arms held her fast and when he kissed her again, his mouth was demanding, his tongue insistent as it pressed against her teeth. She shoved against him, peeling her lips from his. "Stop—oh, please, stop."

He lifted his head slightly, then glanced at her wet lips and, with a groan of regret, whispered, "I'm sorry."

Then his mouth found hers again.

Passion exploded deep in her soul. Wanton desire flooded her senses and somewhere in the back of her mind she knew she was doing something irrevocably wrong, betraying a precious trust, but she couldn't stop.

Devlin's hand splayed possessively against the small of her back, drawing her close, crushing her breasts against his chest, while his lips moved sensually across hers. Her mouth parted of its own accord and Devlin's tongue anxiously sought and found the wet velvet recess of her mouth.

He groaned against her, shifting his weight, drawing them both down to the hard floor. His legs, taut and muscular beneath his jeans, rubbed against hers.

Chelsea's senses swam dizzily. She couldn't think, could only feel. His hands twined in her hair, forcing her head back, and his lips trailed across her cheeks and throat.

"Chels, sweet Chels—" he growled and a vibrant answering response tore through her soul. She tingled and returned the fever of his kisses with her own. Though what she was doing was forbidden, she couldn't seem to stop herself.

Devlin rolled atop her and she clung to him, all thoughts of refusing long since shoved from her mind. Moving sensually, he cupped her breast and it swelled in his palm.

He started to lift her sweater and his fingers grazed the skin of her abdomen. Warning bells clanged through Chelsea's mind. "No—" she cried as his fingers found the lace of her bra and her traitorous nipple hardened against his rough skin. "Please, Devlin—" but it sounded like a plea.

He stopped moving and threw his head back, squeezing his eyes closed. With a groan, he rolled off her, and took in one long, steadying breath. Shoving the heels of his hands into his eyes, he swore between clenched teeth. "How could you do that to John?"

"How could *I?*" she flung back, wounded. "How could *you!*"

"I—I was just trying to prove a point." But his hands shook as he shoved his hair from his forehead and his eyes, blue as a sizzling flame, still gleamed with eroticism.

"This was a *test?*" she cried, horrified.

"Yes."

"And what did it prove?"

"That you're not in love with John," he said simply.

"Oh, but I am in love with you?" she mocked, quivering inside when she realized how closely she'd come to making love with him.

He barked out a short, mirthless laugh. "You don't have to love someone to have sex with them."

"I do!"

His brows lifted cynically. "No, you just have to tell yourself you're in love so that your conscience is salved."

"What! No—"

"You want another demonstration?" he asked.

"Is that what it was?" she threw back at him.

His lips clamped shut. "Nothing more!"

"Liar!"

Devlin's eyes shuttered. "You think I feel something special for you?" He let out a sound of disgust. "Why do you women delude yourselves into thinking that sex is more than it is?"

"You bastard! You'd sleep with your best friend's—"

"What? What, exactly, are you to John? His mistress?"

"No—"

"Not his fiancée," he reminded her callously.

"But we're involved!"

"Not so involved that you wouldn't go to bed with me."

"You're the last man on earth I'd—" But his raised eyebrow called her the liar that she was.

The phone rang, jangling her already rattling nerves. She stared at the telephone as if it had miraculously come to life.

"You'd better answer it," Devlin said with maddening calm. "It's probably John."

"You said it was dead!"

He lifted a shoulder. "You're right. I'm a liar."

The phone rang shrilly again and Chelsea in a fit of anger stormed across the room. "Hello?"

"Chels!" John said.

Chelsea's throat closed and tears of regret sprang to her eyes. "Where—where are you?" she choked out, wishing he were here, wishing she could erase the taste of Devlin from her lips. Oh, she'd been so foolish!

"Still in the city. This project is taking longer than I thought."

"No—" She stared across the room to Devlin, who

sat near the fire, his arms crossed over his chest, his face without emotion.

"Look, hon, I'm sorry, but I can't get out of here until morning."

"Oh, John, please," she whispered desperately, her voice nearly cracking.

"Are you all right?" he asked, and she hated the concern in his voice. Devlin was right, she didn't deserve a man like John.

"I—I'm fine," she said, though she knew her face was ashen. Lord, she'd acted so wantonly, so...

"Well, don't worry. Devlin'll take care of you."

"I don't need anyone to—"

"Sure you do, Chels. That's why I love you."

"I love you, too," she whispered, staring straight at Devlin and defying him with her eyes. She'd never, never betray John again. Not with Devlin. Not with any man.

"I'll see you in the morning. Just hang in there," he said, then hung up.

Chelsea replaced the receiver with icy calm. "He won't be here until morning."

Devlin shrugged. "I guess we'll have to make do."

"Have you lied about anything else?" she asked, motioning toward the phone.

"I don't make it a practice." His jaw hardened. "But what do you care? You're an expert."

"I don't understand."

His eyes blazed. "Every time you kiss John, or tell him that you miss him, or profess to love him, or lie in his bed, you're lying through your beautiful white teeth."

She wanted to throw herself at him and pummel

him with her fists, call him every name in the book, but she stood in the kitchen, gripping the counter and said, "I made a mistake with you, McVey, a horrible one. And I regret it. I'll regret it for the rest of my life. But it won't happen again."

"No?" He smiled crookedly, but she willed herself to ignore any speck of his masculine appeal.

"No!"

"Want me to prove you wrong?" He crooked one eyebrow.

Her stomach began to knot. "No reason. You've shown me that I can be as much of an animal as you are, but there is one difference."

"Oh, and what's that?"

"I won't be looking for an opportunity."

"Neither will I," he said coldly and for an insane instant she felt a stab of disappointment. "You see, I only wanted to show you that you're not the woman for John."

"That's John's decision."

"John doesn't have all the facts."

"I don't understand—" But she did. In a blinding flash of realization, she knew that he intended to blackmail her. "You wouldn't tell him about this, would you?"

His jaw grew taut. "Only if I thought it would save him a life of misery. But the problem is, when I tell John what happened between you and me, either he won't believe me and I'll lose the best friend I've got, or he will believe me and hate me."

"So we're at an impasse."

"No, lady. I expect you to think about what happened tonight and reexamine your reasons for pretending to be in love with John. Then, I think, you'll come to the same conclusion I've already drawn—he'd be happier with a more traditional wife."

"How noble of you," she mocked.

For a minute, he let down his guard. His eyes darkened from an inner pain. "It's not all nobility, Chelsea," he said, his jaw sliding to one side. "I've seen a lot of bad marriages in my time—"

"Like yours?" she flung out angrily and watched as he winced. "Is that what this is all about? Did your wife hurt you so badly that you think every woman will betray…"

His jaw was so tight, a muscle jumped near his temple. "Don't bring up my wife."

"Then don't preach to me about John."

For seconds they glared at each other and Chelsea wished she could drop through the floor, but she held his gaze. At last Devlin said quietly, "I'd hate for John to be disappointed or you to be trapped."

"I wouldn't—"

"Just think about it," he suggested, shoving himself upright and crossing the room. Chelsea's heart tripped into double-time, but he didn't touch her. Instead, he found the bar and poured himself a stiff drink.

The rest of the night she could think of little but what had happened between them and her traitorous body tingled at the memory of his kiss, but he didn't so much as come near her again. In fact, he acted as if they had been friends for life.

Slowly, she began to trust him and fortunately, Devlin had the decency to never bring up the subject of that night alone in the cabin.

Only much later—around Christmas—when John

announced that he and Chelsea were to be married, did Devlin react violently.

They were at John's condominium for a holiday celebration. A fourteen-foot tree, resplendent in twinkling lights and glittering silver decorations, stood near the fireplace where a yule log crackled and burned. Soft Christmas carols drifted from hidden speakers, filling the rooms.

John was ecstatic. "Can you believe it?" he asked Devlin. "All these years and she finally said yes."

"No," Devlin said, shifting his knowing gaze to Chelsea. "Congratulations." He lifted his champagne glass and John squeezed Chelsea possessively. "Many years of happiness." Sipping his champagne, he let his gaze move over Chelsea—two blue orbs that cut through her facade and saw right to her soul.

"Th—thank you," she said, disgusted with herself for stumbling over the words.

The phone rang and John rolled his eyes. "I'll get it in the den," he said, hurrying down the short hallway.

Devlin turned and walked quickly onto the deck. Chelsea, hesitating only a second, followed him outside. He stood, staring at the stormy waters of the bay, bracing himself with both hands against the rail. Shoulders bunched, knuckles white, hair ruffled in the stiff breeze, he tensed when he heard her approach. His jaw was so tight, a muscle flexed beneath his temple. "You're sure about this?"

"Absolutely." She stood next to him and her stomach fluttered.

Devlin's lips compressed. His eyes turned a darker shade of blue. He glanced back to the sea again and muttered something under his breath.

Chelsea shivered and rubbed her arms. Why did it matter what he thought?

"What made you change your mind?" Devlin asked.

"I didn't change it. The time's right."

"Since when?"

Since I decided I needed a safe, secure life, a life with no surprises. "Actually, today," she said, feeling the salt-laden breeze tangle in her hair.

"Well, I hope you're happy with your decision and—" he turned, facing her, his expression grave "—you'd better do your damnedest to make John happy, because he deserves it."

"You don't think I will?"

His jaw slid to the side. "You don't want to hear my opinion."

Chelsea could never resist a challenge. She tilted her head upward and said evenly, "Of course I do. You're a friend of John's. Your opinion matters."

His eyes narrowed on her lips and her breath got lost between her lungs and her throat. She was reminded of the night he'd kissed her so passionately, fired her blood as no other man had dared.

"Let's not play any games, Chelsea," he said slowly, his gaze daring her to argue with him. "You and I both know you're marrying the wrong man."

"I don't think so."

"Don't you? Well, I remember a time when I could have proved—"

"You're wrong!"

He stared at her a few seconds and time seemed to stand still. "I hope so, lady," he whispered. "I hope to God I'm wrong about you. Because John deserves better. If you ever cheat on him, I'll make sure he finds out about it."

"But I would never do anything to hurt him!"

"Just don't forget that I have a long memory," he said as John opened the sliding doors and joined them.

"What's going on?" John asked.

"I was just congratulating your bride-to-be," Devlin drawled.

Chelsea felt herself pale, but John didn't notice. "Good," he said. "Then let's celebrate." He whipped out a piece of mistletoe from his pocket, dangled it over Chelsea's head and before she could object, kissed her long and hard. To her dismay, she felt nothing. She tried. Good Lord, she clung to John, tasting of him, willing her blood to race like wildfire, but her heartbeat barely accelerated.

When he lifted his head from hers, she glanced over his shoulder to the railing where Devlin had been standing. But Devlin was gone—only his empty glass testament that he'd been there at all.

From that night until the stormy day he disappeared in the bleak waters of San Francisco Bay, Devlin never allowed himself to be alone with her again.

Chapter 6

The next morning, Chelsea sat at the vanity and brushed her hair. She'd slept poorly, with thoughts of John and Devlin running through her mind.

Why wouldn't Mitch admit that he was Devlin? What was Devlin trying to hide?

Devlin would never have done anything to jeopardize John's life, she was sure of that. But something had happened on that boat, something that had forced Devlin to drop out of sight and pretend he was dead, only to end up here with an assumed identity.

So what was it? What would cause Devlin to take such drastic measures?

She tied her auburn hair away from her face in a ponytail, and frowned at her reflection. A line furrowed between her dark brows, her eyes were a moody shade of green, and she gnawed anxiously on her lower lip. "Oh, stop it," she muttered, touching up her makeup.

Frustrated, she pulled on a turquoise swimsuit and terry cover up, plopped her straw hat onto her head and grabbed her beach bag. She'd spend the day relaxing on the beach, sorting out exactly what her next step would be. As a private detective, she decided, locking the door of her room, she was a failure.

"Well, I wondered where you've been keeping yourself," a high-pitched voice called to her. "I haven't seen you since the cab ride over here!"

Chelsea glanced up and discovered Emily Vaughn bearing down on her. Decked out in a yellow and orange muumuu, sandals, wide-brimmed hat that shaded her apricot-tinted hair and white-rimmed sunglasses, Emily charged down the hall. "Well?" she asked as she caught up to Chelsea, her sandals clicking to her short steps. "What've you been up to?"

"Exploring," Chelsea replied evasively as they walked together down the stairs to the main lobby.

"Fascinating island, isn't it?" Emily quipped.

"And then some."

"And what did you find?"

Not much. "A great little boutique near the waterfront," Chelsea replied.

"Ever locate that man you were looking for?"

Chelsea nearly stumbled on the bottom step. "Man?" she repeated. How could Emily know?

"Mmm." Emily nodded quickly. "Come on, let's have breakfast by the pool. Jeff will find us there."

Chelsea wasn't really hungry, but she decided that she didn't have anything better to do. Until she found a way to observe Mitch Russell, she was at a standstill.

They were served croissants, jam, juice and coffee at a round, glass-topped table positioned near the shimmering water of the swimming pool. Emily, adjusting the umbrella of the table, finally explained. "Jeff saw you in the bar the other night and said you ran up to some man thinking he was someone else."

Chelsea inwardly groaned. "That's essentially correct."

"So—who is this man?"

"The man I ran into is Mitch Russell. I thought he was a friend of mine I hadn't seen in a while," Chelsea evaded.

"But he wasn't?" Satisfied with the angle of the striped umbrella, Emily sat down and began attacking her croissant, spreading thick currant jam over the flaky roll.

"No."

"You didn't come all the way down here just to find him, did you?"

"This is my vacation."

"And a wonderful place for a vacation it is," Emily remarked, temporarily distracted as she munched on her croissant. "Jeff and I have been saving all year just to come down here. Marvelous weather, steeped in history—a lovely spot. Heaven on earth is what I call it." She prattled on and Chelsea only half-listened, her eyes drawn to the path that led to the beach, as if just thinking about Mitch Russell would make him suddenly appear.

"…so I guess I just can't let him out of my sight again," Emily was saying. "First the bar downstairs and then some run-down place on the waterfront. Oh, he saw that man there, too, what did you say his name was—Russ something or other?"

Chelsea's gaze flew back to Emily's face. "Mitch Russell?"

"Right. Jeff saw him last night with a couple of other men."

But last night she and Mitch had been together at his house.

"What time?"

"Oh, it was early. Six or seven, I think. I don't let Jeff out alone too late. I worry too much." She smiled at Chelsea, obviously satisfied that she'd regained the younger woman's attention. "You know, it was the strangest thing. Jeff said your friend and the men he was with were speaking Spanish—well, at least Jeff thought it was Spanish—but the native language on this island is French. Don't you think that's odd?"

"Jeff's sure?" Chelsea asked.

"Oh, I think so. He took Spanish in college. Of course that was years ago, but—" she lifted a shoulder "—Jeff's not one to get his facts wrong." She washed down a bite of croissant with a swallow of coffee. "So—I take it you haven't talked to your friend in a while—the friend you're looking for. Otherwise you would know where he's staying and would have called to arrange a meeting, isn't that right, dear?"

"I suppose." Chelsea shifted uncomfortably in her chair.

"And he's not in the phone book."

"No."

"So why do you think he's here—on Paradis?"

"I heard he might have ended up here, and since I

was planning a vacation anyway, I thought I'd look him up."

"And he looks like this Russell man?"

"Very much," she admitted, deciding Emily talked too much for her to confide her secret. Besides, Chelsea's story sounded so farfetched, who would believe her? "Do you know the name of the bar where Jeff saw Mitch?"

"He'd have to tell you that. But it wouldn't be too hard to figure out. This is a pretty small island."

That much was true.

"Oh, here's the sleepyhead now!" Emily waved wildly and her lined face broke into a radiant grin. Chelsea glanced over her shoulder to spy Jeff walking briskly to the table.

"Look who I found, dear!" Emily said as he sat down. "And see, we saved you some rolls and jelly." She handed him the platter of croissants as a waiter refilled their cups. "Now, you just help yourself. I was telling Chelsea that you ran into that man you saw her with in the bar on the first night we were here! She says his name is Russell Mit—no, Mitch Russell."

Jeff slathered butter on his croissant and grunted an affirmative.

"And they were speaking Spanish, isn't that right, dear? What's the name of that bar?"

Jeff lifted a shoulder and his face pulled into a thoughtful frown. "Can't remember."

Emily glanced at Chelsea. "What did I tell you?" She tossed up her hands. "Oh, it doesn't matter anyway! He'll think of it soon enough. And it's going to be a simply marvelous day! I can just feel it. Maybe we should all go fishing. There are boats you can rent."

"Thanks, but I can't. Not today," Chelsea said.

Emily's face fell. "Why not?"

"I've got plans," she lied, feeling a twang of guilt. Emily and Jeff had been nothing but nice to her and yet she couldn't spend an entire day drifting on the ocean. She was in Paradis for a purpose.

"Oh, can't they wait! We can sunbathe and talk and—"

"Another time," Chelsea promised, standing and reaching for her beach bag.

"Oh, all right, but we'll hold you to it."

"Good." Chelsea smiled and dug through her wallet, but Emily shook her head.

"You put that thing away. We'll just charge this to our room."

"Oh, no, I couldn't—" Chelsea replied quickly, before Jeff could respond.

"I won't hear of it any other way," Emily insisted. "You kept me company and I appreciate it. Now, just go on and see if you can find your friend. If you do, I certainly want to meet him."

Chelsea swallowed a smile. She couldn't picture Devlin and Emily having one thing in common.

"The Dauphin Bleu," Jeff said suddenly as he turned his teacup in his hands.

Emily's brows knit. "What're you talking about?"

"The bar last night. I think the name of it was the Blue Dolphin."

Chelsea grinned. Finally—she was getting somewhere!

"Could you pick out the men again if you saw them—the men who were speaking Spanish to Mitch?" she asked.

"Maybe," Jeff evaded, turning his cup nervously on the table and avoiding Chelsea's eyes.

"Good."

"Stop fiddling with your tea. You're making me crazy," Emily said, shaking her head. "What's wrong with you?"

Jeff scowled. "Well, it wasn't just two men who were with Chelsea's friend. There was also a woman with them."

"So?" Emily asked, but Chelsea's heart had nearly stopped. Jeff was obviously uncomfortable.

"Your friend—Russell—he was with her. She was very attentive to him." Jeff rubbed his hand across his chin.

"I see. And what about him?" Chelsea asked, her fingers gripping the handle of her bag so tightly her hands ached.

"They seemed to be pretty wrapped up in each other." He blew across his tea.

Chelsea's heart dropped. What did she care if Mitch had a woman on the island? Devlin had dated more than she could count. And yet... "Well, thanks for breakfast," she said, forcing a bright smile. "Next time it's on me."

"Oh, go on!" Emily said waving her away, chuckling.

"I'll see you later!"

"We'll count on it," Emily replied.

As Chelsea left the table, Emily was rattling on about the weather and Jeff was eating in long-suffering silence.

Chelsea, though she was loath to admit it, felt more than one pang of jealousy at the thought of this mysterious woman in Mitch Russell's—or Devlin's—life. Who was she? Were they lovers? She certainly hadn't returned to Mitch's place with him. "Don't even think about it," she grumbled to herself later, as she lay on a beach towel and eyed the horizon.

The afternoon sun was hot and intense, beating against her skin until she was covered in sweat and the sunscreen she'd applied was dripping from her skin. She waded in the aquamarine water to cool off, but her mind kept wandering back to Mitch and his woman.

Her heart twisted a little though she didn't understand why. He was young and virile—why wouldn't he have a woman?

Foolishly, she felt betrayed. Licking her lips, she remembered the touch of his mouth on hers, the electricity that licked through her body at the taste of him. So much like Devlin. So damned much like Devlin. His looks, his touch, his voice—everything about him screamed that he was Devlin and yet he denied it. Frustrated, she kicked at a stone in the surf and sent a tiny crab scurrying for cover.

Why does it matter so much? You loved John, not Devlin. Chewing on her lower lip, she wondered if the love she'd felt for John—real though it had been—was more of a sense of loyalty—a duty that she'd felt compelled to fulfill after Devlin had nearly made love to her in the cabin.

Her skin turned hot at the memory. Awash with guilt, she sat in the warm water and propped her chin on her knees. Had she been deceiving John, lying to Devlin and deluding herself? Had she, as Devlin had so coarsely suggested, never really loved John enough to become his wife?

"That's ridiculous!" she chided herself, then sighed. "Oh, Lord, what a mess!" Shoving her hair from her eyes, she thought about Mitch and Devlin and all the conflicting emotions each man wrought from her.

The brilliant day seemed to evaporate, leaving her in a desert of memories. If Mitch had been at the Dauphin Bleu earlier last evening, he'd then come home for a quick swim and subsequently discovered Chelsea on his front porch. At first he'd been angry—and then he'd put on the act of pretending that she'd led someone inadvertently to him. But whom?

And who was the woman he'd been with? Was she young? Beautiful? Was he in love with her? Was he waiting for her when Chelsea had planted herself on his front porch? Was that why he tried so hard to get rid of her?

His big act of shutting the blinds and pulling her into the cabin had all been for show—to scare her off—and to make sure that his girlfriend hadn't spotted her, Chelsea decided angrily, a headache beginning to pound behind her eyes.

Well, he'd find out she didn't scare easily. Struggling to her feet, she walked out of the surf and trudged through the sand to her beach towel. After shaking the sand from the towel, she stepped into her cover-up, then tucked her towel and sunscreen into her beach bag. More determined than ever to find out everything possible about Mitch Russell, she set off down the beach, intending to hike over a mile through the sand to the town of Emeraude. She'd check out the Dauphin Bleu as well as the other watering holes in town. Surely someone would know something about Mitch, or Devlin, or whoever he really was!

* * *

The Dauphin Bleu wasn't much. Set two blocks away from the waterfront, with yellow stucco walls, a brown patched roof, and a quivering neon window sign—a blue dolphin leaping from a pink wave—the bar had seen better days.

Chelsea shoved hard on the scarred plank door before she noticed the "Closed" sign, which listed the hours of operation.

Sighing, she checked her watch. The bar wouldn't open for two hours. And what will you do then? she asked herself as she headed back toward the waterfront, her sandals scuffing on the cracked concrete sidewalks. Wait for Mitch again? Suffer through the questioning gazes cast in your direction? The thought turned her stomach, but she was determined to do whatever it took to find out what had happened to Devlin as well as to John.

If only John had lived, she thought, pausing at a corner before crossing the street and joining the crowd moving through the shaded, open-air market. Her life would have been simple if John had survived the boating accident. They would be married by now, living in his condominium, planning, perhaps, to buy a house or have a baby.

But all her dreams were behind her now; they'd sunk into the stormy depths of San Francisco Bay when John had been killed. The old pain clutched at her heart as she thought about John—the man she was to marry—the man she'd loved. And she *had* loved him. Despite what Devlin had thought. Perhaps that love hadn't been a raging passion, maybe it hadn't been a billowing lust that had swelled through her each time she'd kissed him, but she'd loved John and had known that they would spend the rest of their lives in friendly companionship, in laughter and love.

But that future was long gone, destroyed when John—an expert seaman and swimmer—had drowned, leaving so many unanswered questions. Questions only Devlin McVey could answer.

The hours dragged by, but finally the bar opened for the evening. She forced herself inside the breathless, dark room and found a barstool in a back corner that faced the door. After ordering a glass of wine she waited, as she had for two other nights, her gaze wandering around the worn interior. What kind of a man would hang out here night after night? But maybe Mitch wasn't always here or at the Villa. She swirled her untouched wine and wondered how Mitch spent his days as well as his nights.

Men and a very few women began to wander inside. Laughing and talking, they ordered drinks. Chelsea nursed a glass of wine and had started on her second when the same lanky blond man she'd met on her first night at the Villa approached her table. What was his name? Chris something or other. Without waiting for an invitation, he plopped himself down on the barstool.

"You alone?" he asked, offering her a smile that showed off white teeth that overlapped slightly.

"Yes, but I'm waiting for someone."

"Again," he reminded her.

She smiled and nodded.

"Same guy?"

Unfortunately, yes. "Mmm," she replied noncommittally. What was it about this man and his mocking gaze that put her on edge?

"As I said the other night, there's no reason I can't keep you company 'til your friend arrives."

There was no reason he couldn't stay, she decided. Besides, she was tired of being alone, chasing the ghost of Devlin McVey.

"Oh, come on. Give a guy a chance," he suggested with an easy smile, his eyes twinkling. "What's your name?"

"Chelsea."

"From the States—right? West coast, I'd bet—Seattle?"

"Close. San Francisco."

"Here on a vacation?"

"Of a sort," she evaded.

He ordered a beer for himself and another glass of wine for her. "I'm from Wyoming—not far from Laramie. But that's a long story…" When their drinks had been deposited on the table, he said, "So what's holding up your friend?"

"I don't know," she admitted, wishing Mitch would miraculously appear.

"I'll tell you this much about your friend," Chris said, sipping from his glass. "He's crazy to keep a woman like you waiting. Who is he?"

For the first time, Chelsea decided Chris might be able to help her. Since she wasn't getting anywhere on her own, she decided to try something new. "I'm waiting for Mitch Russell. You know him?"

A flicker of recognition lightened Chris's eyes, but other than that small indication, his cool expression didn't change. "I've met him a couple of times. But he mainly keeps to himself." He eyed her thoughtfully.

"Umm." She nodded, sipping from her glass as a

steel drum tuned up in the corner. "I knew him a long time ago."

Chris studied his beer. "In Chicago?"

"Actually I met him in San Francisco," she said, deciding to keep the details to herself.

"Was he out there on assignment?"

"Assignment?" she repeated.

"Yeah, I thought he worked for some newspaper in Chicago, but he gave it all up when he was in an accident—the one that killed his wife."

So Mitch Russell claimed to be a journalist. "Which paper?" she asked.

"You know, I don't think I ever heard the name of it." Chris thought for a moment, but shook his head. "I know he did some traveling for the paper, but essentially he lived in Chicago or Detroit or Cincinnati or someplace like that."

Chelsea grinned inwardly. Devlin had lived in Cincinnati before he'd moved to San Francisco and an accident had taken his wife's life. Finally, she was getting somewhere.

"And now he's writing a book," she added.

"That's what he says."

"But you haven't seen it?"

"Nope, but I don't really know him that well."

She sipped her wine. "You don't hang out with him often?"

"Me? Nah. He's kind of a loner—but I guess you know that. He's all wrapped up in his book, or so he says, and spends his time with a few of the locals— probably for research or local color or whatever you want to call it."

"His book is set in the islands?"

Chris lifted his shoulders. "Beats me. Like I said, I barely know the guy."

You and me both, she agreed silently, steering the course of the conversation to neutral territory.

The band started playing a familiar tune and Chris asked her to dance, but she declined, claiming to be tired, which she was.

"How about a rain check?" Chris asked as he walked her outside and she found a cab. "Can I see you again?"

Why not? "Sure. I'm staying at the Villa," she replied, more than a little uncomfortable. She hadn't dated since John's death and she wasn't really interested in starting any kind of relationship. But Chris lived on the island. He might be able to help her find out more about Devlin.

"I'll call," Chris promised as she slid into the cab.

Chelsea nodded and waved as she asked the driver to take her back to the Villa.

Tired, she stared through the gritty window of the cab and decided she hadn't learned much about Mitch today, but the little she had gleaned hadn't convinced her that he wasn't Devlin. In fact, little by little, she was piecing together Mitch's past—a past that seemed very much like Devlin McVey's.

Tomorrow, she silently promised herself, barely able to keep her eyes open. She'd find out more tomorrow.

However, in the next few days her luck didn't improve. In fact, she hadn't spotted Mitch once. Now she was contemplating returning to his house. "And do what?" she asked herself as she walked through the streets of Emeraude. What good would another showdown do?

She walked back to the Dauphin Bleu and sighed when she noticed the Closed sign. Could she stand another night lingering in the seedy bar hoping for Mitch to show up, only to end up disappointed again?

Frustrated, she slammed a fist on the door of the establishment and nearly jumped out of her skin when the door swung open and a round-bellied man with dark skin and frizzy gray hair stared at her.

"Can I help you?" he asked in a thick, rumbling accent.

Chelsea didn't even pause to think. "Yes! I'm looking for this man," she said quickly, whipping out her glossy picture of Mitch.

"Aaah. Mr. Russell."

"Yes! Mr. Russell." Maybe she'd finally struck pay dirt!

"Most days he spends at his house or in his boat," the man said thoughtfully. "He lives to the north around the point..." He gave her directions to Mitch's cabin along with a few pieces of information Chelsea had already discovered herself. "He stay mostly to himself."

"Doesn't he have any friends?"

"A few. He be with Mr. Landeen sometimes or Mr. Raoul," he said thoughtfully. "But mainly he be with himself."

This was nothing new, except she was surprised that Chris's name had come up. She thanked the man and with little more information than she had before, she strolled through the open-air market, eyeing the wares. She bought a small bag of oranges, a bottle of wine and two baskets, which she tucked into her beach bag.

The sun was low in the western sky but the heat of the day, still rising in shimmering waves from the pavement, caused sweat to collect between her shoulder blades. Walking lazily along the bleached planks of the docks, she gazed at the sea, where silhouettes of sailboats skimmed the horizon and larger fishing vessels lumbered into port. Sunbathers, catching a few dying rays, were scattered along the beach and swimmers dotted the turquoise water. The pungent odors of fish, seaweed, and brine filled her nostrils.

Paradis had a certain charm, she thought, leaning against a rail worn smooth with time. She watched the boats rocking lazily against the docks—outriggers, sloops, ketches—bobbing to the gentle swell of the tide, when she saw him.

Mitch Russell, big as life, was barely a hundred yards from her. His eyes were guarded by sunglasses and he wore tan slacks and a plaid shirt with the sleeves rolled over his forearms. He was talking to two men—both dark-haired and tanned.

Chelsea couldn't believe her good luck. She hoped she blended into the crowd along the piers as she stared at Mitch and the people with him. One man was tall with a thick moustache and greasy black hair. He wore faded denim jeans and a blue jacket. The other man was shorter and thicker, his belly protruding and the beginning of a beard starting to darken his chin. He was dressed in a straw-colored suit and black tie and tugged nervously at his chin as they talked.

However, the two men held little interest for Chelsea. It was their companion, a beautiful woman who stood so close to Mitch that no daylight squeezed between them. With jet-black hair, large eyes and a pointed little nose, she grinned up at Mitch, her generous mouth curved into a smile—as if she and he shared some private joke.

Chelsea's insides twisted as Mitch whispered something to her and she tossed back her head and laughed, her straight black hair shining vibrantly in the fading sunlight.

So he did have a woman.

A painful little ache throbbed in Chelsea's heart. *What did you expect?* her mind taunted. *Mitch Russell means nothing to you—and you mean nothing to him! As for Devlin—well, he never really cared for you, now, did he? If he did survive the accident, he ran from you and the life he'd led in San Francisco and even if he died in the bay with John, you've lost him forever.*

"No," she whispered vehemently as she stared at the man whose features and voice were so like Devlin's, whose smile and laughter reminded her of Devlin's and whose kiss was as powerful and consuming as Devlin's had been.

She reached into her bag and found her camera. Focusing quickly, she snapped off several quick shots of Mitch and the raven-haired woman, of his two acquaintances, and of the sleek red sailboat moored nearby as it moved in tempo with the lapping of the tide.

As if he could feel her eyes on him, Mitch glanced her way. In the viewfinder, she saw his lips tighten, though he barely missed a beat before turning his attention back to the group. Slinging one arm around the beautiful woman's waist, he pulled her tight against him and squeezed, his fingers splaying intimately beneath her breast.

Nausea swam in Chelsea's throat. She shoved the lens cap onto her camera. She felt suddenly dirty and sick. How could she care the least bit for that wretched man? Just because he looked like Devlin?

Disgusted, she threaded her way between the other people crowding the docks. The heat seemed abruptly staggering. She swiped her bangs from her eyes and felt sweat against her palm. She just needed a few hours to get a grip on herself, to shower and change and somewhere find the guts to come back to the Dauphin Bleu and observe Mitch again.

And what if you see him take that woman into his arms and kiss her?

"It won't matter," she said aloud, sounding more certain than she felt. Bracing herself, she hazarded one last glance over her shoulder to see Mitch alone on the docks. The other members of his party had boarded a sleek red speedboat, which boasted the name *Lucia,* and Mitch stood, shoulders bunched tightly as he watched the racy boat roar out of the bay.

Though it was ridiculous, Chelsea felt a certain satisfaction that the woman was no longer with Mitch. She was trying to swallow a smile when the boat rounded the far point of the island.

As soon as the speedy craft disappeared from view, Mitch turned and spying Chelsea, strode swiftly her way. His jaw was set, his eyes blazing as he approached and Chelsea felt more than a tiny prickle of fear.

"Just what the hell do you think you're doing?" he demanded in a harsh whisper. Grabbing hold of her upper arm, he propelled her away from the docks and across a dusty street crowded with tourists. Only a few people even glanced their way.

"I was just sightseeing."

"Ha!" He yanked harder on her arm, forcing her down the street and through the tightly packed shops of Emeraude. "And I suppose you were just taking a few photographs of the view?" he snarled.

"Yes. The bay, the beach, the docks—"

"Me."

"No, I—"

"Sure." He yanked harder on her arm and they passed through the open market, leaving the water-front behind.

"Where're you taking me?"

"Someplace safe."

"Safe?" she repeated, half running to keep up with him before she understood. "Oh, I get it. Safe because of the other night, when you thought someone followed me to your house and you insinuated that there was some kind of danger?"

His lips pressed so tightly together they turned white against his black beard.

"So what are you afraid of, Mr. *Russell?*" she chided, unable to keep her tongue still. "Were you concerned that your girlfriend would see me?"

He muttered something under his breath, rolled his eyes to the summer-blue sky, then swore softly. Yanking harder on her arm, he said, "Look, I don't need you fouling up my life."

"I'm not."

"Like hell!" He strode, dragging her to keep pace with him, along an old cobblestone street until it gave out and petered into a path that led into an overgrown park. Trees offered shade and fragrant blossoms scented the air. Insects buzzed as they passed, birds pecked at crumbs on the paths and a few people sat on old wrought iron benches.

"Isn't this far enough?" she demanded, trying to tug her arm away from him.

"Not private enough!" he growled and a feeling of panic swept up Chelsea's spine. Throwing her a dark look, he explained, "I don't want to cause a scene and you, lady, bring out the worst in me."

"You mean you actually have a better side?" she flung out.

That was a mistake. He slid a furious glance in her direction and his fingers dug into the soft flesh of her arm. "Believe it or not, there are times when my sole purpose in life *isn't* centered around wringing your pretty neck!"

"How chivalrous," she mocked.

Growling something unintelligible, he continued to tug on her arm as the path led through a grass clearing and past an old gazebo in sad need of paint. "We could stop here," she suggested, but Mitch didn't pause for a second.

Beach grass tickled her calves as the sandy trail led upward, switching back and forth through stands of leafy trees and shrubbery. Chelsea's legs began to ache as the path grew steeper. Several times she stubbed her toe, but Mitch continued to climb. "You should have told me to wear my hiking boots," she grumbled.

"I didn't know you had any."

"Well, they're back in San Francisco—"

"A lot of good that does you." He glanced down at her sandals and a frown creased his brow. "Women's fashions," he grunted disgustedly, but the fingers around her arm slackened a little and his pace slowed slightly.

Eventually, just when Chelsea thought her calves and thighs could stand no more, the trees gave way to a clearing.

Chelsea walked onto the grass and her breath caught in her throat at the panoramic view of sky and sea. Far below, past acres of emerald-green treetops, the small shops and docks of Emeraude stretched around the glistening waters of the bay. Boats dotted the horizon and, closer, seabirds swooped to rookeries tucked into the rocks and marshes of the deeper recesses of Paradis.

"Okay," he said at last, finally releasing her. "You and I are going to have it out—once and for all!" Without so much as asking, he reached into her basket, found her camera and opened the back.

"Hey—wait!"

He stripped the film from the camera.

"That's mine—"

Exposing the film to the sun, he tossed the empty camera back to her. "So now you've got it back!"

She caught the camera on the fly. "You have no right—"

"I? *I* have no right? What about you? Sneaking around like some phony private eye, taking pictures, asking questions, generally being a pain in the backside!"

"But you can't just—"

"I can do what I damn well please," he snarled back. "This is my home. You're the foreigner—"

"Foreigner? So you've taken up citizenship? Is that it? Well, even so, you can't—"

"I can!" Advancing on her, Mitch ground out, "Now, you listen to me! You're the one who can't! You can't trespass on my land, you can't take pictures of me or my friends without telling me about it and you certainly can't start asking questions about me of every person you meet on the street!"

"But, I—"

"I know. You think I'm lying to you. You have this insane belief that I'm someone I'm not!"

She just stared at him. Could she have been so wrong? Doubt prickled her mind as she stared at this bearded man who glared at her from the protection of dark glasses. She licked her lips nervously. "Who—who were the people you were talking to?"

"What people?" He shoved his sunglasses onto his head.

"On the docks."

"Look, don't you go bothering them," he warned, his eyes snapping blue fire.

"Who are they? Friends?"

"Acquaintances, and probably not the nicest people you'd ever want to meet. But I need them, they help me with research for my story."

"Your story?"

"The book I'm writing. Part one is set in South America in a fictional small dictatorship. Those people—the men on the docks—have given me insight to the people, customs and government of their country."

"In exchange for—?"

His lips compressed. "Money."

"Couldn't you just go to the library?"

The look he cast her called her every kind of fool. "Not for the kind of information I need."

Chelsea's stomach knotted. "What about the woman that was with them?"

"Same thing."

She arched a disbelieving brow.

"Haven't you ever heard of the woman's perspective? Well, believe it or not, a woman from an impoverished Third World country has a different outlook on life than most American women who can walk into Nieman Marcus and charge whatever they want."

"What're their names?" she asked and his eyes turned dangerous.

He acted as if he hadn't heard her question. "Since you've been poking around into my personal life, you probably know I'm a reporter."

"I'd heard."

"I protect my sources. And my advice to you is to leave well enough alone. I don't want those people or you hurt."

"I wouldn't—" Then she understood. "What 'customs' do they tell you about? Drugs? Prostitution? Shady government deals with the United States?"

"It's none of your business, Chelsea."

"It is if you're Devlin."

"You are too much!" He threw his hands into the air as if asking supplication. "I'm sorry about your friend—really, I am. It's hard to lose someone—I know. I lost my wife about eighteen months ago. But you just have to go on."

"Like you did," she ventured. "By running down here?"

His jaw clenched and he walked away from her, staring at the sea, his shoulders broad and stretching the cloth of his shirt, the tails flapping in the breeze. He pinched the bridge of his nose and Chelsea's throat tightened. How many times had she seen Devlin, in exasperation, make the very same gesture?

"I had my reasons for leaving," he said slowly, and when he turned back to face her, his eyes were clouded with guilt. His lips pressed firmly together and her gaze was drawn to his mouth. "But I guess you could say that I ran away." His jaw slid to one side. "I wouldn't deny it, but I don't like my life pried open and dissected." He shoved his hair from his eyes. "What is it I have to do to get rid of you?"

"Prove that you're not Devlin," she said, not missing a beat.

"I tried, the other night. Obviously you didn't buy it."

"Would you?"

"Yes! Damn it, woman, why won't you accept what is so patently obvious?" Striding back to her, he shoved his face so close to hers that his beard touched her cheek. "I am *not, never have been* and *never will be* Devlin McVey! Until the other night in the bar at the Villa, I'd never laid eyes on you before and I'd never heard of the man and I wish to Almighty God that I never had. Now, the way I see it, you can keep up with this fantasy of yours or you can accept me for who I am."

"Which is?" she asked, her voice so soft she could barely hear it.

"A man who is disgusted with his way of life in America, a man who lost his wife and it nearly killed him because he was behind the wheel, a man who's trying to rebuild a life that makes some kind of sense and a man who wants and needs his privacy!" His blue gaze delved so deeply into hers, it seemed to scrape her soul and for the first time since meeting him, she felt something akin to pity for this man who called himself Mitch Russell. He must have read her expression because he swore under his breath and plowed his fingers through his hair. "Why won't you believe me?"

"Because I can't!" she cried, aching inside because she hurt so much. Had she come so far for nothing? Good Lord, was this man really who he said he was? She blushed and felt like an utter fool.

When he reached forward with one finger and slowly tilted her chin upward, so that her eyes met the mystery in his, she nearly came undone. Inside, she trembled. Her skin felt cold and hot at once, prickly and tense as his gaze searched the contours of her face.

"You want me to leave you alone?" she whispered.

"Yes…and no. I want you to give up pretending I'm someone I'm not."

She swallowed hard. "And…"

"And…if you won't leave me alone, at least meet me on my own terms, treat me as if I'm not some long lost dream."

She licked her lips, aware of his one finger so near the pulse beginning to throb in her neck. "If you only knew how like him you are."

"Give it up, Chelsea." His fingers slowly descended, trailing along her neck to rest at the hollow of her throat. "I'm not your perfect Devlin," he whispered, his throat suddenly raw and hoarse.

"He wasn't perfect and he wasn't mine."

His eyes darkened. "Oh, I think he was. He was probably just fool enough not to know it." His arms circled her waist and he drew her to him. His lips crashed down on hers with a possessive fury that made her knees suddenly weak. His tongue, supple and wet, invaded her mouth, touching and dancing eagerly, sending chills down her spine.

Winding her arms around his neck, she molded her lips to his. He reached lower, his hands cupping her buttocks, drawing her closer still. Hard-muscled thighs pressed firmly against her, intimately caressing her own bare legs. Her breasts were crushed against the wall of his chest and her heart thudded loudly.

Stop! Stop him now! Don't make this mistake! a voice inside her head screamed, but as one hand reached upward and tangled in the long strands of her hair, she couldn't resist. His weight drew them both downward to a bed of long sun-bleached grass with a canopy of cloudless blue sky.

His beard was rough against her face, his calloused hands hard and demanding as he touched her through her clothes, smoothing the cotton fabric across her breasts and buttocks, creating an ache that streamed through her in wanton invitation. He was half lying atop her, his legs pinning hers as his lips and tongue played havoc with her senses.

Her nipples reacted, puckering to the feel of his hand through the cloth, her breath constricted in her throat and all the while her brain screamed at her that this was wrong—this hot seduction was purely animal lust and had nothing to do with love.

He tore his lips from hers and stared down into her eyes. Slowly he reached for the top button of her cover-up, plucking the button and sliding it all-too-easily through its hole. The second and third buttons gave way.

Chelsea's heart was pounding, her blood pulsing hot through her veins. "You are beautiful," he murmured as he stared at her breasts swelling so boldly. He reached for another button.

"No!" With all the strength she could muster, she grabbed his wrist and stopped him from going further.

A small smile played upon his lips. "Second thoughts?" he challenged, and she saw his gaze flicker to the rapid rise and fall of her chest.

"And third and fourth and so on," she said back, willing her voice to remain steady, while his finger still touched the bare skin between her breasts and his leg was flung over one of hers, pinning her to the steamy earth.

"What is it with you, Chelsea Reed?" he asked, undaunted as he propped his head with one hand and let his gaze rove lazily up and down her body.

Chelsea swallowed with difficulty. She knew her hair was tangled, her clothes were pushed and pulled, revealing the hollow of her breast and the length of her thigh. She could feel a burn of embarrassment stain her cheeks. Her lips were swollen—still tasting of his mouth and tongue—and her eyelids were still at half mast. She tried to squirm away, to snatch at the gaping cloth over her breasts, but he pressed his weight against her, pinning her at the thighs.

"Don't you want me?"

"I—I don't even know who you are!"

"Well, that's progress," he said, his eyes glimmering seductively. "Maybe you're not so hung up on this Devlin character as much as you believe—or maybe he's just a figment of your imagination."

"What?" she nearly screamed before she noticed the mockery in his eyes. This—this seduction was all just an act! He wasn't interested in her, he was just trying to prove a point! Just a man with a woman—any woman. Just as Devlin had tried to prove a point when she said she was in love with John!

Though Mitch's voice had turned gruff and his eyes still glinted in sensual invitation, it wasn't because she was Chelsea Reed, it was only because she was available and throwing herself at him.

Sick with shame and disgust, she tried to roll away. "Get off me," she commanded and he laughed.

"What's wrong, Chelsea? Tired of your little game? Can't you believe in your fantasies any longer?"

She struggled free and he let her go. Standing, towering over him, her breath coming in short gasps, she tossed her hair away from her face and tilting up her chin said coldly, "You're the most disgusting, self-serving, arrogant son of a bitch I've ever met!"

"Is that a compliment?"

She clenched her jaw tight and asked with quiet fury, "Why is it you get such a thrill out of mortifying me? No, don't answer that—" She scooped up her bag and started for the path "—I don't want to know."

"Just remember who's been chasing whom."

"Chasing?" she repeated in a low whisper. *"Chasing?"* Whirling, she faced him again and almost melted when she noticed the boyish mischief twinkling in his eyes, the way his black hair fell over his forehead so fetchingly. "I've never chased you, Mitch. But I did come down to this island with a purpose and I haven't given up."

His smile faded. He rose slowly and crossed the grassy strip to stand just in front of her. His eyes narrowed on her lips. "Are you willing to take a chance on that—" he motioned with one thumb to the trampled bed of grass where they'd so nearly made love "—happening again? Because it will, you know. There's something electric between you and me—don't try to deny it. You felt it, too. Call it sexual attraction or raw animal magnetism or just plain sex, but it exists."

"In your mind."

"And your body."

She wanted to slap him, but she couldn't. He was only telling the truth.

"Leave me alone, Chelsea. For your sake and mine. I don't want to get involved with you any more than you want to have a quick meaningless affair with a man you don't even know. Go back to San Francisco. Find another John. Or another Devlin for that matter. But leave me the hell alone!"

For the first time she thought she saw a glimmer of pain in his eyes. "Why did you bring me up here?"

"To point out that you're playing a dangerous game and you'll lose."

"Why is it dangerous?"

"Because you're too involved in this fantasy—this myth—you're deluding yourself, woman. And I don't want to be a part of any dreams that will only end in disappointment."

"And yet you tried to seduce me."

One side of his mouth lifted. "Oh, I beg to differ. You tried to seduce me."

"Me?"

"You're just lucky I'm not that kind of guy."

"What?" she whispered but realized again, when she caught the glimmer of laughter in his eyes, that he was teasing her. There was more to Mitch Russell than he let on, a side to him that she found lighthearted and free. But it was buried deep beneath layers of distrust and anger. "You're absolutely insufferable."

"Probably. Now, Ms. Reed, why don't I take you back to the hotel and you give up with the cameras and the questions and the bulldozing your way into my life."

"Is that what you really want?"

He hesitated, but only for a second. The brackets around his mouth deepened. "It would be best. For both of us."

"Why?"

"Because, even if I wanted to, I couldn't be the man you're hoping I am."

The sincerity in his blue eyes cut her to the bone. For the first time since she'd met Mitch Russell, she thought he might be telling her the truth. Maybe he deserved the same. Drawing a shuddering breath she said, "As you know, I spent a lot of time and effort getting here. And it's hard for me to believe that someone who looks and sounds and feels so much like Devlin isn't he. All I want from you is some time to get to know you, so that I can go back to the States convinced that he's really gone."

He glanced out to sea and his hair ruffled in the wind. "You want time—time with me?"

"Yes."

"How much?"

"Two weeks."

Sighing, he turned to face her again, and this time his face was set in stone. "Three days."

"But that's not enough."

"That's the deal. Take it or leave it."

"A week, then."

"Three days or nothing. And you've got to promise me that you'll quit spying on me, taking pictures and acting like some kind of bumbling James Bond." He glared up at her. "I mean it, Chelsea. I've got a job to do—a book to write. So, when I'm ready, I'll come looking for you—"

"When *you're* ready?" she repeated.

"Right. I'm not on a vacation."

"But—"

"Take it or leave it!" he snapped.

She didn't have any choice. She could see by the rock-hard set of his jaw that he wouldn't budge and three days was better than nothing, wasn't it?

Besides, where was it written that she had to keep her end of the bargain?

"All right, Mr. Russell," she finally agreed, feeling more than a little trepidation at the white lie. "You've got yourself a deal!"

Chapter 7

Feeling as if she'd made a pact with the very devil himself, Chelsea slid a furtive glance in his direction as he drove her back to the hotel. What would he look like without his beard? His build was the same, his eyes so provocative and blue, they had to belong to Devlin.

As if he sensed her staring at him, he shifted down and looked at her in such a way that the back of her throat went dry. "Why don't you tell me about yourself?" he suggested.

"Why?"

"Well, you've been asking a lot of questions. I figured it was my turn."

"There's not much to tell," she said, smiling slightly. "Besides, it's a boring story."

"You? Boring?" He let out a long breath. "You may be a lot of things, lady, but 'boring'? Never!"

Reluctantly, she sketched out her life, told him about her family, her overprotective older sister, her father the cop, her martyred mother, left for a woman less than half her age.

Mitch listened attentively as his Bronco rambled up the slight incline to the Villa. When she stopped talking, he glanced her way. "And what about your fiancé?"

"John," she whispered, feeling a tug on her heart. Sighing, she shook her head sadly. "John was special."

"You loved him very much."

She hesitated for only a second. "Yes."

"But still you look for his friend."

"For answers," she admitted.

"Answers?" Mitch's hands tightened over the wheel as the Bronco broke through the trees and the hotel loomed ahead. Magenta and violet reflected in the windows and the dusty white walls seemed less scarred in the coming twilight.

"I think Devlin might know something about the boating accident that the police don't." She chewed on her bottom lip as he guided the rig into the pitted asphalt lot and cut the engine.

"Then you don't believe it was an accident?"

"No! I mean, it's possible, but it just doesn't make sense, does it? Why would Devlin run if what had happened in the bay were only an accident?"

"Wait a minute—you think McVey might be responsible?" he asked.

"No." She shook her head emphatically. "But I really don't know what to think. That's why I have to find Devlin. There's a reason he took off—a reason John died."

Mitch's hand surrounded her arm and through the open window of the Bronco, fragrant scents of lemon and gardenia wafted in the warm air. "You know, lady, you're setting yourself up for a major fall. In my book, your friend McVey drowned. Period. End of story. No fairy-tale ending. No mystery. No nothing."

The fingers on her inner arm were warm against her sensitive skin and the stare he sent her fairly smoldered. Yet he didn't move to get closer to her. His hand dropped and he turned away. "Good night, Chelsea," he said, waiting for her to leave.

She reached for the handle of the door. "You know, he even drove a Bronco not so different from this. Not a Jeep, but a Bronco."

"So?"

"Seems like more than a coincidence."

He snorted and shook his head, but when he glanced back at her, she touched him on the arm. "If you are Devlin, Mitch," she said slowly. "I'm going to find a way to prove it and then you're going to have to face whatever it was that happened in that storm." Her eyes held his for a heart-stopping moment. "There will be no more running."

"And what will you do, when you finally accept the fact that you're wrong, hmm? How will you handle the fact that you're attracted to me—and don't try to deny it," he added as if anticipating the protest that leaped to her lips. "Because when you do, you'll be the one who'll be thinking of running."

With that, he rammed the Bronco into gear and as soon as she climbed from the cab and slammed the door he tore out of the lot, thick tires chirping against worn asphalt.

He seemed so sure of himself, so confident. And yet there was an inner man, a kinder man she'd only glimpsed, hidden deep within the arrogant exterior of Mitch Russell.

She watched his taillights disappear around a bend in the drive. Unfortunately for him, he hadn't counted on her tenacity. She'd find a way to prove he was Devlin—even if she had to take dental X-rays to do it.

At the thought, a slow smile crept across her face. No, she wouldn't have to resort to coercing a dentist into helping her, she thought with a smile. There was another way to prove he was Devlin, if only she had the guts to try and find out. Hadn't John, on the night she'd met Devlin, mentioned that he had a birthmark—a distinctive crescent high on his hip?

At the time, she thought John had been teasing, but once, a few months before the boating accident, John had ribbed Devlin about the birthmark. To her surprise, a dark flush had tinted the back of hard-edged Devlin's neck, thereby proving, to Chelsea's way of thinking, that he did, indeed, have the embarrassing mark.

And now, in all the months since the accident, she hadn't really thought about Devlin's birthmark, probably because she'd never seen it. If Russell was, in fact, Devlin McVey, then certainly he'd still have the birthmark, unless along with growing a beard he'd also decided to have some plastic surgery!

Chelsea considered this new idea from all angles as she shoved open the hotel doors and walked through the shabby lobby. Did she have the nerve to suggest to Mitch that he remove his pants in her presence?

A tingle of anticipation darted up her spine, and she grimaced.

There had to be another way.

But how?

Short of rifling through his belongings, she had no other way to prove he was lying.

Steeling herself as she climbed the stairs, she decided she'd give herself two and a half days and if, in that time, she wasn't able to know without a doubt that Mitch Russell was just an alias for Devlin McVey—she'd have to find a way to see that damned birthmark.

Sighing, she unlocked the door of her hotel room and dropped her beach bag on the floor. She didn't much care for her plan, but then, she didn't have much choice. Like it or not, she was running out of time.

Of course, she could further the deception and pretend to fall in love with him. Considering how charged the air was whenever they were together, and the explosion of passion that ignited whenever they touched, it wouldn't be too hard to act as if she were caught up in making love to him and then stopping suddenly when he'd bared himself so she could view his naked hip.

That thought turned her stomach. She wasn't used to trickery and there was the distinct chance that her plan could backfire. She had only to think of this very afternoon and how her emotions had nearly gotten the better of her. What if it was she, not he, who was lost in passion?

She'd nearly made love to him on the cliff overlooking the sea. Her face burned as she flopped back on her hotel room bed and stared at the ceiling.

Well, there was a chance she'd see him in a swim

suit—something revealing enough that the birthmark would show. She smiled to herself. That was it! She'd ask him to go swimming with her.

"This is for John," she told herself firmly, deciding that if all else failed, she had no recourse but to pretend to fall in love with Mitch to prove that he was Devlin. There was only one way. She had to see his bare hip.

The next morning, after a night of fitful sleep, her conscience still nagged at her.

A headache was pounding behind her eyes when Chelsea met Terri on the beach near the hotel and tried to sunbathe. While soaking up the sun's rays, Chelsea explained everything to Terri, including how Devlin supposedly disappeared and why she'd come to Paradis. She ended by telling Terri how little progress she'd made.

"Sounds like you should have kept that investigator hired on," Terri said, slathering sunscreen on her belly and thighs. She smiled to herself and adjusted her green two-piece suit. "Why would Devlin—if that's who you really think he is—try to hide way down here in the middle of nowhere?"

"I wish I knew," Chelsea replied, squinting against the sun. Sitting upright, she wrapped her arms around her knees and dug her toes into the warm sand.

"Is there a reason he'd want to avoid you?"

"Not that I know of."

"Maybe he feels guilty for—what was his name—Joe's death?"

"John's," Chelsea corrected automatically. Some of the pain of losing John had eased over the past few months and lately, since meeting Mitch, John's image had faded. But Devlin hadn't. In fact, just being around Mitch made memories of Devlin swim dangerously close to the surface of her mind.

"Tell me about your friend," Terri suggested. She fiddled with the beach umbrella to shade her face, but let her long legs stretch into the white sand. "This Devlin. Why're you so interested?"

"I thought I already explained—"

Terri waved impatiently, then dug into her cooler for a can of soda. She offered cherry cola to Chelsea. "I know what you said, and maybe that's what you believe, but, if you ask me, you're not being honest with yourself. Devlin must be much more important than just your fiancé's best friend for you to come traipsing all the way down here, accuse a man with a different name of running away, and never let up." She popped the lid on her can of orange soda. "Tell me the truth, what do you really feel for Devlin?"

"Friendship," she said automatically, then sighed and blew her bangs from her eyes. "Well, it really was kind of a love-hate relationship."

"Love?" Terri asked, her eyebrows lifting over the rims of her sunglasses.

"Not the way you mean."

"Sexual attraction, then?"

What was the point of lying? She'd been kidding herself for nearly a year and a half. "Devlin was the kind of man I always avoided—you know the type."

"Tall, dark and handsome?"

"To begin with. He seemed kind of dangerous and unapproachable. He had a rough edge to him that made me uncomfortable and he was a cop, a detective, like my dad."

"And that was a problem?"

"The problem was that I'd planned to marry John, have a family, a house in the suburbs, a station wagon with wood trim on the side, you know, the whole bit."

"You?" Terri hooted. "Who were you kidding?"

Chelsea bristled a little. "What do you mean?"

Shaking her red hair, Terri wagged a finger at Chelsea. "You're the least likely candidate for P.T.A. president I've ever seen. Oh, sure, you probably want marriage and a family someday, but you've got too much sense of adventure to tie yourself down to an accountant."

"John was an architect."

"Doesn't matter. Unless I miss my guess, you're not cut out for the wife-of-the-executive routine." She shoved her sunglasses onto her crown.

"Why not?"

"Because you're here, that's why. How many women do you know who own their own business and fly off on some whim—some tropical adventure—to meet a mystery man who's supposedly been running away from her and the dark secret of his past?"

"You've seen too many movies," Chelsea retorted, but sipped her too-sweet cola slowly, wondering why everyone, Felicia, now Terri, even Mitch himself, had accused her of being somehow destined to be with Devlin.

"Don't forget, I was married," Terri reminded her. "I know the difference between caring for someone and grand passion."

Chelsea lifted her brows.

"My husband cared for me—he really did. But I

wasn't the—great passion of his life. That was reserved for his secretary."

"Oh. I'm sorry."

"Don't be. I'm not," she said with a trace of bit-
terness. "I'm still looking for my own grand passion
and so are you." Terri drained her drink, then put both
empty cans back into her cooler. "And if it does turn
out that Devlin McVey is dead, you shouldn't give up
on Mitch Russell."

"Meaning?"

"Meaning that he's a man who could set a woman's
blood on fire."

Chelsea laughed. "Is there such a thing?"

"Absolutely!" Terry grinned. "And let me tell you,
when I find a guy who does that for me, I'm going to
sink my hooks into him and never let go!"

Chelsea chuckled as she drew a circle in the sand
and thought about Mitch. "You know, I saw him yesterday, with a couple of men and a woman."

"Mmm."

"A beautiful woman," Chelsea corrected.

"Jealous?"

"No! Well, it did bother me."

"Aha! I knew it!"

"I just wondered if you knew her."

"What's her name?"

"I don't know, but she was gorgeous." Chelsea went
on to describe the woman's attributes, remembering
her black hair and dark, laughing eyes.

"She could be anyone," Terri said frowning. "But
I haven't heard of Mitch being linked romantically
with anyone special. I've seen him with a couple of
women—like I said, no one special—and I might have

even seen him with this one. I really don't remember. But I wouldn't worry too much about the competition."

"It isn't a competition."

"Sure." Terri glanced at her watch and let out a groan. "I'm late! I've got to be at the store in less than half an hour!" Gathering up her things quickly, she added, "I promised to close the boutique this afternoon. I'll see you later!"

"Let me help."

"No reason, I've got everything." Hauling her cooler, umbrella and towel, she headed up the beach toward the Villa. Chelsea insisted on carrying Terri's beach bag and helped her load her equipment into her car.

Once Terri had taken off, Chelsea returned to her room. No messages. Frowning, she stopped at the mirror and checked her reflection. Her turquoise suit brought out the green in her eyes and her auburn hair fell to her shoulders in vibrant waves. Not that it mattered, she told herself. If Mitch found her attractive, fine. If he didn't—she couldn't worry about it. She was only here to prove that he was Devlin.

And what then?

Worried sea-green eyes stared back at her. If Mitch proved to be Devlin, then she would be faced with the fact that Devlin had run from her, from the accident, from his past. And she'd never dealt well with Devlin when he hadn't been hiding his true identity. How would she handle him now?

Would he tell her what she wanted to know? Or would he throw in her face the very fact that she'd been attracted to him from the first instant their gazes had collided?

And now that John was gone—no longer between them—what would happen? She stared at her reflection, and chewed on her lower lip. What did she expect of Devlin? That he would return to San Francisco with her? Clear up the mystery surrounding John's death? Or would he tell her to get lost, mind her own business, remind her that John's death was just an accident he couldn't face?

Her insides knotted and she leaned against the bureau under the mirror. "Oh, Devlin," she murmured, a thick lump knotting her throat as the reality of how much he'd meant to her surfaced. She had cared for him and not only as John's friend; no, despite all her arguments to the contrary, their relationship had run through much deeper, more turbulent emotional waters than pure friendship. Had she met him before John, she might have fallen for him. Now that John was gone...

And now there was Mitch—if, indeed, he truly was just a man who looked and sounded so much like Devlin that her senses were fooled. This man added a new dimension to an already difficult situation. Mitch was attractive—she couldn't deny it.

However, he was callous and cynical and sometimes bordered on being cruel. Yet there was a side to him that she'd seen only in fleeting glimmers, and she felt that his blatant sexuality, his bold innuendos had been meant to send her scurrying away from him, rather than draw her into his arms.

Mitch was dangerous and exciting and she hated herself for falling into his male trap, yet she couldn't stop herself.

Tossing on a cover-up and grabbing her snorkeling gear, she decided she could wait no longer. She hurried downstairs and checked at the desk, hoping Mitch had called. The thin, bored-looking clerk assured her no one had asked for her.

It figured. She fumed all the way back to the beach.

So what had happened, didn't she still have a "deal" with Mitch? Had he conveniently forgotten that they'd made a pact? Or was his bargain just a ploy to get her out of his hair? Well, it wouldn't work.

Seething, she dropped her equipment near the water's edge. Damn the man, he wasn't going to get rid of her that easily!

Stripping out of her cover-up, she glanced northward, to the stretch of sand that dwindled to the rocks jetting into the sea. Beyond the point was Mitch's cabin. Maybe it was time to visit him again. They had struck a bargain and time was slipping by—much too quickly. She wasn't about to sit around and wait for him to call her—if and when he got around to it.

She grabbed snorkel, mask and fins, then walked across the wet sand to the tide, where the foamy surf tickled her toes. White pelicans squawked and swooped from the rocks nearby, and a double-masted replica of a nineteenth-century clipper ship, filled with tourists, glided across the blue-green water.

She stepped into her fins, adjusted her mask and snorkel, waded deep into the sea, then began to swim just below the surface of the water. Schools of fish in brilliant shades of yellow and orange darted through the coral reefs and hid in the tangles of seaweed rippling with the tide.

Trying to concentrate on the vibrant sea life, Chelsea swam northward, around the point, but she barely noticed the beauty of the shadowy depths. As had been the case since she'd first met him, she continued to think about Mitch.

She was attracted to him, though the man made her blood boil and sometimes tied her stomach in knots. Had her feelings for Devlin been more than she wanted to admit? Well, yes, considering her response to him when they'd been alone at the cabin in the Sierra Nevadas. Did Devlin care for her? Not at all. As for Mitch, he didn't seem very interested, either. Except that she represented just one more female conquest. He'd made it clear he'd only suffered her company because he thought she was coming on to him and he was willing to take her to bed.

The thought did strange things to her. She was offended, but intrigued. Making love to Mitch Russell had crossed her mind more than once, but she feared that the act itself could hardly come under the heading of "love," and just plain sex was out of the question. She was liberated, but not that liberated, and she hoped she never would be. And yet—isn't that exactly what she was planning—a quick seduction for the single purpose of seeing him naked?

But she wasn't planning to go through with it and the only reason she was considering it was for the sake of the truth, the sake of finding out what had happened on the day of John's death.

Sure. John would have approved.

She felt sick inside as she passed the northern point on the beach and swam inland.

Surfacing near the weathered dock, she tossed her hair away from her face and stripped off her face mask. Taking in huge gulps of air, she told herself she would never purposely try to seduce Mitch Russell—

well, at least not yet. But, if she couldn't get him in a pair of revealing swim trunks, the time was fast approaching when she might have to pretend to fall in love with him. And then what?

Her heartbeat quickened, and she licked the saltwater from her lips. Maybe her plan was too bold.

She climbed onto the dock, then wrung her hair with her hands. Goose bumps appeared on her skin where the sea water still trickled down her neck and arms as she stared at Mitch's cabin.

His Bronco, not so very different from Devlin's, was parked near the house and Chelsea felt her breath catch in her throat. She left her snorkeling gear on the weathered dock, then walked barefoot through the hot sand to the cabin nestled in the trees. The windows of the tiny house were open, the shades stirring in the breeze and as she climbed the steps of the front porch, Mitch's voice caught her attention.

"…you're sure?" he was saying. "Of course we'll be alone—"

Chelsea froze. Coming here had been a mistake. Her heart thudded against her ribs.

"—I'll take care of all the details. But let's meet somewhere else. Someplace private. Away from the island. So that no one surprises us." His voice was so silky, so smooth.

Her skin crawled. She started edging toward the steps. Better to leave now, before Mitch and his raven-haired mistress discovered her eavesdropping. She'd stepped onto the sand when she heard the distinctive sound of a telephone receiver being slammed back into its cradle.

So he'd been on the phone, setting up a tryst with

a woman. She had taken two steps when his voice arrested her.

"Was I mistaken or did we have a bargain?" Mitch demanded.

Chelsea turned quickly, nearly stumbling, and when his eyes clashed with hers, she saw him take in a swift, short breath. His gaze raked her body and his lips tightened almost imperceptibly as he apparently noticed the swell of her breasts and nip of her waist beneath the taut, wet fabric of her suit. Was it her imagination or did she notice more than simple male appreciation in his eyes?

Standing in the doorway, his shirt open, his hands stuffed into the pockets of a pair of tan slacks, he glared at her. To her horror, she found him amazingly handsome.

"I got tired of waiting," she responded, angling her chin upward against his height advantage. "And we're running out of time."

"I thought I told you I didn't want to be spied upon."

"And I thought you told me we had three days together."

"We do."

"It's afternoon. The first day is slipping by. I didn't want to waste any time."

One dark brow cocked insolently. "Some of us have to work for a living. Remember?"

"I thought writers had flexible hours."

"I work better under a schedule."

She gathered in her breath. "I thought you could use a break. Maybe we could go swimming. You could show me some of the sights," she said, hoping to sound innocent. "I brought my gear." She waved toward the dock where her equipment lay.

Mitch eyed her for a minute. Rubbing his beard, he lifted a shoulder. "Well, since you're already here, I guess I can take the rest of the day off."

This was an unexpected surprise. Her heart sky-rocketed. "Good."

"I'll be just a minute." He stepped back into the house and Chelsea decided to follow him inside. She saw him duck into a back bedroom and she peeked around the corner. The room was sparse—decorated with a single chair, desk and computer. He punched a few keys, snapped disks from the drive and flipped the machine off. The glowing terminal went blank.

"How's it coming?" she asked.

"What?"

"Your story—whatever it is." She motioned toward the cluttered desk, where reference books, notes, magazines and two empty coffee cups were strewn.

"At least you had the presence of mind not to call it the 'Great American Novel.'"

"Isn't it?"

He grinned and his teeth flashed beneath his beard. "That remains to be seen. Okay—" He shepherded her outside. "Give me a minute to change."

"Take all the time you need," she said, relieved.

He was gone less than five minutes. When he reappeared, he was wearing a pair of khaki-colored shorts that reached his upper thigh, and a windbreaker.

"I thought we were going swimming," she said, disappointed. Now what?

He smiled devilishly. "I've got a better idea."

"Do you?"

"Hmm. But let's get one thing straight," he said. "No more questions, okay?"

"No questions? Then how're we going to get to know each other?"

He cast her a hard glance. "Believe me, Chelsea, when you find out my life history, you'll be bored to tears."

"I doubt it."

"Don't. I'm not mysterious, intriguing, or even interesting."

That's where you're wrong, Mitch Russell, she thought, but held her tongue as she half ran to keep up with him as he strode toward the sea.

"My story's been told a thousand times. I grew up in the midwest, played on the high-school basketball team, got a small scholarship, went to college, got married, and graduated with a degree in journalism. In a few years, I worked at a couple of different papers and then everything went to hell in a handcart."

"Meaning the accident," she said as they walked across the hot sand to the dock where her snorkeling equipment lay unattended.

"Right. The accident." His eyes darkened and he leaned over to untie the lashings that kept the small sailboat, the *Mirage,* moored to the pier. Glancing up at her, he smiled and Chelsea warmed from the inside out. "Come on, let's try out your sea legs. Ever been sailing before?"

She climbed into the small boat. "You know I have."

"How?" He shoved off, then glanced over his shoulder.

Because you were there, damn it! On your boat in the bay! "The pictures I showed you, remember?"

"Oh, right, your fiancé had a boat."

"The sailboat belonged to Devlin."

His lips compressed as he adjusted the boom, then guided the small craft through the clear water. "I'd forgotten. Seems as if McVey had everything. What was it you saw in his friend? Was he rich?"

"John? No. He did well enough, but he wasn't wealthy."

"So it wasn't money, and it wasn't passion—"

"I didn't say that," she cut in.

He slid her a knowing glance. "Then why do I have the feeling that you were more interested in his friend than your intended?"

"Because you're bullheaded," she said quickly, then regretted it, when he grinned at her. "John was kind and considerate and intelligent and...and he loved me."

"Sounds like you were planning to marry your best friend."

"Something wrong with that?"

"You wouldn't have been satisfied."

"How do you know?" she shot back. "You don't know anything about me." Or did he?

"I've met your kind before."

"Give me a break."

"You like a challenge, Chelsea, and a little adventure." Mitch studied the horizon, the lines near the corners of his eyes deepening as he steered through the very coral reefs she'd swum through less than an hour before. He slipped a pair of mirrored glasses onto his nose and his black hair ruffled in the wind.

The prow of the boat sliced through the water and the mainsail billowed in the wind that kicked in off the tide. White clouds had gathered overhead, blocking some of the sun's heat as they slowly shifted across the sky. The smell of salt and sea mingled together, filling Chelsea's senses.

She didn't want to think that he might be right, that John wouldn't have created in her that same rush of adrenaline that Devlin had induced. But that very rush was exactly what she'd been trying to avoid. She didn't need a man who was explosive and unpredictable— she wanted a safe and sane man—a man who would give her security and laughter, warm smiles and encouragement, not some rake who could set her blood afire, then move along to the next conquest.

Frowning, she wondered at Mitch's words, so like Devlin's. "Let's not play games, Chelsea, you're marrying the wrong man. You and I both know you're marrying the wrong man," Devlin had insisted, and though she'd denied it then and still rejected his accusation even now, there had been a ring of truth to his words, she thought ruefully.

And Mitch felt the same way. Coincidence? Unlikely. Oh, what she wouldn't do to see him without his beard. And without his pants? her mind teased cruelly, causing her to blush.

"Where to?" he asked, as they rounded the point and cut south along the edge of the island. The beach where she'd sunbathed earlier was visible as was the rambling hotel.

"You're the skipper."

"Be careful, I might kidnap you."

She crooked a disbelieving brow. "And take me where?"

Amusement flickered in his sky-blue eyes. "That

would ruin the surprise, wouldn't it?" He started to turn the craft into the wind, but Chelsea stopped him.

"Before we go anywhere, I think I should change."

He flicked a glance down her body. "You look fine to me. And you're the one who showed up like that."

"But we're so close to the hotel. Really, it would only take a minute." Since they weren't going swimming, she had to switch gears and now that she'd finally gotten his attention, she didn't want to lose it and by changing into something warmer, she could spend the rest of the afternoon and evening with him, watching him, looking for little idiosyncrasies that would convince her he really was Devlin.

With a shrug, Mitch headed the boat inland and in a few minutes, docked the *Mirage* against the pilings near the hotel.

Chelsea climbed out of the boat and grabbed her snorkel, fins and mask. "I'll only be a little while," she said as they plowed through the sand to the back side of the Villa.

"You don't want me to come up to your room?"

She caught the glint in his eye. "No more than I did the first night you suggested it," she said, though she knew she was missing out on a chance. If she could get him into the room, pretend to seduce him—all the while waiting to catch a view of his hip... And then what? Lead him into the bathroom for a cold shower?

No, the hotel room was much too obvious. The only reason she would take him upstairs would be to sleep with him—he wouldn't misconstrue her intentions and she needed a place that seemed more spontaneous so that when she backed out at the last minute, he wouldn't suspect he'd been set up.

She didn't much like the turn of her thoughts as she scurried up the stairs. This new, devious side of her nature bothered her, but she shoved her own recriminations aside. If Mitch were actually Devlin, then he deserved every bit of her deception and if he wasn't Devlin, then he needed a lesson in manners. From the first minute she'd spied him, he'd been inconsiderate, rude and irritatingly arrogant.

She stripped off her suit, showered and changed into a denim skirt and white blouse with wide sleeves that she rolled to her elbows. Adding a trace of makeup and a set of silvery bracelets, she slipped into sandals and hurried downstairs.

He was waiting in the bar—the very bar where she'd first made a fool of herself by running up to him and expecting Devlin McVey to wrap his arms around her and tell her how good it was to see her again.

She felt more than one cautious stare sent her way by a few of the regulars, but she didn't meet the interested eyes that followed her. Mitch grinned when he saw her, left some bills on the bar and ignored the rest of his beer.

"You didn't bring an overnight bag," he said.

Her heart began to drum. "Will I need one?"

"That's up to you."

"Are you propositioning me, Mr. Russell?"

"Take it any way you like." His fingers wrapped around the crook of her elbow and he propelled her through French doors that led to a flagstone patio. A few round tables were positioned near the old wrought iron railing, but Mitch passed them and headed through a rusty gate.

"Where're we going?"

"Didn't I say you'd be kidnapped?" he asked, his touch heating her skin and sending ripples of that very same heat up her arm and through her body.

"But you were kidding—"

"Was I?" His lips twisted beneath his beard and his eyes glinted appreciatively.

Chelsea had second thoughts. Despite her earlier plan that she would try and seduce him, at least until a point, she felt as if she were suddenly walking on very thin ice. Mitch was taking control of the situation.

"Why don't we just stay at the Villa? I could buy you dinner."

He barked out a laugh at that. "Always the liberated female."

They crossed the sand and Mitch propelled her along the dock, toward the *Mirage*. "I thought we'd go somewhere more private."

Chelsea started to panic. This wasn't how it was supposed to happen. "Where?"

"Come on, Chelsea. Where's your sense of adventure?" he mocked, teasing and irritating her all at once.

"I'm not the kind of woman who likes to be rough-handled by a man and ordered around."

"No one's rough-handling you. And face it, you *are* the kind who likes a challenge, and a fight, and you enjoy a bit of a mystery—a little intrigue. In fact, unless I miss my guess," he added, untying the lashings, "you love to be surprised."

"I like to be in control."

"So do I," he said, helping her into the boat, his gaze locking with hers for a throbbing instant. Chelsea's mouth turned to cotton and she thought he might kiss her again. Unconsciously, she licked her lips.

Mitch caught the sensual movement and his back teeth ground together. His brow became more furrowed and he forced his attention to the sailboat, guiding the small craft through the shimmering waters toward the open sea.

Though she was loath to admit it, Chelsea decided Mitch Russell was right about her. She did like a challenge and, despite her fears, enjoyed the adventure of it all. Felicia would call it her personality flaw and right now, alone with Mitch, Chelsea was in no position to argue.

Spray, cast up from the prow slicing through the water, clung to her face and hair, bringing with it the scent of fish and brine.

She dragged her fingers through the water and wondered where he was taking her. Trepidation skittered up her spine, but didn't account for the breathless feeling that kept her senses alive. True, she didn't know him all that well, and yet she trusted him, at least a little.

The sailboat rounded the southern tip of the island and he dropped anchor, letting the *Mirage* undulate on the sea. Paradis loomed in the distance, dark and green against a lowering sun. Fiery shades of magenta and gold washed over the sky.

"How about dinner?" he asked.

"Here?" She grinned. "What're we going to do—fish?"

He laughed. "And risk the chance of starving? I don't think so. Wait just a minute." He opened a small hold and withdrew a bottle of wine and a couple of white sacks. To her amazement, he spread a blanket between them and placed cartons of pasta salad, marinated shrimp, sliced cheese and crusty bread and two clear, stemmed glasses, on the makeshift table.

"Where'd you get all this?"

"At the hotel—while you were changing," he said with a crooked grin. "I hauled it back to the boat, then returned to the bar."

"It didn't take me *that* long."

Jaw sliding to the side, he found a wine cork and opened the bottle. "It took long enough." He poured them each a glass, offered her one and, clinking the rim of his glass to hers, said, "Salut!"

Chelsea felt her face drain of color. Her glass trembled in her fingers. "You remember," she accused, her throat dry.

He glanced up at her. "Remember what? Is something wrong?"

"The first night we met—the toast—"

"The first night we met you were drinking alone in the bar waiting for—"

"No!" She couldn't be wrong. Her eyes searched the clouded depths of his. "When I met you at John's apartment. He was making dinner and he toasted you—by saying 'Salut!'"

Mitch's mouth turned down. "I thought we weren't going to bring up all this again."

"But you said—"

"It was a coincidence, Chelsea! Nothing more!" His eyes snapped fire and he shoved a hand through his hair in frustration. "I'm sure I say a lot of things—and do a lot of things—that your friend did. But you can't keep looking for farfetched links to your past!"

Quaking inside, Chelsea took a sip of her wine.

The cool Riesling slid down her throat, but she barely tasted it.

"Come on," Mitch invited, his voice softer. "Let's eat."

He offered her a paper plate and though her mind was far from food, she managed to serve herself as the boat slowly rocked with the movement of the sea. Don't give up, she told herself, but found she was torn. This new man, Mitch Russell, was free of all the pain of the past. He wouldn't know how Devlin had mortified her, how he'd proved that she was as susceptible to his charms as the next woman. Mitch was taking her at face value—even though he thought she was more than a little obsessed with her past.

She relaxed as the sunset turned to dusk and she even began to taste the food that he'd been thoughtful enough to bring with him. There was more to Mitch Russell than his gruff exterior, she realized, and smiled at the thought. He was handsome and intelligent, if quick to anger.

Stars began to appear as the sky turned from rose to lavender to deepest purple. Chelsea leaned back against a soft cushion while sipping her second glass of wine. Had circumstances been different, she thought, watching as Mitch moved easily about the small boat, adjusting the sails and raising anchor, she could fall for a man like him.

The thought struck her like a thunderbolt. She didn't know anything about Mitch, except that his temper was all too quick to flare and his attitude toward women, if she could judge by the way he treated her, was the worst! What had she been thinking? Mitch Russell was as diametrically opposed to John Stern as he could be. But not so different from Devlin, her mind nagged.

"Ooh!" Angry with herself, she decided she'd had too much wine and quickly dumped the remainder in her glass into the ocean.

"Something wrong?" Mitch asked as he turned the craft back to the island and the winking lights of Emeraude.

"Nothing," she snapped.

He chuckled to himself, and that was all the more infuriating! Damn the man, how was he able to get under her skin so easily? From the corner of her eye, she could see the pull of his pants against his buttocks and the stretch of his shirt across his shoulders as he worked with the boom, but she kept her gaze fixed on their destination, the poorly lit beach near the Villa.

Once he moored the craft, she hopped out quickly, ignoring the hand he offered.

"Was it something I said?" he asked, his voice mocking as they walked along the path to the hotel.

"What?"

"Something's bothering you. What is it?" he asked, once they were near the hotel again.

"I'm just having a tough time accepting the fact that you're not Devlin," she admitted, knowing she was skirting the real issue.

"Why?" he asked suddenly, his voice as smooth as velvet.

"Because I miss him." She gazed upward to his night-darkened eyes and caught him staring at her. Her throat grew thick with emotion at her admission. How long had she denied that she'd missed Devlin, even cared for him? She'd pretended that she was down here only on a mission to find out what happened to John, but there was more to it. Oh, God, what she wouldn't do to know for certain that Devlin was alive.

Mitch's arms wrapped around her waist, drawing her quickly to him and his lips crashed down on hers so swiftly she could barely take a breath.

Warm, wondrous feelings shot through her and though she knew she should struggle and break the embrace she couldn't. His lips were magical, the splay of his hands thrillingly possessive. His tongue pressed hard against her teeth, demanding entrance. She could do little but part her lips and tremble when his plundering tongue darted in and out of her mouth, tasting and caressing, titillating and creating sensations of warmth and desire that rippled through her body. Her heart thundered and she pressed tightly to him, her breasts flatted against the hard wall of his chest.

"Oh, God," he groaned, shifting so that his thighs molded to hers.

She kissed him back, twining her arms around his neck and twisting his hair between her fingers. His beard was rough against her face, but she barely noticed as desire swept through her. A soft moan escaped from her lips and he answered, pulling her closer still until she could feel that he wanted her as desperately as she wanted him.

"Stop it," he growled. As suddenly as he'd grabbed her, he let her go, stepping away and breathing in short, shallow breaths.

She nearly stumbled backward. Was this another of his damned tests—to prove that he could send her heart racing—to demonstrate how he could dominate her senses and bring her down to the purely primal nature of woman? She gazed into his eyes and saw more than raw sensuality in the stormy blue depths—there was wonder and confusion, anger and despair. "Stop it?" she repeated, hurt.

"I wasn't talking to you!" he muttered.

"But—"

"I was telling myself to let go of you while I still could!" He made a sound of self-deprecation and he shoved the heels of his hands against his eyes—just as Devlin had years ago at the cabin near Lake Tahoe.

Chelsea couldn't speak, could only stare at his bunched shoulders and inside she was sure, sure he had to be Devlin.

"I won't be used, Chelsea," he said, his voice raw with emotion. "You can't pretend I'm someone else!"

"But I didn't—"

"Yes, you did!" Drawing in a long, whistling breath, he turned and faced her, frowning darkly, and gave her one last piece of advice. In a voice that was rough and low, he whispered, "If you want anything more to do with me, lady, you'll have to forget Devlin McVey."

Chapter 8

Chelsea nearly stumbled up the faded hotel stairs. Good lord, what had she gotten herself into? Was she falling in love with Mitch—or Devlin—or both men? She stopped on the first floor and took in a long, bracing breath.

What about John? She was beginning to wonder if she ever had really loved him. Her heart wrenched at the thought and she hated Mitch for planting the seeds of doubt in her mind. Or had it been Devlin who had started her second guessing herself? Had Devlin been right all along when he'd accused her of planning to marry the wrong man?

Stomach so tight it hurt, she climbed the second flight of stairs and considered her plan to seduce Mitch. She snorted at her own naïveté. Yes, she'd intended to pretend to fall in love with Mitch, but now she wondered if an act were necessary. In less than a week, she really had begun to fall for him.

She unlocked the door to her room and stepped into her shabby haven away from the emotional turmoil of dealing with Mitch Russell. Sighing in disgust, she flung herself onto the bed and stared at the ceiling. Ever since dating John, she'd known what she wanted in life. She wanted a business of her own, a husband, two children and a nice house. She wanted security and safety and a nice little world that was so predictable it might border on boring.

Until now. Well, no—she had to be honest with herself—Devlin had made her question her values, and yet she'd ignored him. But now, with Mitch, her entire world was spinning out of control—all the things she'd wanted in life—in fact, the very reasons she'd come to Paradis, seemed to mock her.

Furious with herself, she peeled off her skirt and started on her blouse when she noticed the red light flashing on her phone. She wanted to ignore the message, because she wasn't in the mood for one of Felicia's lectures.

Unfortunately, she had to take the call. What if something were wrong? What if their mother were ill? What if there were serious problems at the boutique in San Francisco?

Reluctantly, she dialed the front desk and was told that Ned Jenkins had called her. Her heart started to pump crazily as she scribbled down the private detective's number in San Francisco. What could he possibly want?

She dialed the number, heard the long distance connection crackle through, then impatiently drummed her fingers as she waited for Ned to pick up. On the fourth ring, his answering machine clicked on and a recorded message asked her to leave her name and number.

"Ned, this is Chelsea Reed. I'm at the Villa on Paradis and the number is—"

"Chelsea!" Ned picked up the phone, his voice battling with the poor connection. He sounded relieved. "God, I'm glad you called. I thought I'd better give you the latest on Devlin McVey."

Chelsea's heart stopped beating and she felt the color wash from her face. Please, God, don't let him tell me that Devlin's body was finally found! "What is it?" she asked quietly, bracing herself for the worst. Oh, Lord, what would she do if Devlin were truly dead? The future seemed suddenly empty and dark...

"I talked with a friend of mine at the police department—the guy worked with Devlin for a while—anyway, I finally managed to get him to open up a little. He wouldn't say much, of course, but the scuttlebutt is that McVey was on the take."

"What?" she cried, disbelieving.

"You heard me. Not everyone in the department goes along with the theory, of course, but he was working on some big drug case at the time of his supposed death. Some of the guys at headquarters think McVey faked his death because someone had figured out that he was working for the other side."

"That's crazy!" Chelsea whispered hoarsely.

"I'm just repeating what my friend said. He claims that McVey was going to be up on charges—or at the very least, investigated by internal affairs. If he's alive, he'll still face criminal proceedings."

"I don't believe it!" Chelsea's fingers held the receiver in a death grip. "Your 'friend' is spreading rumors! Filthy, vile gossip. That's all this is!"

"No way. I had to pry this information out of him. He didn't want to talk. As I said, he worked with McVey and kind of liked him—well, at least respected him, if not his methods. He confided to me that McVey used some very unorthodox procedures while he was working for the department."

Chelsea sank onto the bed. "This is just gossip, Ned, that's all."

"Maybe so. But when McVey disappeared, he did have several debts that hadn't been paid—a bill for nursing care for his mother before she died, another for his car, and a sizeable contract on that houseboat he lived on."

"Just because he owed some money is no reason to think he'd do anything illegal!" she snapped, instantly defending the very man who had once put her on the defensive.

"I know, I know, but I'm just telling you the facts."

"You're insinuating that Devlin killed his best friend on purpose!" she hissed, disgust roiling in her stomach. Devlin might have been ruthless, even slightly unscrupulous where she was concerned, but he'd been a staunch defender of the law and a loyal friend to John. He would never hurt John. Never. What Ned Jenkins was peddling was an outrageous lie!

"No, I don't think McVey planned anything. I think the accident occurred and McVey made the most of it. He wouldn't kill Stern—the police don't even think that—but he might have found a way to get out of his problems, the very problems he was going to talk to your fiancé about on that boat."

Chelsea was trembling. John *had* mentioned that Devlin wanted to discuss something with him—something private. Chelsea had assumed it had something to do with one of his women, though she had worried that he might finally tell John about the night in the cabin and how Chelsea had all too willingly kissed him and nearly fell victim to her unbridled passion. But this…this bizarre tale that Devlin, in desperation, had turned against the law? No way!

"Look," Jenkins was saying. "I just thought you should know what's going on up here."

Chelsea's hands began to sweat. Had she inadvertently brought serious trouble to Devlin by insisting he had to be found? "Did you tell your friend that you'd located Devlin?"

"Nope."

Relief stole through her. "Why not?"

"You're my client. I'm working for you. I figure the police department has enough men on the payroll. If they want to find McVey, they can spend their own time, money and men on the job."

Thank God for Jenkins's perverse code of honor. "Thank you."

"So—you talked to Russell yet?" he inquired.

"Just about every day."

"And he claims that he's not McVey, right? Acts like you're a fruitcake?"

"That's pretty much it."

"Well, be careful. If my sources are right and McVey was a bad cop, he won't appreciate you stirring up any trouble."

"Devlin would never hurt me!"

"If you say so, but desperate men do desperate things. Just take care of yourself, okay?"

"I will," Chelsea promised, staring through the open window of her hotel room as she hung up the phone. Hot injustice swept through her blood. Devlin—a good cop gone bad? Never! Ever since college, he'd been on the right side of the law! Or had he? She'd only heard the story from John and John had definitely been prejudiced where Devlin was concerned. But on the take? Working with drug dealers? Devlin? Not in a million years!

She closed her mind to Jenkins's call. Obviously the police department needed a reason to explain Devlin's disappearance and they'd come up with this ludicrous story about him turning bad. It made her nauseous.

Devlin had been many things—arrogant, cynical, almost cruel when he felt he had to be—but he would never turn criminal, no matter how desperate his money situation had been. In fact, if he'd wanted to talk to John about his problems on the day of the accident, his reasons had probably been to borrow money. After all, John had been well off, and he would have been more than willing to help out his friend.

But Devlin would never have asked for John's help. His pride would have stopped him. So what had been the topic of conversation on that fateful journey into the bay?

If not money, had Devlin intended to tell John that his fiancé had nearly made love to him at Lake Tahoe? Even now, Chelsea felt the heat of a guilty flush climb up her neck.

Tired of the horrid questions that kept circling

through her mind, Chelsea stripped off the rest of her clothes and climbed into bed. She picked up a paperback she'd bought in the airport, but her mind kept returning to Devlin and Mitch.

Who was the woman Mitch was planning to meet? And if he had a lover already, why did he kiss Chelsea as if there was a consuming passion between them that couldn't be ignored?

What was going on in San Francisco? Were the police looking for Devlin now? Would they follow her and track him to Paradis?

Sighing angrily, she tossed her book aside. Her emotions were a tangled mess of yesterday and today, the past, the present and the future. Three men kept invading her mind—confusing her and making her doubt everything she'd once considered so very real.

Yes, John had been safe and secure. And though her love for him hadn't been passionate, she'd cared for him very deeply. But not in the same way she was beginning to care for Mitch, the way she'd secretly cared for Devlin.

Both Mitch and Devlin were explosive, passionate men who bent the rules and did as they pleased. Could there be two men so alike and yet so different?

A headache began to pound behind her eyes. She snapped off the light. Somehow, she had to find out.

The next day, she spent the morning waiting for Mitch to call. He didn't. She had half a mind to ring him up, but before she dialed the phone, she heard a brisk knock on her door. "Chelsea—are you in there?"

She groaned inwardly when she recognized Emily Vaughn's voice.

"Just a minute!" She hurried to the door and found Emily and Jeff waiting in the hallway.

"We're on our way to St. Jean," Emily said with a bright smile. "Thought you might like to tag along."

Chelsea racked her brain for an excuse to stay here...and do what—wait for the phone to ring?

"We'll only be gone a few hours—back by nightfall," Emily prattled on and Jeff just shrugged. "It'll do you a world of good."

"Do I need one?"

"Everyone does, hon. Now, come along. I hear there are some simply magnificent gardens to explore. Isn't that right, dear?" she added automatically to Jeff.

Gardens were the last thing on her mind, but Chelsea could think of no reason to stay chained to the phone. As for Mitch's deal of three days, he'd obviously had a change of heart. Besides, this was her chance to look around Lagune and some of the smaller villages on St. Jean. This might also be her chance to discover where Mitch went on his regular visits to the larger island. There was even a chance, though a long shot, that she might just spy Mr. Russell in Lagune and find out firsthand what he found so fascinating on St. Jean.

"Okay," she said to Emily, "you can stop twisting my arm. Just let me get my bag."

She grabbed her straw beach bag, a hat and her favorite white jacket, then locked the door behind her as they headed downstairs.

In the lobby, she ran into Chris Landeen. He seemed surprised to see her, but grinned. "Going out?" he asked.

"We're taking the grand tour to St. Jean," Emily replied, her eyebrows rising slightly.

"Are you?" Chris said. "You know, I was thinking of going there myself!"

"You could join us," Emily said. "I'm Emily Vaughn, this is my husband, Jeff, and you obviously already know Chelsea…"

Chelsea wanted to die as Chris introduced himself. The last thing she needed was for Emily to play matchmaker!

"I've got a little business to take care of first," Chris said, "but maybe I'll catch up to you later!"

"We'll be looking for you!" Emily replied with a wave.

Chris winked at Chelsea. "If I don't see you in Lagune, I'll call you later."

"A nice man," Emily said as Chris strode away.

"I suppose."

"But not your Mr. Russell."

"Definitely not." Chelsea shook her head and followed Jeff outside.

A creaky old station-wagon-cum-hotel-bus took them into Emeraude and the driver dropped them off on the docks. They caught the *Anna Marie* to St. Jean and Chelsea couldn't contain the little shiver of excitement that accelerated the beat of her heart. There was a chance that Mitch was already on the larger island and if, by some fluke, she found him, she might have a better understanding of who he really was.

She gripped the rail of the boat and stared ahead, watching as the prow knifed cleanly through the blue-green water. The spray touched her cheeks and curled the hair at her nape and she actually smiled to herself.

Emily, true to nature, was chattering on about the history of the islands, specifically of pirates who had long ago been officers who had lost favor in the French Navy. Chelsea wasn't sure that all the stories were true, but she let the older woman spin her tales.

"And how're things going with you and your friend?" Emily finally asked, when she'd run out of pirate stories and the boat was nearing the harbor of Lagune. "Mr. Russell. Did you ever locate him again?"

"Mmm," she replied. She really didn't want to discuss Mitch.

"And?" Emily asked eagerly, tilting her tiny head upward like a little bird waiting for an expected morsel.

"And nothing." The boat's engines slowed as the captain guided the craft into the harbor. "He doesn't remember me."

Emily's mouth dropped open. *"Humph!"* she snorted indignantly. "Then you'd best find yourself another man!"

Chelsea grinned. "I'll tell him that. Next time I see him."

"Good, because if you don't, I will," Emily vowed and Jeff, long suffering as usual, rolled his eyes. "Besides," she added, "there are other fish in the sea—that good-looking man we met in the lobby of the hotel, for one."

"Chris?"

"Yes. Nothing wrong with that one."

If only it were that simple, Chelsea thought, gazing toward their destination.

Lagune was a city in comparison with lazy little Emeraude. The streets bustled with traffic and tourists were jammed along the sidewalks. Palm trees offered shade from the sweltering sun and a few cafés with outdoor tables offered refreshment.

As they strolled along the side streets, Chelsea barely kept up with her end of the conversation. Through her sunglasses, she studied the crowd and the city, hoping for some clue as to why Mitch would come here so often. Was he bored with the sleepy pace of Paradis? And if so, why not move to the bigger island? Or was his damned privacy so valuable?

Frowning thoughtfully, Chelsea followed Emily's brisk pace as they hurried to a stop for a tour bus. She felt an odd sensation—as if she were being watched—but one look at the other tourists convinced her they were all strangers. No one was staring at her and no set of eyes was quickly averted.

"You're letting this cloak and dagger stuff go to your head," she admonished herself.

"Pardon?" Emily said, craning her neck back toward Chelsea as she boarded the bus.

"Nothing. Just talking to myself."

"Bad habit," Emily reproved with a kind smile. "One I've got myself." She climbed aboard the huge, slightly battered bus. Chelsea followed, feeling out of place as she slid into a seat near the rear. Cracking a window, she was rewarded with a huge whiff of diesel.

Emily and Jeff occupied the seat in front of her and while Emily chatted with the woman across the aisle from her, Chelsea stared out the window and wondered what her next move would be.

In a cloud of black smoke, the bus lumbered away from the curb and headed out of town. Chelsea barely noticed the passing countryside as she thought about

Mitch. Where was he today? What was he doing? And how could she possibly pretend to fall in love with him in only a few days? Closing her eyes, she leaned back in her seat.

Emily jabbered incessantly all the way to the old Mediterranean-style villa that had been turned into a museum. Together with the rest of the tourists, Emily, Jeff and Chelsea wandered through cool, high-ceilinged rooms, their sandals scuffing against thick tile floors. The rooms were furnished with antiques and cooled by slow-moving paddle fans.

Outside, they threaded their way through a maze of showy gardens that terraced from the villa to the sea. Flowers in shades of scarlet, lavender and yellow offered splashes of vibrant color and added a sweet fragrance to the salty air.

"Isn't this place glorious!" Emily cried, clasping her hands as she stared at a terrace surrounded by lush greenery and vines that showed off heavy purple and pink blossoms.

The sensation came again—the eerie feeling that she was being observed.

"Absolutely," Chelsea replied, though she glanced over her shoulder, half expecting someone to be watching her. The idea was ludicrous, of course, and yet, she couldn't shake the nerve-racking feeling.

"You know this mansion was built by an infamous French pirate who held his mistresses captive here."

Chelsea giggled. Some of Emily's tales were so outrageous. "Doesn't look much like a prison to me."

Jeff chuckled and offered Chelsea a smile as they joined their tour group and returned to town.

At a bistro near the harbor, they ate an early dinner

of soft-shelled crab and rice in a spicy red sauce. The food and accompanying wine were delicious but filling, and Chelsea finally shoved her plate aside, though she'd consumed less than half her meal. "I can't swallow another bite."

"But we haven't ordered dessert or coffee yet!" Emily countered.

"You go ahead," Chelsea offered, sliding her chair back. "I'll be right back." She was walking through the crowded tables toward the restroom when she felt the weight of someone's gaze on her back. Whirling, she found herself staring at the tables she'd just passed, a crowded cluster of people eating and drinking, barely glancing in her direction.

"You're really losing it," she grumbled to herself, then she froze. Through the window, she spied the woman she'd seen Mitch with earlier. Her long black hair was streaming behind her as she stepped into a speedboat. Before Chelsea reached the door, the boat had pulled away from shore and was heading northeast. To Paradis? To Mitch?

Her heart wrenched at the thought and she wanted to kick herself. So what if Mitch and the woman were together? Chelsea certainly didn't have any claims to Mitch Russell. Nor did she have any claims to Devlin McVey.

Nonetheless the thought that she'd been spied upon made her skin crawl and she shivered. She hurried into the restroom and splashed water on her face. So the woman was watching her.

But why?

Was she on a mission from Mitch?

Angrily she brushed her hair and slapped on fresh

lipstick, then returned to the table where Jeff and Emily were lingering over a half-eaten slice of key lime pie. "About time you got back here. I'm afraid we've nearly killed this pie, though we did remember to get you a spoon," Emily chirped when Chelsea sat down. "Have a bite, the pie's simply divine."

Chelsea shook her head. "I really couldn't," she said. Not only was she stuffed, but her stomach was in tight little knots. Had the black-haired woman been following her today? She slipped her arms through the sleeves of her jacket, though the temperature in the room had to be over seventy.

"Are you all right?" Emily asked, her voice edged with concern.

"I just overate. I'll be fine," Chelsea lied.

A few minutes later, they left the restaurant and boarded the *Anna Marie*. Clouds had rolled in, turning the sky dark.

"Looks like it's going to storm," Emily said, eyeing the horizon, but Chelsea was only half listening. Her eyes were riveted to the far side of the boat where Chris Landeen had settled against the rail. As if feeling her eyes on him, he looked up, smiled and sketched out a wave.

Inexplicably, Chelsea's stomach tightened. Was it just coincidence that Chris and the black-haired woman had been in Lagune? She expected him to head in her direction, but he turned his attention back to a short, balding man and laughed at something he was saying.

Don't make more of it than there is, she told herself as she turned her eyes back to the sea.

The boat pulled out of the harbor and Chelsea sat with Emily and Jeff, anxious to get back to Paradis.

On the ride back to Emeraude, Chris sauntered over and leaned his elbows on the rail. He slid an appreciative glance her way. "How about dinner with me tomorrow night?" he asked.

"I'm not sure I can," she replied.

"Why not? Plans with your friend?"

Her fingers gripped the rail more tightly. "I'll have to check."

Chris frowned and patted the rail. "I can take a hint," he said and walked back to his seat.

"That wasn't smart," Emily told her later as the boat pulled into the harbor. "I wouldn't be too hasty turning that one down. Not unless you're involved with someone else."

Not yet, she thought uneasily, her mind returning, as it had for the past few days, to Mitch.

She didn't see Mitch that night and he didn't call. By ten o'clock, Chelsea was mentally climbing the walls.

Mr. Russell certainly wasn't living up to his part of the bargain, she thought sourly, as she dialed Sally in San Francisco.

Her partner answered on the fourth ring and just the sound of Sally's voice brought a smile to Chelsea's face.

"Well, have you convinced Devlin to come home and tell all?" Sally asked.

"I'm not even sure he is Devlin," Chelsea confessed as she leaned against the headboard of the bed. She explained about her experiences on the island and Sally sighed dramatically. "There are some things he does—some mannerisms that are just like Devlin's, and he has the same style, he dresses the same, and yet…oh, I don't know! One minute I think he's Devlin, the next I'm sure he's a different person entirely!"

"Well, don't expect me to feel sorry for you. You're in a tropical haven, sipping rum and coke or whatever it is they drink down there, and sunbathing, while I'm holding down the fort and slaving away."

They talked for nearly an hour. Sally explained that the boutique was low on inventory and high in sales. She stressed again the need to expand. Chelsea, for her part, told Sally about Terri and the Boutique Exotique.

"Don't you dare come back here with some wild animals to brighten this place up," she warned. "I'm not into getting bitten, scratched, clawed or mauled."

"Don't worry," Chelsea said with a laugh.

"The only beast I expect you to bring back is the infamous Mr. McVey."

If only it were that simple, Chelsea thought. They talked a little longer and finally hung up. She drew her knees beneath her chin and wrapped her arms around her calves and sighed loudly. How would she ever get close enough to Mitch to prove that he was Devlin McVey?

She still didn't have an answer when she threw back the covers and crawled between the sheets. Stretching, she frowned when she felt a piece of paper tucked beneath her pillow.

More annoyed than concerned, she withdrew the small piece of white paper and unfolded the creased note. In bold type, the short message read: LEAVE PARADIS.

She gasped and her gaze flew around the room. Who had planted the note? Fear shot through her. Her pulse raced wildly and she broke out in a cold sweat. Despite the fact that she'd locked the door, she walked through the room, looking under the bed, in the closet and shower, and checking the balcony before she felt herself calm a little.

"Don't panic," she told herself, but her fingers shook as she picked up the telephone receiver and punched out the number of the front desk. When the clerk answered, she said, "This is Chelsea Reed, room 243. Has anyone been asking for me?"

"Just a minute," the bored voice replied. "…no."

"There are no messages?"

"I'm sorry."

"And no one has asked to see me?"

"As I said, no one," he replied, his voice sounding more than a little irritated.

Chelsea considered complaining to the hotel security that someone had been in her room, but instead she drew on her courage and said, "Thank you." The clerk clicked off and she slowly replaced the receiver.

Leaving the warning could be Mitch's way of scaring her. She wouldn't put it past him after he'd pulled that stunt of dragging her into the house and snapping off the lights when she'd first shown up on his doorstep.

No, she decided, forcing herself to remain calm, she wouldn't let some little scrap of paper scare her off.

At least not yet.

But that night, she slept with the lights in her room burning brightly.

* * *

The following morning dawned gloomy and hot. Gray, burgeoning clouds swarmed over the sea, and the air was heavy as it clung to Chelsea's skin. The restless ocean was the color of steel.

Mitch didn't call. Though she spent most of the day in and out of the hotel, he didn't leave a message. "Some three days this has turned out to be," she grumbled, infuriated that she was hanging by the telephone for a man to call. Disgusted with herself, she threw on the white dress she'd purchased from Terri, grabbed her beach bag and headed into town.

Obviously, Mitch had been buying time. He'd never intended to let her get to know him. Or was there something more to it? she wondered as she waited for a cab near the entrance to the Villa. Ned Jenkins's call bothered her more than she wanted to admit. His insinuations were ridiculous, of course. Devlin had always been on the right side of the law. Though he'd bent more than his share of rules, he wouldn't turn bad. No, something was rotten at the San Francisco Police Department, but it had never been Devlin McVey.

As for the note, it was tucked safely into the pocket of her wallet and she'd forced it from her mind.

A dusty gray wagon pulled in front of the curb and she climbed in, instructing a round-faced cabby to drive her into Emeraude. She'd spend the day in town, go back to the Dauphin Bleu if need be, to find out more about Mitch Russell and try to discover who had been in her room.

She remembered overhearing his telephone call and her mind conjured up the beautiful raven-haired woman with her bronze skin, full lips and flashing

eyes. The same woman she'd seen yesterday in Lagune. Had she met with Mitch last night? Was he just
stringing Chelsea along until he could find a way to
get rid of her?

"Oh, God," she whispered, resting her head against
the glass of the stifling cab.

"What's that?" the cab driver asked. A portly black
man with an easy smile, he glanced at her in the rearview mirror.

"Nothing," she said automatically, then decided she
had nothing to lose at this point. "I was supposed to
meet a man today and he didn't show up." That was a
bit of a lie, but stretching the truth earned her a sympathetic look in the mirror. "I don't suppose you know
him? Mitch Russell."

The driver shook his head. "Sorry."

"Nothing to be sorry for," Chelsea replied as the old
wagon wound through the dense rain forest.

In town, she had a late lunch in a small bistro on
the waterfront, then browsed through the craft shops
and an art gallery before ending up at the Boutique
Exotique.

The parrot whistled sharply as Chelsea entered.

Terri, who was balanced precariously on a ladder
as she pinned lime green shorts and tangerine-col-
ored tops to the wall over the register, glanced over
her shoulder and grinned. "Well, look who's here. I
hope you came with credit cards in hand." She shoved
a final tack into the wall and with one appraising look
at her work, climbed down. "How's this?" she asked,
waving at her display.

"Bright."

"Good. It's supposed to be." Terri wiped her hands on her short red skirt. "So what're you doing in town?"

"Looking for company, I guess."

"Uh-oh, don't tell me, the elusive Mr. Russell has vanished again."

"How'd you know?"

Terri eyed her work and frowned. "Because I saw him leave this morning as I was opening up the shop."

"Leave?"

"Umm. I told you he leaves once or twice a week—at least I think it's that often. I don't really keep tabs on the man."

"He left in his boat?"

Terri shook her head. "No, it was a red speedboat, I think. I've seen it around before."

Chelsea's heart sank. She instinctively knew which craft he was on—and with whom. The same beautiful woman who'd stared at her through the restaurant window in St. Jean. "Was the name of the boat the *Lucia*?"

Terri thought for a minute. "I don't know—could've been. I didn't get a good look, and until I met you, I wasn't really paying that much attention to Mr. Russell and his friends."

"His friends?"

"Yeah. The men and woman I've seen him with a few times." She slid Chelsea a sympathetic glance. "If it's any consolation, I don't think they're lovers."

"I couldn't care less—" Chelsea began, but the look in Terri's eyes silenced her.

"Next you're going to tell me what he does with his love life is his business," Terri teased. "Ever since you landed on this island, you've been obsessed with the man, so don't tell me it doesn't matter whom he's seeing."

The parrot squawked loudly as two women entered the store. Terri said, "Just let me help these two and I'll be right back."

While Terri assisted a series of customers, Chelsea spent nearly an hour in the store and ended up buying a necklace, two pairs of shorts and a scarf. "You know I was just teasing when you came in and I told you I expected to see your credit card," Terri said with a grin as she rang up the sale.

"Everything in this bag—" Chelsea patted the plastic sack "—is an absolute must."

"If you say so." Three more women entered the shop and Terri rolled her eyes. "I bet I don't get out of here until midnight," she whispered.

"You love it, and you know it."

"Yeah, but I can think of better ways to spend my evening."

So could Chelsea, but she didn't want to dwell on the night stretching before her. As far as she could tell, she'd wasted another day learning nothing more about Mitch. "I'll see you on Wednesday," Terri promised. "That's my day off. Maybe we'll go over to St. Jean and poke around the beach."

"I'd like that," Chelsea replied, waving as she left the boutique.

Outside, the heat was oppressive, the air dense. Chelsea considered starting with the Dauphin Bleu and asking questions about Mitch. There were some other bars located along the waterfront but the thought of making small talk with strangers in a series of seedy watering holes turned her stomach.

The wind picked up and the sky darkened with the promise of the storm. She wandered along the docks and, as she stopped to swipe at the sweat that had collected on the back of her neck, she spied Mitch's sailboat lashed to the wharf.

"Looking for me?" a voice boomed behind her.

Her heart nearly stopped as she saw him, arms stretched over his head, shirt pulling out of his jeans and exposing a length of lean abdomen, as he worked on the sail. His gaze met hers.

"Now, why would I?" she asked sauntering closer.

"Well, it could be my devastating personality..."

"Ha!"

"Or my looks."

She raised her brows skeptically.

"Or you could just be after my body."

"That's it," she teased back.

An amused smile touched his lips and she instantly bristled at the thought that he was mocking her as he hopped lithely onto the dock.

"We did have a deal," she reminded him.

"We still do." His eyes gleamed. "Don't tell me you've been waiting for me."

"Not a chance," she lied.

"Then what's the problem?"

Curse the man. "Oh, I don't know. The way I see it, three days constitutes seventy-two hours and in the past sixty-four, I've seen you maybe six or seven tops."

"You didn't specify—"

"Well, I'm specifying now! You promised me seventy-two hours. The way I figure it, you still owe me a minimum of sixty-six."

"So I am in demand," he teased.

"This is business."

"I'm crushed." But he was still taunting her. "Come on," he suggested, motioning her onto the *Mirage,* "since the meter's running, let's not waste any more time."

"Good idea."

"Hop in the boat."

She eyed the small craft and thought of the note left under her pillow. Suddenly she didn't feel quite so safe, but she stepped onto the sailboat anyway. "Where're we going?"

"Back to my place." He climbed aboard and unleashed the ropes securing the boat. "If you're lucky, I'll cook you dinner."

"If I'm lucky?" she repeated. "So you've been planning this all day?"

"Yep. I had some business that I had to take care of first, then I planned to pick you up." He eyed the horizon. "We'd better shove off before the storm breaks."

"A storm?" she said, her voice catching as she thought of John and Devlin and how their boat had splintered apart in the middle of San Francisco Bay.

As if he noticed the sudden morbid turn of her thoughts, he said, "It's nothing to worry about."

"You're sure?"

"Trust me."

Oh, God, could she? She bit her lower lip as they cast off. Trust me. Did she know him well enough? Did she know him at all? Or was she attracted to him because he was so much like Devlin? Her mouth turned dry as he moved so effortlessly on the slippery deck, so athletically. His narrow hips, long legs, wide shoulders, just like Devlin. The wind pushed at his white shirt, whipping it and tossing his black hair from his eyes. Oh, God, he seemed so much like Devlin. If only...

She forced her mind back to the present, to the roiling sea and earlier this afternoon when he'd been with the exotic, black-haired woman. With an effort she tried to keep the challenge from her voice as she asked, "What was your business this afternoon?"

He lifted a shoulder. "Just a little research for my book."

"And you had to leave the island?"

"That's right." Shoving a pair of aviator glasses onto his nose, he guided the *Mirage* through the choppy waters of the bay, past an inbound schooner and several fishing boats. "Why the third degree?" he asked and Chelsea tried not to notice the sensual curve of his lips or the quirk of amusement touching the corners of his mouth.

"I'm just trying to get to know you."

"Or spying again," he guessed. "You found out I was with Bambi and you're jealous. Admit it."

"Bambi? Her name is *Bambi?*" Chelsea repeated, so incredulous that her jaw dropped.

She was rewarded with Mitch's hearty laugh. "No, her name isn't Bambi. But you *were* spying again."

"Someone happened to see you," she sniffed.

"And you were jealous."

"Not in the least!" But she almost smiled. He had baited her on that one, and she'd swallowed the bait along with the hook, line and sinker.

"So you just happened to be asking questions about me," he prodded.

"I thought you'd reneged on your part of the bargain." She considered telling him about the worrisome note, but decided that it was best if she bided her time. Maybe he would slip up and admit that he was trying to scare her off the island. But why? There wasn't a logical reason unless he truly was Devlin and had something to hide.

"If and when I renege, I'll tell you to your face," he replied, sliding her an assessing glance. "You know, I'm beginning to think that the only way to make sure you stay out of trouble is to keep an eye on you."

"Of all the—"

"Not a good feeling, is it?"

Chelsea was more than a little irritated, but she didn't argue. Battling with him wasn't getting her anywhere. No, she'd have to try and get alone with him if she was going to pry any more information from him.

And if you're going to pretend to be in love with him.

A thousand butterflies erupted in her stomach and her throat tightened as she watched him from beneath the sweep of her lashes. His tanned face was set as he guided the sailboat along the small channel between the coral reefs, and his legs were planted wide, for balance.

The air was thick with the scent of a storm and the sea. The tiny boat bobbed as furious gusts of wind billowed the sails and snatched at Chelsea's hair. Sea spray splashed the deck and clung to her face.

"This storm might be worse than predicted," Mitch nearly shouted as the wind tore past in a loud rush. For the first time, Chelsea saw the worry in his eyes.

She stared out to sea and frowned. The aquamarine water had turned dark, reflecting the ominous sky, and sky and sea blended at the horizon. Other boats were heading inland, to the safety of the Emeraude harbor as Mitch rounded the point and steered the *Mirage* toward his own small dock.

"Hope you don't mind dinner in a hurricane," he said with a cynical grin.

"A hurricane?" she repeated, her mouth dry as she scanned the sky. "You took me out in a hurricane?"

"It's not *that* bad. Besides, it's not hurricane season."

"John was killed in a storm like this," she reminded him and the skin of his cheekbones grew taut.

"I'm sorry," he said, eyeing the charcoal gray sky. "I forgot."

"How could you?" she nearly screamed.

"It's not something I remember."

Her hands clenched over the rail. How could he not remember, unless he truly wasn't Devlin? Her stomach twisted. Was he, as he'd been insisting since the first time she'd met him, Mitch Russell? Her heart felt as if it had cracked with a new, fresh pain. Was it possible that she'd been wrong, so horribly wrong?

Mitch guided the small boat toward the dock. "Well, it may not be a hurricane, but it's gonna be rough."

"How long will it last?"

"Who knows?" He lowered the sails when the boat was positioned at the dock, then lashed it securely to the moorings and took Chelsea by the hand. "I'd better get you inside." Rain began to pour from the heavens, dripping on the weathered pier and peppering the sand.

Suddenly, she panicked. The bold chilling reality of what she was about to do hit her with a force that nearly stole the breath from her lungs. How could she,

in the privacy of Mitch's house, so far from civilization, pretend to want to make love to him—only to
stop once he was stripped and she could view his bare
hips? He'd be furious—or worse yet, persuasive and
she wasn't sure she could deny him, nor that she'd
want to.

How could she get away from him—from her own
passionate emotions—in the middle of a storm? After
all, this was a man she barely knew.

"Chels—?" he asked and his voice sounded so much
like Devlin's that her heart squeezed. He took her hand
and she let him help her from the boat. "Come on." He
tried to protect her from the rain that began to fall by
holding one arm over her head, but her legs felt like
rubber and she suddenly wished she was anywhere
else on earth but in the middle of a tropical storm with
Mitch Russell. She couldn't go through with her act—a
false seduction. Be this man Mitch Russell or Devlin
McVey, she couldn't lie so brazenly and deceive him
with such cool calculation.

"I—maybe I should go home," she said as they
stepped onto the wet sand.

"It's too late."

"But—I—well, I can't stay here indefinitely." She
stopped in a thicket of palms lining the beach, not
far from his cabin. She had to find a way to end this
horrid charade, even if it meant running away from
him right now.

His fingers tightened over her wrist. "What're you
afraid of?"

You! Me! Us! Her throat worked, but no sound escaped.

"The storm will pass."

Staring into the depths of his eyes, lost in his darkening gaze, Chelsea wasn't so sure. The maelstrom of emotions raging in her soul was tearing her apart.

"I won't hurt you," he said so softly she barely heard him.

She swallowed with difficulty. "I—I'm not afraid," she murmured.

"Oh no?" One dark brow cocked insolently.

"You're not *that* devastating, Mr. Russell."

"Well, Chelsea, you are," he whispered and to her shock, he jerked her hard against him and lowered his mouth over hers. Chelsea gasped, her heart knocking wildly in her chest, but she didn't tear herself away.

Instead, against every promise she'd so recently made to herself, her body reacted and she kissed him back. As the wind slashed through the fronds of palms high overhead, whipping the sea into a wild froth, she pressed her mouth to his and thrilled when his tongue claimed hers.

His hands roved anxiously over the back of her dress and her own arms wound tight around his neck.

"Oh, God, Chels," he whispered over the whistle of the wind. Rain began to fall, but Chelsea barely noticed, so captivated was she by the movements of his hands and lips.

He kissed her eyes, her cheeks, her ears. His fingers tangled in her long hair and he pulled gently, exposing her throat to his marauding mouth.

His tongue flicked and danced, tasting of her sweetness, leaving a damp trail that the rain washed away.

Chelsea quivered inside. She felt his hand move upward to surround her breast and knew her nipple had already grown taut. Beneath the damp, white fabric of her dress, she swelled to fill his palm, and a warm wetness oozed deep within her.

"God, help me," he whispered, falling to his knees and dragging her onto the sand. He placed his mouth over her breast and through the rain-dampened fabric, his tongue and teeth sought and flicked, teasing and dancing, drawing a deep, raw moan from her throat.

Desire ran in a wanton dance through her blood and she trembled with the need of him, writhed on the sand with a want so intense it chased away any lingering thoughts of denial.

She held his head close against her as hot, electric pulses shot through her body. Tingling at the touch of him, she tried to force more of herself onto him until, through the white cotton, he was suckling as a babe.

He groaned, and still kissing and nipping at her breast, he found the buttons of her dress and began sliding the small buttons through their holes.

Chelsea, caught in the wonder of his lovemaking, didn't notice. She felt the rain against her face, felt his fingers surround one buttock and pull her anxiously against him, fitting their hips together as he thrust closer and his hard shaft pressed intimately against her abdomen.

Her throat was dry, her mind spinning in delicious circles of desire.

His hands found bare skin and he shoved her dress from her, exposing one lace-encased breast. Anxiously, he yanked on her bra strap, forcing her breast to spill out, bare and full. Groaning, he breathed, warm as a summer wind, against her and his lips found the button of her nipple. He tasted her and anxiously shoved her dress over her other shoulder and past her hips.

His fingers slid easily down her legs and he managed to cast aside his own clothes as the storm picked up and the sky turned dark as midnight.

She didn't stop him when he unhooked that flimsy, wet scrap of material that was her bra, nor did she protest when he yanked down her underpants.

She could think only of how much she cared for this enigmatic man and the firestorm of passion he aroused in her. He lay with her, his hands sculpting her wet body, her own fingers exploring and touching him intimately.

He was beautiful and hard, his body all sinewy muscle and bone. The dark hair of his chest rubbed against her breasts when he leaned over and kissed her again, his lips molding and searching, his tongue hard and demanding.

He rolled her onto her back, and prodded her legs apart with his knees. Then, poised just over her, he gazed down, his face taut with strain, his eyes scorching. With one hand, he touched her breast almost reverently, watching as the proud dark nipple puckered to attention. Then he leaned forward and kissed that dark little peak.

Desire throbbed deep inside Chelsea, yawning and aching to be filled. With one finger, he stroked her thigh and she writhed beneath him. "Please," she whispered in a voice she didn't recognize as her own.

His throat worked when he tilted his head upward again and stared into her eyes. "I've wanted to do this from the first moment I saw you," he whispered and then, without another word, he lost all restraint of his tense muscles and plunged into her, driving deeply, filling her, sending shock wave after sweet shock wave through her body.

She clung to him, her fingers digging into the corded, rain-slicked muscles of his shoulders as she fused her body to his, arching upward, meeting him in a supreme, blinding ecstasy that tore the breath from her lungs.

She didn't think, only felt the warmth of his body in hers, tasted the male saltiness of his skin as her mouth pressed hard against his lips, throat and chest.

Her eyes closed, though she wanted to see more of him as his tempo increased and she was pushed higher and harder, moving faster, spinning out of control, until a dazzling light splintered behind her eyes and she bucked, convulsing, crying out. But her words were drowned by the roar of the wind and his own primal cry. "Chelsea—oh, God—Chelsea! Oh, sweet, sweet, Chelsea. I knew it would be like this!"

"So did I," she whispered, a warm glow enveloping her, the storm seeming light-years away, the rain a welcome mist as she held him tightly to her and felt his rough beard against her wet breasts.

He licked the raindrops from her skin and she became alive again, her body already anticipating another sweet deluge from him.

Their hearts pounded in time with the fury of the sea. Chelsea clung to him and felt his body instinctively curve around hers, protecting her from the elements.

"Come on," he said softly as her heartbeat returned to normal. "I'd better get you inside. You're going to spend the night with me, in my bed, and I won't listen to a single argument."

Before she could say anything, he stood and picked her up in one lithe movement. All thoughts of denial slipped from her mind. She wrapped her arms around his neck to avoid falling and closed her mind to all the logical arguments that had begun to fill her mind.

Tonight she wouldn't listen to logic.

Tonight she would love him and let tomorrow bring what it may.

She nestled her head against his neck as he did exactly as he'd promised. He carried her, naked as the day she was born, into his house and straight to his bed.

Chapter 9

The storm raged all night long and Chelsea, kept awake by the pounding of the wind and Mitch's lovemaking, only dozed near dawn. Wrapped in the security of Mitch's arms, she didn't have time for self-doubt or recriminations—at least not until she awoke to find herself in Mitch's bed, with him lying naked beside her.

Oh, Lord, she silently prayed as her gaze traveled over his tanned skin and muscles, now relaxed. Dark lashes swept his cheek and his breathing was slow and even. Black hair fell over his eyes and matched the thick beard covering his chin.

What had gotten into her? she wondered as morning light stole through the room. She'd never, never made love to a man she didn't love before—not even Devlin. Appalled that she'd let her wayward emotions control her body, she realized, regretfully, that there was no turning back.

Also, there was no chance that she could let herself fall in love with him. No, she wouldn't delude herself, she thought, angrily flopping back on the pillows and letting out a heartfelt sigh. What she felt for Mitch was raw, sexual attraction. Love hadn't entered into it. Her heart ached at the thought.

Just because he looked, smelled, felt, and tasted like Devlin was no excuse for the way she'd acted.

Glancing over her shoulder at Mitch again, she was more convinced than ever that he must be Devlin. He had to be. But that didn't mean that making love to him had been right. In fact, making love to Devlin was much more complex than making love to Mitch. She could leave Mitch Russell here in Paradis and never look back—well, she could try. As for Devlin, she doubted he would ever be out of her life, not even if he were dead.

She could attempt to write off Mitch Russell as an island fling—or at least she could try. But her feelings for Devlin were seeded much too deeply.

She bit on her lower lip and slid toward the edge of Mitch's double bed. She had to get away before she let her war-torn emotions control her again. But just as her foot dangled to the floor, she remembered her reason for pretending to fall for Mitch and her cheeks burned all the more brightly. Not once in all their long hours of lying naked together had she looked for the birthmark which would prove without a doubt that the man in bed with her was Devlin McVey.

Didn't she care? How could she have forgotten something so important? Lord, what was wrong with her!

Furious, she tossed back the covers, exposing not only herself but all of Devlin or Mitch or whoever he was in his splendid nakedness. His legs were long, tanned and covered with soft dark hair, his buttocks white, his back long, muscled and sleek. He stirred, growling a little, then looked up at her with eyes so blue they took her breath away.

"Can't get enough of me?" he asked, smiling beneath his beard as he reached for her.

"I don't even know what I'm doing here," she admitted, her mouth cotton dry as she forced her gaze back to his lean hips, searching for that damned birthmark. Where was it?

He shifted and she felt her skin tremble in expectation when his fingers grazed her bare thigh. "This is insane," she muttered, still searching desperately as he rolled over suddenly, exposing all of himself to her.

"Haven't you ever seen a man before?" he mocked and she wanted to die at his lack of modesty.

She didn't answer, just stared in horror at his hip, searching for his birthmark.

It wasn't there! No crescent shaped mark, only an ugly network of scars that mottled his skin.

How could she have been so wrong?

Dying a thousand deaths, she squeezed her eyes shut, then opened them again, willing the damned birthmark to be there.

"Is something wrong?" he asked, concern lining his brow.

Everything! "I—I think we made a horrid mistake," she stammered, her insides raw and hurting. This man *wasn't* Devlin. Oh, God, what had she done?

Mortified beyond words, she tried to scramble from

his bed, but he grabbed her quickly. "Mistake?" he repeated.

"Oh, yes, this should never have happened!"

His eyes were clouded with confusion. "I don't get it," he muttered, staring down at her with an intensity that scorched all the way to her soul. "We're consenting adults."

"That doesn't make it right." Oh, God, if she could only get away from him before she broke down!

"What does?"

"Love."

He snorted and she went cold inside. "A dreamer." Levering up on one elbow, he shook his head and stared at her. "You really do live in a fantasy world."

She hated to think that he was right and struggled to free herself, but he pinned her against the bed, his hard body pressed intimately against hers. "Why don't you just relax and enjoy yourself?" he suggested.

Just let me go! "Really, I can't. This is wrong, all wrong!"

"Why?"

"Oh, Devlin, don't you understand?" she flung out before she realized her mistake.

His face washed of all color and his expression turned to stone. "What did you call me?" he ground out.

"Devlin," she whispered, shaking.

"That's what I thought." He swore violently and the passion left his face. He stared at her as if she'd gone mad. "I'm not— Oh hell, what does it matter? Get out!"

"What?"

"You heard me, get out!" He rolled off the bed and

reached for a pair of faded denim jeans. As he did, he half turned and she saw his hip again, white except for a ragged network of scars which ran down to the top of his thigh. She dragged the sheet over her breasts for modesty's sake and for several long seconds, she stared at the scars which convinced her that he wasn't Devlin after all.

Shame and mortification shot through her. Oh, God, why had she been so impetuous, gone so far? Her throat felt raw and her eyes burned with unshed tears. Her entire world tilted.

She forgot that he was angry with her. "What happened?" she whispered, praying for some sign of a birthmark and seeing none.

"I'm just tired of playing your ridiculous games!" He stepped into his jeans.

"No—I mean your scars—what happened?"

"The accident," he clipped. "You remember—the one that took my wife's life?"

"Oh, right," she whispered, filled with self-loathing. How had she made love to this man—this stranger? She glanced up at him, unshed tears filling her eyes, and she felt a painful tug on her heart. Good God, had she convinced herself that she loved him? How pathetic. She shoved her hair out of her eyes and wished she could disappear.

"And don't try and tell me I got hurt in a boating accident with a man I've never met."

"I—I didn't," she said, shaking her head.

"Good, because if you ask me, the only reason you've convinced yourself that I'm this Devlin character is to smooth over your guilty conscience for making love with a man you barely know!"

"No," she argued, grabbing hold of some of her tattered pride. "That's not true. I've thought you were Devlin from the moment I first saw you!"

He snapped his jeans and pulled up the zipper. "But you wouldn't believe me, would you? And you kept pushing it. Even when it was obvious I wasn't your man."

"He *wasn't* my man."

"Oh, no? Well, from where I sit he should have been. And if what happened between us last night was because you thought I was Devlin, I feel sorry for that poor idiot you were engaged to. God, you must've used him to get at his friend."

"That's not the way it was!" she cried, mortified.

"Well, I wouldn't know, would I? I wasn't there!" he snarled.

Stunned, she couldn't move, couldn't find her voice. She was outraged, but her fury was matched by the dark red patch that swarmed up his neck.

"Now, if you're through digging into my personal life and having sex with a fantasy, just get the hell out of my bed!"

"Only too gladly," she replied tightly. Astounded that he wasn't Devlin and stung that he would make love to her, then order her cruelly away, she rolled out of bed and grabbed a shirt he'd slung over the back of a chair.

He saw her buttoning the shirt and rolled his eyes. Scowling, he shoved his hands into the pockets of his jeans. "I'll get your clothes—"

"Don't bother! I don't want or need any help from you!" she insisted, holding her wobbling chin high as she swept past him and strode out the front door. Tears of embarrassment burned at the back of her eyes, but she set her jaw and trudged along the beach, feeling mortified as she found her sandy bra and underpants and her ruined white dress. Her bag had blown over and she had to scrounge along the beach to find her wallet, keys and sunscreen, gritty from the sand.

She'd really been out of her mind last night—leaving her things unattended, making passionate, wanton love with Devlin—no Mitch—oh, God, what had she done! Raw inside from his callousness, she wanted to crumple into a heap near the water's edge and break down and cry. But she wouldn't give him the satisfaction of showing how much he'd wounded her. Chin held stiffly erect, she waded until she was knee-deep in the surf and tried to rinse out her soiled clothes.

Choking back sobs, she didn't even hear him approach, didn't know he was in the water beside her until he touched her shoulder. She jumped away.

"Look, I'm sorry," he said, but she stepped further away, recoiling from his touch.

"You don't have to apologize!" she spat, casting a "drop dead" look over her shoulder and seeing the first sign of vulnerability crossing his hard-edged features. Turning her back on him again, she swished her clothes in the salt water.

"Chels—"

Oh, God, so much like Devlin—why did he sound so much like Devlin? Tears clogged her throat and filled the corners of her eyes. "Leave me alone!"

"It's just that you're so crazed about me being this other guy," he explained, touching her shoulders and forcing her to turn to face him.

"Stop it!" she whispered. "I—I said we made a mistake. I made a mistake."

"I just want to make something clear. I'm done with being used by you, Chelsea!"

"Used? Used?" she repeated, incredulous. "You think I used you?"

"Yep. So you could play out your fantasies—pretend that you were really making love with Devlin McVey."

That was so close to the truth, it shattered her. Hadn't she convinced herself he *was* Devlin—as if that made making love to him all right?

"I think I'd better leave," she said. "But, just so you don't think I'm totally out of my mind, you should know that I'm not the only one who thinks Devlin may be alive." She turned, starting for the path that led south toward the Villa.

He caught up with her before she'd taken two steps. He grabbed her arm and yanked hard, spinning her around. "What's that supposed to mean?"

"The police in San Francisco haven't completely given up on the idea that Devlin's alive," she said, seeing no reason to hide anything from him. "In fact, they've come up with some theories of their own—the first of which is that Devlin was on the take."

The fingers digging into her arm tightened.

"They think that the drug case he was working on went sour because he tipped off the crooks."

Mitch's eyes darkened dangerously. "And what do you think?"

"Devlin would never have sacrificed his principles. He was a good cop and he would never, never have done anything to hurt John." She swallowed hard. "I know that from my own experience."

"How?"

What did it matter? She forced her gaze to his. "Because you were right about Devlin and me. One night...before I was engaged to John, I was alone with Devlin, not that either of us wanted to be, but, well..." Even now the words stuck in her throat and tears of shame burned the back of her eyes. "One thing led to another and we nearly made love. We didn't, but it could have happened. Devlin was sick with disgust— with himself and with me. I, um, don't think he ever trusted me again. At least he never so much as touched me."

"Maybe he couldn't trust himself around you," he said thoughtfully. "You do have a way of getting under a man's skin."

She shook her head. "Not Devlin's." Taking in a deep breath, she added, "But Devlin, above all else, was a good cop. And now, back in San Francisco, there's even been some talk that he rigged the boating accident and faked his own death."

"Go on," he said, his nostrils flaring slightly.

"I talked to my private investigator the other night. And it seems Devlin's caused quite a stir in the city. Some people even think he might have killed John on purpose!"

The fingers digging into her flesh were almost cruel and the look on his face was desperate and ravaged. "Chelsea, you've *got* to listen to me! For your sake and mine. Whoever this McVey character was, he sounds like trouble and I think it would be wise for you to write him off. Grieve if you have to—cry your tears—but face the fact that he's gone. Forever."

The tears that had been threatening all morning collected in her eyes and her throat closed painfully. She didn't want to break down and cry, but she was so overwrought, so twisted and turned, so pulled one way and the other, she felt as if she might faint. Last night she'd convinced herself that this man was Devlin, this morning she vowed that he was Mitch. How could two men tear her apart so?

At the sight of the tears beginning to track from her eyes, his angular face softened a bit. "I know it's hard—"

"You don't know a damn thing!" she cried, wanting to lash out, to return the pain that had cut her to the bone.

"—but you've got to face the truth."

She knew what he was going to say before the words passed his lips. "Devlin's *not* dead! He's not! He can't be!" she rasped, hearing the desperate, nearly hysterical edge to her voice.

Mitch's arms surrounded her and though she fought him, shoved against his shoulders and when that didn't work, pummeled his chest with her hands, he wouldn't let go. His strong arms held fast as iron bands and even her attempts at kicking him with her bare feet only caused him to flinch.

"I won't believe it, I won't, I won't, I won't!" she screamed as if she were a child.

"You have to."

"No!" Considering a life without even the hope of ever seeing Devlin again was terrifying. Empty, love-less years stretched long before her. The thought struck her that she had loved him and her knees went weak. Had everyone else seen so clearly that she'd fallen for her fiancé's best friend? Old wounds opened brutally and denial sprang to her lips. "No, no, no!"

Yet the nagging thought wouldn't go away. She'd even considered the possibility herself. In loving Devlin, had she lied to him, lied to herself and lied to John? Letting out a painful cry, she felt as if she were breaking in two. If not for Mitch's strong arms, his tender lips pressed against her crown, the soft, soothing words he whispered against her ear, she would surely have fallen to the sand. "It's all right, Chels. Cry, love, if you have to. Let it all out." His voice, as deep as Devlin's, was filled with emotion. As if he cared!

If only she'd had the courage to admit to Devlin, long ago, that she'd cared, that she'd loved him, that he'd been right and she had wanted to make love to him. If only she'd faced up to the fact and been honest with John.

And now, she had to be honest with this man. If he was a stranger, she had used him, as a replacement for a love she'd never shared. She looked up at him and through the sheen of her tears he still looked so much like Devlin—felt so much like him—that her heart broke into a thousand pieces.

He kissed the tears from her eyes and she wept all the harder at his tenderness. "Don't," she whispered, but he didn't listen and held her close, gently rocking, willing her pain away.

Slowly, as the minutes passed, she regained some of her composure. The tears dried and the anguish tearing through her lessened slightly.

"I'm sorry," he said again, his voice rough, as her sobs subsided.

"So am I."

"It's not easy to lose someone you love."

She remembered his wife and felt a stab of jealousy for a dead woman who could evoke so much reverence in this irreverent man. "No, it's not," she agreed, slowly pushing against him.

His arms relaxed.

"You were right," she said, forcing the horrid words to her throat. "I was using you. I wanted Devlin to be alive so badly that I would have done anything, *anything,* to prove that he was."

"And now?"

"I wish I knew."

"You'll go home?"

"Eventually."

"And in the meantime?"

She glanced past his shoulder to the cozy little cabin nestled between the trees. Sunlight and shadow played upon the roof and debris littered the porch. "I don't know," she admitted, turning away from the house and staring at the sea.

Morning light danced upon the water, causing jewel-like prisms to twinkle on the surface. The *Mirage* rolled restlessly against the dock. "I have a few more days," she replied. "I guess I could stay here."

"Knowing that you'll never finish your quest?"

That was the hard part. Accepting Devlin's death. She ran a shaky hand over her forehead. "I—I'll have to think about it."

Mitch sighed. "And what am I going to do with you?"

Love me, she thought, but avoided his eyes. That was absurd—loving someone he barely knew—a woman he thought was a candidate for the ward of a mental hospital.

One side of his mouth lifted into a crooked grin. "Come on in. I'll make you breakfast and then I'll drive you back to the hotel," he offered.

Chelsea wanted to refuse. She didn't want to be reminded that she'd fallen so effortlessly into his arms, that all the while she'd been making love to him, she'd pretended that he was Devlin. "I should just go back now," she said, wanting to lick her wounds, to find a way to accept that Devlin might be lost to her forever.

"This won't take long. And you can clean these out and dry them," he said, holding up her sandy underwear and bra. Chelsea flushed to the roots of her hair, but she didn't protest when he took her hand in his and walked her back to the house.

It was a cozy, bare cabin, far removed from John's expensive bay-front condo and Devlin's cluttered houseboat. But the simplicity of Mitch's cabin touched her and she thought dreamily of a life here, with him, tucked away from the world.

Inside, Mitch handed her two thick white towels and herded her into the bathroom.

"Call if you need me," he said at the door.

"I'll be fine," she assured him, her heart aching a little at his concern.

While Mitch cooked breakfast, Chelsea showered, letting the warm water run through her hair and down her back. Memories of Devlin assailed her, but those distant thoughts wove intricately with fresher images of Mitch. The two men were so alike yet so different.

Was it possible that she'd been in love with them both? And if so, what did that say about her? Was she so fickle that she could love Devlin, while being engaged to John, then fall for Mitch while she was still intent on locating Devlin? Lathering her body and feeling the soap slide down her wet skin, she was reminded of making love to Mitch in the rain. An explosion of emotions tore through her. She leaned against the shower stall and felt ashamed all over again.

"What now?" he'd asked, and she posed the same question to herself. She turned off the water and buffed her body dry with a thick white towel. She had a life back in San Francisco—a thriving business that needed her and a family who cared. Now that she'd accepted that Mitch wasn't Devlin, what possible excuse was there to linger?

She swiped at the foggy mirror and stared at her reflection. Cloudy green eyes glared back at her. The fact that she was beginning to fall in love with Mitch scared her. Just as she'd never admitted that she'd loved Devlin, now she couldn't accept any emotional strings tying her to Mitch.

He was an expatriate, a cynical ex-journalist who was content to plunk a few keys on a computer during the day, and hang out in the local bars at night. Oh, yes, and occasionally he would be seen in the company of one sultry Latin lady.

Not exactly husband material.

And definitely not safe.

She slipped Mitch's robe over her shoulders and rolled up the sleeves. Cinching the belt, she opened the bathroom door and heard him clanging around in the kitchen. Funny, she thought, John had cooked for her, and now Mitch seemed to be filling that void.

The door to the room across the hall was ajar and Chelsea remembered that this tiny room was Mitch's office. Biting her lip, she shoved the door open and stepped inside. The desk was about as messy as the last time she'd seen it, and she, deciding it was now or never, slid into the desk chair.

Quietly, she started the computer, then hunted through the desk drawers, trying to find the work disk. At last, she located it, tucked behind a stack of file folders. Inserting it with shaking fingers, she accessed the file. There it was—the first chapter of a book, written by Mitch Russell, entitled Blue Lightning.

Chelsea scanned the first few lines, then skimmed the entire chapter. From what she could tell, the book was a thriller—the hero a policeman who broke more than his share of rules in his efforts to solve a series of murders. The setting for the novel was San Francisco.

Not South America.

Not Chicago.

Not Paradis.

Her heart stopped beating. The detective in the story could have been Devlin. But Devlin was supposed to be dead and Mitch had never met him.

Unless Mitch had lied. Again.

Trembling, she sagged back in the chair. Raw emotion tore through her and her heartbeat became erratic. She had to bite her lip to keep from breaking down again. What kind of a game was Mitch playing with her mind?

Steeling herself, she removed the work disk and after slowly counting to ten, grabbed what she could of her elusive composure and strode, barefoot, down the short hallway to the kitchen where Mitch was busy over the stove, flipping hot cake after hot cake from the griddle to a plate on the counter.

"You lied to me," she said, stopping near the table, her voice filled with challenge.

"I did?"

"Yes—about this!" She held the damning disk in front of her. As he glanced over his shoulder, he spied the computer disk. His devil-may-care smile slid from his face and once again she was staring at the dangerous man she'd first met on the island. "I read it, you know, all of chapter one."

"What're you doing?" he demanded, a blood vessel bulging in his neck. "You can't go through my things! You actually turned on my computer and—"

She didn't back down. "I want an explanation. You said you were writing a story about some Third World country in South America, but the setting in here—" she shook the floppy disk angrily "—is the good old United States and more specifically, San Francisco."

His muscles tensed and his eyes glittered. "Most of the book is set on the West Coast—Seattle, Portland, L.A. and yes, even San Francisco. But a lot of the back story is set in Colombia and Peru," he said evenly.

"And Paradis?"

"Yes."

"The man in this book could be Devlin McVey," she nearly shouted.

"The hero could be any cop in America."

"Or, more specifically, any cop in San Francisco. Don't do this to me, Mitch. Don't play me for a fool! There are just too many coincidences that don't make a whole lot of sense unless you're Devlin McVey or his twin!"

"Did he have one?"

"Not that I know of," she said, beginning to shake inside. "I'm sick and tired of being pulled and pushed by you. One minute you convince me you're who you say you are, and the next I'm back to square one, believing you're Devlin!"

"Your problem."

"I don't think so!" She shook the disk under his nose. "Mitch, please. Don't lie to me! How do you know about this? Oh, God, if you're Devlin, don't torture me this way!"

His nostrils flared and the pancakes on the griddle began to smoke, but Mitch didn't seem to care. He turned off the grill without so much as a glance at the hotcakes, then grabbed his keys from the counter. "Get dressed," he ordered.

"Why?"

"You're leaving."

"No, I'm not."

"Don't make me show you that I'm stronger than you are," he said with quiet menace. "Go on, get your clothes right now, or I'll dress you myself!" The determined glint in his eye convinced her that he meant business.

She dropped his work disk on the table. "It won't do any good, you know," she warned with steely determination. "You can't get rid of me. Not now."

"Oh, no?" His grin was almost wicked and it caused a shiver of fear to slide down her spine as he tossed her dress and shoes to her. "Just wait and see."

Chapter 10

Mitch's Bronco squealed to a stop in the parking lot of the Villa. Seething, he yanked his keys from the ignition, opened the door and strode around to the passenger's side. Tugging open the door with one hand, he reached inside with the other.

"I can get out myself," Chelsea told him coldly, but he grabbed hold of her arm and hauled her onto the asphalt.

She tried to walk by herself, but he was at her side, his hand clamped around her elbow as he propelled her into the hotel, past the front desk and up the stairs. "You don't have to keep this up," she grumbled, hurrying to keep pace with him.

"You haven't left me much choice."

On the second floor, he nearly pulled her down the hall. At her door, she flung his arm off her. "Thanks," she said through clenched teeth. "You've done your duty."

"Not yet."

"I'm here. What more do you want?"

"I want you off Paradis."

"But I have every right to stay here—"

"Open the door."

He was dead serious but she didn't budge. "You can't tell me what—"

With infuriating calm, he leaned one shoulder insolently against the jamb and waited as she dug through her bag for her keys. "If you think I'm going to invite you in—"

"I don't need an invitation," he said flatly.

"You have the most gall of any man—"

"Just open the damned door before I break it down!" he growled and his face was suddenly fierce with impatience.

Chelsea shoved the key into the lock, then shouldered open the door. She took one step inside and her throat closed. "No— Oh, God, no—"

"What the hell happened here?" Mitch whispered. Quietly, he shut the door behind him.

All her clothes were strewn on the floor, her suitcases had been ripped and dumped, the drawers of her bureau were tipped over and carelessly left upside down, and her bed had been stripped of blankets, sheets and even the mattress.

"Looks like you had company," Mitch muttered angrily, his eyes scanning the mess.

"But why...?" she asked, stepping slowly through the piles of clothes and upturned furniture. "Who would do this?" Sick inside, she surveyed the damage. The ugly image of some stranger pawing through her things, touching her clothes, caused her stomach to roil. She felt her face go white and steadied herself against the door.

"Stay put," he whispered. Her heart hammered as he walked quickly into the bathroom, opened the shower, then returned. He looked through the open closet, then opened the doors to the balcony. Satisfied that whoever had ransacked the hotel room was no longer around, he frowned as he stared at the destruction.

"Is anything missing?" he asked, his voice surprisingly kind.

"I—I don't know."

"Take a quick look around," he ordered. "Tell me if you think anything was stolen."

She didn't know where to start. She started picking through her clothes and she thought of the burglar, tossing her clothes, jewelry and papers heedlessly around the room. Her dismay slowly gave way to outrage as she saw her address book, pages ripped out, shredded and torn, littering the floor by the window. The balcony doors were open and a breeze caused the curtains to billow and the torn papers to flutter. Impotent anger burned through her blood. "Don't you think we should call the police?"

"Not yet."

"But—"

"Trust me, Chelsea," he insisted, picking up her scattered dresses, shorts and sweaters, his fingers deftly—almost professionally—going through the pockets of each item of her clothes.

"But I think—"

"Just take a mental inventory, will you? You should

be good at that, you own a store or something, don't you?" He tossed a few dresses across the end of the bed, then grabbed her white jacket and began going through the pockets.

She reached for a sundress, but stopped when she heard him draw a quick breath between his teeth. "Well, what do you know?" Mitch said, holding up a tiny vial of white powder and frowning darkly. "This yours?"

She shook her head. "No." She didn't have to ask what it was. With a sinking sensation she knew.

His eyes thinned. "I'd guess someone planted drugs on you. Cocaine probably."

"Are you sure?"

"I don't think it's sugar, do you?"

"But why?" she asked, aghast. To her horror, he pocketed the small bottle.

"Obviously someone doesn't like you poking around."

"But I've only been 'poking around' about you."

"Keep looking," Mitch suggested, and Chelsea, shaken to her roots, started sorting through her clothes. Nothing appeared to be missing. Nor were there any other notes or hidden bottles or packets. But the room was a disaster and her things were strewn around so carelessly she couldn't keep her temper in check. "This just doesn't make any sense," she said, glancing up at Mitch as he shoved the mattress in place, then kneeled to look under the bed. She stopped folding clothes and eyed him. "You acted as if you suspected someone had planted something here."

"I'm suspicious by nature."

"But why would anyone vandalize my room?"

He glanced at her as if she were incredibly naive. "Obviously whoever did this wanted you to be in big trouble with the police."

"Me, in trouble? But I didn't do anything. I don't understand."

"This is probably because of me," he admitted with a scowl.

"You? Why?"

"They must've seen us together."

"They? They who?"

"I'm not sure."

"But you've got a pretty good idea," she said, understanding a little.

"I'll find out."

"How?"

His eyes glittered and she felt a tremor of fear. "Leave this to me."

But she couldn't let it go. All his secrecy hadn't helped at all. "Why would anyone ransack my room and plant drugs here? I just don't get it…" She let her words trail off as she thought that he might somehow be connected with crime, perhaps a drug smuggler hiding under the guise of a would-be author.

She sank onto a pile of clothes. "This has something to do with you, the reason you came down here in the first place—whatever it is you do down here, doesn't it?"

She remembered the first night she'd been bold enough to walk to his house, and the way he'd reacted when he'd thought she'd been followed. Her throat grew tight. The thought that he was tied up in something illegal, something as horrid as drug smuggling, tore at her insides. She forced her voice to remain calm, though her hands were clenched into tight fists. "What's going on, Mitch?"

He let out a snort. "I wish I knew."

"But you know *something*."

He hesitated, then his eyes met hers again and his gaze was hard and determined. "I know one thing. You've got to get out of here."

"Oh, so we're back to that."

Mitch reacted violently. He sprang across the bed and took hold of her wrist. "*I* didn't do this to your room. You know that. I was with you."

That much was true.

"But you know who did," she insisted.

"Maybe."

She was starting to get scared. "And you won't call the police."

"No." He scanned the room one last time, righted one of her suitcases and began throwing her clothes into it. "You'd better pack."

"No."

His head snapped up and sizzling blue eyes pinned her. "We probably don't have much time, Chelsea, and I'm not going to spend it arguing with you." Kicking an empty suitcase toward her, he said through clenched teeth, "Pack what you want in ten minutes. The rest stays."

Despite the fear that inched up her spine, she didn't budge. "I'm not going anywhere. Not until you explain everything."

With an exasperated oath, he flung her jacket into the open case, then planted his fists on his hips and glared at her. "You don't have much of a choice, do you? Either you leave quietly, my way, or we call the

police and they lock you up in one of the worst jails
I've ever seen or they transport you to the nearest
American city and drop you in the lap of the D.E.A."

"But I'm innocent—"

"Save it for the judge." He went back to his task,
flinging her clothes into the case. "Has anyone been
following you?"

"I don't know. I'm—I'm not sure," she said, remembering all too vividly how she'd felt eyes watching her
from time to time.

He glanced up sharply. "But you think maybe someone was?"

This was no game. He was deadly serious, a trace
of fear flickering across his hard features. "It…it was
just a feeling I had the other day when I went sightseeing in St. Jean."

"Did you see anyone?"

"Only friends of yours."

"I don't have any friends," he said flatly.

"Well—Bambi or whatever her real name is—was
there, along with her two buddies, of course." She
watched for a reaction but Mitch didn't move, just
stared at her, his face set in granite.

"Anyone else?" he asked.

"No—well, yes, I saw Chris Landeen on the boat."

"Did you happen to be wearing this—" he held up
her white cotton jacket "—at that time?"

"Yes, but no one had a chance to put anything in my
pocket. Besides, if they had, they wouldn't have had to
go through all the trouble of breaking into my room."

"Maybe," he said, rubbing his beard. "Who were
you with on St. Jean?"

"A nice elderly couple," she retorted, feeling the urge to protect Emily and Jeff.

"Do they have names?"

"Of course they do, but—"

"Quit fighting me, Chelsea!" he warned, his patience long gone. "Don't you see I'm on your side?"

"No! I don't! I don't know whose side you're on or even if there are sides. I'm still not sure I even know your name."

His jaw clamped tight.

"What I see is that you're trying to scare the hell out of me and you're doing a damned good job of it," she said, her throat catching.

"Oh, God," he whispered, then wrapped her in his arms. His breath fanned across her hair and it felt right to be held by him. Within his arms she felt safe and warm. "Look," he admitted. "I'm scared, too. I don't like this any more than you do, but you've got to help me. Now, come on, Chels, who were you with?"

The way he said her name—so familiarly, as if they'd known each other for years, caused her heart to tear. She had no choice but to trust him now. "I was with Jeff and Emily Vaughn," she said, feeling a traitor. "But they're not involved in any of this!"

"You don't know, Chelsea," he said with such dead calm that her heart began to pound.

"What about you?" she asked, pulling herself free of his comforting embrace. "What're you involved in?"

"Right now, I'm just trying to save your backside." He finished stuffing her clothes into her suitcases and lifted them from the bed. "Can't you take a hint? Someone's giving you a pretty strong warning."

"Do you know who?" she asked boldly, her insides

quivering. She didn't want him mixed up in this and yet there seemed no way that he wasn't involved.

"No."

"But you said you could take a guess."

"I could take several, but I won't." He grabbed the plastic sack used to line the trash can, walked into the bathroom and scraped her makeup, shampoo, toothbrush, and anything else he could find off the counter and into the bag.

"And I don't suppose you know who wrote me the note?"

"What note?" he asked, barely listening as he snapped her suitcase closed.

"The note I found under my pillow. The one that suggested rather strongly that I leave Paradis."

He froze, every muscle suddenly taunt. "You received a threat?"

"A warning."

"And you didn't tell me?"

"I thought it might have been from you!" she cried, her fear spreading when she saw the worry in his eyes.

"Someone broke into your room *twice?*"

"Yes—"

"God Almighty! Did you call the front desk, alert security?"

"No."

"Why the hell not?"

"Why the hell aren't you calling the police right now?" she flung back.

"I've got my reasons."

"Yeah, right. Well, I've got mine."

He ignored that and asked, "Do you still have it?"

"I think so." She dug into her purse, pulled out her

wallet and opened a small pocket. The scrap of paper was tucked away where she'd left it. As she pulled the folded note from her wallet, Mitch snatched it from her hand.

He paled slightly. "That does it." He picked up the telephone receiver, dialed quickly and after a few seconds spoke in rapid Spanish.

"What're you doing—" But he held up a hand, refusing to listen to her protests.

When he hung up, he said with quiet authority, "You're getting out of here and now!"

"Who did you call?"

"Someone who's going to help us."

"Can't you even tell me who?"

"No. Let's go." He picked up her suitcase, handed it to her, then propelled her to the door where he grabbed the second case. "When did you get the note?"

"The other night."

"When?"

"Tuesday," she said. "I went to bed and found it under my pillow."

"You should've told me," he muttered as they headed for the elevator.

"You haven't made yourself all that available."

"That's because I didn't want to be seen with you," he explained.

Chelsea's heart plummeted and she felt an overpowering sense of disappointment. Crazy as it was, she'd begun to care for Mitch Russell. Despite the fact that he was overbearing, cynical, and a regular pain in the backside, she saw deeper into the man. There was a tender side to him, a gentleness hidden under crusty layers of cynicism and pride. "Am I such an embarrassment?" she asked as they hurried downstairs.

He actually smiled. "Sometimes," he admitted, as he ushered her quickly through the lobby.

"I'll take care of the bill later," he said crisply when she tried to pause at the desk.

"Where am I going?"

He didn't waste any time, held the door open for her and escorted her to the parking lot. "Off the island."

She stopped dead in her tracks. "No way!" She couldn't leave, not yet, not when she was so close to finding out the truth—and so close to Mitch. Their lovemaking last night...

"As I said, you've run out of options." He opened the door to his Bronco and helped her inside. "No funny stuff," he said, his gaze locking with hers as he reached for the door. "This is serious, Chelsea. For once in your life, do as I say and don't ask any questions. I'm thinking about your safety."

"And your hide?" she asked, arching an insolent eyebrow.

His lips curved into a wayward smile. "That's a distinct possibility, isn't it? Think what you want." He slammed the door shut and walked around the Bronco. Once behind the wheel, he plunged the key into the ignition and took off, guiding the Bronco down the winding road that led through the trees to Emeraude.

On the way into town, Chelsea considered all her options. She could throw a fit on the docks, scream bloody murder so that Mitch couldn't send her away, but that would only attract attention.

The warning note, her ransacked room, and the vial

of white powder convinced her that she didn't want to cause a commotion. She had to take Mitch at his word that he wasn't behind everything, and she did believe him.

Hazarding a glance from the corner of her eye, she saw the tension radiating from him. His hands were tight and white-knuckled around the steering wheel, his jaw was set and grim and there was a leashed fury in his stiff shoulders.

Not only that, but she'd noticed the glimmer of fear in his eyes. He was worried—worried about her.

Sighing, she shoved her hair from her eyes and wished he'd trust her enough to confide in her. Their lovemaking had only been hours ago, and yet she felt as if it had happened in a distant and faraway world; a world in which he had shown that he cared for her.

He parked on the docks and took hold of her hand. His voice was soft, his eyes piercing. "Please, Chelsea," he said quietly, "Don't try anything stupid. Trust me on this, okay?"

"But—"

His fingers tightened. "This is for real. I don't want you to get hurt."

Her heart squeezed. If he only knew how easily he could wound her. "I—I want to stay with you," she said impulsively. "Whatever this is, we can battle it together."

He hesitated just a second and slowly, as if it was painful, he reached toward her and brushed a wayward strand of hair from her cheek. His fingers were strong and trembled a little when they grazed her skin. "Don't make this any harder than it is, Chelsea. You have no idea what's going on."

"That's because you won't let me!" she cried.

He closed his eyes, then forced them open. "Let's go."

"No, Mitch, please. Let me stay. After last night I know that whatever happens—"

"You were right. Last night was a mistake," he said coldly and she felt as if she'd been slapped. He dropped her hand and leaned back in the seat. "It should never have happened."

"But it did happen!" she cried, disbelieving that he would be so cruel. "You can't deny it!"

"I can and I will!" He reached over and opened the passenger door. "This is where we say goodbye, Chelsea."

"Just like that?"

"Yep." He slanted her a cold glance as she stepped out of the Bronco and he followed suit. Grabbing her bags, he started for the docks, to a pier where a charter boat was anchored. When she stood rooted to the spot, he glanced over his shoulder and asked, "Are you coming with me or will I have to carry you?"

"I'm not going anywhere."

"Have it your way." He dropped the suitcases, fired off some quick Spanish to a deckhand, and started toward her, an unmistakable gleam in his eye. The deckhand hopped onto the pier, grabbed her luggage and hauled it aboard.

"You wouldn't dare!" she said when Mitch reached her.

"Try me," he ground out, taking hold of her elbow and yanking her toward the waiting boat.

"You can't do this—"

"Just watch." His grip was hard and punishing, his

stride long and determined. "Remember, this is for your own good."

"Don't patronize me!"

"Wouldn't dream of it." At the end of the dock, she stopped, refusing to take the necessary steps onto the boat. Mitch didn't miss a beat, he spoke again in Spanish, this time to the captain of the *Sea Breeze*. The huge, bear-like man with oversized features, snow white hair and thick glasses nodded his agreement.

"I'm not a willing passenger!" she cut in.

"Captain Vasquez isn't interested," Mitch replied.

"But you can't just leave me here!"

"I'm not. You're setting sail in fifteen minutes. The captain has money for you and a one-way plane ticket to San Francisco, by way of St. Jean, Miami, and Dallas."

"I'm not getting on any plane!" she said staunchly, refusing to leave him now. He needed her. Whether he knew it or not, he needed her and, God help her, she needed him! "You don't have a plane ticket—"

"As I said, I already gave it to the captain."

"When?"

"A few days ago."

Something inside her died. Pain, hot and searing, cut through her soul as she stared into his eyes. "You planned to send me away, and you even bought the ticket, but last night…you made love to me?" she whispered brokenly.

He swallowed hard. "I didn't plan on that."

God, how could he be so cruel?

"It just happened."

"You planned it!" she cried, knowing it to be a lie, but wanting to wound him as he'd hurt her. How could he have loved her so thoroughly last night, how could he have caressed her so sweetly, knowing that he planned to shove her aside? Tears welled behind her eyes.

"I didn't plan on anything," he said.

"Then, please, let me stay with you," she begged, mortified at the sound of her own voice.

"You can't," he whispered, his throat thick. Then suddenly he stiffened and his eyes flashed. "For once, Chelsea, use your head."

"Okay," she said bravely, her heart shredding but deciding it was do or die. "I've thought it through. I want to stay with you."

For a second, something akin to tenderness crossed his features and for the briefest of moments, Chelsea thought he'd change his mind. She flung her arms around his neck and buried her face in his chest. "I love you," she said desperately.

For a heartbeat he didn't move and she thought there was a chance his arms would wrap around her and he'd tell her that he loved her, too.

Instead he ground his teeth together, pushed her to arm's length and, though his blue, blue eyes were shadowed, he said, "I don't want you here, Chelsea."

"I don't believe you!"

"Accept it, Chelsea. It was over before it really began. What we felt—that was all just sex, but now it's dangerous for you here and you can't stay." A muscle worked near his temple but his fingers held tightly onto her, as if he couldn't let go.

She held up her trembling chin and stared at him through the sheen of tears. "I don't care if you're Devlin or Mitch, I love you," she said again.

"Oh, God." He closed his eyes a second, as if in agony, but when his lids rose again, his gaze was cold and distant. "Leave Paradis and forget that you ever knew me," he said, the words biting deep.

"You don't mean it," she said bravely, wounded inside.

"I do, lady. I don't want anything more to do with you." He dropped her wrists. Turning on his heel, he marched stiffly back to his Bronco.

Chelsea stood numbly on the dock, watching him storm away without so much as one backward glance. She felt like crumpling onto the sea-weathered planks and tears streamed from her eyes.

Was it possible that he really didn't care about her? Pain, mocking at her for her naïveté, scraped her soul.

"Come on, Missy," the captain said over the rumble of the *Sea Breeze*'s massive engines. "Time to go."

She was vaguely aware that her feet were moving, that she was being guided onto the boat, that the captain was calling off orders in Spanish. Her gaze followed Mitch and she watched in silent desperation as he climbed behind the wheel, gunned the engine and tore out of the parking lot until at last, the old rig rounded a corner and disappeared from sight.

Mitch Russell was out of her life.

Chelsea didn't remember the ride to St. Jean. As the charter boat pulled into the harbor at Lagune, she finally surfaced from the jumble of emotions that had kept her preoccupied since the beginning of the trip. She stared at her hand, still closed around the plane ticket and money the captain, by way of Mitch, had given her.

The boat pulled into the dock and sailors began to leave. Captain Vasquez said, "I will call the cab for you to get you to the airport."

Slowly, she realized that she was still being ramrodded into doing exactly what Mitch wanted. "No—no, thank you," she said, rebelling as she forced a wobbly smile. "I'll do it myself."

"And you will take the plane?"

Not on your life, she thought, though much of the fight had been squeezed out of her. "I don't have any other option," she said slowly, hoping to sound convincingly beaten.

The bear-like captain didn't look like he believed her, but at that moment two deckhands began yelling loudly in Spanish, obviously about ready to tear into each other. Circling on the deck, fists clenched, black eyes glittering ominously, they threatened and snarled.

"*Dios!*" Captain Vasquez muttered under his breath, momentarily forgetting her. "Juan, no—" He started for the two men and Chelsea grabbed her bags, hurrying down the plank leading to the dock.

She half ran along the crowded waterfront, hoping to disappear before the captain remembered that she was his responsibility. How much money had Mitch paid to get rid of her, she wondered, then gritted her teeth. Well, it wasn't enough! She'd come here with a purpose and, by God, she wasn't leaving until she had finished her mission.

Or before you have one last chance to make Mitch realize that he loves you?

She closed her ears to that nagging little voice in her mind and hailed a passing cab. The driver slammed on the brakes and she yanked open the back door, tossed her bags inside and hopped into the backseat.

"Where to?" the cabby asked, eyeing her in the rearview mirror.

"A hotel."

"Which one?"

Chelsea thought quickly, her mind spinning ahead with a half-formed plan. "I, um, don't have reservations. I just need a room—inexpensive—for a day or two."

"There are many hotels on the island."

"How about one with a view of the docks," she said suddenly as inspiration hit.

"Not inexpensive," he said.

"That's all right. Just as long as it's a small hotel that doesn't attract too many tourists."

"Now you are asking the impossible," he grumbled, pulling into the lazy traffic while trying to avoid pedestrians.

Chelsea settled back in her seat. The beginning of her plan was forming in her mind and with a little luck, she might find out more about Mitch Russell or Devlin.

And what if you do? Suppose you even prove without a doubt that Devlin and Mitch are the same person. Do you really expect him to take you into his arms and say that it was all a horrid mistake, that he loved you all along?

Chelsea frowned, her brows pulled tightly together. No, she thought sadly, the best she could hope for was an answer about John's death. Whether the man she'd fallen in love with was Mitch or Devlin, he didn't feel the same way about her. She'd given him ample opportunity to say he cared and he hadn't.

He's not Devlin, she reminded herself, clenching her hands so tightly they ached.

Her throat closed and she battled tears. She wouldn't cry. She wouldn't. But she had to find out about Mitch Russell. She had no choice. Once she understood him further, found out why her room was ransacked and why he wouldn't let himself love her, she'd leave to start her life over again, without dreams of the past weighing her down.

Chapter 11

The hotel was named The Dockside and it was perfect. Slightly run-down and only four stories, it blended into the skyline and waterfront as well as any other and it would serve her purpose.

Chelsea managed to rent a nondescript room on the fourth floor with a view of the bay.

After showering and washing her hair, she ordered lunch and then started working on her plan.

Her first call was to Emeraude and the Boutique Exotique. Terri answered on the third ring.

"Terri, this is Chelsea and I need a big favor," she said.

"Sure, anything," Terri readily agreed. "Just hang on while I help this customer."

Chelsea waited for what seemed like half an hour, though it was probably less than five minutes.

"Okay, what's up?" Terri asked.

Chelsea took in a deep breath. "It's a long story," she confided.

"No problem, things are slow here today. I'm all ears."

Chelsea launched into her tale, filling Terri in. After quickly explaining how she was forced to leave the island, Chelsea ended with, "So, if you can, I'd like you to be my eyes in Emeraude. I can't take the chance of showing up there again; I'm sure Mitch would find me in no time, but if you can tell me anything you see around the docks, I'd appreciate it. The most important thing I need to know is if and when Mitch leaves the island in this direction."

"I'll be glad to help," Terri said, "but I'm kind of stuck here, so I might miss him."

"That's okay, just do the best you can," Chelsea said. "But be careful."

"Now you're really getting me interested," Terri replied, laughing.

Chelsea was worried. She hated dragging Terri into this mess, but didn't see any other option. "Just remember that someone's desperate. They tore my room apart and planted drugs there."

"Don't worry," Terri said. "I can handle it. Look, I've got another customer, I've got to run."

"I'll talk to you later."

She'd barely hung up when room service delivered her lunch. After tipping the waiter, she sat on the balcony and studied her view of the bay while she picked at her avocado salad, sliced cantaloupe and bread. Though she was famished, she barely tasted her food. How long would she wait for Mitch to show up? And what if she missed him?

She thought about returning to Paradis, but knew going back would only make the situation worse. No, if she really wanted to find out what was going on in Mitch's life, she'd have to be patient and wait.

Unfortunately, patience had never been her long suit. She tossed her napkin onto the table and sighed. After reading the chapter in Mitch's book, she'd been certain he was Devlin—and his reaction had been violent. Until then, she'd felt that he'd been falling in love with her, too. Or was he capable of such an emotion?

Mitch. Devlin. The two men blended into one in her mind and she knew that she'd never be able to forget them. Whatever happened in the next few days would probably dictate the course of the rest of her life.

Rather than dwell on the complications of loving Mitch, she took her tray into the room, braced herself, and called her sister.

The recorder flipped on and Chelsea rolled her eyes as she listened to the recorded message. When at last it was her turn to speak, she said, "Hi, Felicia, this is Chels. I've moved to another hotel in Lagune on the island of St. Jean. The number is..." She reeled off her phone and room numbers, then explained that she wouldn't be home for another week. "Tell Mom I'll call her soon," she ended, before hanging up and punching out the number of the shop she owned with Sally.

Sally was in. "Hi," she chirped over the wires. "I wondered when I was going to hear from you again. Don't tell me, you're running off with a rich billionaire who's vacationing down there and fell madly in love with you."

"How'd you know?" Chelsea quipped, feeling better just talking to her friend.

"Because you're living out *my* fantasy!" Sally threw back at her. They chatted for a while and Sally insisted that, though they all missed her desperately, the business was perking along and sales were up. "I'm about to go mad just ordering things," Sally said. "We're already out of some of our fall suits. It's impossible to keep up!"

"Well, when I get back, it'll be your turn," Chelsea said, smiling for the first time in hours. "You can come down here, or visit Tahiti or wherever you want to go."

"Oh, no, when you get back, we'll talk about expanding. I found the perfect spot in Oakland and it's only a half-hour drive and you'll absolutely love it."

"I'll take your word for it," Chelsea said. "I should be home in a week. I'll let you know the exact date when I buy my ticket."

"Don't worry about it. I'll see you when you get here."

Chelsea hung up, grabbed her purse and dashed downstairs to set her plan into motion. The lobby, as uninspiring as her room, was nearly empty as she shoved open the glass doors.

Outside, the heat was blistering, burning against her scalp and rising in waves from the pavement. She joined the rest of the tourists on the sidewalk that bordered the waterfront. The glare off the water was blinding and only a few trees offered sparse shade.

Chelsea barely noticed as she passed windows of the shops lining the bay. She only slowed as she discovered a camera store that featured binoculars in the front display.

"Perfect," she told herself, and purchased the most powerful pair she could afford. On her way back to the hotel, she stopped at a bakery, a fruit stand and bookstore.

Back in her room, she shoved two chairs and a small table onto her small balcony, hung the binoculars around her neck and settled into one chair while propping her feet on the other.

Then she was ready. She checked the binoculars and grinned as she stared through the thick glasses. Depending upon where Mitch decided to berth the *Mirage,* Chelsea would spot him. All she had to do was wait.

She didn't think in terms of how long. She didn't care. She was going to find out his secret and why he insisted upon pushing her away. Once and for all, she'd find out if he was Devlin, and then, she told herself firmly, when she knew the truth, she'd fly back to San Francisco without him.

Only then would she be able to bury the past.

Her heart squeezed painfully and she ignored it, setting her jaw and resolutely staring through the binoculars.

Her eyes were just beginning to tire when the phone rang so loudly she nearly jumped out of her chair to answer it. "Hello?"

"Chelsea! Thank God you're there!" Felicia said breathlessly. "I just got in and heard your message. You have no idea what's going on! I tried to leave a message at the Villa and the snotty desk clerk insisted you'd already checked out. Mom and I were worried to death!"

"Slow down," Chelsea said. "Why were you worried?"

"Because of Devlin! Oh, Chelsea, all hell's broken loose up here. I've already talked to two policemen—detectives—who used to work with Devlin. It seems they think he must be alive. They asked me all sorts of questions about him—about you."

Chelsea's knees gave out. She sank onto the bed. "And what did you tell them?" she said slowly, her hands beginning to sweat over the receiver.

"Well, the truth, of course!" Felicia replied, slightly miffed. "I'm surprised no one contacted you."

"You told them I was here—looking for Devlin?"

"Yes!"

"Oh, God, Felicia, you didn't!"

"I just told you I did. Why wouldn't I? They were the police, for God's sake!" Felicia was nearly shrieking.

Chelsea tried to stay calm. "When did you talk to them?"

"When? Two—days ago."

"And you didn't call me until now?"

"I said I tried earlier at the hotel—you weren't there!" Felicia snapped.

"But two days!" Panic ripped through her. Chelsea licked her lips nervously, wondering if there were a way to get word to Mitch, to warn him that he would soon be accosted by police who might think he was Devlin. If he hadn't been already.

"What's going on? Chelsea," Felicia asked. "Are you in trouble?"

If you only knew. "No," she said, "but I decided to take a room in Lagune, on St. Jean."

"Why?"

"Paradis is pretty small."

"This has something to do with that Mitch person, doesn't it?"

"He and I had a disagreement," Chelsea admitted.

"You're in trouble!" Felicia pronounced.

"I'm fine," Chelsea lied.

"Well, as long as you're not involved with whoever that man is. Whether he is Devlin or not, and I seriously doubt he is, it's no good trying to resurrect the dead. All those emotions, all those feelings belong in the past. Face it, Chelsea, it's time to move on. And all this business with the police—it's just so awful!"

"Nothing's been proven yet," she said, instantly defensive.

"I know, and they wouldn't tell me much, but I got the impression that Devlin did something illegal. Something worse than faking his death—"

"I don't believe it!" Chelsea snapped, annoyed with herself. She'd probably drawn a map for the police, a map that led right to Mitch Russell's doorstep.

"This is a nightmare! I knew you should never have taken off on this wild goose chase! You'd better come back to San Francisco. I talked to Sally the other day and she's hot to expand. Maybe you should concentrate on the store. Start in a new location, make some new friends, start dating again. It wouldn't hurt you to have a life."

"I do have a life."

Felicia's voice was hard. "I mean a new life—without any strings to John or Devlin."

"I'll think about it." Chelsea bit her tongue and said goodbye before she said something she'd regret.

Nervous as a cat, she took up her position as lookout again and stared through the lenses. The waterfront was packed with people, tourists and seamen, milling around the piers that stretched out to the sea. Boats of all sizes and shapes were lashed to the moorings, while others headed inland and out to sea.

"This may be impossible," she thought as the sun lowered. She sipped from a bottle of diet cola and considered the fact that she was wasting her time. What if Mitch came after darkness fell? What if he didn't come at all? What if she missed him?

She toyed with the idea of returning to Emeraude and having it out with him once and for all, but he would probably just send her packing again.

But if the police were on his tail, shouldn't she warn him? She could call—tell him she was in the Dallas airport and that she'd talked to someone at home and discovered that the police, too, were looking for Devlin.

He probably wouldn't even take her call. And she had warned him already when she'd told him earlier that the San Francisco Police Department thought Devlin McVey had turned bad.

She chewed on her nails, then left her post to make the call. She couldn't stand the waiting, the not knowing. Face it, Chelsea, you're in love with him. Be he Satan or saint, criminal or upstanding citizen, Mitch Russell or Devlin McVey, you've lost your heart to him.

She shoved her hair from her eyes with shaking fingers and slowly lowered herself onto the bed. She loved him, just as she'd vowed earlier. The impact of loving him hadn't really hit her until now. Until she realized that within days, she'd never see him again.

The thought of learning the truth and leaving for San Francisco, as she had promised herself she would, tore her apart. Even now her insides were churning...

The phone rang and she picked it up quickly, half-expecting to hear Mitch's voice.

"Chelsea? It's Terri. Believe it or not, I think Mitch is heading your way."

"He is?" she whispered, hardly believing that he would risk boating to Lagune only hours after having her shipped here.

"Yep, at least I think that's where he's headed. I was over at the bistro talking to Simone when Tacita—that's the girl we've seen Mitch with—stormed in and demanded to use the phone. She was red-faced and furious and God only knows what she was talking about. My Spanish is pretty rusty, but you can bet she was madder than a wet hen."

Chelsea's breath constricted. "And Mitch was with her?"

"Oh, no! After she took off, I left for the boutique and I saw that red speedboat heading in the direction of St. Jean. I couldn't make anyone out at that distance, but there were three people on board and Mitch's sailboat is still moored down at the docks."

Chelsea's skin broke out in a cold sweat. "When did they leave?"

"Fifteen or twenty minutes ago," Terri said. "Is everything okay?"

"I hope so," Chelsea said fervently. "I'll let you know. Thanks a lot."

"No problem."

Chelsea hung up and walked back to the balcony. The sun had begun to set, the sky was turning dark and the sea had become a deep shade of purple. Lifting the binoculars to her eyes, Chelsea trained her glasses toward Paradis and saw several boats approaching, but the craft that caught her attention was a shiny red speedboat that knifed through the water, leaving a thick white wake behind.

Biting her lower lip, she watched, barely daring to breathe, as the image grew larger. Only when the boat docked did she see the faces of the three men on board, and sure enough, Mitch Russell in the company of the two swarthy-looking men she'd seen him with before.

She didn't think twice. This was it. Her one chance. She wasn't going to blow it. Grabbing her purse, she nearly flew out of the room and pounded down three flights of steps. Outside, she squinted against the gathering darkness and the crowd on the waterfront until she found Mitch's profile, and her heart turned over. Tall and lean, his shoulders wide, his eyes protected by dark glasses, he was as handsome and mysterious as ever. Her heart jackhammered as she stared after him and his two acquaintances.

Trying to keep a buffer of people between them, she followed slowly, keeping her gaze trained on the three men. They stopped at the door of a seedy bar. Mitch glanced over his shoulder once, but Chelsea was partially hidden by a tall woman with a parasol. Obviously satisfied that they hadn't been observed, Mitch shoved hard on the door and followed his two compatriots inside.

Nervous sweat ran down Chelsea's spine. But she couldn't give up—not now. And she couldn't brazenly follow the men inside, either. So she had to use another entrance. Quickly, she rounded the corner of the block, walked up a side street and ducked into a back alley.

The back door to a row of shops was open. Chelsea found the rear entrance to the bar and slipped inside. The rooms were dark and she followed a short hallway of red linoleum through a small pool room to the main area. She stood at the corner and quickly eyed the place. The bar was filled with smoke, tinny music and harsh laughter.

A few men sat around short tables and Chelsea realized, belatedly, that, as a woman she stuck out like a sore thumb. Mitch and his friends were just seating themselves at a booth in the corner and Chelsea ducked into a table at the opposite side of the bar, behind a chipped stucco post and a row of half-filled bottles of liquor.

Mitch's back was to her and she was grateful for small favors. She ordered a beer and paid for it, ignoring the frosty glass that was set before her on the table and wishing she could find a way to get closer. She already assumed the two men that Mitch was using for "research" were thugs, the kind of surly, angry men that gave her the creeps. From her partially hidden vantage point, she pretended interest in a local paper, but studied them.

The tall man signaled to the bartender and ordered three drinks. He snarled out an order, then frowned when a petite waitress didn't serve them fast enough.

Why would Mitch keep company with such men?

For the first time since she'd arrived in the Caribbean, Chelsea wished she had never come. Seeing Mitch pal around with these two men made her skin crawl, and yet she stuck it out, gritting her teeth in determination. There had to be a reason he was here with them, a good reason! He couldn't be a criminal—she wouldn't believe it!

Her hands were shaking when she reached for her glass and took a sip. At that moment, the taller of the two men spied her. He had been stroking his moustache thoughtfully, but stopped and a look of consternation crossed his features while his black gaze roved over her face.

Chelsea pretended nonchalance, catching his gaze, then ignoring it, as if it were an everyday occurrence for her to stop into a seedy bar by herself.

The tall man muttered something to his friend and both he and Mitch turned at the same time.

Mitch froze. Beneath his beard his skin went white. He said something to his friends and shrugged, dismissing her. As if he'd never seen her in his life before.

But a sliver of fear shot through Chelsea. Should she leave or stay? Either way, she thought—seeing the gleam of menace in the tall man's black eyes—might put Mitch's life in danger.

She started to scoot her chair back and the short, thick-set man panicked when she reached for her purse. He yelled something in rapid-fire Spanish to his friend, motioning to Chelsea.

"No!" Mitch cut in, sending Chelsea a warning look that turned her blood to ice. "She is nothing to me. She knows nothing! Believe me!" He grabbed the tall man's arm. "Let's go—"

But Mitch was too late. The fat man's lips curled suspiciously. "She has heard too much," he said in a thick Spanish accent. From beneath his light-colored suit jacket, he withdrew a pistol.

Chelsea's blood turned to ice.

"Chelsea!" Mitch screamed, knocking the man's arm, so that his aim went wild. "Jesus! No!"

The gun went off with a *crack!*

Glass shattered behind the bar. People screamed and shrieked, overturning tables and spilling drinks. Men leaped for cover or ran for the exits. Beer and wine sloshed on the cement floor.

Chelsea tried to run, scrambling to the bar as she got to her feet. But the fat man aimed again and Mitch flew over an overturned table, protecting her body with his. The gun went off loudly and Chelsea felt him stiffen as he emitted a loud moan.

Good Lord, he was hit!

"Move it!" Wind whistled through his teeth. "This way," he muttered hauling her to her feet and running with a limp through the bar to a back exit. "Move!"

The tall man sprang forward, hollering loudly in Spanish as he gave chase.

Outside, police sirens wailed. Dogs barked, children screamed and dust caught in Chelsea's throat. Mitch yanked hard on Chelsea's hand, half dragging her down a dark labyrinth of cobblestone alleys that wound in and out of dusty yellow buildings that somehow all looked the same.

"What the hell were you doing in there?" he demanded as they ran. Sweat dampened his brow and his face was twisted in pain. He ran with a limp and blood stained the ground, leaving a scarlet trail behind them.

"I had to know what was going on."

"Hell, you just about got us both killed!" Breathing with difficulty, he yanked her around a corner and through the side street.

Behind them, footsteps pounded the pavement and people yelled or screamed. Two more shots rang through the town and Mitch began to slow, his left leg dragging, blood running from the wound in his thigh, his pants stiff and stained.

"You—you never listen do you?" he gasped, breathing with an effort. Sweat beaded his brow and his face was white. His lips were flat against his teeth as he fought the pain.

"And you never tell me the truth—"

"That's it! Stop right where you are!" a male voice boomed.

Chelsea turned and found a giant of a man bearing down on them. In one hand he had a gun, in the other he flashed a policeman's badge. All she saw were the words San Francisco Police Department and she nearly collapsed. Her worst fears were confirmed. She'd led the police to Devlin—or to Mitch—and because of her, he would probably spend the rest of his life behind bars.

"He's hurt—take him to a hospital," the voice said again and for the first time Chelsea realized there were two other men with the huge police officer, and one of them was a stocky man with red hair and cold blue eyes.

Ned Jenkins.

So he'd told them he thought he'd found Devlin.

"What're you doing here?" she demanded.

"My job," Ned explained.

"But you said—"

"That changed," he replied. "When the D.E.A. got involved."

Chelsea's heart turned to stone. She turned to Mitch. "I—I didn't mean—"

"It's all right, Chels," he said quietly, wincing in pain, his dark hair in sweaty strands against his forehead. "It had to come down to this."

The big man took charge. "Have him stitched up and then meet us down at headquarters with her," he said, nodding in Chelsea's direction. "Let's just see what they have to say." He turned to Chelsea. "Come on, lady, I can't wait to hear how you got yourself involved in this mess."

Chapter 12

"So that's it?" the policeman asked, watching as Chelsea nervously shredded her foam coffee cup. "You came down here looking for Devlin McVey because you thought he was still alive, and you ended up with Mitch Russell."

"Yes," she said, sitting in an uncomfortable chair in the police station.

Officer Jack Bates, a black man with light brown eyes and a perpetual scowl, shook his head as he finished typing. "I have to hand it to you, you've got guts." He whipped her statement out of his typewriter.

"Thanks," Chelsea said.

"Read this over and if it's right, sign on the bottom," he instructed, handing her a pen.

She read over the typed pages, telling her side of

the story, and sighed. Then, with only a second's hesitation, she signed her name quickly.

"Okay, you're free to leave the station. But don't leave the island. We've arranged a room for you at the Duchess Hotel at Roger's Point. We took the liberty of moving your things over. You'll be a guest of the department for a few days."

"I suppose I should be flattered," she said biting her tongue. She had no right to question the police. As a policeman's daughter, she knew that this man, along with the rest of the force, was only doing his job. "I'm sorry," she said, "It's been kind of a rough day."

He flashed her a sympathetic smile. "Don't worry about it."

Smiling, she picked up her purse and asked, "What about Mr. Russell?"

"On his way here from the hospital," Officer Bates replied.

"Is he okay?"

"So far." His golden eyes showed a little bit of understanding. "I wouldn't be too concerned about him, if I were you. Seems to me Mitch Russell's the type who always lands on his feet."

"I guess you're right," she said sadly.

"You want me to give him a message for you?"

What was there to say? "No, thanks," she said. "Maybe I'll see him later." But she doubted it.

"There's a car waiting for you. Someone will drive you over to the hotel."

"Thanks." Feeling suddenly tired, she walked through the small cinder-block station. Outside, a blue-and-white police car was waiting. The driver, a woman with cropped brown hair and a perpetual frown, gunned the car when Chelsea hopped in. They drove in silence through the winding streets of Lagune to the outskirts of town where the road angled sharply upward, through a forest of lush trees and vegetation.

As she rested her head on the back of her seat, Chelsea thought of Mitch and Devlin and John. San Francisco and John Stern seemed far away, a part of her past that had little to do with her now. Even her image of Devlin was unclear and the feelings she'd once held for him seemed foolish and trite.

But Mitch was a different story. If he were Devlin, then he'd changed and she couldn't even think of him as she'd once thought of Devlin. No, Mitch was another man entirely, a mystery, an enigma, but a man she knew she could love for a lifetime.

And she'd betrayed him. Innocently, perhaps, but betrayed him nonetheless. Obviously he was at odds with the law and she led them straight to him. Her heart ached. Deep inside, she couldn't, wouldn't believe that Mitch was involved in anything illegal. Hadn't he tried to save her just this afternoon? Didn't that single noble act prove him guiltless?

She closed her eyes for a second and when she opened them again, the driver was pulling into the circular brick drive of the Duchess Hotel. In the center of the grounds a tiered fountain spewed water in thin, perfect streams and well-tended gardens filled with red, blue, orange and yellow flowers offered sweet fragrance. Shiny clinging vines grew in abundance against a tall, whitewashed hotel with a red tile roof and skirted with wide verandas.

Any other day, this spectacular hotel would have thrilled her.

"You're already registered," the woman officer explained, leaning over the back of her seat and handing Chelsea a key to a room on the third floor. "And all your personal belongings from the Dockside as well as the Villa on Paradis are here."

She could barely believe it. "Thank you," she said as she slid out. She watched as the police car rolled around the gardens and disappeared down the hill.

Squaring her shoulders, she walked stiffly up the few short steps. Inside, the hotel was grander than any she'd seen on either Paradis or St. Jean. The lobby floor was polished tile, the desk a burnished mahogany. Thick walls of clean white stucco surrounded tall, paned windows that offered panoramic views of the gardens or sea. Huge paddle fans circulated the air and thick carpeting in fawn and cream led upstairs.

Chelsea took the elevator to the third floor. Her room turned out to be a suite that filled the entire west wing. Antique furniture, brass lamps and fresh cut flowers were placed in intimate groupings and each private area was graced with French doors leading to a private balcony.

The police department of St. Jean certainly knew how to live well, Chelsea thought as she picked a mango from a basket of fruit.

She set the mango aside, kicked off her shoes, showered and slipped into her bathrobe. Then, her hair still damp, she wandered out onto the balcony and stared at the palm-lined view of the bay. If only Mitch were here to share this with her, she thought. The breeze, smelling faintly of the sea, caressed her face and lifted her hair from her shoulders. The ocean had darkened with the night. A few stars winked in the sky and a sliver of moon hung low over the sea.

Mitch, Mitch Mitch. Would she ever be able to get him out of her mind?

Leaning against the rail, she stared at the darkening horizon and tried to picture Mitch sailing back to Paradis. Without her.

Click.

She turned, thinking she imagined the noise. Her heart leaped to her throat as the doorknob turned. Her fingers twisted in the belt of her robe. "Who's there?" she called, but her voice was faint. She felt her heart leap as she expected Mitch to stick his head in.

To steady herself, she leaned against the rail behind her and nearly fainted when she spied Devlin— no Mitch—enter the room.

Startlingly clean-cut—without a beard, his hair neatly trimmed—he limped into the room. "Chelsea—" he called before he saw her through the open balcony door.

She could barely believe her eyes. His newly shaven face was tanned only to his beard line and he was wearing faded jeans, a T-shirt and a beat-up leather jacket—Devlin's jacket.

"There you are." His gaze skated down her robe to the V above her breasts and he smiled, that brilliant slash of white that could only belong to Devlin.

Oh, God, he *was* Devlin. And Mitch! Tears sprang to her eyes.

"Thank God you're alive!" she cried, running to him and flinging her arms around his neck and nearly knocking him over. Tears of happiness tracked down her cheeks and she buried her face against him. "You miserable, lying, cheating, son of a bitch," she said, choking on tears and laughter, her heart soaring in the knowledge that Devlin was alive, that he was Mitch, that the two men she loved more than anything in the world were one and the same!

"That's some greeting for a man who just saved your neck!"

"Why did you lie to me?" she cried, still hanging desperately onto him. "Why did you pretend to be Mitch? God, how could you deny it over and over again?"

"It wasn't easy!"

"But you made it look easy. Over and over. You kept denying and telling me that I was crazy, and if I weren't so glad that you're alive, I'd kill you myself!"

He laughed then, tilting her face up to his and kissing her so deeply that she couldn't breathe, could barely think, and suddenly she didn't care about his reasons. "I had to do it, Chels," he said, when he finally lifted his lips from hers.

"Why?"

"For John."

"Why?"

His eyes darkened with a private pain. "John wasn't supposed to be killed that day," he said with a sigh. "I was."

"What?" she whispered.

"Come on, sit down." He helped her to the side of the bed and his face grew hard. "I was working on a case, a big drug-smuggling case, trying to break up a ring that moved drugs from South America through Paradis to the U. S. Unfortunately, the men involved were beginning to suspect that I was a cop. What I didn't know is that they planned to kill me, by booby-trapping the boat."

"But why did you want to talk to John that day?" she asked, her throat raw.

"Because I was going to explain that I'd have to disappear for a while. I didn't want anyone to know who my friends were. It was to protect him—and you—and it backfired. While we were sailing, the storm picked up, and we started for shore, but the boat blew up, just out of the blue, probably some sort of timing device on a bomb—it wouldn't take much and not enough of the wreckage was found to prove it. Anyway, I survived. Unfortunately John wasn't so lucky."

"So you were out for revenge."

He nodded. "I swam ashore, got hold of my superiors and demanded a new identity to protect myself."

"Didn't you tell them what you were doing?"

He frowned. "This was personal," he said, his jaw sliding to the side and his eyes gleaming with an inner anger. "So I used all the information I'd gathered during the investigation and moved down here. I assumed the role of an expatriated American and within about three months, I made contact with the drug cartel."

"The same one?"

"Yes, but I was dealing with different people and I'd changed my looks significantly enough that they wouldn't recognize me. Until you showed up."

"Uh-oh."

"Right. I was just about to expose the drug kingpins to the police in a sting operation when you fouled up everything! I couldn't believe it! And I couldn't get rid of you."

"You tried," she charged.

"You bet I did. I was frantic for your safety. I thought that if I was rude and cruel enough, you'd take the hint. But not you, oh, no—I'd forgotten how damned stubborn you can be."

He rolled his eyes and stared at the ceiling. "And then, even when I came on to you like a macho creep, you wouldn't buy it. You kept after me. I tried to stay away from you, I even hired some people to watch you."

"You did what?" she cried.

"Chris Landeen—he'd met you and I asked him and a couple of clerks at the hotel to keep an eye on you. I couldn't risk seeing you myself, for fear that by being with you, showing that I cared about you, I'd look vulnerable to the thugs and, if I ever made them angry, they might turn on you. So I hired Chris and a few others because I had to know that you were okay. And then came the storm." He turned back to her and his eyes blazed with a familiar blue flame. "The damned storm. There you were and I couldn't resist. Hell, I didn't want to."

"And then you threw me out."

"Because Carlos and Ramon were on to you! Who do you suppose put the drugs in your room? Who sent you the note?"

"Them?"

He grinned wickedly. "Well, actually I'd bet Tacita left the note for you—she probably bribed a maid in the hotel."

"Tacita—you mean Bambi?"

"One and the same." His eyes twinkled and she shoved a wet lock of hair from her face. "She's very jealous, you know."

"What was she to you?"

"Nothing," he said softly. "Too wishy-washy. You know me, I go for the mule-headed type."

"Thanks a lot!"

"You nearly ruined everything, you know."

"How?"

"Today, in the bar. That was the final showdown. The local police were in position and, thanks to you, the San Francisco cops were there as well. Everything was set, until you showed up and nearly ruined the arrest and damned near got us both killed!"

She eyed his leg. "You will be okay, won't you?"

"Just a little sore for a while. The bullet grazed my thigh, but didn't hit anything serious." His eyes gleamed seductively. "In fact, I think we should make sure that all my parts are working."

"Maybe you should rest in bed," she suggested.

His eyes gleamed. "Precisely what I had in mind," he said, kissing her again. "And I'm not going to get up for days!" His lips touched her eyes, her throat, her cheeks, "You know, I believed you today when you told me you loved me."

"I do," she said simply, winding her arms around his neck.

He sighed and said hoarsely. "And I love you, Chelsea, God, I've loved you for so long." He lifted his head and gazed into her eyes. "I lied when we were in Lake Tahoe. I wasn't testing you, I just couldn't keep my hands off you. And I was disgusted with myself because John was my friend. I betrayed him by wanting you."

"It's all right," she said, automatically, as she smoothed the hair from his face.

"No, it's not. Before she died, my wife cheated on me with a 'friend' of mine. I know how it feels," he ground out, his eyes dark.

"We didn't cheat on John."

"Close enough," he said in disgust, then asked. "Would you really have married him?"

"I don't know. I thought I wanted to at the time, but even then, I had doubts. I guess we'll never know." She felt a tug on her heart at the thought of John and she knew that she'd never forget him. During the course of her relationship with him, she'd known there had been something missing, something vital and passionate and real, something she had with Devlin.

He touched her gently on the cheek. "And what about me? Will you marry me?" he asked so suddenly Chelsea glanced up sharply to see if he were joking. But his expression was serious and the love in his eyes was overwhelming.

"Of course I'll marry you, Devlin," she said, then added impishly. "You know, I'll even marry you if your name turns out to be Mitch."

He laughed and the sound touched a special part of Chelsea's heart. "We could get married tomorrow morning," he said, "and spend our honeymoon down here while the investigation wraps up."

"What then?"

"Back to San Francisco where I'll finish up my book—that is legit by the way." Wrapping his arms around her, he kissed her lightly on the lips. "But one thing worries me," he said.

"Just one?"

"Will you be happy married to a cop? I've been of-fered my old job back."

"I love you, Devlin, not your job. I don't care if you're a detective with the police department in San Francisco or a writer on Paradis. You know," she said honestly, "I wouldn't even care if we never left the islands."

He grinned widely. "Good, because I think we should keep the cabin on Paradis. It could be our own private tropical paradise for the rest of our lives."

"And our children's lives," she added, with a wink.

"Children? You want children?"

"Many—and the first one will be named Mitch or Michelle," she teased.

"No," he said softly, "the first one will be named John." Devlin wrapped his arms around her and Chelsea felt tears build behind her eyes. She loved him, oh, God, how she loved him!

From this day forward she intended to spend the rest of her life proving how much he meant to her.

His weight shifted and they tumbled onto the bed. "Aren't you going to ask to see my scar?" he asked and Chelsea giggled.

"This time I'll remember to look," she said as his mouth captured hers in a kiss that was both fierce and gentle.

Closing her eyes, she yielded, body and soul, lost in the wonder that was and always had been Devlin McVey.

* * * * *

SECRET DELIVERY

Delores Fossen

Prologue

Willow Ridge, Texas

Sheriff Jack Whitley figured he had three minutes, maybe less, to save the woman's life.

He slammed on his brakes, and his Ford pickup skidded to a stop just inches from what was left of the bridge's ice-scabbed guardrail. Seconds earlier, a car had broken through the metal and plunged over the side. Since he'd been traveling from the opposite direction, he'd caught just a glimpse of terror on the driver's face before Mill's Creek had swallowed her and her car.

There was no time to remove his gun or shoes. No time to call for help. He grabbed the life hammer from his glove compartment, barreled out of his truck and, running, he dived right into the cold dark water.

Hell. He couldn't see. The creek was thick with winter silt that concealed just about everything, but he went on instinct. At the speed the woman was traveling when she slammed through the guardrail, she was probably thirty, maybe forty feet out. He surfaced only long enough to drag in a deep breath so he could go down after her again.

Seconds ticked off in his head, each one a frantic reminder that he had to get to her. He had to save her. *Now.* No one, not even he, could last long in this frozen water.

He ignored the numbing cold that was starting to smother him and focused, finally spotting her black Lexus angled nose-down with the headlights and front fender already sinking into the clots of mud on the creek floor.

Jack fought through the water to get to her. She was there, behind the steering wheel, her light-colored coat billowing around her like a ghost. Her eyes were closed. Maybe she was unconscious.

Or already dead.

He pushed that possibility aside and latched on to the door handle.

It was jammed.

Cursing to himself, he bashed the life hammer against the window. The sharp metal head of the emergency tool made a large enough hole so he could reach in, open the door and undo her seat belt.

The woman spilled into his arms.

He grabbed her and began to haul her to the surface. Each inch was a struggle. His lungs burned now, and his muscles began to knot. Somehow, though, he broke through the water and breathed in some much needed air, while the woman lay limp and lifeless in his arms.

Jack dragged her to the muddy embankment, tilted back her head and started mouth-to-mouth resuscitation. He literally gave her what little breath he had left.

Her eyes fluttered open. She coughed. And Jack said a very sincere prayer of thanks.

"We got lucky," he gasped.

She opened her mouth, but didn't speak. Her stark-blue eyes widened, and the sound she made was one of raw agony.

"What's wrong? Are you hurt?" Jack asked.

She didn't answer. She fought with her coat, shoving it open and clamping her hands over her belly.

Jack saw then that she was pregnant. She had to be in her last trimester.

"Help me. I'm in trouble." She looked up at him, her eyes shimmering with tears, her face twisted in pain. "*Please*. Don't let my baby die."

Her words slammed into him. They'd dodged one bullet, but another was headed right at them.

Jack scooped her into his arms and ran like hell toward his truck.

Chapter 1

Eight months later

Alana Davis checked the rearview mirror again. The dark-colored car was still following her.

"Oh, God," she mumbled.

It couldn't be the security guard. It just couldn't be. Because if he'd managed to catch up with her, Alana figured this time he would kill her.

She couldn't stop, not even to find a pay phone and call the police. Not that there'd been a pay phone anywhere along the way from the secluded house in the woods where she'd been held captive. Nor was there one along the highway that had taken her nearly an hour to find. Luckily, the car she'd stolen from the front of the house had nearly a full tank of gas.

And thankfully, she'd seen the sign to the town of Willow Ridge.

The guard and a nurse had force-fed her a partial dose of sedatives only hours earlier, so it'd taken Alana a while to fight through dizziness and make the connection. Willow Ridge was just one of those floating memories that she couldn't immediately link to anything or anyone. But then she remembered Jack Whitley, the town's sheriff. He'd helped her.

She couldn't remember what he'd done exactly, but she instinctively knew she could trust him.

Alana couldn't say that about anyone else.

She certainly couldn't trust the guard or nurse. Or her brother. In fact, one of them must have been responsible for her captivity.

But which one?

And why?

She didn't know the answer to either question, but Jack Whitley would be able to find out.

Lightning rifled through the night sky. A few seconds later, thunder came, a thick rumbling groan. Shivering, she made the final turn that would take her to Willow Ridge. Even with the rain and her spotty vision, she could see the other vehicle make the turn right along behind her. He stayed close. Too close.

Alana added some pressure to the accelerator and sped through deep puddles that had already collected on the road. The car's wipers slashed over the windshield, smearing the rain on the glass so it was even harder for her to see. Her pulse raced out of control.

She maneuvered the car around a sharp curve. The tires squealed in protest at the excessive speed, and she checked the mirror again. The other vehicle stayed right with her, the high-beam headlights glaring into her eyes.

It certainly wasn't safe to race through a raging summer storm at ten o'clock at night, but she didn't want to face that guard on this deserted road. She had no weapon, no way to defend herself. Worse, she was exhausted and wondered if she'd be able to stand, much less fight.

Ahead of her, she finally saw the town lights. Welcome signs of civilization and help.

Going even faster, she sped toward Main Street, flanked on both sides with shops, a diner, even a white church with a steeple. Letting some vague, fuzzy memories guide her, she drove toward the center of the tiny town and spotted the sheriff's office.

Alana braked to a stop, glanced behind her and saw nothing. No car. No headlights.

No one.

Relief flooded through her. Maybe the guard had gotten scared and driven away. Still, she didn't just sit there. He might be lurking on a side street, waiting to grab her and take her back to that house in the woods.

Rain pelted her when she got out of the car. She was already cold and shivering, and the wetness didn't help. Alana ran toward the glass-front door of the sheriff's office. Each step was an effort. Her muscles were stiff, her hands throbbed from where she'd gripped the steering wheel and the dizziness was worse than it had been during her escape.

Why did everything seem out of focus? And wrong. Something was wrong. But what?

She threw open the door, and the burst of air from the AC spilled over her. It was dark in the front section of the building, but there was a light on in a room at the middle of a short narrow hall.

"Sheriff Whitley?" Her voice was barely a whisper.

She saw something move in the shadows, and a moment later, a man stepped out. Alana got just a glimpse of him before another stab of lightning flashed in the sky and the lights went out.

Oh, mercy. Had the guard done this? Was he coming after her?

"Calm down," the man said. It was Jack Whitley's voice. "If you keep breathing like that, you'll hyperventilate and I'm fresh out of paper bags." She heard his footsteps come closer. "You afraid of the dark?"

"No." Her voice still had little sound.

"Well, not to worry," Jack said as if he didn't believe her. "The storm must have knocked out the town's transformer, but we have a generator. It'll kick on in a minute or two."

He came closer still, and she caught his scent. He smelled like coffee and chocolate cake. "Did your car break down?"

Alana's teeth started to chatter. And she glanced back at the door to make sure the guard wasn't there. "Someone was following me."

Even though she couldn't see his reaction, she could feel it. He tensed and hurried past her to go to the door. "I don't see anyone," he said, looking out. "Is that your car parked out front?"

"No."

She was about to explain, but something else about him changed. The silence was heavy, making it easier to hear him draw his gun.

"I'm pretty sure the license plate matches a vehicle

that was reported stolen just about an hour ago," he informed her. "The owner said the person who stole it—a woman—should be considered armed and dangerous. I'm guessing you're that woman, huh?"

Her heart jolted. Dizziness came again, and she had to lean against the wall to keep from falling.

This was certainly a complication Alana hadn't expected. That guard had some nerve to report his car stolen after he'd held her captive. And better yet—to call her armed and dangerous. The guard had been the one with the gun.

"I did steal the car," she admitted. "But I had to. They were holding me captive."

"They?" It was his cop's voice. Laced with skepticism and authority.

"A guard and a nurse. I don't know their names, but I can describe them." Well, she could if she didn't pass out first. "They held me at a house in the woods for…a long time. But I escaped."

"How'd you manage to do that?" He didn't believe that, either. She could tell from his tone.

"I spit out some of the meds they always gave me at night. And I pretended to fall asleep. Then I sneaked out of my bedroom, grabbed the guard's keys and ran. I drove away before he could stop me. But there must have been another car somewhere on the grounds, and he used it to come after me."

Jack Whitley made a sound that could have meant anything. "I need you to turn around and place your hands flat against the wall."

"You're arresting me?" She clamped her teeth over her bottom lip to keep it from shaking. Too bad she couldn't do something to stop the rest of her body from trembling. Mercy, she was freezing.

"I'm placing you in custody," he corrected, "until I can get this straightened out. Go ahead. Hands on the wall. I need to search you."

Alana had no idea what else to do, so she complied. The painted concrete block wall was smooth against her palms, and she rested her head against it, as well, hoping it'd help her think straight.

The overhead fluorescent lights crackled on, and she heard him walk closer. "Legs slightly apart," he ordered. "And don't make any sudden moves."

Alana held her breath while he ran his left hand over her wet cotton nightgown. Down her bare legs, all the way to her equally bare feet. He repeated the process on the inside of her legs and thighs. She made a slight involuntary hitching sound when the back of his hand brushed her *there*. It was a reminder for her that she wasn't wearing any panties.

The sheriff made a similar sound, but his was more of surprise. Maybe now he'd believe that she had truly escaped with literally just the gown on her back.

"I think you've got a fever," he let her know. "You might be sick."

A fever. That might explain why she felt so horrible.

"Turn around, slowly," he said, his voice a little gentler now. "We'll go into my office, and you can sit down. If you're not feeling better after a few minutes, I can drive you to the hospital and have your temperature checked."

Alana did turn, but she kept her weight against the wall in case her legs gave way. She got her first good look at the man she had thought she could trust. Now she wasn't so sure.

It was Jack Whitley all right.

She recognized that midnight-black hair. Those intense gunmetal-blue eyes. He wore jeans and a white shirt with his badge clipped onto a wide leather belt with a rodeo buckle. Definitely a cowboy cop in both appearance and attitude.

"I told you the truth about being held hostage," Alana insisted.

But if he heard her, there was no indication of it. His eyes widened, then narrowed. "Alana Davis?" he snarled.

"You remember me." The intense look in his eyes was scaring her.

"Yeah. I remember you."

Too bad she couldn't recall exactly what she'd done to rile him. And there was no mistaking that she'd done just that. "You helped me."

He glared at her. "Eight months ago, I pulled you from your car when you went over the bridge at Mill's Creek."

Yes. Images flashed through her mind. Icy water. She couldn't breathe. Trapped in her car. She tried to make the pieces fit and finally nodded. "You saved my life."

He didn't take his eyes off her. "And you ran away from the hospital the first chance you got. You didn't tell anyone why you were leaving or where you were going."

Alana didn't remember that at all. Why would she have done that?

"Look, I don't know what game you're playing, or

why you showed up here like this. But it doesn't matter," he stated. "You're not getting Joey back."

"Joey?" She shook her head.

That riled him even more. "Are you saying you don't remember him?"

Alana forced herself to concentrate on that name. *Joey.* But it meant nothing to her.

"I'm confused about some things. Not about being held captive," she admitted. "Or you rescuing me from my car eight months ago. I know those things happened. But I think this fever's making it hard for me to concentrate."

"Right." That was all he said for several long moments. "I'll call the doctor and see if he's still at the hospital," he grumbled.

Jack shoved his gun back into his shoulder holster, caught her arm and led her to his office. He put her in the chair adjacent to his cluttered desk, and snatched up the phone.

While Jack made a call to the doctor, Alana tried to force herself to think, to assemble the memories that were fragmented in her head.

Had she really left the hospital after Jack saved her?

"My brother," she mumbled. Then she groaned. Maybe her brother, Sean, had heard about her accident and had done what he usually did.

Taken over her life.

If she'd been incapacitated, he would have had her removed from the hospital. And yes, he would have done that without telling anyone, including the sheriff. Sean wouldn't have approved of the medical care, or lack thereof, that she might be getting in a small country hospital.

And had Sean then taken her to the house in the woods?

Probably not.

Alana leaned forward so she could lay her head on Jack's desk. There weren't many bare spots on the scarred oak, but there was plenty of stuff. A flyer showed a picture of a woman with the word *missing* beneath her name, Kinley Ford. Several old newspapers. An outdated chunky computer monitor, stacks of files, not one but two chipped coffee mugs, a half-eaten slice of chocolate cake on a saucer.

She saw the fax about the car she'd supposedly stolen and would have gotten angry all over again if she hadn't spotted a framed photograph of Jack holding a baby boy. The baby wore denim overalls, a miniature cowboy hat and red boots. Both Jack and the baby were grinning.

Staring at the baby, Alana reached for the picture, but Jack snatched it away from her and put it into his center desk drawer.

"The doctor's on his way here," he relayed the second he hung up the phone.

That was good. But it wasn't the doctor or her fever that had her attention now. It was the little boy in the picture. "Who's Joey?" she asked.

Jack Whitley cursed under his breath. "What the hell's the matter with you?"

She flinched at his hard tone. "The fever, I guess. But you already know that. Please tell me—who's Joey?"

For several long moments, he didn't say anything. Alana was afraid he might not tell her. For reasons she didn't understand, it was suddenly critical that she know.

"Joey's the baby you gave birth to eight months ago," Jack informed her.

"W-what?"

Jack leaned in and got right in her face. "Joey's the little boy you abandoned at Willow Ridge Hospital." He stabbed his index fingers at her. "And if you think you can get him back after all this time, then think again. Because Joey is *mine*."

Chapter 2

Jack felt as if someone had dropped a mountain on him.

The same woman who'd already given him the surprise of his life eight months ago on Christmas morning.

Alana Davis.

Now here she'd turned up again like a bad penny. Driving a stolen car and rattling off a story about being held captive.

A story he wasn't buying.

Alana had some explaining to do.

She didn't look much different now than she had when he'd fished her out of that frozen creek. She'd been wet then. Shivering, and scared, too.

Of course, she'd had a darn good reason to be scared. She'd nearly drowned and then had gone into shock and labor at the same time. It'd been a miracle that Jack hadn't had to deliver the newborn right there in the cab of his truck. Thankfully, he'd gotten her to the hospital and Dr. Bartolo in the nick of time.

"I had a baby?" Alana asked.

It was a question that confused and riled Jack. Of course, just about everything Alana had ever done had confused and riled him. Maybe it was the fever causing her to act this way. Maybe not. But it didn't matter. She'd made her decision about Joey the minute she walked out on him when he was barely a day old.

Now she'd have to live with that decision.

She couldn't have a lick of a claim to Joey. Jack had been the only father the little boy had ever known. He wouldn't lose him now, especially not to the mother who'd abandoned him, and Jack was certain he'd be able to convince a judge of that. She might have some legal rights as the birth mother, but those rights could be taken away.

"You don't remember giving birth to a baby," he said. Jack made sure it sounded as if he was accusing her of a Texas-size lie.

Tears sprang to her china-blue eyes, and her bottom lip trembled. She awkwardly swiped at her wet shoulder-length brown hair to push it away from her face. "Why are you saying this? Why are you telling these lies?" The tears and the trembling increased. "If I'd had a baby, I would have remembered."

But the stark fear on her pale face said differently.

"Oh, you had a baby all right. Six pounds, two ounces," he supplied.

She only shook her head.

And Jack saw something in those blue eyes that he hadn't wanted to see. Something familiar that he'd garnered from eight years of being the sheriff of Willow Ridge. The harsh reaction of a woman who just might be telling the truth.

Oh, hell.

Groaning, he sank down in his chair and stared at her. "While we're waiting for the doctor, maybe we should start from the beginning," he suggested. Somehow, he had to make sense of all of this and arrest her for auto theft or send her on her way. "You said you remember your car going into the creek?"

Alana nodded. "I remember that. You pulled me onto the muddy bank and gave me mouth-to-mouth resuscitation. You saved my life."

So far, so good. "And then you went into labor."

Silence. For a long time. He could see the worry lines bunch up her forehead. "I don't remember that part." It seemed to break her heart to say it.

It damn near broke Jack's, too. Of course, he had more at stake than she did. Joey was his son in every way that mattered. And he wouldn't ever turn his back on that little boy the way Alana had.

"I took you to the hospital that day," Jack continued, wondering what he was going to do if he actually jogged her memory. "We got there, and you had the baby on the way into the examining room."

He watched those blue eyes to see if there was any recollection of that. But there didn't seem to be any. Only more tears. Disgusted with the sympathy those tears were producing in him, he grabbed a handful of tissues from his desk drawer and shoved them at her.

"Wipe your eyes," he insisted.

She did. It didn't help, though. More tears followed.

So did a helpless-sounding throaty moan. "Why don't I remember? Why?"

"To hell if I know. You didn't seem to have a memory problem when you were there at the hospital." But even then, he'd thought there was something fishy about her story of how she'd gotten into the creek. Or what she was doing in Willow Ridge in the first place.

Alana stared at him. Blinked. "Maybe I had amnesia from the accident."

Now it was Jack's turn to shake his head. "The doctor thoroughly examined you. No head trauma. No trauma of any kind except for a bruise on your shoulder from the seat belt. I never heard of a seat belt bruise causing amnesia."

"Emotional stress, then." She sounded desperate to come up with an explanation, any explanation, of why she'd done something so despicable.

"You were fine after the delivery." Jack didn't bother to answer nicely. Every moment with her was like another mountain falling on him. "You even filled out the hospital paperwork."

Including the birth certificate.

"You nursed Joey," he continued. "Ate Christmas dinner that my aunt Tessie brought in for you. You slept a few hours. And then a little after one in the morning, you sneaked out of the hospital."

She repeated that last sentence under her breath. A moment later, a spark flared across those blue irises. "That must have been when the guard and the nurse kidnapped me."

Jack didn't bother to suppress a groan. So they were back to that story. Of course, he couldn't completely dismiss it. After all, she was sitting in his office wearing just a nightgown. A wet one at that.

The flimsy cotton clung to her breasts. It was so clingy that he could see her nipples.

He got up, grabbed a raincoat from his closet and put it over her so that it covered the entire front of her body. For reasons he didn't understand or care to explore, seeing her breasts reminded him that she was a woman. An attractive one at that.

Jack didn't want to think about that.

He only wanted to remember that this was the person who could destroy him. All because of DNA. As far as Jack was concerned, she was just an egg donor, nothing more.

"Willow Ridge might be a hayseed town to a city girl like you, but we still have a few amenities," he explained. "Like a security camera in the hospital parking lot, for instance. That camera photographed you leaving the hospital *alone*. No guard. No nurse. Definitely no indication of a kidnapping. You left of your own free will and without anyone's coercion or assistance."

And he should know. He'd studied the tape hundreds of times trying to figure out what the devil had happened.

"You mean I left alone in the dead of winter?" she clarified. There was strong skepticism in her frail voice, and she waited until he confirmed that with a frosty nod. "Did I get into a car?"

Now, here was the confusing part. "No. You just walked away."

Jack still had that image of her in his mind, too. Wearing the bleached-out green hospital gown, cotton robe and flip-flops, she'd walked out of the front of the one-story hospital, and stumbled on the sidewalk. The cold wind had whipped at her nightclothes and her hair. She'd looked unsteady.

She'd staggered several more times as she made her way through the parking lot.

There'd only been one clear shot of her face that night.

Jack would never forget it.

It was the same frightened, tearstained, shell-shocked face that was staring back at him now.

"You said the baby's name is Joey?" she asked.

All of his muscles went stiff. He didn't want to discuss Joey with her. But he also knew he didn't have a choice. Eventually, he had to give her enough details to satisfy her curiosity so he could get her out of there.

"You named him," he reminded her.

Another blink. "Did I?"

He couldn't contain his smirk, but beneath it, his concerns were snowballing. "You did. You said you named him after your kid brother who died when you were a child." And he braced himself.

Alana hugged his raincoat closer to her. "I remember my little brother, Joey. And I remember I was wearing a green hospital gown and robe when I woke up at the house in the woods."

Jack actually welcomed the change in subject, even though he knew it could only be temporary.

Eventually she'd ask more about Joey.

"What else do you remember about the house, the guard and the nurse?" he asked.

She hesitated a moment. "Everything, I think. It was December twenty-sixth when I woke up in that house.

So I must have been there all this time." Alana's eyes met his. "Why did they hold me captive?"

Jack shrugged. "You're the only one who'll be able to answer that."

Their eyes stayed connected until she lurched at the sound of the front door opening. Because he was on edge, Jack automatically reached for his gun and went to the door. But the gun wasn't necessary. The tall, lanky visitor was Dr. Keith Bartolo.

"Doc's here," Jack relayed to Alana, only because she looked ready to jump out of her skin.

"Jack," the doctor grumbled. He pulled off his rain-beaded felt hat, and with his leather medical bag gripped in his right hand, he made his way down the hall.

Jack had known the doctor most of his life, since the man had moved to Willow Ridge over twenty-three years ago and set up a practice. Jack also knew when Bartolo wasn't in a good mood. Apparently, the fiftysomething-year-old doc didn't like being called out after hours during a storm. Jack knew how the man felt. He rarely worked late these days because of Joey, but here he was at ten thirty going a second round with Alana Davis when he was supposed to be finishing up paperwork so he could take the weekend off.

"You said you had a sick prisoner," Dr. Bartolo prompted. He headed in the direction of the lone jail cell at the far end of the hall.

"She's in my office," Jack corrected.

The doctor lifted a caramel-brown eyebrow, and Jack stepped to the side so the man could enter. The doc and Alana looked at each other, and Jack didn't know which one of them was more surprised.

Alana swallowed hard. "I know you."

"Of course you do." Dr. Bartolo stared at her. "I was the attending physician when Jack brought you to the hospital last Christmas."

That was it. Apparently that was all the bedside manner he intended to dispense. The doctor plopped his bag onto Jack's desk, unzipped it and pulled out a digital thermometer. After putting a plastic sleeve over the tip, he stuck it in Alana's mouth.

"Why is she a prisoner?" the doctor asked as the thermometer beeped once.

"She stole a car."

Even though Alana didn't say anything out loud, her eyes said plenty. Jack could almost hear her giving him a tongue-lashing. Yes, she'd stolen the car. She'd admitted that. But according to her, it'd been to escape.

So, was it true?

He could check with the sheriff who'd posted the stolen car report and get the name of the person who had filed the claim. That would lead him to Alana's so-called guard. Jack hoped this wasn't some kind of lovers' quarrel. But he immediately rethought that. Maybe that would be the best solution for him. Find whoever was behind this so she could drop the amnesia act.

If it *was* an act.

The thermometer made a series of rapid beeps. Dr. Bartolo pulled it from her mouth and looked at the tiny screen. "Your temp's just a little over a hundred. Not too high. Any idea what's wrong with you?"

She shook her head.

"Okay." Dr. Bartolo didn't appear to be any more convinced of that than Jack did of her amnesia story. He flicked the plastic disposable tip into the trash and placed the thermometer back into his bag. "Are you taking any meds?"

Alana glanced at Jack. "No."

Jack frowned. "She said a guard and a nurse gave her some sedatives, and they'd been doing that for some time now," he explained. And he didn't think she'd forgotten that already. Her eyes narrowed slightly as if she hadn't wanted to share that information with the doctor.

"Sedatives?" the doctor questioned. "What kind?"

She shook her head again, causing Jack to huff. Before the doctor's arrival, she'd been chatty, so why hush now? "The kind of sedatives that might cause memory loss," Jack provided. "Or not. She could be making that part up."

That caused some concern in the doctor's eyes. "If there's a possibility of memory loss, she needs to be hospitalized. I'd also need to do a tox screen to see if there's anything in her blood."

"Would a fever that low cause her to hallucinate?" Jack asked Dr. Bartolo. "Or could sedatives do that?"

He lifted his shoulder. "Not the fever but possibly the sedatives. Why? What makes you think she's hallucinating?"

"A couple of things, but we can try to figure out all of that at the hospital." And once he had more details, he'd have to deal with the stolen car issue. It was entirely possible that the sheriff of the town where the stolen car complaint was filed would come and take Alana back to face those charges.

Jack hated that he felt relief about that.

But he did. The sooner he got Alana Davis out of Joey's life, the better.

"I have to go to the bathroom," Alana announced,

standing. But she had to catch his desk to stop herself from falling. Or maybe it was all an act to get him to feel sorry for her.

"Across the hall." Jack pointed in that direction. Both Jack and the doctor watched her as she made her way into the tiny room.

"Okay," Dr. Bartolo said the moment the bathroom door closed. "What's this all about? Did she come back to town to try to get Joey from you?"

"I don't know." There was so much about this that didn't make sense. "She says she doesn't remember giving birth to him."

"Is that so?" Bartolo stayed quiet a moment. "I guess that means she can't or won't say why she left town the way she did."

"She says she doesn't remember that, either. But she does remember being taken captive after leaving the hospital." Jack paused to figure out how best to phrase this. "Is it possible she's crazy?"

"It's possible," the doctor readily agreed. "After all, most normal women wouldn't just abandon their newborn the way she did."

True. Her behavior here tonight hadn't convinced him that she was doing any better than she had been eight months ago.

"But maybe it's something equally obvious," the doctor continued. "Maybe she's broken the law. Maybe she's a criminal, and she's telling you she has memory loss to cover up something else."

Jack mulled that over and cursed.

He bolted toward the bathroom. The door was locked, of course. So he pounded on it. "Alana, open up!"

Nothing.

Not so much as a sniffle.

Though he was riled enough to bash down the door, he resisted. Because he knew it wouldn't do any good. There was a small window in the bathroom, and if his instincts were right, Alana had already used it, to escape.

Jack raced down the hall, past the jail cell and headed for the rear exit. It was raining harder now, but that didn't slow him down. He ran to the east exterior side of the building, to the sliver of an alleyway that separated the sheriff's office from City Hall. The narrow space was made even narrower by a dark green Dumpster stuck right in the middle. And it was pitch black.

Someone screamed.

Alana.

With his heart pounding now, he drew his gun and raced around the Dumpster. Jack spotted her white nightgown. She appeared to be struggling with someone.

"What's going on?" he called out.

Just like that, the struggle stopped, and Alana fell back against the wall. Hard. She stayed on her feet and pointed in the opposition direction from where he was standing.

Jack thought he heard footsteps, but he couldn't be sure because of the pounding rain. Keeping his gun ready just in case, he went to her.

"Did you see him?" Alana asked.

"See who?" Jack automatically looked around.

"It was the guard from the house," she said, still pointing. "He was trying to make me go back."

Jack heard another sound.

A car engine.

He sprinted to the alley opening that led to Main Street, and stopped just short of the sidewalk. Using the sheriff's office for cover, he glanced around the corner.

A dark-colored car sped away.

Mud or something had been smeared over the license plate, and he couldn't even get a glimpse of the driver because of the heavily tinted windows and the darkness.

It was possible the driver was just a visitor. Some innocent guy who was in the wrong place at the wrong time. But just in case, Jack turned to get his patrol car. He simply wanted to ask the driver a few questions. But then he looked back and saw Alana, just as she collapsed on the ground.

Chapter 3

Alana heard voices. They were only whispers at first. But they became clearer within just a few seconds.

She didn't open her eyes. Not yet. She waited, listening, trying to figure out what was going on.

Was it safe?

Or did she need to be prepared to run again?

Judging from the sterile smell and the feel of the bed beneath her, she wasn't back at the house in the woods. Nor was she in the alley next to the sheriff's office. She was in a hospital. And the voice, at least one of them, belonged to Jack Whitley. He was talking to Dr. Bartolo.

She peeked out. Definitely a hospital. The walls and bedding were stark white, and there was an IV in the back of her hand. Sunlight threaded through the blind slats and onto the thermal blanket that covered her.

Neither the guard nor the nurse who'd held her captive was there. Everything felt safe. Which was a facade, of course. It wasn't safe unless Jack had caught the guard after he'd attacked her in the alley.

Maybe he had.

The last thing she remembered before losing consciousness was Jack going after him. If he'd succeeded, then perhaps the nightmare was over.

Well, part of it, anyway.

There was still the issue of her son.

Her mind no longer felt like sludge, and Alana didn't have to think hard to remember everything. She was a jewelry designer. Born and raised in San Antonio. One sibling, her older brother, Sean. She had friends and a life that had disappeared eight months ago.

The day she went into labor.

She could recall each pain. Every moment. Including the birth of her precious son. She'd loved him instantly. A kind of love she hadn't thought was possible until she'd held him in her arms for the first time.

But there were blanks. The missing twenty-four hours of her life that followed the delivery. And even some of the time immediately before it. They were crucial gaps of time—she had no idea what had put her in that creek or what had happened to make her leave her newborn son and walk out into the cold December night. She only knew the end result. She'd been held captive, escaped and then nearly been killed again.

"You're awake," she heard Jack say. He walked closer, crammed his hands into the pockets of his jeans and stood over her.

He was still wearing the same clothes he'd had on the night before. And he hadn't shaved. A dark, desperado stubble covered his chin, and there were smudgy circles under his eyes. He probably hadn't slept.

"Why am I in the hospital?" she asked.

"The fever for one thing. It's gone now, but Dr. Bartolo thinks you had a virus of some kind. You also hit your head when you fell in the alley. He needed to check and make sure it wasn't serious. It's just a bad bump." He glanced at Dr. Bartolo on the other side of the room before his attention returned to her. "Don't you remember?"

She didn't have to think hard for those memories to flood through her. Plus, the left side of her head was throbbing. "Yes. I remember. I was trying to get away because I was scared of the doctor. *And you.* But you caught me. Did you catch the man, too?"

Jack shook his head. "Sorry."

Fear instantly returned. If the man had gotten to her once, he could get to her again. But Alana didn't think that was her biggest concern right now. There was something guarded about Jack's expression. For one thing, he wasn't glaring at her. In fact, he was treating her like a patient.

"Did you see the person who tried to grab me in the alley?" she wanted to know.

"Not really."

"It was the guard," Alana concluded, though she hadn't actually seen his face. "You'll have to find him."

Jack nodded, but it seemed to be a gesture to appease her. He eased his hands from his pockets, dragged a chair closer and sat down beside her bed.

Oh, no. She got a really bad feeling about this. He was obviously about to have a heart-to-heart chat with her.

"After I got you to the hospital last night, I called your brother, Sean, in San Antonio," Jack explained. "Do you remember him?"

"Of course," she said after she got her teeth unclenched. Great. Just great. Now her overly protective big brother knew everything she'd told Jack. But that also meant that Sean had known she'd been held captive.

He was probably already on his way to Willow Ridge.

Sean would powerhouse his way into the hospital and try to take over. His goal would be to get her away from there so he could convince her that she didn't want to try to claim her son.

"I remember almost everything," Alana mumbled. Including her brother's objection to her being pregnant. Sean had hated the fact that she planned to become a single mom. Not because he was truly concerned about the challenges that might bring, but because of appearances. He believed their conservative business associates would think less of Alana and therefore think less of their company and him. Plus, Sean had also expressed concern that Alana's focus might be on a child and not solely on her career.

"Good." Jack followed that with a crisp nod. "I'm glad you're getting your memory back."

She'd been ready to try to get out of the bed, but that stopped her. "Good?" Alana contested. "Okay, what's wrong?"

He scrubbed his hand over his face. "You recall why you walked out of here eight months ago?"

Alana hated to admit this, but she had no choice. If she told Jack as much as she knew, he might be able to help her put the pieces together. "No. But I know I gave birth to Joey. And I know I love him. I also want to see him. Now."

Jack stayed quiet a moment. "That wouldn't be a good idea. You have a virus, remember, and in case it's something more, it'll be another ten hours or so before the antibiotics take full effect. You wouldn't want to make him sick, would you?" His tone was sympathetic enough, but there was a lot of emotion and anger simmering right beneath the surface.

"Oh, I get it," Alana grumbled. "My brother told you to be nice to me."

"Among other things," Jack admitted. "He's coming to take you home."

Alana wanted to curse. "How much time do I have before Sean gets here?"

"An hour. Maybe two. He said he'd be here around noon, and it's a little after ten right now."

She sat up. "I don't want him to see me like this. And I don't want to go with him."

Jack caught her arm and eased her back down onto the bed. "Sean told me that Joey's birth father was dead."

That clenched her teeth again. "You obviously had a long conversation."

"We did. But Sean and I had that particular discussion eight months ago when I was trying to track you down."

Everything inside her went still. She hadn't thought of it sooner, but of course Jack would have tried to find her. Too bad he hadn't. It would have saved her eight months of captivity, and that was just the beginning.

It had also cost her time with her precious baby. She'd missed so much already.

Too much.

She wouldn't miss any more.

"Sean didn't know why you ran off the way you did," Jack continued. "But he had a theory. He thought it was because you were clinically depressed."

Maybe. But that didn't feel right, either. "Depressed, why?"

"Because of the death of Joey's birth father, Neil Franklin."

She shook her head. "My relationship with Neil had been over for months before he died. In fact, I ended things with him when I learned I was pregnant and he said he didn't want to be a father."

There were no gaps in those particular memories, including the big blowup when Neil had even questioned if he was indeed the father of her unborn child. That accusation had been more than enough to cause Alana to walk out. But then she'd had to listen to months of her brother saying "I told you so" and trying to pressure her to give the child up for adoption.

And then all those memories collided with her present situation.

"Why all these questions about Sean and Neil? Did Sean do something to get me to abandon Joey here at the hospital? Is that why I left?" she demanded.

Jack didn't jump to deny it. Nor did he confirm it, either. He took his time answering, and the moment he opened his mouth, his phone rang. He jerked it from his pocket as if he'd been expecting an important call.

"I have to take this," he said, and he got up, stepped outside and shut the door.

Alana wanted to listen to his conversation—it might pertain to her. But Dr. Bartolo put her chart aside and walked closer. "I got your lab results back. You had traces of a drug called Rohypnol in your system."

"Rohypnol," she repeated. "The date rape drug?"

The doctor nodded and must have noticed that she was on the verge of panicking. "You weren't sexually assaulted," he continued. He reached over and began to remove the IV. "But there was enough of the drug in your system to explain your memory loss."

God knows how many doses of the Rohypnol she'd been given. The nurse and guard had forced her to take it almost daily. She was certain of that. What Alana wasn't certain about was discussing it with the doctor. For some reason, she didn't trust him. Had he done something to make her feel this way? Or was she just being paranoid?

If so, she had a reason for the paranoia. Someone had also tried to take her from that alley. He'd grabbed her, hard, and was dragging her away when Jack arrived.

"I delivered your son," the doctor added a moment later.

"Yes." She studied his body language. His forehead was bunched. His breathing, short and a little rough. "I don't suppose you know why I left the hospital?"

She expected a quick denial. But it didn't come. His breathing got even shorter. "You said some things when you were in labor. Maybe it means nothing. But you said someone had run you off the road."

Alana forced her mind to the crash. The images were all there. Cold and crisp. Images of her in her car in the water. But nothing of what'd happened moments before impact.

"I told Jack what you said, and he checked out the creek road again," the doctor explained. "He didn't find any tread marks or any other sign to indicate that you had slammed on the brakes or swerved to miss going into the creek."

"That proves nothing. Someone could still have been after me," she quickly pointed out. She winced a little when he pulled the IV needle from her hand.

"You're right." He dabbed the IV puncture with some cotton and then slipped a bandage over it. "Something sure had you spooked. You remember what that was?"

This suddenly felt like an interrogation. Or a threat to remind her that remembering wouldn't be a good idea.

Alana shook her head. "I don't know. Do you?"

His head jerked back a little in a gesture of surprise. "Of course not. I told Jack everything that went on and everything you said to me."

She wasn't so sure. "What else did I say?"

"Some of it was rambling," he readily answered. But he didn't say anything for several moments. "I got the feeling you were withholding information, that you were in some kind of trouble. Were you?"

Probably. But she kept that to herself.

Alana went back through those memory gaps. If someone had indeed run her off the road, then something had happened to precipitate it. Maybe it was as simple as a case of road rage. Some hotheaded driver had cut her off and caused the accident.

Yes, that was possible. Better than the alternative.

But why hadn't there been any sign of her slamming on the brakes? And what had she been doing in Willow Ridge?

"When you were in labor, you mentioned an important meeting," the doctor continued. He took her chart and jotted down something on it. He didn't look at her. He kept his focus on whatever he was writing. "Guess you don't remember that, either?"

She didn't, and even though Alana tried hard to recall any details about that, she drew a blank.

"An important meeting," Dr. Bartolo repeated. "Maybe it had something to do with your job?"

This chat was making her more uncomfortable by the minute. She looked around in case she needed an escape route. But that wasn't necessary. Jack came back through the door.

Alana cursed the relief she felt at seeing him. For some reason, she trusted him. However, he didn't extend much trust to her. He shoved his phone back into his pocket and stared at her. He didn't sit or offer her any more pseudo sympathy.

"You're looking at me as if I'm crazy," she said.

"Sorry." But he kept staring at her. "Do the names Ted Moore and Margaret Vargas ring any bells?"

"No. Should they?"

"Yeah." He paused. A long time. "They should."

Mercy. Was this another blank spot in her memory? If so, it must be a critical one. "Do they have something to do with Joey?"

"Not really." Jack nodded at the doctor, a gesture the two of them must have understood, because the doctor excused himself and left the room.

This conversation must be about to turn ugly.

And then it hit her. A horrible thought. "Did the man in the alley go after Joey?"

"No. Joey's fine."

But she didn't believe him. "I have to see him. I have to make sure he's okay. And don't remind me about this virus. I don't have to get close to him to make sure he's safe."

He clamped his hand on her arm when she tried to get up. "You aren't going to see him, Alana."

Alana pushed his hand away. "You have no legal right to keep my son from me."

"Wanna bet?"

She froze. Because that didn't sound like an idle threat. "What does that mean?"

"It means when you filled out the birth certificate, you listed me as the father."

Had she? Yes. She had. Why, though, she didn't know. "But you're not his father and a DNA test will prove that."

"Biologically, Joey's not my son, but he is legally. When we couldn't find you, I petitioned the courts for custody, and since your brother, Sean, was Joey's next of kin, he agreed. He gave me sole guardianship."

She clenched her hands tightly. Alana didn't doubt that Sean had done this. He'd never wanted her to have the baby. "Well, I can change that. I can petition the courts, too—"

"No judge will give you custody, Alana."

Again, it wasn't an empty threat. He had something to back it up. "Why not?"

"Because you weren't held captive. The guard and the nurse I mentioned. Ted Moore and Margaret Vargas. They've contacted law enforcement agencies to report your disappearance."

Alana shook her head. She didn't understand. "My disappearance?"

"More like your escape," Jack clarified. "Alana, you were declared insane. For the past eight months you've been confined to a private mental institution."

Chapter 4

Alana didn't have much color in her cheeks, but Jack's announcement drained what little she did have. She swallowed hard and eased her head back onto the pillow. Her eyelids fluttered down.

She looked beaten and overwhelmed.

Jack knew exactly how she felt.

For eight months, he'd dreaded Alana's return, but with each passing day, it'd been easier and easier for him to convince himself that she wouldn't come back. That she wouldn't fall back into his life and try to claim Joey.

Yet here she was. A force to be reckoned with. A woman to fear. He should be bracing himself to do battle. But unfortunately, like her he was feeling overwhelmed himself. And empathy was starting to creep into this equation. But that wasn't the only problem.

There was this physical pull he had for her.

He was sure those two emotions were connected. That, and the fact that Alana was attractive. It would have been hard not to notice that about her. But empathy and attraction could cause him to lose focus. That, in turn, could cause him to lose Joey.

"So now I'm crazy," she mumbled. Alana chuckled, but there was no humor in it. She opened her eyes and blinked back tears. "I'm not crazy, Jack. I'm not."

He didn't want to offer an opinion on that. Instead, it was best to go ahead and put everything out in the open. "There was a court order committing you to the institution."

Her gaze slashed to his, and she swiped the tears from her face. "I want to see it."

He nodded. "It's being faxed." He wanted to see it, as well.

"And I want to speak to Ted Moore and Margaret Vargas. I want them to explain why they gave me a date rape drug. That's hardly the medication a reputable institution would dispense to a so-called patient."

Jack knew about the drug. Dr. Bartolo had already told him. He wanted to ask that same question himself. In fact, he wanted to ask Ted and Margaret a lot of questions.

Because something wasn't adding up.

More than anything, he needed Alana's situation to make sense. If she was legally insane, then he could send her back to an institution. She wouldn't be able to take Joey. He didn't relish the thought of Alana being crazy, but he was desperate to hang on to his son.

But as a lawman, he also needed the truth.

He cursed himself. This need for justice had been

an obsession most of his life, and it'd had devastating consequences. His own father was in prison because of it, and while most would say that the man deserved to be behind bars, Jack would always remember that it was his testimony that had turned the key to his father's prison cell.

"Margaret was the one who had the authorities put out an APB on you," Jack explained. "She's also the one who'll be faxing the court order."

She stared up at the ceiling, and her mouth tightened. "Let me guess. My brother initiated that court order? He's the one who had me sent to that place."

"I'm not sure." But it was a darn good guess. When Jack had met Sean eight months earlier, the man had made it crystal clear that he didn't want Alana raising Joey. Sean thought she was not "emotionally equipped" to be a single parent. Still, it seemed extreme that Sean would have his sister committed. Unless he truly thought she was insane. Then, Sean might have wanted to hide her away so she wouldn't be a liability to their business and so she could discretely get some help.

"Margaret didn't know where Ted was," Jack added. "She said she hasn't seen him since last night when he went after you."

"Well, I know where he was. He was in that alley. He tried to hurt me."

Jack didn't dispute that. But he was sure, though, that his body language was suggesting some doubt. "See, that's one of the things that doesn't add up. The APB was out there. Plus, you were right next to a sheriff's office. If it'd been Ted in that alley, he would have just walked inside and asked me for assistance." He paused. "And I would have given it to him."

"So, who do you think it was in the alley?" she demanded.

A hallucination caused by the fever and the drugs already in her system. Except Jack had seen that car with the mud-smeared plates. Still, a strange car didn't mean this Ted had tried to grab her.

"If Ted had come to apprehend you, why would he have run?" Jack asked. "He had a court order to keep you confined. The law was on his side, not yours."

Another punch of frustration rushed through her eyes. "Maybe that court order isn't worth the paper it's being faxed on."

"Maybe. That's one of the things I might be able to determine when I see the document."

And when he questioned Ted and Margaret. Whenever that would be. The woman hadn't exactly volunteered to come to Willow Ridge, which meant Jack would have to make a trip to the Sauder Mental Health Facility about an hour's drive away. Margaret hadn't been chatty about the exact location, claiming that the place was private to prevent the media from finding it and the occasional famous patients who entered the facility for drug rehab.

Margaret's explanation had made him even more uneasy. But he couldn't go until he had things stabilized with Alana. Fortunately, he'd already gotten Ted and Margaret's photos from the online database of drivers' licenses, and he'd run computer checks. Neither had criminal records, but Jack had asked his deputy to do a little digging to see if anything flagged.

"When the fax arrives," Alana continued, "I want

you to read that court order word for word. I'll do the same. But first, I'll have to battle my brother." She lifted her head from the pillow again, and this time she pushed his hand away when he tried to stop her. "I need some clothes. I don't want Sean to see me like this. I'm sure I look frail and weak. It'll only give him more ammunition to try to have me recommitted."

Jack couldn't argue with that, but Alana wasn't ready to be up and moving around. Still, he didn't stop her. "I can't guarantee the doctor will let you leave the hospital, but I'll see what I can do about getting you something else to wear."

She'd gathered up the blanket to drape around her. Her gaze met his. "Thank you."

He didn't want her thanks. He didn't want empathy. He didn't want to feel that she was getting railroaded.

But he did.

Damn it. He did.

Jack stepped outside the room, and welcomed the moment he had to himself. He didn't usually have trouble being objective, especially since Alana was officially part of an investigation now. But she was also a huge threat to his happiness. That was coloring his objectivity.

When he spotted Sara Murphy, a nurse and a woman he'd known his entire life, he walked up the hall to her. "Could you possibly scrounge up some street clothes for the patient?" Jack hitched his thumb toward Alana's door.

Sara nodded and shifted a pink wad of sugary-scented gum in her mouth so she could answer him. "Sure will." She volleyed her doe-brown eyes between

Jack and the door. "I heard what's going on, and I'm sorry. She's here to try to take little Joey, isn't she?"

Jack settled for saying, "It's complicated."

"Not so complicated. You love that boy. Everybody around here knows that." Sara patted his arm. "Have you learned anything more about the night she wandered out of the hospital?"

"No."

Sara glanced around as if to make sure no one was listening, and stepped closer. "Look, I'm on your side. I don't want that woman back here. But you know I've had my worries about her from the start."

Yeah. He did. He'd interviewed Sara several times. "You don't think Alana left the hospital voluntarily that night eight months ago."

"And I still don't. I saw her an hour before she disappeared, and she was fit as a fiddle. She talked about Joey, about their future together. She was talking about taking Mommy and Me classes, for heaven's sake." Sara shook her head. "And then bam! an hour later, she walks out into the freezing night without giving a second thought to leaving her baby behind."

Since it'd been a while since those interviews, Jack asked the obvious. "You're sure you didn't see anyone go into Alana's room that night?"

She flexed her eyebrows. "Just Doc Bartolo."

There it was again. That same punch of doubt that had come eight months ago. Dr. Bartolo had been the last credible person to see Alana. She'd been fine, he insisted. Since the doctor had never given Jack a reason to distrust him, he'd believed him.

Except there was a niggling doubt in the back of

his mind. Jack had discovered that looking at Joey had dimmed those doubts.

"You did the right thing, taking that baby the way you did," Sara insisted.

Did I? Jack asked himself.

Thankfully, he didn't pose that question to Sara. He spotted Deputy Reyes Medina making his way down the hall toward him. At six-three and well over two hundred pounds, Reyes was impossible to miss. He had the face and the coloring of his Comanche ancestors, but his expression was all cop. He walked, looked and talked as if he were ready to kick someone's butt into the next county.

It took Jack a moment to realize Reyes wasn't alone. He saw something behind the deputy, and after Reyes moved a little to the side, Jack got another surprise he didn't want.

His aunt Tessie was there, and she was holding Joey.

Jack groaned some ripe profanity. This was not the place he wanted his son.

"I'll get those clothes for Ms. Davis," Sara mumbled, excusing herself.

Jack heard her, but he didn't respond, instead making a beeline for his aunt.

"Is it true?" Tessie asked. She'd obviously dressed in a hurry. No makeup, not that she wore much anyway. Her salt-white hair was in disarray, and her Coke-bottle-green eyes were wide with concern. "Is that woman really here in the hospital?"

Jack caught her arm to stop her from moving any closer to Alana's room. "She's here. I was going to tell you, but I haven't had a chance."

Unlike Reyes and Tessie, Joey wasn't showing much

concern. He grinned from ear to ear and reached for Jack. Jack pulled his son into his arms and gave himself a moment to be a father. He could have sworn his blood pressure dropped to normal. The knot in his stomach eased up. And for a few precious seconds, all was right with the world.

"I told Tessie she shouldn't be here," Reyes grumbled.

Tessie started her defense before Reyes finished the last word of his sentence. "I wanted to see her. I want to make her understand that she can't come back after all these months and take Joey."

"It's not a good time to do that," Jack countered. He couldn't tell Tessie that Alana would try to take Joey. Jack didn't even want to say the words aloud.

There was a sound behind him, and judging from Tessie's and Reyes's reactions, Jack knew what it was. He quickly handed Joey to Tessie. "Take him home please."

She nodded but kept her attention fastened to the other end of the hall. One glance over his shoulder confirmed that Alana was there, standing in the doorway of her room. She had the blanket draped around her like a robe and was looking at Joey. She started toward him.

"The virus," Jack reminded her. "You'll make him sick."

Alana froze. Thank God. If it hadn't been for her illness, Alana would have tried to wrench Joey from Tessie's arms. Joey would have been confused. Frightened. And the contact would no doubt have given Alana even more determination to take the child she'd given birth to.

Tessie turned and hurried back toward the exit. Jack

went to Alana, to make sure she stayed put. When he reached her, he saw her tears, even though she was doing her level best to blink them away.

"He's so beautiful," she whispered, her attention still focused over his shoulder where Tessie had been standing just seconds earlier.

"Yes, he is."

"Joey has my hair color." She touched her fingers to her own saddle-brown locks. "What about his eyes? What color are they?"

"Blue." Like Alana's. Jack didn't volunteer that, though. His heart already felt as if it were being crushed.

"Blue," she repeated with a determined nod. "I'm seeing him tomorrow." It wasn't a request. "The medicine will have kicked in. I won't be contagious. I'll see my baby."

Jack was already trying to figure out a way to stop that. Or a way for him to deal with what might be inevitable. Because even if Alana was sent back to that institution, it didn't mean she was out of the picture when it came to Joey. She'd hire a lawyer. She'd fight. And now that she knew she had a son, she wouldn't back down. But as the only father Joey had ever known, he wouldn't back down, either.

Reyes handed Jack some papers. The first was a fax with the photo of a woman. The FBI had already sent him her picture, and it was on his desk. "Kinley Ford?" Jack read aloud.

"She's the missing woman the Rangers and FBI are looking for. It's possible she's in the area."

Well, it wouldn't be the first time. Nine months ago Kinley Ford had been in town, and even though she hadn't been responsible, three people had been killed. It'd been one of the few murder cases Jack had ever had to handle, and he didn't want to have to deal with her now. "Does she have anything to do with Alana?"

"Not that I can tell, but a lot of people are anxious to find her. The FBI wants us to put flyers with her picture around town."

Jack intended to do that, but it would have to wait. He looked at the other papers Reyes had given him. Alana's commitment papers. With them were two black-and-white pictures. When Jack glanced at them, he remembered that Joey wasn't the only issue here.

"I got her commitment papers a little over an hour ago and made some calls," Reyes explained. "I'm trying to track down the judge who signed them."

Good. That was a start.

"I also showed those around." Reyes pointed to the photos of Ted Moore and Margaret Vargas. The deputy glanced at Alana.

"And?" Jack prompted, giving Reyes permission to go on.

"They just arrived in town. So did her brother, Sean. All three are in the hospital lobby."

"Here?" Jack and Alana said in unison. Apparently Margaret had decided to come to town after all.

Alana's tone was laced with anger. She seemed to welcome this unexpected visit. Jack did, too, in a way. But he wanted this meeting to happen at the sheriff's office since it would likely turn into an interrogation. Maybe even an arrest.

Reyes nodded. "Margaret said she left the institution as soon as she faxed the commitment papers to us. Said she figured it was best that she speak to Alana and you in person."

Jack wasn't so sure of that.

"I told them to wait in the lobby until I cleared everything with you," Reyes explained. "According to the pair, they didn't arrive with the brother. It's a coincidence that they're all here together at exactly the same time."

Jack wasn't a strong believer in coincidences. It could be that Sean had a reason to want to dissociate himself from the pair. Especially from Ted—the man might have crossed a legal line or two if he truly had gone after Alana the way she said he had.

"Before you see to them, I think you should know what I learned," the deputy went on. "When I showed those pictures around town this morning, the new waitress that Bella hired over at the diner said she saw that man, Ted, late last night."

"Where?" Jack asked, though he already suspected the answer.

"In front of your office. She said the guy came running out of the alley, jumped in his car and drove away. She said he looked like he was up to no good."

"He was," Alana assured them. She turned to him. "I told you."

So she had. Jack would have liked to explain the man's behavior. But he couldn't. Unless Ted was trying to cover up the fact that a patient had escaped and he didn't want to get in trouble for a security infraction. But that didn't make sense. Once the man realized he hadn't contained Alana, then why hadn't he stayed? Why get in his car and leave without alerting someone in the sheriff's office?

Jack heard the footsteps, looked up and realized he might not have to wait long for those answers. Sean and his guests hadn't stayed put in the lobby despite the deputy's order. They were coming up the hall, and judging from their expressions, they were there to take Alana back to the institution.

Of course, that led Jack to another question.

Was he going to let them?

Chapter 5

Alana knew she should be bracing herself for the meeting with her brother and the two people who'd held her captive. She should also be preparing for a fight in case Margaret and Ted attempted to apprehend her.

But she had trouble focusing.

The fever and drugs weren't to blame this time. Her thoughts were scattered. Only moments earlier she'd seen her son.

"Joey," she said under her breath.

Just that glimpse of him had been enough for her to know this child was hers. Love was instant. Strong. And she would use that love to give her strength. She would get her son back. But first, she had to deal with the three obstacles coming her way.

Four, she corrected.

Because Jack might turn out to be the biggest obstacle of all.

"Alana," her brother greeted, but there was no warmth in it. Not that she expected it from him. Sean was her only living brother, but over the years, they'd become more business partners than siblings. And because he was older, he had declared himself her boss and keeper.

"Why don't we take this into the room?" Jack suggested. He looked back at his deputy. "Stay close just in case."

Alana wasn't leaving with her brother, Margaret or Ted, and she would use physical force if necessary to stop them from taking her.

With the hulking deputy choosing to wait outside the door, they filed into her hospital room, each casting glances at her. She threw some glances right back at them.

"Where do I start?" she mumbled. She had a list of questions and accusations. She decided to begin with Ted because she could still feel his hands on her when he tried to grab her in the alley. "Explain what you were trying to do to me last night."

Ted's Adam's apple bobbed on his thin throat. It was the only thing thin about him. He had bulky shoulders and arms, and his shaved head made him seem even more fearsome. "I was trying to do my job and bring you back to the Sauder facility."

"So you admit you were here in Willow Ridge?" Jack asked.

"Of course. Ms. Davis is a patient, and it's my job to make sure she stays confined until the judge says differently. We were instructed that she could be a danger to herself and others."

That must have been Margaret's cue to bring out the paper she had tucked beneath her arm. Like Ted, Margaret was no lightweight. She was close to six feet tall and had an athletic build. There'd been times when Margaret had held her down and forced her to take the sedating drugs.

"And here's a notice from the judge that your confinement has *not* been terminated," Margaret announced. "I had him fax it to the hospital so I could show you." There was a victorious glimmer in her ice-gray eyes when she looked at Alana. "That means you're to be returned to Sauder immediately."

Alana wasn't unaffected by the threat. Other than Jack, and he was iffy, she didn't have an ally in the room.

Jack took the paper from Margaret and glanced over it. While he was doing that, Alana turned her attention to the biggest rat in the room, her brother.

As usual, Sean was dressed to perfection. Italian suit. A pair of those pricey leather shoes he had custom-made for him. Genetically, they looked alike with his light brown hair and blue eyes. But their personalities were as different as night and day.

Just being near him caused her blood to boil, and she had to fight to hang on to her temper. "You surrendered custody of my son to Jack. I'd like to know why."

He shrugged, showing no concern as to what he'd put her through. "Because I couldn't find you, and because I didn't want to raise the kid myself. Besides, I figured Jack would make a good father."

It was the flippant answer she'd expected. Still, it

329

didn't make it easier to hear, or accept. "So you had me locked up in a mental institution."

"Not me. I didn't do that."

"I don't believe you."

Another shrug. He slid his hands into his pants pockets. "Believe what you will, but I had nothing to do with it. I couldn't even find you, much less have you committed."

Strange. Her brother was a coldhearted jerk, but she hadn't known him to lie, even if he was good at it. But if he was telling the truth, then who had put her in that place?

"You have the judge's name?" she asked Jack.

"Marvin Pierce," he read from the paper that he'd taken from Margaret. "Ring any bells?"

"None." But there were a lot of confusing things about this situation. She turned back to Margaret. "Who paid for me to stay at the facility?"

"I don't know."

Jack spoke up before Alana could. "Then, I need the name of the facility's business manager."

Margaret shook her head. "I manage it and have done for the past eight months. Ms. Davis was our only patient, though I'd been informed that in the past, there were others. Some of them were celebrities who wanted to go through rehab while they hid from the paparazzi."

Alana obviously wasn't the only one who found it odd that she was the sole patient. Even her brother lowered his chin and angled a questioning glance at both Ted and Margaret. Jack did more than glance.

"Then who paid your salaries?" he asked.

Margaret looked at Ted before she answered. "All payments came from the Sauder Foundation. I just assumed Ms. Davis's family was paying the foundation for her residential care since there wasn't any paperwork for medical insurance."

"Not me, I wasn't paying," Sean volunteered. "If my sister had needed psychological help, I would have sent her to Europe. No need to announce that sort of thing to business associates and friends by keeping her in the state."

All of them looked at Alana. "Trust me, I didn't pay to have myself committed. I'd just given birth to a beautiful healthy baby boy. The only thing I wanted was to be with him. So I wouldn't have hired someone to lock me away."

Jack made a throaty sound of agreement. And she knew that cost him. He probably wanted nothing more than for these people to take her, but she was praying the lawman in him would want the truth. Even if the truth cost him custody of the child he'd raised.

"We have the paper to return her to the facility," Margaret reminded them. She stepped forward.

Jack blocked her path. "Alana can't leave. She's here because she's sick. She has a virus, and it's highly contagious."

Margaret dropped back a step. So did Ted. Sean stayed put, probably because he felt he was immune to such mundane things.

"I can take her home," her brother insisted. "She can receive medical treatment there."

"I don't want to go home." Alana took a deep breath to continue the fight, but it wasn't necessary.

"She's staying put," Jack interjected. "Once the doctor releases her, I'll give all three of you a call. We'll work something out."

Ted's mouth opened in a show of outrage. "But what if she escapes again?"

"She won't." Jack aimed a warning glare at her. "Now it's time for you all to leave so she can get some rest."

"But we have orders to take her back," Margaret protested.

Jack put his hands on his hips. "I'm the sheriff here. Hate to state the obvious, but I'm in charge, and the only way I'll release her to you is if that order has been signed by the governor or God. Since it isn't, you're leaving."

"We'll be back," Ted threatened, and he caught Margaret's arm and ushered her out of the room. The door swished closed behind them.

Her brother stayed put.

"I won't be so easily turned away," Sean commented. "We need to figure out what happens next." He didn't wait for them to answer. "My suggestion is to transfer you to another hospital. Maybe one out of state where you can get expert care and won't be under the prying eyes of small-town gossips."

"Gossips?" Alana repeated. "Sean, that's the least of my problems."

"Maybe. But it could be a big problem when word gets out that you might have taken a trip over the cuckoo's nest. Think of your business. Of your clients, who also happen to be mine. You won't keep those clients for long if they think they're dealing with a lunatic."

Sheez. He just didn't get it. "My jewelry designs don't mean much now."

"You say that, but while you've been gone, I've managed to sell nearly every piece you ever designed. To the *right* people. You've won awards, Alana, and if you're smart, you'll use your God-given talent to build on the business reputation I've boosted for you."

Alana couldn't help it. She laughed, even though she was not amused by any of this conversation. "For the past eight months, I've had my life and my son taken from me. If you've had any part in that, I'll never forgive you."

Sean spared her a final glance and looked at Jack. "When will she be well enough to travel?"

"Don't know. You'd have to ask Dr. Bartolo about that."

Sean apparently took that suggestion as gospel. Without so much as mumbling a goodbye, he turned and left.

Alana stood there, looking at the door, and trying to make sense of what'd just happened. Maybe, just maybe she was in the middle of a nightmare, and she would soon wake up to her son and her life. But the look in Jack's eyes confirmed that this was her reality.

"No matter what Dr. Bartolo says, I'm not going with Sean," Alana insisted.

Jack nodded, walked closer and caught her arm. It took Alana a moment to realize why he'd done that, and then she noticed she was shaking. Not just trembling. Actually shaking. He eased her into a sitting position on the bed and put his palm on her forehead.

"Is the fever back?" she asked. Part of her hoped it was because that would be an easy explanation, but she also needed to get well so she could stop whatever was about to happen to her.

"You're not hot."

She was punchy and ready to burst into tears. "I

don't think I've ever been so happy to hear a man say that to me."

The corner of his mouth lifted, and it changed his face. He looked even better than he usually did. Her son probably saw a lot of those smiles, and it made her wonder what kind of father Jack had been.

"I haven't thanked you," she said. Best to keep talking because she was afraid if she stopped that she'd fall apart. "For saving my life. For taking in my son. If you hadn't, Sean would have let him become a ward of the court. God knows what would have happened to him."

Jack just stared at her. "I don't need your thanks for taking Joey."

She'd jabbed at the wound again. She'd reminded him they were on opposite sides of a very important issue. "You're right. I'm sorry."

"I don't want your apology, either." He frowned. Cursed. Squeezed his eyes shut for a second and groaned. "Yeah, I'm taking shots at you only minutes after that tornado trio came barreling in through here and tried to tear you to pieces. But the truth is, I don't want to feel anything for you, Alana. Especially concern."

Concern. Well, at least he wasn't feeling this crazy physical attraction. "I could use some concern. And some help. Jack, I'm scared, and I know I shouldn't be admitting that to you. I should be trying to bluff you into thinking I'm strong enough to fight for custody."

He looked at her. Alana expected him to continue to snap at her. After all, she was as much of a threat to him as he was to her. But he didn't.

Jack reached out, put his fingers beneath her chin

and lifted it. It wasn't a hug, but it was as close to a comforting gesture as she could have hoped for.

"Careful. I have a virus, remember?" she whispered.

"Yeah, I remember. Just don't breathe on me."

Despite the grumbled warning, his touch was warm. Welcoming. And Alana didn't back away. She sat there and took everything he was offering.

Until there was a sharp rap at the door.

"Yeah?" he called out, and moved his hand. He moved his feet, too, and walked away from her.

The deputy opened the door and stuck in his head. "Just got a call about that commitment order. Thought you'd want to know."

Jack glanced at her, probably debating if this was news he wanted to hear in private.

"If this is about me, I have a right to hear it, too," Alana reminded him.

Jack seemed to consider that and then gave his deputy the nod.

"I checked out the judge, Marvin Pierce. I doubt he signed anything. The guy's been dead and buried for two years now."

Alana's heart began to race. Finally, there was some proof that she'd been railroaded, but that only created more questions.

"So, if he's dead, who signed the order that imprisoned me?" she asked.

The deputy shook his head. "Don't know that, *yet*. It could be a paperwork snafu of some kind. Maybe someone typed in the wrong judge's name when the file was logged into the computer."

That put a slight dent in the hope she'd just felt.

"Let me know as soon as you hear anything else," Jack instructed.

Reyes assured him that he would, and he shut the door.

Alana let out the breath she'd been holding. And then she studied Jack's expression. He didn't look as surprised and vindicated as she felt. "You suspected it might be a suspicious signature on those commitment papers?"

"I considered it." He paused and looked as if he wanted to be anywhere but there. "With all the other things that have happened, it'd be foolish for me not to be skeptical. Your unexplained departure from the hospital eight months ago. The date-rape drug Dr. Bartolo found in your blood. The incident in the alley last night, and Ted's strange way of trying to recapture you."

She continued to study that intense expression. "You're beginning to believe me."

He shrugged. Then nodded. Then shook his head. "I don't want to believe you, but I don't see how all of this could be aboveboard. Something's wrong. Still, that doesn't mean it's all wrong. The commitment papers could have been legal," he added.

In some small way, he believed her. And that meant he might help her.

Alana pushed harder and decided to ask for what she wanted most from him. "I need to see my son, Jack. *Please.*"

She sat there, waiting, and it seemed like an eternity before he finally nodded. "I'll let you see him. But there are some rules."

Alana silently cheered. She was willing to do what he asked. "Anything."

"You won't leave the hospital until the doctor releases you. No more attempts to escape."

"Agreed." Besides, there was no place she wanted to be other than with her son.

"I'll bring Joey here for a short visit. I don't want you holding him because of the virus."

That would be hard, but she wouldn't do anything to put Joey at risk. "What else?"

Jack looked her straight in the eye. "You won't take him from me."

She could have sworn that her heart stopped. "I can't agree to that."

"I mean, you won't do anything about the custody issue, not until I've discovered what the heck is going on."

"Sean probably set up that phony Sauder institution. He's the one who's behind all of this."

"Maybe. But until I have solid proof of that, I want you to promise me that you won't challenge me for custody. I can't handle that kind of distraction when I'm trying to work on this case."

Because she had no choice, she nodded. "But you know that eventually I *will* challenge you. I'll do whatever it takes to get him back."

"I know. And I'll do whatever it takes to stop you."

So they were at a stalemate. Well, sort of. Jack had the power. He had physical custody of her son. "Will you still bring Joey to see me?"

"Yes." Judging from the set of his jaw, it'd taken a lot for him to say that. "But I'm warning you, Alana, if you try to escape or try to pull anything funny, the visit is off. No more playing nice."

She had no intention of going anywhere. After the

emotional firestorm she'd just endured, Alana felt drained and raw. But she also felt hope. Soon, she'd get to see her son up close. He would be in the same room with her.

This would be the beginning.

She'd follow Jack's rules. She wouldn't try to escape. And she wouldn't do anything to break this tenuous, temporary agreement.

"So, how soon can I see him?" she asked.

He checked his watch, rubbed his eyes and mumbled something. "Aunt Tessie's heading back to the ranch. I'll give her a call and have her return."

"You mean now?"

"Now," he verified. He headed for the door and delivered the rest of what he had to say to her from over his shoulder. "Just don't make me regret it."

Alana couldn't promise that she would be on her best behavior. She couldn't speak. Soon, she would get her own version of a miracle.

She'd get to see her son.

Alana thought of the day she'd learned she was going to have a child. Even though the pregnancy wasn't planned, she'd been thrilled. But not Neil. He hadn't wanted children, and the pregnancy had ended their relationship. Good riddance, was what Alana thought at the time. She still felt that way now. Neil was dead, out of the picture.

But not Jack.

Jack had stepped up to raise a stranger's child. He'd prevented her son from going into foster care. And now it was all those good deeds that she'd have to challenge if she wanted custody. Which she did. But then, Alana glanced around the hospital room and considered her predicament. She wasn't exactly in a good place to be fighting for her child, even though that's exactly what she had to do.

Since she was still feeling light-headed, Alana lay back on the bed. No one had brought her clothes yet, so that meant she'd meet her son while she was wearing a hospital gown. Since Joey was only eight months old, he wouldn't notice. She, on the other hand, would commit every little detail about him to memory.

The door flew open. Her heart jumped. But she didn't even have time to make it off the bed before someone turned off the overhead light.

"Jack?" she called out. She was about to ask why he'd done that, but a hand slid over her mouth.

Her instinct was to scream, but the rough hand prevented that. Adrenaline ripped through her. Everything sped up. Her heart. Her breathing. The need to fight and stop whatever was happening to her.

God, what was happening?

"Make a sound, and you'll die right here," someone said. A man.

A stranger's voice.

At least she thought he was a stranger. It was hard to tell—his voice was hoarse and whispered.

"What do you want?" she asked, her own voice muffled beneath his hand. He wore a latex glove.

"You're coming with me," he insisted.

She was about to assure him that she wasn't, but then she felt a sharp jab in her left arm. A shot. He'd given her some kind of injection.

Alana shoved at him, but whoever he was, he was strong. He latched on to her as if she were a rag doll and picked her up from the bed. He forced her to stand.

She was weak and dizzy, and he trapped her into the crook of his left arm. Imprisoning her.

"We're leaving," he said in a growl, "and if you don't cooperate, I'll take your son instead of you."

Oh, God. He couldn't hurt Joey. She couldn't let that happen. But how could she stop him?

How?

She forced herself to stay calm. That wasn't easy to do when her son's life was at stake. Still, she had to come up with some way to prevent him from taking her. Alana didn't know who this man was or what he wanted, but she figured he was taking her to another private mental institution.

And this time, she might not escape.

Moving almost soundlessly, the man carried her to the door and peeked out. Unlike her room, the hall was well lit, and she got a good look at her attacker. Tall, dark haired. His faced was pocked with acne scars. She'd never seen him before. So why was he doing this? Was he working for someone who wanted her back under lock and key?

She was being kidnapped.

Or worse.

He could murder her.

Alana saw someone at the other end of the hall. The person's back was to them. She opened her mouth to call out, but her mouth was numb.

So was the rest of her.

Whatever drug he'd given her had acted fast, and she feared she would soon lose consciousness. If that happened, she wouldn't be able to put up a fight, and even though there were lots of people in the hospital, he might be able to get her out of there without any-one noticing.

Knowing she had to do something, she tried to ram her elbow into his stomach. That didn't work, either. And even though she fought the numbness and the haze, she knew the exact moment she failed.

Alana went limp, and the man scooped her into his arms. The last thing she saw was the bloodred exit sign before everything faded to black.

Chapter 6

What the heck was he doing?

Jack stopped just outside the doors of the hospital entrance and went through everything that'd just happened with Alana.

He cursed again.

Why had he agreed to let Alana see Joey? Why?

Legally, he was Joey's father. Legally, he could control when and if Alana saw him. Of course, he couldn't control that forever. She'd soon file a petition to regain her parental rights. And eventually if she could prove she'd been kidnapped and that she was sane, she would get at least joint custody.

He might lose his son altogether.

That was one of the reasons he'd agreed to let Alana see the baby—Jack had hoped to keep things as amicable as possible between them. Another reason was the blasted compassion he kept feeling for her. He was a sucker for a damsel in distress, and Alana had *damsel* written all over her.

He'd gotten her reassurance that she wouldn't try to escape. Not that she would at this point. If the court order that had put her in the institution wasn't real, and she obviously thought it wasn't, then she probably was already planning her next move to get her son back. Heck, she might be talking to her attorney right now.

And here he had been about to deliver Joey to her.

That wouldn't make her less committed to getting custody. It would cause her to leap at it.

Jack didn't think she'd consider his feelings or think of him with compassion. Nor would she let attraction play into it. No. She'd come after him with a legal team and a lot of money to back up her custody fight.

He needed to have another chat with Alana before he allowed her to see Joey.

Jack turned around, the doors swished open and he retraced his steps through the lobby. Best to get this conversation out of the way. Several people greeted him, but Jack didn't stop, didn't slow down. He went straight for Alana's room.

The door was ajar.

He'd shut it only minutes earlier. He was sure of it. Of course, that wasn't enough reason for concern since this was a hospital where doctors and nurses came and went all the time. Jack peered into the room and spotted the empty bed.

"Alana?" he called out.

Nothing.

He shoved the door wide open and looked around.

There was no sign of her. He checked the bathroom, but she wasn't there, either.

Damn. Had she escaped after promising him that she would stay put?

Furious that he'd believed her, he went back into the hall and saw Dr. Bartolo coming out of one of the other rooms.

"Where's Alana?" Jack asked.

The doctor lifted his shoulder. "She's not in her room?"

Jack cursed again. He'd only left her five or six minutes ago, and he'd been certain that she would sit there and wait for him to return with Joey.

Which is exactly what she would have done.

He stopped and considered that. Alana might have an overwhelming need to escape so she wouldn't be returned to the mental institution, but he was betting that need was paltry compared to the desire to see her son.

And that meant something was wrong.

He pulled out his cell phone and called his deputy. Reyes answered on the first ring. "I need you back at the hospital. Especially the parking lot. We might have a situation with Alana Davis."

"What's the problem?"

"I have a bad feeling her brother might have decided to force her to go with him."

He shoved his phone back into his pocket so his hands would be free. In case of what, he didn't know. Five minutes wasn't that long for Sean to have gotten her out of there, especially if Alana was trying to fight him off, which she would be doing.

They might still be in the building.

But they wouldn't be for long.

Jack glanced around and spotted the nearest exit. It was at the end of the corridor and led to a waiting room. It was usually a busy place, so he looked in the opposite direction. At the emergency exit. Not much foot traffic there, and it led directly to the parking lot.

Oh, man. That bad feeling got a lot worse.

He raced toward the exit and threw open the door. The hot, muggy air engulfed him. So did his concerns as he picked through the sea of cars and saw something he didn't want to see.

Alana.

A big, hulking guy was in the process of cramming her into the backseat of a tan four-door Ford.

Jack drew his gun and barreled down the steps. The position put him at ground level. He could still see the man, but there was a row of cars in between them.

"Sheriff Jack Whitley," he called out to identify himself. "Don't move."

The man practically threw Alana onto the seat and reached for something. The handle on the driver's-side door. Hell.

He wasn't going to stop.

"Rethink that," Jack yelled. "Because I'll shoot. You're not leaving with her."

The man froze and eased his hands into the air. Surrendering. Thank God. Jack didn't want a shoot-out in the hospital parking lot where Alana or an innocent bystander could be hurt. The man didn't seem to be armed. At least there wasn't a weapon visible in either of his hands. However, that didn't mean he didn't have one hidden inside his bulky shirt and jeans.

"Who are you?" Jack demanded.

With his gun ready and aimed, he started toward

the Ford. He could see Alana, but she didn't appear to be conscious. Maybe that's why she wasn't moving.

Hopefully, it wasn't something more serious.

He didn't take the time to blame himself for not realizing she was at risk. But he would do that later. After he'd stopped the kidnapping or whatever the heck this was.

"Who are you?" Jack repeated when the guy didn't say a word.

But Jack had hardly finished the question when the man dropped to the ground. He was fast, a blur literally jumping down out of sight.

Jack's body was already primed for a fight, and that caused his adrenaline to soar. He didn't fire. He didn't want to risk hitting Alana. Plus, if the guy was unarmed, then he needed to try to apprehend him first. He might be able to get some answers from him about what was going on.

Jack heard the man was shuffling around. Just in case he was trying to grab Alana from the car, Jack went closer, keeping his own steps light so he could hear what was happening. The shuffling continued, and by the time Jack reached the Ford, the guy wasn't anywhere in sight.

Jack fired his gaze all around the parking lot. Other than the vehicles, there weren't any places to hide. No trees or shrubs. Just a half dozen light poles. While he was looking, he tried to see if he could spot Reyes. He'd told his deputy to head to the parking lot, and Jack knew that Reyes wouldn't let him down.

While he watched for a possible ambush, Jack reached in the car and put her fingers to Alana's neck. She had a pulse. That was the good news. But she wasn't moving, and her color wasn't good. There was a dab of blood of her left arm that looked to be the site of an injection. The guy had drugged her with God knows what, and she might need medical attention.

"Don't make this hard on yourself," Jack called out to the man. He needed to get this guy under control so he could see to Alana.

Jack eased away from the car and repositioned himself so he could do a visual search. He couldn't go far from the Ford. He couldn't risk the would-be kidnapper doubling back, getting into the car and driving away.

"What's going on?" he heard Reyes yell. Judging from the sound of his voice, the deputy was behind him.

Jack was about to give Reyes a brief description of the perp, but the next sound he heard had him cursing.

It was the sound of a car engine.

Jack turned, reaiming his weapon. It was already too late to respond. At the far end of the parking lot, a dark green car pulled out. The driver slammed on the accelerator, causing the tires to squeal over the concrete surface.

The car sped away.

"Follow him," Jack called out to Reyes, who was already sprinting across the parking lot to get the cruiser he'd left out front. "And call for backup."

That would mean bringing in Kirby Ward, the night deputy, but Jack didn't have a choice. He didn't want Reyes to do this on his own, and he couldn't leave Alana.

While keeping watch, Jack grabbed his cell phone and pressed in the numbers for the hospital dispatch. "I need a doctor in the parking lot *now!*"

He moved closer to Alana and touched her face, hoping it would wake her. Alana stirred, trying to open her eyes, but the attempt wasn't successful.

Alana mumbled something he couldn't understand, but Jack hoped she could tell him the identity of the man who'd just sped away. If they knew that, then he could figure out who was responsible for this. Someone wanted her away from the hospital, fast, and to accomplish that they'd been willing to risk a kidnapping in broad daylight.

That gave him two bits of critical information.

The person behind this was desperate. And he or she wanted Alana alive. Because if the kidnapper had been able to drug her, he could just as easily have made it a lethal dose. She could be dead by now. But instead, he'd risked taking her through the hospital to a car.

Desperate all right.

And usually when desperation was that huge, it meant this had to do with love or money. Since her brother, Sean, was now at the top of his list of suspects, it could be both.

Sean could have paid the man to take Alana. Why, was the next question. Jack swore he'd find the answer to that soon.

Dr. Bartolo came out of the hospital. He didn't look like a man with fire under his feet, so Jack yelled, "Alana's unconscious. I'm pretty sure somebody drugged her and then tried to kidnap her. She needs help."

That got the doc moving a little faster, but Jack didn't like the lack of urgency. Mercy. What was wrong with the man? Just because Alana was Joey's birth mother, Jack didn't want the town to square off against her.

She had enough enemies.

Dr. Bartolo finally made it to them, and like Jack, the first thing he did was check her pulse. Then he lifted her right eyelid and looked at her pupil. "Yes, she's been drugged. Any idea what she was given?"

"No. The guy who tried to take her didn't say a word."

"Hmmm." The doctor reached for his phone. "I'll have the medics bring out a gurney. She doesn't appear to be injured but better safe than sorry."

Jack couldn't agree more.

The hospital wasn't safe, and he didn't have the manpower to provide round-the-clock protection for her. Willow Ridge was a small town with just him and two deputies. Jack had often pulled double and even triple shifts.

Now he was going to have to take it one step further.

He'd have to take Alana in his protective custody.

Maybe then he could request assistance from the Texas Rangers. Or convince the city council to pay for a bodyguard service or a temporary deputy. But for now, the only solution he could see was to take her to the ranch.

Where she'd see Joey.

It wasn't his first choice. Or even his second. Heck, it wasn't even on the list. But it was his only choice.

He couldn't let her get hurt. He couldn't let that kidnapper come after her again.

"Joey," Alana mumbled.

Jack leaned over her. "He's not here."

Frantically, she shook her head and tried to say something. What, was anyone's guess.

"You're safe now," Jack told her, and to try to reassure her of that, he touched her arm with his fingertips.

Rubbed gently. "We'll get you inside, and the doctor will examine you."

She shook her head again, and her face twisted as if she were in pain. "Joey."

It was her hysterical tone and expression that grabbed his attention. "What about him?"

"That man…the kidnapper…he threatened me. He said if I didn't go with him, he'd take Joey."

Jack's heart dropped.

Not this.

Please, God, not this.

"See to Alana," Jack instructed the doctor. And he practically ripped the phone from his pocket. He forced himself to stay calm. Which was impossible. But somehow he managed to stab in the numbers without breaking his cell.

"I think I lost him," Reyes announced when he answered the call.

That didn't get Jack's heart back in his chest, and it kicked up his adrenaline. "Get to the ranch," Jack ordered. He started to sprint toward his car. "I'll meet you there."

"What's wrong?" Reyes asked.

Jack almost hated to say the words aloud. Because the words were a father's nightmare. "The kidnapper's going after Joey."

Chapter 7

Alana forced open her eyes. She was inside the hospital again. In the E.R. That in itself was enough to cause her to panic, but that particular panic was nothing compared to what she remembered.

The kidnapper had threatened Joey.

She pushed away the hands that were trying to examine her. Dr. Bartolo's hands, she realized.

"Just relax," he insisted. "You're okay."

No. She wasn't. She wouldn't be okay until she stopped that monster from taking her son.

"Joey," she said. Alana sat up and quickly tried to get her bearings. She was dizzy and weak, but that wouldn't prevent her from leaving.

"Jack's already on the way to the ranch," the doctor explained. "I'm sure he'll call the moment he gets there and confirms that all is well."

But everything might not be. The kidnapper's threat was clear. He would use Joey as leverage to get her to cooperate, and Jack might need help.

Alana took a deep breath, hoping it would clear her head, and she got up from the gurney.

"I wouldn't advise that," the doctor warned.

She ignored him and looked around for a pair of shoes or a robe. There was nothing like that in the ER, so that meant she would have to wear just the gown she had on. She started for the door.

Dr. Bartolo caught her arm. She didn't trust him, didn't know the reason for the distrust, and hated that if he hadn't caught her, she would probably have fallen flat on her face.

"Jack's not going to let anything happen to that little boy," the doctor assured her.

He led her back to the gurney. He was right about Jack and she honestly couldn't stand on her own, so Alana had no choice but to sit down. Maybe after a minute or two, she could think straight and figure out how she could help Jack.

"I took a blood sample," the doctor continued. "It'll tell me what kind of drug you were given."

She glanced down at the injection site on her arm. It was a reminder of just what this man was willing to do to kidnap her. He wouldn't be any less ruthless with her child.

"You got a good look at the man who did this?" Dr. Bartolo asked.

Had she? Yes. She had. Alana clearly remembered his face. That was something at least. She'd be able to give a detailed description to Jack. Of course, it was possible that Jack already had an up-close and personal view of the kidnapper since the man might have driven straight to the ranch.

"I need to talk to Jack," she said. "I need to find out what's going on."

She was about to get up again, but she heard the footsteps, looked up and saw Jack. His breath was fast, and there was sweat on his face.

"Where's Joey?" she asked, almost too afraid to hear the answer.

"He's okay."

Alana's heart beat even faster. She was relieved, but that wasn't relief she saw in Jack's expression. "Where is he?"

"Here, at the hospital. Aunt Tessie hadn't gone back to the ranch yet. When I called her, they were at the grocery store, so I went over and got them." Jack looked at the doctor. "How soon before she can leave?"

Dr. Bartolo volleyed glances between them. "I take it you want her out of here?"

"Immediately. We weren't able to find the guy who did this. Reyes is still out looking for him, and the Rangers are sending someone down to assist with the search. But for now, I can't guard Joey and Alana if they're in two separate places."

That got Alana on her feet again. "What are you going to do?"

"I'm taking you, Joey and Tessie to my office. There's a small break room with a sofa sleeper. It's pretty sparse, but you'll have to use that until I can make other arrangements."

She didn't care about sparse. Her only require-ment was that it be safe for her son. "And Joey will be there, too?"

Jack spared her a glance, but he didn't look directly at her. His body was tense and tight. His chest, still pumping. "I don't have a choice. Joey will be there."

How ironic. The threat of imminent danger would be the reason she could see her son. But Alana gladly would have postponed that meeting if she could be guaranteed that this man wouldn't go after Joey.

"She'll probably be woozy for a while," the doctor said. "She should rest. This sounds like the start of big mother and child reunion, but my advice is for her not to hold Joey until we're sure this virus has run its course."

Even that didn't dampen Alana's spirits. For now, she would be satisfied with simply meeting the child she'd given birth to.

"Bring her back tomorrow for a checkup," the doctor added.

"Will do." Jack went to her and took her by the arm. He pulled the blanket from the gurney and wrapped it around her like a cape. "Once things have settled, I'll see about getting you some clothes."

Settled. Heaven knows when that would be. "Thank you for this, Jack."

He didn't answer. He got her moving. There was a sense of urgency and unease in his every step.

Her feelings mirrored his. She was afraid, but the fear lifted in a snap when Jack and she walked out of the ER and into the adjacent waiting room. His aunt Tessie was there.

She was holding Joey, just a few feet away.

So close that Alana could practically touch him.

The little boy was a good antidote for the drug still left in her body. Suddenly, she didn't feel hazy. Every inch of her was on alert, and she took in as many details as she could. She'd only gotten a glimpse of him earlier, and he hadn't been nearly this close to her. She wanted to hold on to this moment forever.

He was bigger than she'd imagined he would be, and Jack had been right about the eye color. Blue, an identical shade to hers. His face was round with a flash of rosy color in his cheeks, and that beautiful face was framed with soft brown hair that was thin and spiky.

He was precious.

Joey looked at her with those now suspicious blue eyes and wound his arms tighter around Tessie's neck. He didn't cry, but he certainly wasn't sending her any welcoming signals. But that didn't matter. He would get to know her.

And she would get to know him.

"Alana," Tessie greeted. There was a hint of anger in her eyes and more than a little fear and concern.

Alana understood why. This woman had been a mother figure to Joey. She'd helped Jack raise him, and she would see Alana as a threat.

"Tessie," she greeted back. "I remember you brought me Christmas dinner after I gave birth to Joey. You were kind to me, and I appreciate that."

"We need to go," Jack said, voiding the rest of the polite conversation. It wasn't the time for it, anyway. After all, the kidnapper could return to try to make good on his threat to take Joey.

"My car's right in front of the hospital," Jack explained as he led them in that direction. "We'll do this as fast as we can. Alana, you get in the front with me. Tessie and Joey will take the back since that's where his infant seat is. If you see anything of concern, let me know immediately."

Concern.

Translation: danger.

Alana wanted to take her son and shelter him in her arms, but she knew that wouldn't be wise. She was still light-headed from the effects of the drug. Plus, there was the virus.

Jack didn't waste any time. The moment the front doors swished open, he drew his weapon and looped his left arm around Tessie. The maneuver sandwiched Joey between the two, and they hurried to the black SUV. Alana got in as quickly as she could, and the moment that Tessie had Joey strapped into the seat, Jack drove away.

Alana kept watch in the side mirror, to make sure no one was following them. Jack did the same. His gaze darted all around them. From the backseat, she could hear Tessie talking softly to Joey. The woman was trying to reassure him that all was well, but he had to be aware of the increased tension.

But hopefully not the danger.

"I'm sorry this is happening," Alana said to Jack.

He didn't look at her. He didn't answer her.

"Maybe this man is responsible for what happened eight months ago," she added, talking more to herself than Jack.

"Maybe." But it didn't sound as if he believed that. "I'll check the surveillance video again, but I don't remember seeing him."

Still monitoring their surroundings, he took the turn toward Main Street. There was only a trickle of traffic here, and the two-lane road was practically rural since the hospital was positioned on the outskirts of town.

"He wanted you alive," Jack continued. "So that means he had ransom or some other form of reward in mind."

"He knew I had a son. He said 'if you don't cooperate, I'll take your son instead of you.'"

Because she needed reassurance that he was okay, she glanced over her shoulder at Joey. Tessie was singing him a song, and he was smiling at her.

When they reached Main Street, Jack pulled into the small parking lot of the sheriff's office and drove to the back. There was a door labeled Emergency Exit, and it had a sign that instructed visitors to enter through the front. Jack parked as close to the door as possible, unlocked it and started the transfer. He had them all inside within seconds.

"Take Joey to my office," Jack instructed Tessie. He relocked the emergency exit and activated a security alarm. "The break room's through here."

In the opposite direction as his office.

She would be under the same roof as Joey, but Jack didn't intend to let her spend time with him. Still, it wasn't far. Just on the other side of the hall.

The break room was indeed sparse. It had a sofa and a small table with two chairs. There was a coffeepot and various packs of crackers and chips on the narrow counter beneath two white-painted cabinets. A miniature brown fridge hummed in the corner.

Jack opened a closet and pulled out a pillow and a patchwork quilt. "Dr. Bartolo said you should rest," he reminded her. He also grabbed a pair of black sweatpants and a man's white button shirt that was dangling on a hanger. "The doors are all locked. No one's going to get in without me knowing it. It's safe here."

"Rest," she repeated, knowing that wasn't going to happen. "I can give you my statement now. Or whatever you call it. I'll do whatever you need me to do to help find this man."

He tossed the bedding onto the sofa and handed her the clothes. He also took a plastic bag from the top of the closet. "For now, I need you to rest. Oh, and I need that hospital gown. It might have some DNA or trace that could lead us to the kidnapper."

She took the clothes from him, mumbled a thanks and motioned for him to turn around. He did. And Alana caught the counter so she could keep her balance while she stepped into the pants. They were several sizes too large for her, but anything was better than the open-back hospital gown. She pulled it off, placed it next to the coffeepot and slipped on the shirt. It, too, was big and the bottom hit her at midthigh.

These must be Jack's clothes.

The shirt carried his scent.

"Now rest," Jack insisted. He checked over his shoulder as she was managing the last button.

Alana didn't budge. She couldn't. She was afraid if she sat, she'd fall back asleep. The drug the kidnapper had given her was still in her system, and she was lightheaded. She didn't want to feel this way. She wanted to be able to help Jack keep Joey safe, and for that to happen she had to stay awake.

Jack huffed, riled that she wasn't cooperating. He walked to her, took her gown and stuffed it into the plastic bag. He laid it aside on the counter and caught her arm. He tugged her toward the sofa, but Alana stayed put.

"I need to help. I need to do something," she insisted.

"You've done enough." He was angry.

It took her a moment to fight through the fog in her head and study his expression. He didn't turn away. Jack just stood there and stared at her.

And then it hit her.

"Oh, God. I'm sorry." She pressed her fingertips to her mouth to stop it from trembling. "I'm so sorry."

"Don't," he warned. And it was indeed a warning. He wasn't pleased about this situation—or about her—and she suddenly understood why. It wasn't just the fact that she would be so close to her son.

It was because she'd brought this danger to Joey.

She hadn't meant to do that. Her escape from the house in the woods had been so frightening. So chaotic. She hadn't had time to think. If she had, if she'd realized there was real danger, she wouldn't have come anywhere near her son. Though she had no idea what she would have done.

Her life was spiraling out of control, and she didn't know what to do to make it stop.

Alana started to tremble. Not just her mouth as she tried to speak. But her entire body. And she had no choice but to try to get to the sofa. She had to sit after all.

"I didn't know that coming here would put Joey in danger," she said. "I swear, I didn't know." Mercy, she sounded hysterical and was very close to it. How could she have done this to her son?

Jack opened his mouth, closed it and then cursed

under his breath. His grip tightened around her arm, and he physically sat her on the sofa.

"Look, I want to be angry with you. I'm not especially happy you're here." He dropped down beside her and groaned. "But I also know you wouldn't intentionally endanger Joey."

That admission was more than she could have hoped for, and the relief had an instant effect. It was as if her muscles suddenly had permission to unknot. She went limp, and her head landed against Jack's shoulder. Alana didn't let it stay there. She started to move.

But Jack caught her again.

He slid his arm around her and pulled closer to him. "I'm scared," she admitted.

"Me, too." That was all he said for several moments. "I'm usually objective about my job. I do what I have to do to keep the peace in this town. But Joey's not the job. I don't how it happened, but eight months ago when I held him in my arms, he became my son."

She blinked back tears. "I wish he were yours." Alana felt both of them go stiff. She didn't know who was more surprised with her admission: Jack or her. "I mean, uh, you're a better man than his biological father."

Jack turned his head. He snared her gaze and stared at her. Something changed between them. Maybe the air. Maybe it was all in her head. But she saw something in his eyes that she thought she hadn't seen before.

Solidarity.

They were on the same side, at least when it came to Joey. That was a powerful union. She was Joey's mother, and Jack was his father in every way that counted. In that moment, Alana knew she would have to make concessions. She couldn't cut Jack out of Joey's life.

She didn't want to.

Her son deserved a father like Jack.

"We'll work this out," Alana promised. And she meant it.

Something else went through his eyes. Emotions that she tried to catalog. Gratitude, maybe. Relief, definitely. At that point, it probably would have been a good idea for her to look away, but she didn't.

There was a sense of everything slowing down. And getting warmer.

Not warmer, she amended.

Hotter.

Alana recognized the feelings that trickled through her. This was attraction. Basic. Human.

Strong.

Jack shook his head, as if to clear it. But she saw the heat in his eyes, as well. Now he would back off. He'd say something to explain this all away, something to do with the near life-and-death experience she'd just had.

But that didn't happen, either.

Jack leaned in, lowered his head. His breath brushed over her mouth.

The jolt was sharp and intense. For a moment she thought it was static electricity, but this wasn't painful. This was some kind of pleasure that was so intense, it was downright scary. It slid through every inch of her.

Alana pulled back and drew in a sharp breath.

"Yeah," he said. "That was stupid."

"The craziness got to us," she heard herself say. Now she was the one trying to explain what'd happened. Great. She didn't know what'd happened. Heck, it wasn't even a kiss.

"Alana…" His tone was apologetic, but he waved it off and stood. He went to the other side of the room, as far away from her as he could get without leaving. Which she figured he would do next.

"Alana…" This time, he was disgusted with himself.

She stood, as well. "Jack…" She winced because they were just saying each other's names as if they'd both turned brainless. "I hope you don't get sick."

Alana winced again at the idiotic comment. At her schoolgirl nerves. At the fact that Jack was the last man she should be lusting after.

Wasn't he?

Hot raging hormones had a way of doling out excuses, and she had a whopper. Since Jack and she both had Joey's best interest at heart, it seemed logical that they would feel a closeness. After all, he was a man and she was a woman. They were both single.

As if he could read her mind, Jack shook his head. "We already have too much to work out." His words were calm, void of any emotion.

And it was true.

Less than an hour earlier, someone had tried to kidnap her. The person might try again. Or might even go after Joey. This was not the time or place for hot raging hormones.

She nodded, told her body to knock it off and sank back onto the sofa. She needed to sleep off the kidnapper's drug. Just a short nap. And then maybe she could watch Joey from a distance. But her head had barely hit the pillow when there was a sharp rap.

"Someone's at the front door," Jack informed her.

The kidnapper. God, had he returned? She jumped up from the sofa again and was about to run to Joey.

"A kidnapper probably wouldn't knock first," Jack reminded her. He walked out, heading in the direction of the front door.

He was right again. The kidnapper would be a fool to try to come after her while she was in the sheriff's office.

Alana tamped down the fight instinct and cursed the light-headedness that was causing her not to think straight. She went to the doorway of the break room so she could listen. Jack was already out of sight, but she heard when he opened the door.

And she heard him snap, "What the heck do you want now?"

Alana used the wall for support and made her way up the hall, toward the sound of Jack's voice.

It was her brother, Sean.

She rounded the corner just in time to see Sean hand Jack some papers. Jack glanced at the top page and then mumbled some profanity. Alana went closer to see what had caused Jack's reaction.

"This is for your own good," Sean told her.

Her stomach clenched. Whenever her brother said anything like that, it was usually for his own good, not hers.

"What is it?" she asked Jack, dreading the answer. They had enough to face without adding anything else to the mix.

Jack held up his index finger and continued to read the papers. While he did that, Alana decided to deal with her brother.

"Did you send a kidnapper after me?" she asked. She caught the wall for support and waited for his answer.

Sean didn't look particularly surprised or outraged. Only mildly annoyed. "Of course not. Why? Did someone try to kidnap you?"

"Someone did," she assured him, mimicking his annoyed tone. "Someone also had me committed to that Sauder institution by forging the signature of a dead judge. Would you happen to know anything about that?"

"Nothing."

"You're lying." But she couldn't be sure of that at all. Her brother had always been a good liar. And a manipulator. But she had to admit that this seemed extreme even for him. This was a lot of go through for the sake of maintaining appearances.

"I suppose you think I'm lying about that, too?" Sean tipped his head to the papers Jack was still reading.

He was too smug for that to be a bluff. Those papers were obviously trouble.

She went to Jack so she could have a look for herself. "It's a court order," Jack explained. His gaze snapped to Sean's. "How did you manage to get this done so quickly? You only left the hospital about an hour and a half ago."

Sean lifted his hands and stayed smug. "What can I say? I know people who know people. A family friend signed it and faxed it to me."

"And is this judge dead like the other one who signed the original court order?" Jack asked.

"No. He's very much alive and on the bench in San Antonio. He's sympathetic to my family's situation.

My sister's well-being in the most important thing in my life right now."

Alana ignored him and tried to read the paper, but dizziness was causing the words to squirm on the page. "What kind of court order is it?" she asked Jack.

The muscles in Jack's jaw went to war with each other. "It's a commitment order. Until the new judge can interview you and examine your case files, you're to be returned to the mental institution immediately."

Chapter 8

Jack looked at Alana. What little color she'd had in her cheeks had drained to white. Sean, on the other hand, looked pleased as punch with himself.

Jack wanted to bash the guy in the face.

Since that wasn't an appropriate reaction for a peace officer, he settled for pushing the newly issued commitment papers against Sean's chest. Jack wasn't gentle about it, either, and Sean staggered back a step.

"Please don't make me go," Alana said. Her voice was broken and near panic.

"You're not going anywhere," Jack assured her.

That earned him a raised eyebrow from Sean. "You intend to ignore a judge's order?"

"Damn right, I do." Jack chose his words carefully because one slip, and he could find himself on the wrong side of the law. "Your sister's a witness to an attempted felony—her own kidnapping. And because she's the only person who can identify her attacker, she's in my protective custody."

Alana didn't relax. She eyed Sean to see what he would do next.

Sean waved the papers at them. "I'm not a lawyer, but I don't think a sheriff of Podunkville can ignore a judge's order."

Jack didn't appreciate the insult, but he took some pleasure that his refusal to hand over Alana was causing Sean to lose his cool. "This Podunk sheriff can. Your judge is on the bench in San Antonio. That's Bexar County. He has no jurisdiction here. And Alana's not even a resident of San Antonio. She hasn't lived there in over eight months."

Alana's arm was touching his, and Jack felt her relax a bit. Not Sean, though. His eyes narrowed. "You don't want to make me your enemy."

"Really?" Jack couldn't help himself. Sean was testing his patience. "I don't mind enemies."

"You won't think that way for long," Sean threatened. "I'll get another judge to sign the order. One in this county. And I'll be back." He turned to walk away.

"It'll be a waste of time," Jack commented.

Sean slowly turned around to face him. "What does that mean?"

"It means I know every judge in this county."

A little of Sean's smugness returned. "Yes, I'll bet you do. And not because you're the sheriff. I know what you did to your own father." He paused, smiled. "Does Alana know?"

Jack had to fight to hang on to his composure. "No. It's not pertinent to this case, and neither is the fact you brought it up. If you're trying to undermine me, it won't work. I'm not my father, and I have a solid reputation in this town and in this county. Any judge will agree with me once I tell them why Alana is in my protective custody."

That took care of Sean's smile. He gave Jack one last hard look, and he stormed toward his car.

Alana sagged against him. Jack looped his arm around her to stop her from falling.

"Thank you, again," she whispered. "You seem to be coming to my rescue a lot."

He was surprised and thankful that she didn't ask about his father. "Rescues are part of the job description." Best to keep things light. And after that stupid near kiss, he needed to make her understand that this was the job.

Well, for the most part.

Jack couldn't lie to himself. He'd already tried that and failed. But he couldn't kiss her. Wanting to kiss her was an entirely different matter. He didn't think he could talk his body out of wanting to do that. But he would fight hard not to cross that particular line.

He locked the door and led her back to the break room. On the other side of the hall, he could hear Joey and Tessie. It sounded as if Tessie was reading to him. She'd probably found a kids' book in the small toy chest that Jack kept in the closet in his office.

"Are you okay?" Jack called out to them.

"We're fine," Tessie answered. "What's going on?"

"I'll be over in a minute to explain everything." But first he wanted to get Alana settled and hopefully on her way to a much-needed nap.

"Good. By the way, a fax just came for you," Tessie let him know. "It says urgent on the cover letter."

Alana stopped. "Do you think it's about the man who tried to kidnap me?"

"Maybe." But more likely it was about Alana herself. Reyes had put out a lot of feelers on this case, and the fact that it was marked *urgent* meant he had to deal with it ASAP.

With his arm still looped around Alana, he started for the break room again, but she stopped. "Could I go with you to get the fax?"

"I don't think that's a good idea."

She pushed her hair from her face and sighed. "I won't touch Joey. I just want to look at him."

Of course she'd want to look at her son. The logical part of Jack's brain knew that was a natural reaction. The illogical part wanted Alana in that break room. But he couldn't keep her away for long. Nor was he sure that was even a good idea. For better or worse, Alana was here, in Joey's life, and somehow he had to deal with that and keep his son in the process.

"We'll get the fax, and then we can go to the break room so you can tell me why Sean is so hell-bent on putting you back in a mental institution."

"I can tell you that now." They took it slow walking down the hall. "Sean will say that he's concerned about appearances, and in part, that's true. But the real reason he's doing this is for the money."

Jack figured that would play into this somehow. "How would keeping you locked away get Sean money?"

"We both inherited fifty percent of our parents' jewelry business when they died. It's worth a lot. Millions.

Well, it was eight months ago, anyway. Since I've been out of my mind, literally, Sean would have had sole control of the business and the money."

"And you think he wants to keep that control?" Jack asked.

"Oh, yes. Our parents died eight years ago when I was twenty-one. Sean's six years older than I am, and at that time he had a lot more experience in the business. He had his own contacts. His own way of doing things. He's tried to buy me out numerous times, and every time I've refused. I might not know the business as well as Sean, but I wanted to keep control of my own designs. I knew if Sean bought me out, that wouldn't happen. He tends to go for profit rather than quality."

Jack gave that some thought. "How's the business structured? Do the profits go into one account?"

Alana shook her head. "Two. The profits are split fifty-fifty and deposited into our individual accounts."

Jack made a note to check into Alana's financial records. They might hold some clues as to why this was happening to her.

She paused when they were just a few steps from his office. "I don't want my brother to be guilty of this. I don't want to believe he could choose money over blood."

Neither did he, but Jack had seen it happen too many times to discount Sean as his primary suspect. Besides, he didn't hold a lot of stock with blood. His father was proof of that.

They stopped in the doorway of his office. Tessie was sitting in his chair holding Joey. She was trying to read to him, but Joey had already lost interest in the book. He was squirming and doing his best to get down. Tessie held on, probably because she didn't want Joey trying to crawl in Alana's direction.

When Joey's attention landed on Jack, he stopped squirming. "Da-Da," he babbled. He gave Jack one of those big, priceless grins.

Jack smiled back, went to them and scooped Joey into his arms. He got rewarded with a hug. But Joey's interest was held only for a second. His son's exploring fingers and eyes went straight to the badge clipped onto Jack's belt. Because Jack knew what Joey wanted, he took off the silver star and handed it to him.

Joey beamed and made a few syllables to indicate he had the "toy" he wanted. With Joey now content—for at least a moment or two, anyway—Jack went to the fax machine.

Alana stayed in the doorway, but she had her attention focused on Joey. The little boy spotted her and lifted the badge as if to show her his prize.

"It's shiny, isn't it?" Alana said. There was so much emotion in her voice that Jack worried she was close to crying. However, she blinked back tears.

Joey answered her with more babbles and gave her a smile, as well. Jack knew that was a moment she would remember for the rest of her life.

"Why did you come back?" Tessie asked.

Oh, no. Jack hadn't wanted this conversation to happen now. Not with Alana still woozy from the kidnapper's drug. "It's complicated," Jack explained.

Alana obviously wanted to take that explanation further. "I have no memory of why I left the hospital that night. I don't know what happened, but it must have been extremely serious to make me leave the way I did."

"No memory," Tessie repeated. Jack knew that tone. She was skeptical. But he also knew that his aunt was a fair and reasonable woman. If they learned that Alana hadn't voluntarily walked out eight months ago, then Tessie would step up and try to make things better—just as she'd done twenty years ago when Jack was a kid.

"I think someone might have drugged me that night," Alana continued. "And threatened Joey, too. There aren't any other reasons that would make me walk out and leave my son behind."

While the women continued to talk, Jack looked at the fax. It was from the Texas Rangers in San Antonio. He read through the two paragraphs. And then read it again. When he finished, he realized that both Tessie and Alana were staring at him, obviously waiting to hear why the fax had been deemed "urgent."

Jack decided to start with the simple item first. "The Rangers did a quick check of the Sauder Facility. Everything about it is bogus."

Alana's breath shuddered. "There's proof?"

He nodded and idly gave Joey a kiss on the forehead when the little boy babbled something. "Everything is fake. The permit for the place. The judge's signature on your commitment papers. The foundation set up to pay your expenses."

"So where did the money come from?" Alana asked.

"They don't know yet." Their gazes met, and he saw in Alana's eyes what was no doubt in his. The money had probably come from Sean. "There are now APBs out on Margaret Vargas and Ted Moore."

Alana nodded and swallowed hard. "They had to be in on this."

"Not necessarily. They could have believed the institution and commitment orders were real. There could even have been phony orders or instructions from a doctor. Still, I want to question them." He glanced at the fax again. "The Rangers want to know the location of the place so they can send a CSI unit through it."

Alana nodded, then huffed. "I don't know the names of the roads, but I think I could take you there."

That's what he was afraid she would say. He wasn't exactly champing at the bit to drive her out to a remote facility where she'd been held prisoner. And he didn't want her to face the stress it would cause. It might not be safe. Whoever was behind this might have the place staked out. The trip could turn into a dangerous trap, and this time the kidnapper might succeed. Still, there could be valuable information inside. Info that would break this case wide open.

"After you've rested, try to draw a map," Jack instructed. Maybe it wouldn't be necessary. Maybe the Rangers would find Margaret and Ted and get them to confess to everything.

This was starting to get beyond complicated.

"Does the name Special Agent Parker Howell mean anything to you?" Jack asked, reading from the second paragraph of the fax.

Her eyes lit up with recognition. "Yes." But just as quickly, her forehead bunched up. "He's an FBI agent. I remember him coming to my office about a year ago. He was investigating the sale of illegally obtained diamonds. I didn't have any information to help him."

He read through the fax again to make sure he hadn't missed something. "And?"

"That was it." She paused. "At least I think it was." Her forehead bunched up even more. "Why?"

"Because he's been trying to locate you. He requested assistance from the Rangers eight months ago when you disappeared. He saw the APB that was put out when you left the Sauder Facility, and he's on his way here to Willow Ridge."

Alana shook her head. "What does he want?"

"The fax doesn't say. I hoped you might know."

"No." Her voice and expression were laced with questions and concerns.

Jack shared those concerns. What did an FBI agent want with Alana? He hoped like the devil that she hadn't been involved in anything illegal.

Then rethought that and decided she wouldn't have done anything illegal. Not voluntarily, anyway.

He cursed.

He was neck-deep in personal involvement here. Much to his disgust, any objectivity he should have about this case was long gone. Alana had been railroaded. End of speculation as to her guilt or innocence. That made him either one perceptive lawman or an idiot.

Yeah. That desire to kiss her had really screwed up things.

"Get some rest," Jack told Alana again. "I'll wake you when Special Agent Howell arrives."

She nodded, but didn't budge. The smile she aimed at Joey was weak from fatigue, but she continued to stare at the baby. "What will happen, Jack? It's not fair to the three of you to be cooped up here with me."

Another thing that had to be worked out. "We'll stay here tonight. I'll have Reyes, my deputy, bring in some cots and supplies. Maybe by morning, we'll have this situation resolved. If not, we'll go to the ranch. It's not quite as secure at this building, but I can get the ranch hands to put together some safety measures."

"And then what?" Alana asked.

"I don't know," he admitted. He hated that he didn't have the answers. His son's safety might be at stake, and that meant he had to do whatever it took to keep Joey out of harm's way.

Jack heard the rattle of the knob on the front door, and he groaned. Hopefully, it wasn't Agent Howell already. He wanted Alana to rest before that meeting. However, the rattle was quickly followed by the sound of someone inserting a key into the lock.

"It's me," Reyes called out a moment later.

Since it was possible that his deputy had the kidnapper in custody, Jack handed Joey to Tessie and went past Alana and into the hall.

Reyes was alone. And the man looked seriously riled.

"He got away," Reyes snarled. Though Jack had already figured that out. "I swear I'll get him, though. Just give me some time."

Jack believed him. He only wished he didn't have his own hands so full that he couldn't do some legwork to track down this guy. "I want his car impounded and searched. There might be something in it to reveal his identity. Run the plates, too. We could get lucky."

"We have to get something from that car. It might be our only source of evidence." Reyes glanced at Alana, reached behind him and locked the door. "The surveillance camera doesn't monitor that end of the parking lot. And since he used the emergency exit to get in and out, there won't be any film of him."

"He wore latex gloves," Alana volunteered.

That caused Reyes to look even more riled.

"I bagged the gown she was wearing." Jack hitched his thumb to the break room. "It's on the counter. Let me get Alana in there for a nap, and I'll do the paperwork to have it processed."

The phone rang, and while Reyes answered the call at the front desk, Jack walked with Alana to the break room. Maybe this time he'd actually get her into the makeshift bed so she could rest.

Or not, he decided when he heard Reyes ask the caller, "You're sure it's the Sauder institution where Alana Davis was being held?"

Jack and Alana stopped and waited for the conversation to end. Reyes hung up, and in the same motion, he turned and snared Jack's gaze. "We might have gotten a break. The Rangers learned the location of the institution. It's about an hour from here, out in the middle of the sticks. They're headed over there to check it out."

Good. That could indeed be a break, especially since Alana wouldn't have to get anywhere near the place. Between the facility and the kidnapper's car, they might actually find something useful that would lead to the arrest of whoever was responsible.

Jack didn't have time to savor that possibility because from out the window he saw a man making his way to the front door. Tall. About six-two. Rust-brown hair, cut short and efficient. The guy wore a suit.

This was no doubt Special Agent Parker Howell.

The timing sucked, but this could turn out to be yet more good news.

Jack was more than a little uneasy about what a federal agent would want with Alana, especially if this pertained to those illegal diamonds.

Reyes was the one who opened the door, and the visitor immediately made a sweeping glance around the room. His attention landed on Jack. Then Parker looked past Jack at Alana. He flashed a dazzling smile that made Jack even more uncomfortable.

What the heck was going on here? That wasn't the normal greeting of a federal agent working in an official capacity. It was too friendly.

"Alana," the man greeted.

"Agent Parker Howell," she said stiffly. "What can I do for you?"

The dazzling smile faded. "Agent Parker Howell?" he repeated. "Why so formal?" But he didn't wait for an answer. He turned to Jack. "Was Alana hurt? I heard she was attacked at the hospital."

"How'd you hear that?" Jack asked.

"From the Rangers." He stepped inside and walked closer, his attention fastened again to her. "I'm sorry about the attack, Alana. If I'd found you sooner, I might have been able to prevent it. That's why I'm here. To stop anything else from happening to you. I'm here to take you into protective custody."

Jack didn't say a word. He stood back and listened. For now. But Alana wasn't leaving with this man.

"You're too late," she insisted. "I'm already in Sheriff Whitley's custody."

"That was a good temporary measure." He turned to Jack. "And I thank you for helping us out. But the FBI has authority here."

"How do you figure that?" Jack asked.

Agent Howell shrugged as if the answer were obvious. "Because Alana is a federal informant."

Chapter 9

Alana was too tired and too numb to have an extreme reaction. But, mercy, could her life get any more complicated?

"A federal informant?" Jack asked. It was a challenge.

"Yes." Agent Howell shifted those ice-gray eyes in her direction. "You don't remember?"

"Remember what, exactly?" she asked.

He lifted his shoulder. "Anything about your dealings with the FBI."

She glanced at Jack before she answered. "There are some blank spots in my memory. But I do recall you coming to my office in San Antonio to discuss some diamonds."

"Blood diamonds," the agent calmly provided. He

kept his attention on her eyes as if he were examining her. "That's what we discussed that day."

"I remember that part. I also remembering turning down your request for me to become a federal informant."

"You did, at first. But it wasn't just the one visit. I saw you again Christmas Eve, and we spoke on the phone several times before that. It was during one of those phone conversations when you finally agreed to help us. You don't remember any of that?"

Alana took a moment to try to recall other meetings, but nothing came to mind. Of course, the meetings could have happened. She'd already tried to piece together those last several days before Joey was born, and she had no idea what she'd done or whom she'd spoken to.

"I'm sorry, Agent Howell, but I don't remember," she admitted.

"Parker," he corrected, offering his first name as if they were that familiar with each other. And maybe they were.

Jack caught her when she wobbled a bit. "Did those meetings and conversations have anything to do with what's happening to her now?" he asked.

"Possibly." Without taking his eyes off her, Parker reached into his suit coat pocket and extracted a picture. It was a grainy shot, but the man in the image was still visible. "Is this the person who attacked you at the hospital?"

Alana's breath started to race, and she nodded before she even took the picture from him and brought it closer to her face. Not that she needed a closer look. She'd recognized him after one glimpse. "That's the man."

Jack's grip on her arm got slightly firmer. "Who is he?" he wanted to know.

"Eldon Thatcher."

Reyes crossed the room and looked at the picture, as well. "Can I borrow this? I want to send it out to the sheriffs in the surrounding area. The guy's probably still close, which means we can catch him."

"Be my guest," Parker offered, and Alana handed the picture to the deputy. He took it and disappeared into his office.

"Eldon Thatcher is the one who had the illegal diamonds that he was trying to sell to you." Parker paused. "You really don't remember?"

"Remember what?" she snapped at him. She was very uncomfortable about what she wasn't recalling. And that had a lot to do with the agent in front of her.

Why did she distrust him?

It was the same niggling feeling she'd gotten when she saw Dr. Bartolo. There was just something about both of them that made her uneasy.

Parker took a deep breath. "Eldon Thatcher had these diamonds, and using an alias, he contacted you, hoping you'd buy them despite the lack of paperwork that would prove they were his and not illegally obtained. You got suspicious of him and recorded the conversation. Then you phoned the FBI. We identified the potential seller and asked you to set up a sting operation. We wanted to use your portion of the company to process the sale of the diamonds so we could catch Thatcher."

"And did you catch him?" Jack asked.

"No." Parker had the same look that Reyes had had when he walked in and announced the kidnapper had gotten away. But unlike Reyes's account, something about this didn't sound right.

Alana took a step forward and met Parker's gaze head-on. "Are you saying I agreed to cooperate with this sting operation?"

Parker nodded. "You did."

Alana huffed. "But I was pregnant. Nearly eight months along. And I would have known this might be dangerous."

Another nod. "You still wanted to do it. Of course, we didn't know it would actually place you in danger. All we asked you to do was to agree to speak with Thatcher again. Not even in person. We wanted you to handle the transaction over the phone. An agent would have stood in for you if you could have arranged a sale to take place on Christmas day." He shrugged. "That didn't happen."

"Why not?" Jack demanded, his voice cutting through the silence.

"Honestly, we don't know. We think someone tipped off Thatcher that Alana was an informant. When I realized what'd happened, I tried to call Alana and warn her, but she wasn't home. Her housekeeper said she'd left unexpectedly. After that, she disappeared."

That filled in a few blanks. *If* he was telling the truth. "Why did I come to Willow Ridge?"

He shook his head. "I don't know. Maybe you realized someone was following you, and you started driving and ended up here."

Because she badly wanted to refute that, Alana squeezed her eyes shut and tried to force herself to remember. It didn't work. There was a huge gap of time missing between that meeting with Parker and Jack pulling her from that frozen creek.

"From what I've heard, you've been through a lot," the agent continued. "We can arrange proper medical care for you. Maybe then your memory will return."

Jack stepped closer to Parker. "Are we back to the protective custody issue now?"

"Yes. Alana has to go with me."

"No. I don't," she said as the exact moment that Jack said, "No, she doesn't."

Parker's eyes widened. "Why would you refuse protection? Alana, you could be in grave danger. Your son, too. Thatcher's a dangerous man."

"Obviously. He came after me at the hospital. Now, why would he do that? Before today, I'd never seen his face. I couldn't identify him."

"Who knows?" Parker lifted his hands, palm up. "He might just be trying to eliminate anyone who could connect him to those diamonds."

"That doesn't make sense," Jack insisted. "If all Thatcher wanted was Alana out of the way, then why didn't he just kill her in the hospital room?"

As chilling as that possibility was, Jack was right.

Parker glanced away. Groaned under his breath. "This sounds gruesome, but he might have wanted to torture her first. As I said, Thatcher is dangerous."

Alana hadn't doubted that for a moment. "I'm not going with you," she informed the agent.

Parker's gaze slashed back to hers. "That could be a fatal mistake."

"Could be," she agreed. But she was going to rely on her instincts here, and her instincts were to trust Jack. Besides, she had no intention of leaving her son.

Parker extracted his business card from his pocket and handed it to her. "All right, then. I'll inform my boss of your decision, but call me if you change your mind." He turned as if to leave, but then stopped. He looked at Jack. "When Thatcher tries to take her again, my advice is shoot to kill. Because he won't stop. He'll keep coming after her until he succeeds."

"I wish he were saying that just to scare me," Alana mumbled as she watched the agent walk away. "But he's probably right about this Eldon Thatcher."

Jack shut the door, locked it and in the same motion he caught her arm and led her in the direction of the break room. "Talk to me about Agent Howell. The meeting with him that you can remember, how did it go?"

"Not well, actually. I told him that as a jewelry maker I got contacted often by sellers who were suspicious. These sellers either had no paperwork to prove ownership of what they were offering, or the paperwork was doubtful at best. That's why I declined Parker's request when he wanted me to set up this particular sting."

"He says you changed your mind." Jack's tone mirrored her own doubts about what the agent had claimed.

Alana sank onto the sofa the moment they made it into the break room. "Why would he lie about something like that?"

"Maybe because he's trying to cover his butt."

Alana shook her head. "What do you mean?"

Jack eased the door shut and motioned for her to lie down. He didn't continue until she complied. She could have sworn her feet and back breathed sighs of relief at the prospect of finally getting some rest. Still, she

would have preferred to be in the room with Joey while
they worked to find answers about this investigation.

"Parker said the FBI was going to use a stand-in if
the deal went down," Jack explained. "When you refused to get involved with the case, he might have used
you anyway. He could have had this stand-in pose as
you and contact Eldon Thatcher to arrange the sale."

Alana worked her way through that theory. "And
maybe something went wrong. Maybe Thatcher realized it was a setup, and he came after me because he
believed I had betrayed him." Mercy, it made sense. "I
knew there was a reason I didn't trust Parker."

"I could be wrong." Jack walked closer and looked
down at her. "I can make some calls and find out what
this deal with Thatcher was all about."

More calls. Added to the arrangements he'd have
to make to keep them all safe. "I'm sorry I'm putting
you through this."

He stood there, and a moment later he nodded. "I
don't think this is your fault." He eased onto the edge
of the sofa so that he was sitting next to where she was
lying. "Your brother could be after your money. Parker
could be trying to cover up something, and he could
have inadvertently put Eldon Thatcher on your trail."

"And then there's Margaret and Ted. Maybe they're
working for my brother. Or maybe not. I suppose it's
possible they've been holding me all this time for their
own monetary gain." Her gaze snapped to Jack's just
as his jumped to hers. "My financial records. I need to
go through them to see if someone's gotten into them."

He put his hand on her shoulder when she tried to
get up. "I'd planned to do that after you were asleep."

Yet more work for him. "I can't rest. I need to help you."

"You can rest," he insisted. "Alana, I need you to have a clear head, and that won't happen until you sleep off the sedative Thatcher gave you."

She wanted badly to argue, but she wasn't sure she had the strength to put up a fight. "Can I at least take my nap in the room with Joey?"

"Trust me, you won't get a nap if you're in the room with him."

And at that moment, she heard her son giggle.

The right corner of Jack's mouth lifted. "See?" But the smile was soon replaced with a more serious expression. "Tell you what, I'll bring him in here for just a couple of seconds if you promise me you'll get some sleep."

"I promise." She had no choice. Sleep was going to come whether she wanted it or not. "It must be hard to be so nice to me."

She reached up to smooth away the worry lines on his forehead, but the moment she touched him, she knew it was a mistake. Even now, with all the danger and uncertainty, touching was out.

Jack snagged her hand to move it away. Or so she thought. But he held on to it, lacing their fingers together. He looked as if he were about to say something, but then he released the grip he had on her and started to stand.

Alana caught him. "What were you going to say?"

"Something stupid."

"Go ahead. Say it. With this fog in my head, I probably won't remember it anyway." And for some reason, that made her smile.

He locked gazes with her. "You can't take Joey from me."

Oh, she'd thought this was about the attraction, but she was wrong. Thankfully, one of them had his mind on the right track. And the right track was Joey.

Alana forced herself to come up with a possible solution, one that would get that dour expression off Jack's face. "What if I agree for us to split custody for now? Once Thatcher is caught, we can work out something more permanent."

The dour expression and the pain stayed. This was killing him. But it wasn't a walk in the park for her, either.

"Jack, I have to be a mother to my son." She paused. "But that doesn't mean I'll exclude you as his father. He calls you Da-Da, for heaven's sake. I can see the love you two feel for each other."

He didn't say anything for several moments. "Split custody," he repeated. He started to get up again.

Again, Alana stopped him. She wanted to tell him that she would be fair, that she wouldn't do anything intentional to hurt him or her son. Even if that meant she had to back off for a while.

"I don't get involved easily," he said, surprising her with this turn in the conversation.

"Neither do I." Her tone was cautious, and she waited for more.

"But there's this attraction." His tone was even more cautious than hers. "I'm guessing it's because of Joey?"

Maybe it was the hazy head, but she couldn't make the connection. "No. I don't think it has anything to do with him. You're a hot guy. It's simple attraction."

He seemed to give that some thought, and just when

Alana was certain that he was indeed going to move away, she tightened her grip on his arm and dragged him down to her.

She kissed him.

Alana kept it brief. Hardly more than a peck. But her body reacted as if it were much more. The punch was like hot liquid fire. And she couldn't help but wonder what would happen if they really kissed.

He stayed close, his mouth hovering over hers. "This complicates the hell out of things, you know that?"

"I know. I should probably promise that it won't happen again."

"But it will," he disagreed.

"It will?" The only surprise was that he'd admitted it.

"Yeah. And if you figure out a way to stop it, let me know." He did stand then. "I'll bring Joey in."

Alana hated when he moved away from her. She lost his scent and his warmth all at once. Worse, she lost the sensation of his being there for her. She realized she'd gone a lifetime without feeling that.

Jack hadn't even made it to the door when there was a knock, and it opened. Reyes stuck his head into the room. "We got a problem, boss."

Alana groaned and sat up, bracing herself for the next round.

"A Texas Ranger just called," Reyes explained. He stepped inside, and Alana spotted the piece of paper he had in his hand. "When the Rangers got out to the Sauder Facility, the place was already on fire. They couldn't save anything. By the time the fire department arrived, the entire place was nothing but cinders and ash."

Jack cursed. So did Alana. This was a huge setback. There would almost certainly have been some kind of incriminating evidence in that house that might point to one or more of their suspects.

"There's more," Reyes said. "The mailbox didn't burn, and there was a note inside it. It was from our kidnapping suspect, Eldon Thatcher. The Ranger read it to me, and I wrote it down word for word."

Reyes looked at the paper he held in his hand. Then looked at her. "I'll give you the clean version. Thatcher says he's gonna kill you."

Alana had already suspected that, so she was more than a little surprised at her reaction. Maybe it was hearing the threat aloud that did it, but fear and worry dropped on her like a ton of bricks.

Jack took the note, read through it and then as if he'd declared war on it, he crumpled it into a ball.

"What did it say?" Alana asked, not at all certain that she wanted to know.

"Thatcher's a sick SOB," Reyes mumbled.

"What did it say?" Alana repeated.

"He thinks you sold him out to the FBI." Jack didn't look at her when he spoke. "He wants revenge. And he says he'll get it by taking Joey."

Chapter 10

The sound of Joey's laughter cut through the silence in the hospital waiting room.

Joey grabbed on to a magazine-laded table and pulled himself to a standing position. He slapped at the surface as if to announce his victory. Joey had learned to pull himself up two days earlier, and he'd already mastered it. According to the baby books Jack had read, it wouldn't be long before Joey was walking.

Tessie applauded the feat, causing Joey to giggle again. From the other side of the room, Alana sat and watched. She was smiling, cataloging Joey's every move. She hadn't taken her eyes off him during their ten-minute wait for Dr. Bartolo to appear for her checkup.

Reyes was blocking the doorway that led to the corridor. Unlike Alana, his attention wasn't on Joey. Reyes was standing guard.

Jack had a dozen important things to do. Beefing up security at the ranch. Following up on the search for Eldon Thatcher. Helping Reyes process Thatcher's car and the crime scene in the hospital parking lot. Oh, yeah, and he had to keep his son and Alana safe.

That was primary in his mind.

And that was the reason both he and Reyes were at the hospital waiting. If the doc gave her a clean bill of health, the first thing Alana would want was to hold Joey. Jack wouldn't stop her.

But Alana wouldn't settle for just holding Joey. She'd want to be a major part of his life. And that meant Jack had something else to add to his to-do list. He had to consult his attorney. He had to do whatever it took to keep primary custody of Joey. Then he could control the situation and give Alana visitation rights.

Jack glanced in Alana's direction. She still had her attention fastened to Joey. That intense look told him everything. She might have offered to share custody with him, but she would probably change her mind.

First, though, she had to battle for her safety.

Jack heard footsteps in the corridor and eased his hand over the butt of his holstered gun. "It's the doc," Reyes let him know.

Reyes stepped inside, clearing the path for Dr. Bartolo to enter. The doctor glanced at Jack's posture. Then at Alana. "Go ahead into the examining room." He pointed to a door just a few yards away. "I need to run over to the lab and pick up your results."

Alana nodded and stood. Jack stood, too. He didn't

intend to let Alana out of his sight. Reyes would do the same for Tessie and Joey.

"I see the worry in your eyes," Alana whispered as they went into the examining room.

Jack didn't deny it was there. He left the door open just a fraction so he could respond faster if there was an emergency.

"I had some time to think last night," she added.

He'd heard her tossing and turning. "You were supposed to be resting."

"I managed to do that, too." Her face said otherwise. Still, her chin lifted up, a gesture she probably hoped would make her appear resolved. It didn't work. She still looked tired. "All that thinking led me to a decision. I've decided to move to Willow Ridge."

Jack froze. "Move here?" He didn't like the sound of that. Not that he thought she would just disappear. But having her underfoot was not going to cool this attraction between them. And it would put her near Joey every single day. "We're back to talking about splitting custody?"

She shook her head. "No."

"No?" Jack forced himself to unfreeze, and walked closer so he could study her expression. She was tired, yes. But her eyes were suddenly a lot clearer than they had been.

"I decided you should keep custody for now."

Jack blinked. And replayed each word. After doing that several times, he was still certain he'd misunderstood. "Excuse me?"

She swallowed hard. "For the time being, I want you to have custody."

He'd heard her all right. It was exactly what he'd

wanted to hear, but what he couldn't understand was why she was saying it. "Why the change of heart?"

"More like a reality check." She scrubbed her hands up and down her arms. "I don't need to remind you that my life's a mess. Someone wants me dead, and that's spilled over to Joey. I know you're doing your best to keep him safe. I heard you talking on the phone this morning. You're trying to increase security at the ranch."

He was. He'd even borrowed some ranch hands from neighbors and would have them patrol the pastures. "What does that have to do with custody?"

"Everything." She looked him straight in the eye. "I know you'll do what's necessary to protect Joey."

He would. But he didn't need full custody for that.

"I won't continue to be a burden to you," she added. Her words rushed out as if she'd rehearsed them. "Once we're at the ranch, I'll call and make arrangements for my own security. I can hire a P.I. Several of them. I want them searching for evidence to link Margaret and Ted or even my brother to what's going on. I can also press the Rangers to do more to find Eldon Thatcher. Then I can—"

Jack touched his fingers to her mouth. That simple reminder to slow down worked—she hushed and stared at him. "I can't let you do all the work, okay?" she continued. "Especially since I'm responsible for this."

Oh, man. He didn't want to go there. "Eldon Thatcher is responsible," he reminded her.

She shook her head, but her frustration and fear were evident. Jack knew those emotions well. He felt the same.

"I have this beautiful son," she muttered. Her voice

was beyond shaky. "A son who's in danger, and everything I do still feels as if it's not enough. I should probably get out of town and put some distance between Joey and me, but I'm afraid if I leave, I won't be here to help protect him."

Again, he was right there on the same page with her. Nothing short of jailing Eldon Thatcher would be enough, and even that wouldn't solve all their problems.

"The fight's just started," Jack said. "It's a fight we'll win." Because the alternative wasn't an alternative at all.

And then he did something stupid.

He pulled her into his arms.

The embrace didn't seem so uncomfortable this time.

It felt natural.

What was it about Alana that made him want to get close? He didn't have time for sex. Heck, he didn't have time for a kiss. But that didn't stop him from brushing his lips over her forehead. Nor did it stop him from thinking about where all of this could go after everyone responsible had been caught.

"Let me deal with security," he told her. "Put everything else on hold for now."

She pulled back and stared at him. "I'm not as weak as I was yesterday or the night before when I staggered into your office."

"Yes." For some stupid reason, that nearly made him smile. "I can see that."

That strength would be trouble. As long as she was dazed and weak, he could pretend this closeness was all about protection. He could rationalize that she needed his shoulder. His arms. Heck, maybe she still did need them, but Jack was betting at the moment neither of them was feeling very protective.

She had a unique way of capturing his attention, and she did it by just being her.

Alana no longer wore his clothes. Reyes had brought her one of his girlfriend's outfits. A snug denim skirt, lavender sleeveless top and flat sandals. The items probably weren't her usual fashion fare. After all, Alana came from money, and the outfit screamed *discount store*. But the clothes fit her like a glove.

A tight glove, that accentuated her every curve.

And suddenly those curves seemed as interesting and enticing as her mouth.

Oh, yes. She could definitely get his attention.

The door opened, and they jumped apart as if they'd been doing something wrong. Which wasn't far off the mark. Jack had been on the brink of kissing her blind.

"Everything okay?" Dr. Bartolo asked, noticing their contact and the reaction to being caught.

"You tell me," Alana countered. She cleared her throat, straightened her clothes and tried to look indignant. "What do my lab tests say?"

The doctor stayed quiet a moment. "That you're good to go."

Alana let out a gasp. Of relief, no doubt. Jack wasn't quite so relieved. "What about the virus?"

"No signs of it. The nurse took Alana's vitals when she checked in. No fever. Blood pressure and pulse were normal. It appears the virus was just a twenty-four-hour thing."

"I can hold Joey," she said, heading for the door.

Jack didn't stop her, but he did follow. So did Dr. Bartolo, but he only hung around a couple of seconds before he mumbled "good luck" and started for the corridor.

Tessie must have realized what was about to happen because she got to her feet. Joey was still batting the magazines on the table, and he turned, apparently aware that something major was going on.

Alana didn't make a mad run toward Joey. She slowed her steps and approached him with caution. She paused just a few seconds before she reached down and scooped him into her arms.

Joey looked at Jack for reassurance. After all, Alana was practically a stranger. But Joey didn't cry when she pulled him into a long embrace. His son babbled a little, but Alana's hair soon caught his attention. Joey tugged at one of the strands.

Jack looked around the room at everyone's reactions. Tessie had her hand pressed to her chest and was watching the embrace as if it were a train wreck. Alana's eyes were shiny with fresh tears. And Reyes was watching Jack. The deputy had his eyebrow cocked, questioning how Jack was taking all of this.

Jack didn't have a clue.

He didn't have to examine his feelings, either, because Reyes's cell phone rang. The man answered it, and Jack knew after just a couple of seconds that this call involved something major. He moved closer to Reyes in case they had to discuss business.

"That was Kirby," Reyes informed him. Kirby Ward, the night deputy who was manning the office. "He just got a visitor. Margaret Vargas."

The nurse from Sauder. Interesting. And surprising. "What does she want?"

"To talk to you and Alana. She told Kirby she needed to discuss the fire at Sauder."

Even more interesting. But Jack's first instinct was to refuse to have Alana present when he talked with the nurse. He didn't want to put her through that stress, and he wanted to get her settled into the ranch.

But maybe Margaret would say things to Alana that she wouldn't say to him. Better yet, it would get Alana away from Joey so that Jack could take a deep breath and figure out how he was going to deal with everything that'd happened.

"Go ahead and take Tessie and Joey to the ranch," Jack instructed Reyes. "Alana and I will meet with Margaret, see what she has to say."

Then he could finally get Alana to the ranch so he could get some work done. How, exactly, he didn't know, but he was thinking he might have to rotate Kirby, Reyes and himself at the ranch so they could get the evidence processed. Bodyguard duty was a necessity, but so was catching the man who'd tried to kidnap Alana. Added to all of that, he had to keep the town safe.

Tessie stepped forward to take Joey from Alana. His aunt did so hesitantly, and Alana was also hesitant about giving up the child. She kissed Joey's cheek and gave him a little wave. His son waved back, but not at Alana. At Jack.

Jack could almost feel Alana's heart breaking.

There wasn't time to dwell on it. Jack caught her arm to get her moving. The sooner they met with Margaret, the sooner he could do his job and get her to safety.

Tessie, Joey and Reyes were ahead of them in the

corridor, but Jack had no trouble spotting Dr. Bartolo, and the man talking to the doctor.

Parker Howell.

"What's he doing here?" Alana mumbled.

But she didn't get an immediate answer to her question. The conversation abruptly ended, and Parker hurried off. Jack stopped in front of Dr. Bartolo, and they all watched as Parker exited through the front doors.

"Was Agent Howell looking for us?" Jack asked.

Dr. Bartolo shook his head. "Not exactly. He said he was in town to drop off some more flyers about a missing woman."

Right. Kinley Ford. Reyes had told him that the FBI and the Rangers wanted to find the woman, and he wished he could help. But he had enough to deal with.

"Parker also wanted to know Alana's medical condition," the doctor added. "He especially wanted to know if she was still experiencing memory loss. I told him I'd give the information to him if he got a court order."

Good. Jack didn't want to share anything with the man who seemed determined to take custody of Alana.

"This isn't the first time I've seen Agent Howell around here," the doctor added. "He's was at the hospital eight months ago, the night Alana disappeared."

Alana's eyes were wide when she looked at Jack. "Any reason you didn't mention this sooner?"

"I didn't remember it until I saw him today. All I recall was seeing him in the hall. I didn't make the connection to Alana until he asked about her just now."

"He saw me that night?" Alana clarified.

"Probably. Visitors weren't restricted."

That meant Parker might have been the last person

to see Alana before she disappeared. Funny that the man hadn't come clean about his visit sooner.

That made Jack wonder. What else had Parker failed to mention?

With Alana in tow, Jack hurried toward the doors so he could catch the agent and get some answers that Parker had obviously been dodging.

But Parker was nowhere in sight.

That made Jack even more suspicious. Even though he had a long list of things to do, he really needed to make the time to have a thorough chat with Parker. While he was at it, he needed to call an old friend in the FBI and make sure Parker was legit.

"I take it you don't remember anything about Parker's hospital visit eight months ago?" Jack asked.

"Nothing."

He was afraid of that.

Jack led her out the side exit where he'd left his SUV. Ahead of them, Reyes got Tessie and Joey into the cruiser and drove away in the direction of the ranch. Jack started for his office, which was four miles away in the opposite direction.

"I was obviously drugged that night," Alana continued. "I've been thinking about who and how that could have happened."

So had he. "You remember eating anything?"

"Just the food that Tessie brought me." But then she stopped. "Wait. I also had some orange juice. It was on the tray after I came out of the bathroom, so I had a few sips."

Orange juice could have masked the taste of a drug, and anyone could easily have placed the glass in her room. Her brother, Sean, was still Jack's prime suspect. Or maybe Eldon Thatcher had done it in an attempt to sedate Alana so he could get her quietly out of the hospital.

But how did Parker fit in?

It wouldn't be standard practice for an agent to drug an informant, but that didn't mean he hadn't done exactly that. Maybe Parker thought the drug would make Alana comply with his plan. Then perhaps something had gone wrong? Maybe she'd wandered away before Parker could get to her?

"There are two issues here," Jack said, thinking out loud. "The diamond deal and your disappearance."

She turned in the seat, stared at him. "You think they're connected?"

"Not exactly. But Sean might have used the opportunity to capitalize. He might have rationalized that he was keeping you safe from Thatcher by locking you away at Sauder." Though that would have taken a mountain of rationalization. Still, when money was involved, Jack knew people could do all sorts of things.

"After our talk with Margaret, I want you to check your accounts and see if any money's missing," he instructed. "If it is, that might give me enough for a search warrant to go through your brother's financial records to see if he profited from your stay at Sauder."

Alana nodded. Then paused. "But does Parker fit into that?"

"Maybe. If Sean is the one who put you in Sauder, then maybe he drugged you so he could get you there. Or he could have worked with Parker to do that."

She made a face to indicate she wasn't sure she believed that. "You think Parker drugged me?"

"He was there at the hospital." Still, it was stretch. Unless...

Jack kept coming back to the possibility that Parker was dirty. And if he was truly was, then that made this situation even more complicated.

And dangerous.

"Don't borrow trouble," Alana mumbled. "Let's just focus on my brother and Thatcher for now. We can try to find a money trail leading to my brother while trying to capture Thatcher before he causes us any more problems."

Jack was about to agree when he heard a loud pop. Before the sound barely registered in his head, his SUV jerked to the right.

A blowout.

On the front passenger's-side tire. Alana's side.

He fought to keep the SUV on the road. But there was a second pop and another violent jerk of his vehicle. Jack knew he was losing control.

He also knew why.

Someone had shot out the tires.

He couldn't draw his weapon because he needed both hands on the wheel. He had to stay on the road. Because if he crashed, they would be sitting ducks.

"Do you see the shooter?" Jack asked.

"Shooter?" Judging from the way she blurted that out, she'd just realized what was happening.

His SUV careered off the asphalt and launched into the thick underbrush that flanked both sides of the road. He saw the sprawling live oak, but there was nothing he could do to stop. Still, he tried. He fought with the steering wheel, trying to wrench it in the opposite direction.

But it was too late.

"Hold on!" Jack yelled.

He barely got out the warning before his SUV slammed into the tree.

Chapter 11

The airbag punched into Alana, pinning her against the seat and smothering her. She couldn't move. Couldn't breathe. But she knew she had to do something.

Somewhere amid the trees and the wild shrubs, there was a gunman who was responsible for what had just happened.

And that man was probably Eldon Thatcher.

He'd shot out the tires, and that had caused Jack to lose control and career into the tree. Worse, this might be just the start of the attack.

Beside her, Jack batted aside his airbag. "Are you hurt?" he asked.

Alana quickly tried to take inventory of her body. Other than her constricted breathing, she wasn't in any real pain. But she was terrified.

Jack frantically drew his weapon from his shoulder

holster. "Try to push down your airbag. I need to see if the shooter's coming."

Oh, God. Thatcher might be coming to finish them off.

With her heartbeat pounding in her ears, Alana latched on to the airbag fabric and shoved it away so she could look out the windshield. Both it and her side window were shattered, making it impossible to see if they were about to be attacked.

"Get down!" Jack shouted.

It wasn't a moment too soon.

A bullet tore through the already shattered windshield and sent a spray of safety glass spewing right at them.

Jack cursed and took aim at the gaping hole that the bullet had left. He fired. The blast echoed through the cab of the SUV and caused Alana's ears to pound.

She thought of Joey. Her precious son. Alana prayed that this latest attack was confined only to Jack and her. Maybe Reyes had already gotten her baby to safety at the ranch. She didn't want Joey anywhere near this.

"Stay down. I need you to call nine-one-one." Jack's voice somehow made it over the noise in her own head, as he thrust his phone into her hand.

Before she could dial the first number, another bullet sliced through the metal roof. The large gash brought in heat and blinding sunlight. It was also a reminder of how little protection they had.

Even though her hands were shaking, Alana punched in the numbers, and Deputy Kirby Ward answered. "Someone's shooting at me and Jack," she practically shouted into the phone. And she gave the man their location as best she could.

Another shot fired.

Then another.

Both ripped through her side of the door and came so close that she could almost feel the heat from them. She sank lower into the seat, but she knew that might not do her any good.

Jack levered himself up and returned fire.

"The deputy's on his way," she relayed to Jack. But the question was, would he get there in time? Or would his arrival just make him a target, as well?

"The guy's using a rifle," Jack let her know.

Because the adrenaline and her heartbeat were roaring through her, it took a moment for her to realize what that meant. The shooter was probably hiding behind some of that thick brush or even in a tree. He might not be close enough for Jack's gun to stop him.

The next bullet proved that.

It tore into the seat just above her head.

"Get on the floor!" Jack yelled.

She tried, though the airbag was in her way. Alana shouldered it aside and slid to the floor. For all the good it'd do. Those bullets were eating their way through the SUV, and there was no place safe she could hide.

"You need to get down, too," she told Jack. "You could be hit."

Just the thought of it made her sick. Jack was in this position because of her. She'd put him in danger, and he was taking the majority of the risk by trying to return fire.

Behind them, Alana heard the sound of a car approaching from the road. She didn't dare try to see who it was, but since there was no siren, it probably wasn't the deputy. It was likely an innocent bystander who could also be hurt by one of those flying bullets.

But just like that, the shots stopped.

The silence came so quickly that it caused yet another surge of adrenaline. She knelt there, waiting. Listening.

Jack glanced down at her. "The car must have scared off the shooter."

Good. Except that it meant the gunman might be getting away. Jack must have realized that, as well because he reached for the handle of his door.

Alana latched on to his arm. "You're not going out there."

"I have to."

She was about to argue that point, but she heard a welcome sound. A siren. Backup was close.

Jack pushed her hand from his arm and opened his door. Alana held her breath and prayed that the shots wouldn't start again.

They didn't.

There was only the sound of the siren and Jack's movements.

She levered herself up slightly, and through the hole in the windshield, she saw him take cover behind the tree. His gaze darted all around, looking for the person who'd just tried to kill them.

And then he looked down.

His attention snapped to her. "Get out of the SUV. The gas tank ruptured. If he shoots again, it could cause a fire."

"Oh, God." Alana didn't waste any time. She grabbed the handle, but when it wouldn't budge, she rammed her shoulder against the door to open it. Because of her position, she couldn't get her footing and tumbled onto the ground and scrambled for cover.

"Stay behind the tree," Jack instructed. "Get ready to run if he fires a shot at that gasoline." And then his attention snapped behind them.

For one terrifying moment, she thought maybe the shooter had managed to sneak up on them, but Alana soon realized from the badge he wore that it was the deputy, Kirby Ward. He was young, probably not much older than twenty-one, with a slight build, but he was armed. The moment he was in place, guarding her, Jack stepped out from behind the tree.

Mercy, he was going out there. Alana wanted to tell him to stop, but she couldn't. The shooter was almost certainly Thatcher—a man who'd already tried to kidnap her—and he needed to be stopped. Still, this lull in the shots could be a ploy.

But Jack stepped out into the open anyway, just as another shot rang out.

Alana heard herself scream. She tried to move, to get to Jack so she could help him. But the deputy hooked his left arm around her and held on. She struggled, fighting him, but he wouldn't let go.

"I'm okay," Jack said. "The bullet didn't even come in this direction."

She stopped fighting and went limp with relief. Thatcher hadn't shot at Jack after all.

"What the hell?" Jack mumbled.

The deputy inched away from her and peered around the tree. Alana, too, wanted to know what had caused Jack's reaction.

Both Jack and Kirby had their attention fastened to

something in front of the tree. They had their weapons aimed and ready, but neither looked on the verge of firing.

Jack cursed again and rushed out of her sight. Kirby did the same and shouted, "I'll call an ambulance."

An ambulance? Why? Had Thatcher shot himself?

She couldn't stay put. Alana eased out from the cover of the tree and spotted Jack and Kirby racing toward someone. A man. Staggering, he had a rifle in his hand, but he dropped it to the ground. And Alana soon realized why.

He wasn't surrendering, exactly. There was a bright red stain across the front of his shirt.

Blood.

He'd been shot in the chest.

It wasn't Eldon Thatcher.

It was Ted Moore, the security guard from Sauder.

Judging from Jack's and Kirby's reactions, they were just as surprised as she was.

Since the man was either dead or very close to it, Alana hurried out to the spot where Ted had fallen.

Jack crouched down, but Kirby kept watch around them in case the worst happened: another attack. But Ted certainly wasn't in any shape to continue shooting.

When she approached the man on the ground, Ted immediately angled his eyes in her direction. He opened his mouth and lifted his hand to point at her.

"I…" He drew in a labored breath. His hand dropped, but his gaze stayed fastened on her. "He took your money."

"Who?" Jack and Alana asked in unison.

Ted opened his mouth again, but he said nothing

else. He sucked in one last thin breath and made a choking sound in his throat. And that was it.

Ted Moore was dead.

Jack tried to make himself appear as calm as possible. Tessie looked terrified and her hands were shaking when she hugged him.

"You could have been killed," his aunt said under her breath.

Yeah. Alana, too. But they'd both made it out of the crash and the shooting without so much as a scratch. They'd gotten lucky. Unlike Ted Moore. And while Jack wasn't sorry about having a suspect out of the way, he would have preferred Ted alive. The man's death had left them with far more questions than answers.

Alana's hands were shaking, too, but that didn't stop her from picking up Joey the moment they walked into the family room of the ranch house. His son didn't look so apprehensive this time and offered Alana a tentative smile. When she smiled back, Joey began to babble.

Reyes walked to Jack's side. "I need to get out to the scene of the shooting. You can manage things here?"

"Yes." But the problem was, Jack didn't know what exactly he had to manage. Eldon Thatcher was still out there. Jack didn't know if Ted's death affected Thatcher or not. The men could have two entirely separate agendas, or they could have been partners.

"The medical examiner should have had time to check the body." Jack kept his voice low so that Tessie and Alana wouldn't hear. Thankfully, both women were engrossed in Joey's antics. "I need to know if that gunshot wound was self-inflicted."

"You think it was?"

Jack wanted to say yes. He wanted that to be true. But he had his doubts. It wasn't impossible to self-inflict with a rifle to the chest, but it wasn't the simplest of maneuvers. He settled for answering, "I'm not sure."

Reyes made a sound of agreement. "If Ted was murdered, that means someone else had to be out there."

Yeah. It did. And that's why Jack wouldn't be getting much sleep tonight.

"Check the area for any sign that Ted wasn't acting alone," Jack instructed. "I also want Margaret questioned. She insisted Alana and I meet her at the sheriff's office, so she might have known which route we'd be taking to get there. She might have set all of this up."

"It's possible. She left your office after Kirby responded to your nine-one-one for backup."

Not exactly a surprise, but it was a disturbing development. It could mean that all of them—Thatcher, Ted and Margaret—were working together.

If so, he had two more people to stop.

And then he had to figure out how Alana's brother, Sean, and Special Agent Parker Howell fit into all of this. He needed plenty of information, and he wasn't sure Alana was up to getting it. Still, he didn't have a choice. Yes, she was shaken from the shooting, but he had to do everything within his power to stop another attack.

Reyes made his exit, and Jack went to the front door to lock it and set the security alarm. All the doors and windows were wired, and while this wouldn't necessarily stop another shooting, it would alert him if anyone tried to break in.

Alana looked in his direction as Jack walked back into the family room. His expression must have said it all because she kissed Joey and handed him to Tessie. Jack could see the loss in her face. It was painful to hand over her son when she'd had so few precious moments with him. But there would be other moments.

Moments he'd have to learn to deal with.

"You need me to call about my financial records," Alana said. She blew out a deep breath and pushed her hair from her face.

Jack nodded, and that was Tessie's cue to head for the kitchen. "Joey's probably hungry by now. I'll fix you both something to eat, too." His aunt closed the double doors behind her.

He took your money, Ted had warned. It had to be checked. Alana definitely had more than enough money to make a greedy person do all sorts of criminal things.

Jack pointed to the laptop on a corner desk. "If you remember your account passwords, it might be faster."

She gave a choppy nod, went to the computer and got started right away. He watched her as she clicked her way to a bank Web site. Her hands were still shaking. She was probably close to an inevitable adrenaline crash. Even though this was critical, the task wouldn't stop the crash. Nothing would. Very soon, Alana would realize just how close she'd come to dying today.

"Someone changed the password," she let him know.

That didn't surprise him. A criminal would have done that as soon as he'd gotten control of the account, which wouldn't have been hard to do with Alana drugged. Heck, she might even have given the person the info.

Alana reached for the phone that was next to the laptop. "I'll call my assistant." But she stopped with her hand poised over the phone. "If I still have an assistant." She groaned and shook her head. "God knows what's happened to my business since I've been gone."

"Your brother said he managed it for you," Jack reminded her.

"That's what I'm afraid of." Anger flashed through her eyes, and she snatched up the phone. "I'm calling my assistant on her personal phone. I'm pretty sure I still remember the number."

Several moments later, Alana was speaking to her assistant, Deidre. Alana cut through the woman's questions about where she'd been and said, "I can't explain all of that now. Sorry." She paused. "Deidre, I need you to go through my accounts. All of them." Another pause. "Yes, I know it might take a while, but call me the second you know the balances."

The adrenaline had drained him, as well, so Jack pulled over a chair and sat down beside her. He listened to her responses, and judging from her expression, this conversation wasn't giving her much good news. When she finally hung up, worry had bunched up her forehead.

"Sean told my assistant that I was away on an extended vacation." The emotion caused her voice to break on the last word.

Jack had to tamp down some emotion, as well. But in his case, it was anger. "Wonder why he was so convinced you weren't in danger?" But Jack knew the answer to that. If Sean had been the one who'd kept her at Sauder—and it was looking more and more as if he was—he would have told her assistant that all was well so as not to raise any alarms. He wouldn't have wanted the police brought in.

But that made Jack wonder.

Why hadn't Agent Parker Howell done more to find her? He had to have suspected that Alana was in trouble. Sean might not have been aware of the diamond deal if he'd only been after control of her money, but Parker was certainly aware of it. Yet he hadn't been able to find her.

"I can't believe my brother might have done this to me," Alana said. She stood and shook her head. She squeezed her eyes shut.

Jack stood, too, aware that they were too close. Practically toe-to-toe.

She leaned her head against him, her body brushing against his, but then she immediately jerked back.

"Sorry," she mumbled.

So was he. Sorry that she'd backed away. Despite being on the verge of a meltdown, Alana had remembered the dangerous attraction between them. But Jack was suddenly having a hard time following her lead.

Alana looked up at him. And the restraint she'd shown just moments earlier went south.

It happened fast. She leapt to her toes. He swooped down on her. Their mouths met. Man, did they ever! This was no gentle sweet kiss to offer comfort. This was hot and hungry.

Jack grabbed her. Like his kiss, this was no soft embrace. He snapped her to him. Alana didn't resist. She went willingly and upped the stakes by coiling her arms around his neck. That put their bodies directly against each other.

But he knew he was playing with fire.

He just didn't care.

He wanted this heat. He wanted Alana. Even if wanting her didn't make sense. Soon, very soon, they'd battle for custody of Joey, and the memory of this kiss wouldn't help. But did that make him stop?

No.

Jack only pulled her closer. He slid his hand around the back of her neck and deepened the kiss. That caused the fire inside her to burn even hotter. Her breasts pressed against his chest. Their mouths moved in some frenetic dance to find pleasure.

Her sex brushed against his. There it was. That punch. The reminder of where a good kiss usually led. To sex. In the back of his mind, he knew he couldn't go there, but that didn't stop him, either.

Alana voiced a throaty moan of pleasure and shifted her position, moving against him, her body against his erection. She wanted more of that contact, and she shoved him against the wall. It wasn't gentle. He landed with a thud.

Alana landed against him.

Exactly where he wanted her to be.

Jack trailed the kisses to her neck. It tasted just as good as her mouth and revved his body up another notch. Alana took things even further when her hand trailed down his side and then to his stomach. When her hand started to go even lower, Jack knew he had to do something or he'd end up having sex with her right then, right there.

He spun her around so that it was her back against the wall, and caught her hands, pinning them, so that she couldn't do any more of that mind-blowing touching. He kissed her one last time, and forced himself to pull back.

Their eyes met. He'd hoped to see some sane, rational regret in the depths of all that blue, but all he saw was the heat no doubt mirrored in his.

"Wow," she said. Somehow, that said it all.

He'd expected a kiss with Alana to be good, but he hadn't expected the out-of-control crazy stuff reserved for lust-crazed teenagers.

"We can't have sex, can we?" she asked.

It was a question his body wanted to answer, *Yes, we can*. But he ignored his body and tried to sound like a responsible adult. "Just an hour ago, we were under attack. This is a reaction to that."

She stared at him. Her eyes narrowed slightly. That was the only warning he got before she lunged forward. Even though he had her hands still pinned, her mouth landed right on his. No restraint. Nothing held back.

Alana kissed him.

What little composure he'd garnered just washed away, and when she finally pulled back, he knew this wasn't a reaction to the shooting. It was a human reaction. Pure basic primal attraction. He wanted her naked. He wanted to be inside her. He didn't care if it was wrong or if it complicated the hell out of things.

They stood there staring at each other, their breaths hot and fast. Not moving. He didn't dare move. Because if Alana brushed against his erection one more time, he'd lose control.

"We can't kiss again," she said.

"I don't want this to get mixed up with what's going on with Joey." Jack wanted it out there in the open.

"Trust me. This had nothing to do with the love I feel for my son."

Jack could have said the same thing. But was it true?

Had parenthood forged some kind of strange bond between them?

He looked at her again. At her hair that he'd mussed when he grabbed her. At her kiss-reddened lips. At the flush of arousal still on her face.

Nope.

This wasn't about parenthood. And that meant it was a massive problem. Sex with Alana now seemed inevitable. Instead of facing each other as adversaries on the custody issue, they'd face each other as lovers.

That might make them more amicable to a settlement, but it might also cost him full custody of Joey. Because he'd have feelings for her. He'd be sympathetic. He might not fight as hard, and he needed to fight to keep his son.

The phone rang, the sound slicing through the room, and delivering yet another dose of much-needed reality. It was a reminder that he was in the middle of the most important case of his career.

Though she was obviously still shaken from the kiss, Alana reached behind her, located the phone and answered it. "Deidre," she said. "What did you find?"

Jack moved away from Alana to give them both some breathing room. He wanted her full concentration on the call and the crucial information she was getting from her assistant. While she was doing that, Jack composed himself. What he needed was a cold shower. That might cool him down and bring him back to his senses.

"I see," Alana commented. "And what about the other investment and business accounts?"

Judging from Alana's suddenly slack jaw, this wasn't good news. Jack had expected that. Hopefully, though, it was news that would help them find out what was really going on.

He walked to the window and checked the grounds. There was a ranch hand out front. The man was armed and standing guard. They wouldn't get much ranching done, but he needed the security to keep Alana, Tessie and Joey safe.

When Alana ended the call, Jack turned back around to face her. She'd gone pale. "My half of the profits of the jewelry business hasn't been touched in eight months except to cover normal operating expenses. But my trust fund has been drained, and there's little money left in any of my investment accounts."

"How much is missing?"

"Over three million dollars."

Jack cursed. He'd just found a motive for why someone had wanted Alana locked away.

Alana sank onto the chair and blew out a long, weary breath. "Thankfully, the business account is still there. It's worth nearly twice that amount."

"This is the business you share with Sean?"

She nodded. Her eyes questioned their theory about her brother being behind this. If this was solely about money, why hadn't Sean gone after her business account? That would have been easier than tapping into her trust and investments.

Maybe he hadn't touched the business money because he needed that in place for his own business ventures.

"Deidre said she has my personal laptop. She took it from the office and brought it home with her," Alana continued. "She was afraid without anyone around, someone might steal it. She said she's opening the files now to see if she can find anything about the missing money. If there is, she'll call me right back."

It was a long shot. Truth was, the money probably hadn't started to disappear until after she was at Sauder, or Alana would have noticed the missing funds.

Jack was about to pull her into his arms for a hug of comfort, but his cell phone rang. He checked the screen and saw that it was Reyes. This could be yet another important call.

"I just talked with the M.E.," Reyes explained. "He got out here about a half hour ago and has been examining Ted Moore's body."

"And?"

"He says there's no evidence of close-range residue around the wound. No stippling, either. The entrance wound is about .50-caliber size."

Jack groaned. That meant the gun hadn't been close enough to Ted's skin to leave any soot or residue from the unburned gunpowder. The caliber size was an indication that the shot had come from a long-range rifle. A sniper rifle, it was sometimes called.

Ted hadn't killed himself.

A bullet of that size would have made a much larger hole if Ted had shot himself at point-blank range. So the shooter was some distance away.

"There's more," Reyes continued. "I just checked out Ted's rifle, and I don't even think it's been recently fired. I'll bring it in for testing."

"Good. Collect any bullet fragments from my SUV," Jack instructed, knowing that Reyes already had that on his to-do list. "Also, look for shell casings. I'll be here at the ranch if you need me."

"Bad news?" Alana asked the moment he hung up.

Jack nodded. "No suicide. Thatcher must have murdered Ted with an assault rifle."

Alana shook her head. "But Ted had a rifle, too."

"He had a .22, and Reyes didn't think it'd been fired." Jack had noticed that when the man first staggered out of the woods.

She stayed quiet a moment. "Then what was Ted doing out there?"

He shrugged. "We probably won't know the answer to that until I talk to Thatcher."

Something he couldn't do until the man was captured. Jack didn't doubt that would happen. Thatcher would likely make another attempt to kill them. And Jack would do whatever was necessary to protect Alana and Joey. This wouldn't end until he put a bullet in Thatcher. He only hoped he would get answers first—he didn't want Alana to go through her life wondering why she'd been put through hell and back for the past eight months.

The house phone rang, and when Jack went to answer it, he saw on the caller ID that it was from Alana's assistant, Deidre. He picked up the phone and handed it to Alana.

She looked unsteady. Probably from the news he'd just delivered. But maybe this call would give them something positive.

"December twenty-fourth," Alana mumbled. "I don't remember going to work, but there are a lot of things I don't remember. What did the letter say exactly?" She paused. "Who was to get this letter?" She mumbled something, as if trying to jog her memory. "There was no address information at all?"

Jack heard the woman answer "no."

"Okay. Maybe that's in another note somewhere. What did I write in this letter?" Alana asked.

Jack saw Alana's eyes widen. She drew in a sharp breath and dropped back a step.

"Deidre, could you please repeat that? I want to write it down to make sure I didn't misunderstand." Alana's hands were far from steady when she grabbed the pen and paper next to the phone.

Jack leaned in so he could see what she wrote.

"Special Agent Parker Howell withheld information about the diamond deal he's investigating. He informed me that the buyer is a man named Eldon Thatcher, but after contacting colleagues, I've learned Mr. Thatcher is only one of two interested buyers."

Buyer, not seller. What was going on?

"The other potential buyer is from Willow Ridge." Alana wrote what her assistant was reading to her. "And I intend to contact him."

Jack held his breath and watched as Alana jotted down the name of the person who was ultimately connected to all of this.

"Dr. Keith Bartolo."

Chapter 12

Her life might be far from perfect, but her son certainly was.

Alana tried to read Joey one of the books from a stack in his room but finally gave up. He was far more interested in trying to wrestle with a large stuffed teddy bear. The bear was bright blue, the color of Joey's shirt and shorts, and was twice his size.

Joey giggled when he and the bear toppled onto the thickly carpeted floor.

Alana giggled, too.

Tessie and Jack looked as if they'd just heard a foreign sound. That wasn't far from the truth. It'd been months since she'd laughed, and it might be a while before she did it again. This precious time with her son was a too-brief interlude.

Soon, Joey would be leaving.

The packed bags in the hallway were proof of that. Any minute now, a sheriff friend of Jack's would arrive to whisk Tessie and Joey away. Part of Alana wanted to be whisked away with them. She wanted to get as far from the danger as possible, but going with her son would ultimately put him right back in the line of fire. He'd be safer away from her.

And her heart would break.

She'd already lost so much time with him. She didn't want to lose a moment more. But maybe, just maybe, Jack's deputies and the Texas Rangers could find Thatcher quickly so that her time away from Joey would be very short indeed.

Joey giggled again, and crawling, he tried to drag the bear to Jack, who was in the doorway. Like Alana, he'd changed clothes since the shooting and now wore another pair of those great-fitting jeans and a black shirt. There was no evidence of the struggle on these clothes. No grass stains, no powdery debris from the airbag, no smell of gunshot residue. That didn't mean, however, she couldn't see and smell those things.

It would be a long while before that particular nightmare faded, and judging from the stark emotion in Jack's eyes, he felt the same.

Jack had spent hours making the arrangements for Joey's safety, all while also trying to contact Dr. Bartolo.

But Dr. Bartolo wasn't answering his phone, and his nurse said she didn't know where he was. That didn't make him look innocent, and Alana had to admit that Bartolo might have had something to do with her disappearance. But then, she hadn't trusted him and had gotten the willies when he strolled into Jack's office the night of her arrival.

The doorbell rang, and Alana's heart clenched. It was probably the sheriff coming for Joey, but she automatically scooped her son into her arms and moved to the far side of the room, just in case she had to protect him. Jack nodded, turned and went to answer the door.

Joey didn't fuss about Alana's tight grip. Perhaps he sensed something was wrong. He stared at her with suddenly intense eyes. Joey had gotten his eye color from her, but his expression was all Jack. Jack might not have been Joey's biological father, but she could see so much of him in the little boy.

Jack opened the door and she heard voices. *Friendly* voices. Which meant this wasn't the threat her body had prepared itself for. It was a threat of a different kind. Alana kissed Joey's cheek and said a quick prayer that he would soon be returned safely to her.

"What's gonna happen?" Tessie asked.

Alana didn't think the woman's question was about the little trip Joey and she were about to take. "I don't know," she answered honestly.

"Jack loves that little boy, you know."

"I know. I love him, too."

Tessie walked closer, smiled at Joey and gently rubbed his back. "And how do you feel about Jack?"

Alana opened her mouth. Then she closed it, hoping an acceptable answer would come to mind. It didn't. She was thankful for Jack. But there was also an attraction between them that had reached the boiling point. Worse, it was probably clouding her feelings for him. She was starting to dream of them being a family.

Thinking of Jack as a lover, as her protector and

Joey's father, made a great package. One she should resist. Because if she did become his lover, she didn't want these other things playing into the equation. Sex for her meant making love. It meant a commitment, and neither Jack nor she was ready to go there.

Alana heard footsteps, and a moment later, a lanky brown-haired man appeared in the doorway with Jack.

"This is Sheriff Beck Tanner from LaMesa Springs," Jack said, making the introductions.

He looked capable and trustworthy enough, but Alana wished that Jack could be the one to protect Joey. Love was a huge motivator, and she knew Jack would put his life on the line for her little boy. Still, Jack couldn't be in two places at once, and he had to be in Willow Ridge to catch Thatcher.

Tessie reached for Joey, and Alana gave him one last kiss before the woman took him. There was no way she could stop her tears. Alana was more than a little surprised to see tears in Tessie's eyes, too.

"I'll take care of him. I promise," Tessie whispered. "You take care of Jack, okay?"

In that moment Alana no longer felt at odds with the woman, and she pulled both Tessie and Joey into a quick hug. "I will," she whispered back.

Tessie eased away, and Jack kissed Joey goodbye. There were no tears in Jack's eyes. Just the look of a man determined to succeed.

"You've got the trip mapped out?" Jack asked Sheriff Tanner. He picked up the suitcases, one in each hand, and headed for the door.

"All loaded in the GPS," Sheriff Tanner assured him. "I'm not taking a direct route. And I'll make sure no one follows. My deputy is also with me, just in case. I'll call you the minute we get to the house."

"Thanks," Jack said. Alana echoed the same.

Sheriff Tanner opened the door, and Alana saw his white SUV parked outside. The windows had a dark tint, but with the slant of the late afternoon sun, she could see the outline of a man in the backseat. Tanner's deputy, no doubt.

"Wait inside," Jack instructed.

Alana did and watched as the others hurried to the vehicle. Within just a few seconds, Jack had the suitcases loaded, Tessie put Joey in the child-restraint seat, got inside the vehicle and the sheriff drove away.

It felt as if someone had stomped on her heart.

Jack hurried back up the steps and caught her arm to pull her back inside. He shut the door and locked it.

"Try not to dwell on it," he mumbled.

An impossible task, but he was right. She didn't need to think about her son's departure.

Or the fact that she and Jack were now alone in the ranch house.

There was only one thing that would speed up her son's return and that was capturing the person who wanted her dead. To do that, she had to learn the truth.

Jack immediately got to work. He took out his cell phone, called Reyes and asked for an update on Dr. Bartolo while he went into the family room and turned on the laptop. Alana didn't waste time, either. She looked at the notes she'd made earlier during her phone call with her assistant. The last thing she'd written was Dr. Bartolo's name. The man could be a key to this investigation.

"Dr. Bartolo still isn't answering any of his phones,"

Jack let her know. He sat down at the computer. "No one's seen him in the past two hours."

Bartolo could have disappeared. Maybe he learned Jack and she were on to him. But how would he have known that? Earlier that morning, he hadn't shown any signs of concern during her checkup. Of course, the doctor could also be in danger. If the culprit behind all of this wanted to make sure Jack and she didn't speak to Bartolo, the doctor could have been kidnapped.

Or worse.

That made the situation even more urgent. If Bartolo was in grave danger, in addition to finding him, they needed to figure out how he played into the investigation. And why Parker had lied and said Thatcher was selling instead of buying those illegal diamonds. Had the man just made an honest mistake, or was it more sinister than that?

Alana glanced at her notes again. "Who was this letter to?"

"Maybe you were going to send it to Parker's boss?" Jack turned, looked up at her. "Maybe to me."

That made sense. "I might have wanted you involved if I suspected Dr. Bartolo." And something else made sense. "This could explain why I was in Willow Ridge eight months ago. I probably came to see you about the doctor. Since I was pregnant, I doubt I would have gone to see him on my own."

He nodded, and scratched his head. "You still don't remember any of this?"

"Bits and pieces. For instance, I remember sitting at my desk and typing that letter, but I don't know why I changed my mind about sending it. I don't know why

I decided to come here in person instead of just calling you."

"Maybe because you thought someone might listen in on your conversation."

"Sean," she mumbled. "Or maybe I thought Parker, Thatcher or even Dr. Bartolo had bugged my office." Alana paused and let that sink in. She drifted back to that day and remembered her feelings. Fear. She'd definitely known she was in danger.

And yes, she'd been on her way to talk to Jack.

Though instead of meeting him at his office, she'd realized someone was following her. Just like that, fear rippled through her. "A dark blue van followed me from San Antonio. I remember it."

Jack stood and ducked down a little so they'd be eye to eye. He caught her shoulders. "Keep going. What else do you recall?"

"The van bumped into my car." Her heart started to race, just as it had that day. "I sped up, but there was ice on the road. I skidded, and the van managed to get around me and drive off."

"Probably because the driver saw me coming," Jack provided.

Yes. That made sense. The images were no longer fuzzy and clipped. They came at her like gunshots. "I lost control and crashed through the bridge railing."

She felt the jolt of the impact all over again. The freezing water that gushed into her car. Panicking, she'd fought, first with the airbag and then the seat belt. "I got free, but I couldn't get out of the car. The door was jammed."

"It's okay." Jack's voice sounded miles away. So

Secret Delivery

did his touch, even though Alana was aware that he'd pulled her into his arms. "It's okay," he repeated.

He was trying to calm her down. With reason. Alana thought she might be on the verge of a panic attack. She couldn't catch her breath, and everything was starting to race out of control, just as it had when she was in that water.

"Think back to the van," Jack instructed, his voice level and reassuring. "I didn't see it, but I wasn't exactly looking for it when I spotted your car go off that bridge. Did you see the license plates or get a glimpse of the driver?"

Had she? Though it wasn't easy, Alana pushed aside her emotions and concentrated. She tried to replay everything that had happened from the moment she realized the van was following her. "I couldn't see the driver, but I saw the front bumper. It had Texas plates."

"Good. You remember any of the numbers or letters?"

She shook her head. "No. But it was a rental. I remember seeing a decal for State Rental. Does that help?"

"You bet. I'll make some calls and see if they have a record of someone renting a dark blue van eight months ago. We might get lucky."

Finally. A break.

He went to the computer, clicked his way to an official-looking site and typed in some information about the incident and the rental car. "I'm requesting assistance from the San Antonio P.D. State Rental is headquartered there. They'll send an officer over to check the records."

Alana blew out a long breath and prayed for the best,

even if it led her in the direction of her brother. Right now the truth was the only thing that would bring her little boy back home.

Jack stood again, but instead of moving closer to her, he crammed his hands in his pockets. "What did Tessie whisper to you before she left?"

"Oh." Alana scratched her head, not because she didn't remember, but because it took her a moment to switch from the case to more personal matters. "She wanted me to promise to take care of you. I said I would."

The corner of his mouth lifted, and a dimple flashed in his right cheek. The smile quickly faded, though. "If we get into another situation like we did today, I want you to take cover. I want you behind me."

She didn't want to think of another situation like that occurring. Alana was still too raw from the memories she'd just had to relive. "Behind you?" she questioned, tongue-in-cheek. "You're sure that'd be any safer?" She made sure she punctuated the question with a smile.

His smile didn't return, but he eased his hand from his pocket, reached out and skimmed his fingers over her cheek. He sent little sparks over her entire body. "I'm the sheriff. It's my job to protect you."

There went the sparks and what was left of her smile.

"No," he said quickly. "I didn't mean it like that." He pulled back his hand, shook his head and cursed. "I didn't mean it like that, either."

Because she totally understood his confused state of mind and because she wanted to feel those sparks again, she came up on her toes and kissed him. Not hot and French, the way she wanted. Alana pressed her mouth to his cheek, right at the corner of his lips.

It was an invitation. And then she waited to see what Jack would do next.

He stood there. "If I kiss you, we'll have sex," he announced.

"Oh." She felt a primal tug deep within her belly and tried to look shocked. She wasn't, though. She knew what Jack wanted. What she wanted.

They wanted each other.

They stared at each other, both waiting for the other to back away. But it didn't happen, because Jack's cell phone rang.

Until that ring, Alana hadn't realized just how ready she was to be dragged off to bed. Yes, the timing was terrible, but she wanted Jack more than she'd ever wanted another man. Still, she would have to wait.

Jack snatched the phone from his pocket and glanced at the screen. "It's one of the ranch hands."

A call could mean he'd spotted someone suspicious. Like Thatcher.

Jack hurried across the room and looked out the window. Alana followed, her heart now in her throat. God, how could her emotions rifle so quickly from passion to out-and-out fear?

"What does he want?" Jack asked.

Alana looked over his shoulder and spotted the dark blue car stopped just on the other side of a cattle gate. There stood the ranch hand on the phone. He'd apparently prevented the car from getting any closer to the house.

"All right," Jack said a moment later. "Let him in." He hung up, slipped the phone back into his pocket and drew his gun from his shoulder holster.

"Who's out there?"

"Special Agent Parker Howell, Margaret Vargas and your brother. Parker says he wants to talk, that he knows who's behind the plot to kill you."

Chapter 13

Jack kept Alana behind him and his gun ready when he opened the door.

Yes, Parker was a federal agent, but Jack didn't trust the man any more than he did the pair that Parker had brought with him. But Jack didn't want that to get in the way of Alana and him learning the truth.

Parker froze when he spotted the gun and his left eyebrow shot up. "Is that necessary?"

"Yeah, it is," Jack snapped.

Three suspects were on his porch, and he wasn't about to let down his guard. In fact, he had no plans to let them in, period. Parker stepped forward, but Jack blocked his path.

Parker huffed. So did Sean, while staring at his sister. But Margaret was looking around as if she expected someone to gun her down at any moment. Since that might not be too far from the truth, Jack decided to get to the point.

"You said you knew who was trying to kill Alana," he said to Parker.

"Yes." Parker looked around, as well. "But I don't think it's wise to discuss it out here. I have proof that Eldon Thatcher is in the area. A credible eyewitness put him at a convenience store just outside Willow Ridge."

Jack didn't doubt it. In fact, he believed Thatcher had fired those shots earlier and had probably murdered Ted. The trick now was to find out not only where Thatcher was but how this trio of visitors fit into what was happening.

"I think Thatcher's trying to kill me, too," Margaret volunteered. "That's why I asked Parker to put me in protective custody. I think Thatcher will come after me because he might believe I can connect him to the Sauder Facility. I saw him near the place not long after Alana escaped." Margaret looked nervous, but Jack wasn't completely buying it. She could be faking to throw suspicion off her.

"Did you set us up?" Jack asked her when she didn't continue. "Because I think it's more than suspicious that Alana and I were nearly killed on the way to meet you."

The woman frantically shook her head. "I didn't have any part in that. I just wanted to meet with you. To talk. And to ask for protection."

"She's terrified for her life," Parker added. "Now, can we come in?"

Jack didn't have to think about this one. "No."

"No?" Sean challenged. He shoved his way around Parker but stopped when Jack put the gun in his face.

"No," Jack repeated. He didn't lower the gun until Sean stepped back. "Here's how this'll work. You three will give me answers and then leave. I don't want you near Alana any longer than necessary."

"I'm your brother." Sean aimed his narrowed eyes at his sister.

"Yes," she agreed. She maneuvered herself to Jack's side so she was facing Sean. "But I don't trust you. Someone stole a lot of money from me while I was drugged and locked away at that so-called institution."

"Well, it wasn't me," Sean insisted.

"Nor me." Margaret was adamant about it. "I didn't know you were sane when you there. The commitment letter said you were delusional and violent."

"And you didn't see anything to indicate otherwise?" Jack asked.

Margaret dodged his gaze. "Sometimes, when Alana was heavily drugged, Ted would have her sign papers. I asked him what that was all about, but he said it was just routine, that the owner of the institution required it. I thought that was odd. I mean, Ted was just a guard. Plus, if she was truly insane, then her signature wouldn't have held up in court or anything."

Alana folded her arms over her chest. "Why didn't you get me out of there? Or at least question what was going on? Instead, you turned a blind eye and collected a paycheck."

"And now I might have to pay for that with my life." Margaret swallowed hard, turned and headed back toward the car. "I'm not standing out here in the open any longer. Thatcher is nearby," she whispered, her voice a terrified warning. "Can't you feel him?"

Jack didn't have the woman's same eerie premonition, but the lawman in him made him take a look around. There was no sign of Thatcher, but he didn't like the idea of this outdoor meeting going on much longer.

"We'll follow the money trail," Jack told Parker. "It's not easy to hide a sum that large and not set off alarms." He aimed an accusing glare at Sean.

Parker nodded. "The FBI's already investigating it. In fact, we've learned something that will lead to an imminent arrest. I plan to make that arrest as soon as I leave here. I just wanted to come out and speak to Alana first, so I could update her on the case."

"And the person you'll be arresting?" Jack asked.

"Dr. Keith Bartolo." Parker seemed very confident about his answer. "I can't get into specific details yet, but the FBI believes he's the one who's trying to kill Alana."

Jack and Alana exchanged glances. "How does Thatcher fit into this?" Alana wanted to know.

"At first I thought Thatcher might be operating alone, but now I think he might be working for Dr. Bartolo. That's what the financial records seem to indicate, anyway. Someone is definitely paying Thatcher, and the money seems to be coming from an offshore account set up by Dr. Bartolo."

Hell. If it was true, then Alana's attacker had had hands-on access to her. Bartolo had even been alone with her.

Alana folded her arms over her chest. "Why exactly would Dr. Bartolo want me dead?"

Parker shrugged as if the answer was obvious. "Because he didn't want to go to prison for an illegal diamond deal. When the deal backfired, I think he drugged you and took you to Sauder. And I think he set up the institution so he could milk your accounts and keep you from going to the authorities."

"I think Bartolo took out the money slowly, over several months, so I wouldn't get suspicious," Sean piped in. "If he'd emptied the accounts all at once, the bank would almost certainly have contacted me."

True. But Jack still wasn't sure all of this added up. It was possible that the answer was very simple, that Thatcher had acted alone. That Thatcher had drugged Alana and put her in Sauder and that it was Thatcher alone who wanted her and Margaret dead so all loose ends would be tied up. With Ted dead, he'd have no witnesses to his crime. Thatcher could even have set up Bartolo to take the blame.

But Jack didn't want to risk Alana's life on a theory.

Any of the three in front of him could have put this plan together. Three million dollars was a huge motive to hold a woman against her will and commit murder.

"Earlier you said Eldon Thatcher was trying to sell illegal diamonds," Jack tossed out to Parker. And he waited.

Parker didn't react to that. "He tried. Why do you ask?"

"Because I heard some contradictory information."

"Really?" There was a flicker of emotion in his eyes. "I'd be interested in the source of that information."

"I'll get back to you on that," Jack countered. But it wouldn't happen soon. Not until he was sure Parker was clean and Alana was safe.

Parker reached out to Alana, but then withdrew his hand when she recoiled. "Alana, I want you in the

FBI's protective custody, at least until after Bartolo and Thatcher have been arrested."

She shook her head. "I'm staying here."

"Don't you see what you're doing?" Sean cursed. "You trust this local yokel because you've let your heart get in the way of making a sound logical decision. Or maybe you think cozying up to him is the fastest way to get your son back?"

Alana stepped closer and met her brother eye-to-eye. "I trust Jack."

"Really? And what about your life? Your business? Your future? You trust him with that, too?"

"Yes." She spoke so firmly that Jack looked at her to see her expression. It was firm, too. This was no longer the frightened woman who'd staggered into his office.

Sean cursed again. "You're making another mistake."

And then he did something that surprised Jack. Sean reached out and tried to hug his sister. However, Alana jerked away from him. "The biggest mistake I could make would be to allow you to worm your way back into my life."

"I'm your brother," he reminded her again.

"We share common DNA, but you don't know the meaning of the word *brother*. Rather than inconvenience yourself, you turned your back on my son. He nearly became a ward of the state because of you. And the whole time I was in Sauder, you didn't even try to find me."

"I did try. And you're not thinking straight. Alana, you're not yourself."

"You're wrong. I am myself, and I know what I

want. I want you out of my life." She turned and went back into the house.

Good. She was out of the line of fire, both literally and where her brother was concerned. Alana had some bad blood with Sean, and Jack didn't want her to have to deal with that on top of everything else. Still, it'd probably done her some good to stand up to him.

"You're sure about keeping Alana here?" Parker asked.

Sean didn't wait for the answer. He stormed back to the car.

"I'm sure. Besides, she shouldn't have to be in protective custody too long if you're right about Dr. Bartolo and you can arrest him."

"Oh, I'm right."

"You know where he is?" Jack didn't let the conversation distract him. He glanced around the yard to make sure Thatcher wasn't there.

"Not exactly. But I have someone out looking for him. He's not answering his phone, and he's not in his office. Any idea where he could be?"

"None. In fact, I'm anxious to speak to him myself."

"Yes, I'll bet you are." Parker glanced around, as well. "A word of advice, Jack. This is an FBI investigation now, and I don't want you to get in the way."

Jack tried not to let that rile him, but it did. "I'll get in the way as long as Alana's in danger."

"You're personally involved with her," Parker concluded. "That could be a fatal mistake."

Jack couldn't argue. But he also couldn't go back and undo those kisses that he and Alana had shared. He could only be vigilant and pray that was enough. Because the stakes were way too high for him to fail.

Jack shut the door, locked it and reset the security system. He looked out the sidelight window to make sure their visitors weren't hanging around. When the car finally pulled away, he took out his phone.

"Who are you calling?" Alana asked. She went to the window and watched Parker and the others drive away.

"I'm trying Dr. Bartolo's number again."

Her eyes widened. "You're not going to warn him that he's about to be arrested?"

"No. But I want his side of the story before Parker gets to him."

He scrolled through the cell phone list, located the number and pressed Dial. He waited. One ring. Two. Three.

Someone picked up on the fourth. But whoever it was didn't say anything. But Jack could hear breathing. "Dr. Bartolo?" he greeted.

The seconds dragged by. "Yes."

Jack let out the breath he'd been holding. "Where are you? I've been looking for you."

"I know. I got the messages you left on my voice mail. Jack, I'm in trouble."

It was a Texas-size understatement, but Jack kept that to himself. "What do you mean?"

"I think someone's trying to kill me."

"Welcome to the club." Inside, Jack wasn't so cavalier, and he was more than curious. "Who wants you dead?"

More silence. "Last year I got involved with the wrong people. I heard about some diamonds for sale, and I thought they'd be a good investment. The price was right. The deal wasn't."

"Go on," Jack said when the man stopped. He held the phone closer so that Alana could hear.

"I didn't know the deal involved illegal diamonds. I swear, I didn't know." The doctor sounded convincing. But was he telling the truth?

"How did you find out about these diamonds?"

The doctor hesitated again. "Sean Davis."

Well, Jack had expected that name to pop up. "Alana's brother?"

"Yes. I met him through friends, and he told me about a collection of diamonds that he could get for me at rock-bottom cost. He wanted to go halves with me, with both of us putting up the cash."

Jack looked at Alana. She'd gone pale. "Did you have anything to do with Alana's disappearance?"

"No." But he no longer sounded convincing. "I didn't even know who she was until after she'd disappeared. Davis is a common name. When she came to the hospital in labor, I didn't make the connection. And I didn't know the diamond deal was illegal until the FBI contacted me days after her disappearance."

Jack wasn't sure he believed that, either.

"I think Sean wants me dead now," the doctor continued. "I think I'm the only one who can link him to the diamond deal."

"That seems like an extreme reason to murder someone." But it wasn't, especially if the diamonds were also connected to Alana's being held prisoner and having her trust fund emptied.

"Well, someone wants me dead. Someone took a shot at me a couple of hours ago. I'm pretty sure it was that man, Eldon Thatcher. I think he's working for Sean."

"You didn't report the shooting?" Jack knew he hadn't. If he had, Reyes would have called him immediately.

"No. I decided to get to safety and then contact you."

"Where are you now?" Jack demanded.

"I'd rather not say. Don't try to trace the call, either. I'm tossing my cell phone. I need to disappear for a while."

And with that, Dr. Bartolo hung up.

"Disappear," Jack mumbled. If the doctor was telling the truth and Thatcher was truly after him, then disappearing might not be possible. Dr. Bartolo could be in grave danger.

"My brother again." Alana shook her head. "His name keeps coming up at the wrong time."

"If Dr. Bartolo is telling the truth," Jack reminded her. "According to Parker, the doctor is the one with the criminal motive."

"Yes. You're right." She paused. "You think Parker will find him and make an arrest?"

Maybe. But he might not find Bartolo before Thatcher did.

The only thing remotely positive about Thatcher going after Bartolo was that it meant Joey and Alana might get a temporary reprieve. They needed it. Alana was beyond exhausted and likely missing Joey like crazy. He sure was. And both of them needed some rest.

Jack took a deep breath and took Alana's arm. "Come on. I'll fix us something to eat, and then you can get some sleep."

"I'm not really hungry."

Neither was he, but they hadn't eaten since breakfast, and here it was almost dinnertime. It wouldn't help Joey or the investigation if they starved.

Jack led her to the family-style kitchen, but when he reached the doorway, he frowned. The room was huge, sixteen feet by twenty, and had a fireplace at one end. It also had five floor-to-ceiling windows. Because those windows gave him a great view of the ranch, he'd never considered them a negative, but they were now. If Thatcher managed to get in rifle range, he'd be able to shoot right through that glass.

He went to each one and closed the blinds. Because the sun was already low in the sky, that plunged the room into near darkness. But instead of turning on the overhead light, he only switched on the dim light over the stove. It would cast fewer shadows on the blinds so it'd be harder for a shooter to pinpoint them.

"You're worried that Thatcher will use his sniper rifle again," she mumbled.

Jack didn't answer. She'd already had a too heavy dose of the truth without him confirming it.

Alana didn't look too steady on her feet, so Jack plopped her down on one of the high snack bar stools that were positioned in front of the granite counter. She caught his hand when he started to move away. Even in the darkness, he had no trouble seeing her worried eyes.

"Tell me everything's going to be all right," she said, sounding a little desperate.

"Everything will be all right." He wished he could make that true.

He brought her hand to his mouth, kissed it and placed it back in her lap. Their gazes met again. Uh-oh. Since this could quickly turn from a kiss on the hand to a real kiss, Jack stepped away.

"Juice, milk, water, iced tea?" he asked, heading for the fridge. "Or something stronger?"

"Hmmm. I'd prefer something stronger, but I'd better settle for juice."

They would both need a clear head. Still, that didn't stop him from grabbing a longneck bottle of Lone Star beer. He poured Alana a glass of orange juice and got to work on making them some sandwiches.

"You were raised here?" Alana sipped her juice and glanced around the room.

He glanced around, too, trying to see it for the first time through her eyes. It certainly wasn't fancy with its rustic floors, pine cabinets and table, but he'd added the granite counters to spruce things up a bit.

"Yes. My grandfather built this house back in the fifties, but the land has been in the Whitley family for over a hundred years."

She smiled. "The place suits you."

"Thanks. I think."

"It was a compliment. This place feels like family. Like tradition." Her smile faded when she saw the change in his expression. "What's wrong?"

He followed her gaze around the kitchen until their eyes met again. "If it feels like family, it's because of Tessie. She made this place a home for both of us. And then for Joey, too."

"Not your parents?" she questioned.

He debated how much he should tell her. "My dad's serving a life sentence in Huntsville prison. He's been there for twenty-one years. Since I was ten."

She put her hand on her chest. "I'm sorry."

He shrugged. "I'm sure you'll eventually hear talk around town. My father murdered my mother." Jack tipped his head in the direction of the west pasture. "He took her riding one day, and when they got to the creek, they got into an argument about a man he thought she'd been seeing. He got really angry and hit her in the head with a tree limb. She died instantly."

"My God."

Yeah, that'd been his reaction, too. When he'd seen it. Even now. "I'd gone for a swim that day. My father didn't know I was there, that I'd witnessed the whole thing. He told everyone my mother had died when she fell off her horse."

Obviously stunned, she leaned closer. "You actually saw him kill your mother?"

"I did." Jack had to take a deep breath. "And I testified against him. That day, I lost both my parents, and Tessie moved in so I wouldn't have to go to foster care."

He didn't have to guess what she was thinking. He knew what it was like to be abandoned, and that's why he'd been so quick to step up to take Joey.

Since this was beyond an uncomfortable situation, and one that touched on too many raw nerves, it was time for a change of topic. "I guess you were raised in a fancy house, huh?"

She just stared at him. And blinked back tears.

Great. Now he'd made her cry. "I'm sorry," he told her.

"Don't be. I'm glad you shared that with me. It gave me insight into the kind of man you are."

"I'm the kind who puts justice above all else." He cursed. That comment was a knee-jerk reaction, caused by years of overheard whispered comments. "Some people thought…think," he corrected, "that I shouldn't have turned my father in. Especially since it came out that my mother really was having an affair."

"That doesn't matter. You did the right thing," she said without hesitation.

"Yeah." He wasn't disagreeing with her, but it'd been a damn hard decision to live with. "So, back to you," he tried again. "You were raised in a fancy house?"

For a moment, Jack didn't think she was going to let it drop. But she did. "More like middle class. My mom was from money, but her folks disapproved of my dad. When she married him, they disowned her and put their money in trust funds for Sean and me."

Jack nodded, and kept the subject going. Not just because he didn't want to discuss his parents, but because he genuinely wanted to know more about Alana. "So, how did your brother get so greedy for money?"

She took a deep breath. "I think it's because he saw how our maternal grandparents lived. And how we lived. He didn't like the disparity, and I think it made him hungry for success." But then she shook her head. "Still, there's no excuse for what he's done."

No. There wasn't. Sean had hurt her to the core.

Alana snagged his gaze again. "After we catch the person responsible, will you let me stay here awhile, so I can get to know Joey?"

"Sure. There's a guest room right next to the nursery." He waited for a pang of discomfort, jealousy or whatever emotion might come at his having to share Joey. But it didn't happen. The thought of having Alana under his roof was suddenly very appealing.

For all the wrong reasons.

To get his mind off the idea, he gulped down some

beer and slid the plate with her sandwich across the counter toward her.

"Thanks," she said, looking at it. Then she looked at him.

It got so quiet that he could hear his own heartbeat pulsing in his ears, and every one of his senses seemed to home in on her.

"The sandwich," Alana mumbled. She was apparently trying to put her focus back on anything but him.

Jack tried to do the same. He thought of Thatcher. And the ranch hands who were patrolling the grounds. Of Joey. Of how close Alana and he had come to dying today. He even thought of the emotional conversation they'd just had.

None of that got his mind off Alana.

She stood slowly, and set her juice aside. She stepped toward him, brushing against the counter edge as she came to him. Alana might have started off slowly, but those last few steps were more like a leap.

She landed in his arms.

Jack took things from there, kissing her. Hard. Knowing full well that it was a stupid thing to do. And also knowing exactly where it would lead.

Finally!

That was Alana's first reaction when Jack's mouth came to hers. She'd been waiting for this. Wanting this. And even though it was wrong and reckless, she no longer cared. For now, for this moment, she needed Jack.

And Jack needed her.

He hooked his arm around her waist and snapped her to him. He kissed her until Alana felt as if she were about to melt.

Everything moved quickly, and neither of them tried to slow it down. The kiss was deep, hungry and intense. As was the embrace. It was a race to find some relief from the pleasure that was building inside them, a powderkeg of emotions ready to go off at any moment.

Their bodies pressed against each other, they shifted, maneuvered, tried to get closer. Off-balanced, they landed against the rim of the counter, and they bumped the plate that Jack had placed there. It went sliding across the slick surface and clanged into the granite backsplash.

He lowered his hands from her waist to her butt. Jack lifted her slightly, putting her right against his erection. She hadn't thought her need could get any stronger, but that did it. That contact was more than enough to make her feel like live fire in his hands.

"If you're going to stop—"

Alana didn't let him finish. There wouldn't be any stopping. Not on her part, anyway. Judging from Jack's reaction, he wouldn't be stopping, either.

He turned, moving her out of the kitchen and into the hall. Toward his bedroom, she realized. However, the kisses didn't stop just because they were on the move. Nor did the intimate contact. Jack scooped her up, Alana wrapped her legs around his waist and he took those wildfire kisses to her neck.

She heard herself moan. It was heavy with need. Jack moaned a little, too, when she kissed his neck. That made her wonder what else she could do to turn up his temperature.

Soon, she'd find out.

But probably not now. Her need was too frantic for foreplay or anything that involved slowing down.

He bashed his shoulder into the bedroom door to open it and stumbled toward the bed. They crashed onto the mattress with Jack landing on top of her.

"I'll do better, later," he promised.

Alana didn't know how it could get better. Every inch of her was burning for him. She hadn't felt this alive—nor this wanted—in her entire life.

Jack shoved up the stretchy top she was wearing. He flicked open the front clasp of her bra and took those melting kisses to her breasts. Even more heat blazed through her. Alana made a sound of raw pleasure that she hoped would spur Jack on.

It worked.

While he tormented her nipples, he used his knee to push up her skirt. His right leg landed between hers, right at the juncture of her thighs. Right where she wanted some pressure. And he gave it to her. He had her begging for him to do something to relieve the heat he'd built inside her.

Alana had to get off some of her clothes. Her breasts were already bare. Jack caught her panties and pulled them down her legs. But he was still fully clothed. She wanted to torment his naked body the same way he was tormenting hers.

She fumbled with his shirt buttons, but her hands were shaking. She was shaking. Her body was screaming for her to do something. So she took a shortcut, pulled his shirt from the waist of his jeans and went exploring. She put her hands on his chest. He was solid. All man. His body was sinew and muscle built from years of working on his ranch.

He was perfect.

When her hands went lower, to his toned and rock-hard stomach, she saw pleasure flicker through his jaw muscles. He made a husky, throaty sound.

She went lower still, and since he was driving her crazy kissing her nipples, she decided to turn the tables on him. She somehow got his belt undone and his jeans unzipped.

Before she could get her hands in his boxers, however, Jack upped the insanity. He shoved aside her panties, made his way down her body and gave her a kiss she was certain she would never forget.

Alana saw stars.

She couldn't wait any longer.

She grabbed him and pulled him back up. She got her hand inside his boxers, and touched him. He was huge, hard and just as ready as she was. Her touch made him curse.

He was a little rough and obviously in a hurry. She didn't care. Alana shoved her heels against the mattress so that she could help Jack maneuver them toward the headboard. Except that wasn't his goal. He was after the nightstand. And after fumbling around in the drawer, he produced a condom. Good thing. She certainly hadn't remembered the concept of safe sex.

They didn't even take off the rest of their clothes. Every second was torture.

Until he pushed inside her.

Alana stilled, to savor the moment and the sensations that speared through her. But the stillness didn't last. It couldn't. Her body demanded satisfaction.

They found a rhythm that was as old as time and yet it felt to her as if this was too intense, too special to have been experienced by anyone before.

His eyes met hers. He continued to move inside her,

one long thrust after another. She watched his face and saw what this was doing to him. Alana was certain that her own out-of-control need was mirrored in the depth of his gunmetal-blue eyes.

She said his name on a rise of breath. "Jack."

"Alana." It barely had sound, and yet she could feel his emotion as he plunged them both closer and closer to the edge.

Mercy, she wanted to let go. To feel. To fly.

He didn't make her wait long. He moved faster. Deeper. His eyes, narrowed. His breath gusted against her face.

And when Alana took that leap, when Jack pushed her over the edge, she didn't hold anything back. She let herself go. Felt herself close around him.

Felt herself shatter.

Jack lowered his head. He kissed her so gently that it stunned her even more than the raw pleasure that was coursing through her body. That kiss cut right through the passion-induced haze, and she saw everything clearly. Too clearly.

Oh, no.

She'd let herself fall in love with Jack.

The question was—what was she going to do about it?

Chapter 14

Jack stood in the shower and hoped the scalding hot water would help the knotted muscles in his neck and back. It was too much to hope that it'd help the rest of him relax. He needed a head examination. He'd hauled Alana off to bed and had sex with her.

Great sex.

He'd known it was inevitable, that they would eventually give in to the heat that flamed between them, but he also knew that it would complicate things beyond belief.

What the hell was he supposed to do now?

Invite Alana to move in? That would solve their custody issues temporarily, but it wouldn't solve anything else. Willow Ridge was a small, conservative town, and while no one would begrudge him having an affair, it was a different thing entirely to have Alana live with him. He didn't want Alana, Tessie or Joey subjected to that kind of gossip. Which led him back to his original question.

What was he supposed to do?

Before he could go through his slim options, he heard a knock. He reacted fast, because he'd told Alana to alert him if there even a hint that something might be wrong.

He jumped from the shower, reached for a towel and stopped in midreach when the door flew open.

It was Alana.

She had the phone in her hand. "Sorry. It's Sheriff Tanner. He wants us to know that they all arrived safely."

That was good news, and he was glad she'd delivered it right away.

But she was looking at him as if she wanted him all over again, and even though he'd just had that argument with himself, Jack wanted her again, too.

"The sheriff, uh, wants to talk to you," Alana said, passing him the phone.

Jack grabbed a towel and draped it around his waist before taking the phone. What he didn't do was move away from Alana. She didn't move away from him, either. She stood, just inches away. So close he could take in her scent.

This was going to get hot fast.

"It's Jack," he answered. "Alana said you arrived." He didn't mention the location and wouldn't, just in case someone had managed to tap into the conversation, but Jack knew Sheriff Tanner had taken Joey and Tessie to a safe house.

"Everything went as planned," Tanner assured him. "Just call when you're ready for me to bring 'em back."

"Oh, I will. Thanks, Beck."

Jack considered drawing out the conversation, just so it would keep his mind off sex. But that wasn't going to happen. Not with Alana so close he could practically taste her.

So that's what he did.

He clicked the end-call button. With the phone in his right hand, he curved his left hand around the back of her neck and eased her to him. The towel fell, leaving him with very visible proof of how much he wanted her.

He kissed her, slow and easy. Something that'd been sorely lacking in that crazy frenzy on the bed. He took his time, savoring her, letting the taste of her slide right through him.

She pulled back and ran her tongue over her bottom lip. "Hmmm. That was nice," she murmured.

Yeah, and he was about to make it a lot *nicer.*

But Alana didn't exactly cooperate. She pulled back, stared at him and opened her mouth to speak. Judging from the suddenly serious expression that swept over her, this wasn't going to be something he wanted to hear.

Then she stopped and glanced around. "I think I smell smoke."

Jack lifted his head and sniffed. Alarmed, he sniffed again. There was definitely a trace of smoke in the air.

"Did you put something on the stove?" he asked, hoping she had.

"No."

There was no need to panic—one of the ranch hands

could be burning some brush—but he couldn't stop that jolt of adrenaline.

Alana turned toward the door. "I'll check the kitchen."

But Jack caught her arm. "Wait. I'll go with you."

He was certain that he'd frightened her, but he had no choice. In case something had gone wrong, he didn't want her out there alone. He grabbed his clothes and dressed as fast as he could. He was strapping on his shoulder holster just as his cell phone rang. He snatched it from his pocket.

"It's Deacon," his ranch hand said. With just those two words, Jack could hear the concern in the man's voice. He didn't have to wait long to understand why. "You need to get out of there now! The house is on fire."

"A fire? Where? How?"

"Don't know the how part yet, but it's on the west side of the house."

The kitchen was on the west side. Jack still held out hope that this was caused by something electrical. But with Eldon Thatcher on the loose, he had to anticipate the worst.

"Make sure no one's out there with a rifle," Jack ordered, though with the darkness, that might not be possible.

"Will do. I'll also call the fire department," Deacon said. "You just get yourself out of there."

Jack stabbed the end-call button, shoved the phone in his pocket and drew his weapon. With his left hand, he caught Alana's arm and got them moving. There were plenty of ways to exit the house, but Jack wondered if any of them would be safe.

It certainly wasn't safe to stay put.

There were already wispy coils of smoke in his bedroom and in the hallway, and when he glanced in the direction of the kitchen, he could see that the smoke was considerably thicker there. He could feel the heat, too, which meant the fire was probably already eating its way through the house.

"Stay behind me," he instructed Alana and hoped she wouldn't give him an argument. She didn't. Like him, she was aware of the possibility that this could be some ploy by Thatcher to draw them out.

Unfortunately, it would work.

He couldn't keep Alana inside, but by God, he could do everything within his power to keep her from being an easy target.

"We're going out the back door?" she asked when he took her in that direction.

"Yeah."

It was a gamble. But he wanted to get Alana out and to the nearest barn so she'd have protection.

He thought of Joey and was damn glad he'd sent his son away. As bad as this could be, he wouldn't have wanted Joey anywhere near this.

Alana coughed from the smoke, and Jack used his hand to whip it away. It was a lost cause. The smoke was thicker in the back of the house, and he felt as if it were choking him. Still, he got them to the back door.

He stopped and pressed his hand to the wood. It was cool to the touch, which meant there wasn't a blaze on the other side. But the fire wasn't his greatest fear. Outside, there were plenty of places for a shooter to hide. If Thatcher had made it onto the ranch—and that

wouldn't be that hard to do if he'd come in on foot—
then he could be anywhere.

"Your home," Alana mumbled. "It's being destroyed."

There was nothing he could do about it now.

The ranch hands were no doubt assembling so they
could use a hose to try to battle the flames. Deacon had
already called the fire department, but Jack had to be
honest with himself. The ranch wasn't close to town. It
could take the volunteer fire department at least twenty
minutes to get to them, and if the blaze was as big as
he thought it was, a hose wasn't going to do much.

Jack eased open the door and looked out. There were
floodlights on at the corners of the house, and there was
another light on the front exterior of the barn. Those
along with the moonlight made it possible for him to
see. But he didn't see the gunman, only the ranch hands
scrambling to the fire.

"When we get out, run," Jack instructed. "I don't
want you out in the open any longer than necessary."

She nodded and because he knew they both could
use it, he pressed a quick kiss on her mouth. In the same
motion, he tightened his grip, took a deep breath and
barreled down the steps.

They didn't even make it to the bottom before a bullet slammed into the porch pillar next to Alana's head.

Alana heard the blast.

Her first thought was that the fire had blown out a
window. But a split second later, her fears were confirmed. Jack pushed her to the side, practically tack-
ling her, and they both crashed hard onto the porch.

Another bullet slammed into the wall.

If Jack hadn't reacted so quickly, she would have been shot. Or worse.

Latching on to her, Jack scrambled behind one of the white round porch pillars. Some shrubs were the only other cover they had. She turned her head and looked at the house to see if they could make it back inside.

Not a chance.

The orange and red flames were licking against the kitchen windows. The fire hadn't consumed the house yet, but the smoke would have already made the air inside unbreathable. Still, they couldn't stay put, because the fire would eventually reach the porch.

They'd be caught in the middle. Death by fire. Or death by bullets.

Alana didn't want either.

They had to survive this for Joey's sake. She refused to let whoever had done this take away her son's chance at having a good life.

From the west side of the house, she heard the frantic shouts of the ranch hands. She didn't know how many of them there were, but hopefully they were all armed. She could also hear water running. Someone was spraying it onto those flames.

Another bullet fired at them. This one broke the window just above their heads and showered them with glass, ash and smoke.

"He's on the roof of the barn," Jack called out, so the ranch hands would know where to aim. Within seconds, someone on the side of the house was shooting at the barn.

"Can you see who's on the roof?" she asked.

Jack shook his head. "I know he's there because of the direction of the shots." But they both knew it was probably Thatcher, and he wouldn't stop until they stopped him.

More shots slammed into the porch, one of them skidding across the wooden planks. It sent splinters flying everywhere. As dangerous as the bullets, splinters and glass were, however, it was the fire that would soon be the most deadly threat. Flames shot out of the gaping holes in the glass, and a gust of black smoke wafted right at them.

Jack adjusted their positions, pushing her facedown onto the porch, and he hovered over her so that he was using his body as a shield. Alana didn't approve of him putting her life ahead of his. She wanted to do something to help.

But what?

"Can you throw us a rifle?" she called out to the ranch hands. She couldn't see them. They had taken cover on the side of the house, but if the guys could get them a rifle, they'd have some way to return fire and protect themselves.

Several moments later, a rifle skittered across the porch toward them. Jack reached for it but had to jerk back his hand when a bullet slammed right next to them.

The ranch hands retaliated. She heard at least two shooters take aim at the barn. The bullets smacked into the side and the metal roof. It was just the diversion they needed. Jack rolled to the side, thrust his gun into her hand and snatched up the rifle.

"Fire now!" Jack shouted to the ranch hands.

They did. Jack, too.

The blasts were deafening and nonstop.

Jack came up on one knee, took aim and fired.

Alana wanted to grab him, to pull him back on the porch floor where it was safer, but just like that, the shots stopped.

Terrified, she scrambled so she could see Jack and make sure he hadn't been shot. But relief flooded through her when she didn't see any blood.

Jack didn't move. He knelt there, aiming at the barn. A moment later, she realized why.

She lifted her head just slightly and saw the man. He was dressed like a ranch hand, but even from the distance and near darkness, Alana could see that it was Eldon Thatcher. And unlike Jack, he was bleeding.

Thatcher staggered, and somehow got to his feet despite his injury and the pitched angle of the roof. Alana watched in horror as Thatcher lifted his rifle and took aim at Jack.

"No!" she screamed.

But it was too late. As the sound blasted through the air, she felt everything inside her go numb.

"Jack?" she called out.

"I'm fine," he assured her.

And he was. Thatcher hadn't fired. Jack had.

She snapped her attention back to Thatcher in time to see the rifle drop from his hands. He crumpled into a heap, and as if in slow motion, his body slid from the roof and plunged to the ground below.

Alana didn't have time to feel any relief.

"Come on," Jack said. He grabbed her hand and pulled her to her feet.

Her legs were wobbly. Her lungs felt clogged and heavy. Every step was a challenge, but she somehow made it off that porch.

It wasn't a second too soon.

The fire blazed across the porch, and the roof that had protected them just moments earlier came crashing down right at them.

Chapter 15

Jack pulled Alana into the back yard, fighting to get her away from the collapsing porch.

Cinders, ash and debris spewed in every direction, and that caused the ranch hands to scatter, as well. The porch seemed to groan as it crashed into a burning heap. But Jack didn't even look back. He kept his attention on Thatcher. Even though the man appeared to be dead, Jack wasn't taking any chances.

"Stay down," Jack warned Alana.

He positioned her behind a pair of twin oaks that had a hammock stretched between them. He wanted her to be protected.

While the ranch hands got to work dousing the fire, Jack approached Thatcher, keeping his rifle aimed.

"Need me to call for an ambulance?" Deacon yelled.

Jack went closer. "No." It was clear that Thatcher

was dead. But just in case, Jack knelt down and pressed his fingers to the man's neck.

No pulse.

"But you can call the medical examiner," Jack relayed to Deacon. "And get Reyes out here." He would need his deputy to tie up loose ends, since Jack had been the shooter.

While they were waiting for him, Jack knew he had to work to contain that blaze. If not, the whole house would go up in flames.

He turned to hurry back to the house, but then he saw Alana. Her face was colorless, despite the intense heat from the fire.

"He's dead?" she asked.

Jack nodded and went to her.

She blew out a long breath and nodded, as she stared at the man's lifeless body. "Good."

He understood her relief. Jack hated that he'd just killed a man. But Thatcher would have just kept coming if Jack hadn't stopped him.

Because there wasn't time for anything more, Jack brushed a kiss on her cheek, propped his rifle against the oak and took his gun from her. He reholstered it and got busy. He raced toward the barn, where there was another hose, turned it on and hurried with it toward the house.

Alana grabbed a blanket from the hammock and tried to beat down the flames that were flickering into the yard. It was a good move. The grass was dry in patches, and he didn't want the fire to spread to any of the outbuildings.

In the distance, Jack heard sirens. Thank God. The fire engine was close by, and even though there'd been a lot of damage, they might still be able to save the house.

"Should I try to go inside and get out anything?" Deacon asked.

"No way." It was tempting. A lot of his life was in that house. Joey's life, too. But things could be replaced, and Jack didn't want anyone else dying today.

The fire engine came screaming into the driveway in front of the house, and Jack hurried to it so he could get them maneuvered in the right direction. Not that they could miss the fire. The black coil of smoke rising into the air was a telltale sign.

The volunteer firemen were all men he knew. Friends and neighbors barreled off the engine, ready to respond. It didn't take long before they had their hose connected to the emergency tap, and they began to spray the house.

Jack glanced at Alana. She was still battling those grass fires, and he turned to help her. But then he spotted another vehicle approaching. It was Reyes.

"Thatcher's dead," Jack told the deputy when he jumped from his cruiser. Reyes already had his gun drawn as if he'd expected the worst.

"The M.E.'s on the way," Reyes let him know. "We might have another problem, though. Dr. Bartolo's missing. He's not at home or at the hospital. His cleaning lady was at his house and I asked her to look around, to see if anything was missing. She said the gun from his nightstand was gone."

Yes. The doctor. Jack would have to deal with him soon. After all, the man had been involved in an illegal diamond deal, and he might even have had a part in what had happened to Alana. Heck, for that matter, he could have been the one who sent Thatcher after them.

And with that thought, Jack froze.

What if Dr. Bartolo came after Alana?

Jack raced toward the back of the house, and his heart dropped. She wasn't there where he'd last seen her.

"Deacon, where's Alana?"

Deacon fired some glances around and shrugged. "I thought she was with you."

Jack cursed and tried not to panic. The whole yard was chaotic with the firefighters and his ranch hands. There were nearly a dozen people centered on the activity, and Alana could be among them.

But she wasn't.

"Alana?" he called out.

Nothing.

Jack raced to the oaks and the hammock, and spotted the charred blanket on the ground. She'd been using it to beat out the flames, but there it was, tossed aside. And no Alana in sight.

"Check the barn," he instructed Reyes. His deputy had already drawn his weapon, and Jack did the same. He prayed he wouldn't have to use it.

While Reyes went in the direction of the barn, Jack headed for the east side of the house. Away from fire. Away from the chaos.

He raced around the corner. No Alana.

With his breath gusting and adrenaline shooting through him, he stopped, listened and prayed that all was well. But in his gut, he knew something was wrong.

"Alana?" he called out again.

Still nothing.

Where was she? Where could she have gone? But the real question was, had Dr. Bartolo taken the gun from his house so he could use it on Alana?

Jack heard a sound.

It was like a muffled scream. A cry for help. He sprinted in the direction of that sound. It'd come from the front of the house, but Alana wasn't there.

With panic rising in his throat, he glanced all around. At the fire engine. The deputy's cruiser. His work truck. His damaged SUV that he'd parked out front. No one was around the vehicles. But when he looked up the road, he spotted a dark blue car stopped just on the other side of the open cattle gate.

Jack had seen that car before.

In fact, it'd been at the ranch earlier—when Sean, Margaret and Parker had arrived for their little visit.

He kept his gun ready and headed in the direction of the vehicle. There was a dark tint on the windows, and he couldn't see if anyone was inside.

God, had one of the three taken Alana?

Jack was within ten yards or so of the car when the engine roared on. He raised his gun and aimed, but he couldn't fire. He couldn't risk hitting Alana if she was in there.

"Alana?" he called out again.

He didn't expect an answer and didn't get one, but he knew she was inside. He just knew it. And he also knew the person who had her was up to no good.

"Get out of the car," he ordered, bracing his shooting wrist with his left hand.

But no one got out. The driver, concealed behind that dark tint, gunned the engine.

And drove right at Jack.

Alana blinked and tried to see what was happening.

What was wrong with her?

Everything was hazy again, just as it'd been while she was imprisoned at Sauder. She'd been drugged then. Had someone drugged her now?

She forced herself to concentrate, but everything was swimming in and out of focus. She couldn't see anything clearly. She thought she might be in a car. And someone had put her there.

Who?

Someone sat beside her, in the driver's seat, and she could hear the sound of the engine. Then it hit her. She was being kidnapped.

She groaned and tried to reach out to strike the person, to fight back, but her meager attack only resulted in a light slap to the person's arm.

Again, she tried to focus so she could see who'd taken her, but her eyes wouldn't cooperate. The dizziness was overwhelming and made her sick to her stomach. Added to that, there was a sickeningly sweet taste in her mouth.

The car lurched forward.

Her arm and shoulder rammed into the dashboard, and the pain was instant. But that impact told her something critical.

She wasn't wearing a seat belt. Nor was she tied up. That meant she could escape.

Someone called out her name.

"Alana?" She heard it clearly. A shout.

Jack.

Judging from his frantic tone, he knew that she was in danger.

She tried to answer him, but failed.

The car was the last place she wanted to be. Alana groped for the handle to open the door. She felt the window. Then the leather strip below it. Finally, her fingers closed around the metal lever.

But someone stopped her.

A hand latched on to her wrist and jerked her hand from the lever.

Furious and frantic that she'd failed, Alana tried to fight back at the fierce grip her kidnapper had on her. But her arms were weak, practically limp. As was the rest of her body. Her fight ended with her hands dropping into her lap.

The car swerved to the left, causing her hip to slam into the gearshift. What was going on? Was the kidnapper trying to get away from Jack?

Alana blinked several times, and saw something. Jack. He jumped to the side of the road. If he hadn't done that, the car would have plowed right into him. The blurriness returned in spades, and even though she couldn't see exactly what was happening, she was almost positive that the driver turned around to go after Jack again.

"No!" she yelled.

She grabbed for the steering wheel. It was a huge risk. Because she couldn't see, she could do more harm than good and cause the vehicle to hit Jack. Still, she had to try. She had to do something, because this monster might hurt Jack. And once he had Jack out of the way, God knows where the kidnapper would take her. Or what he would do to her.

She doubted he'd keep her alive very long.

There was the whirring sound of a window being lowered, and hot muggy air rushed into the car. Suddenly, the sounds were a lot clearer. She could hear Jack again. He was shouting for her to get out. So Alana tried again. She reached for the door handle.

But the blast stopped her.

After the shoot-out they'd just had with Thatcher, she knew that sound.

A shot being fired.

Her captor had shot at Jack.

She scrambled to get into a sitting position so she could see what was going on. But dizziness didn't allow her to see much, just the fuzzy image of the person seated beside her. A man, she thought. Outside, there in the darkness, she also thought she saw Jack. He was alive, and scrambling toward the car.

Alana called out his name again. A warning, for him to stop before he got shot. She didn't want to die, but dying wasn't the worst thing that could happen to her. The worst would be for Jack to die while trying to save her.

"I love you," she said. But it came out mumbled. Jack probably couldn't hear her, but she wanted him to know how she felt about him.

Beside her, her captor laughed. Maybe he was amused that she was pouring out her heart. That made her angry. It made her want to lash out at him for trying to hurt Jack.

But another shot sounded.

The blast tore through the car, but even over the

roar it created in her ears, Alana heard the rev of the car engine. The vehicle spun around, and the driver floored the accelerator.

She glanced around, and even through the haze and the darkness in her mind, she realized they were speeding away from the ranch.

That couldn't happen.

What if Jack was hurt and bleeding back there? He might need medical attention. "Stop!" she managed to shout at her captor. "We have to go back."

He laughed again.

Alana gathered up all the energy and anger that she could. She balled her hands into fists, turned and began to pummel him. Her hands and arms might have been weak, but she tried to go after his face so that her blows might do some good.

She felt cold metal jam against her left temple.

"Stop, or you'll die right here," he growled. "And then I'll go after your son."

Oh, God.

She stared at the man. Slowly, very slowly, the dizziness faded so that she could hone in on his face.

"How about another hit of chloroform?" he asked. "That'll make you cooperate."

Chloroform. So that's why she couldn't move or think clearly. That's what he'd used to get her into the car.

And now he had her.

Chapter 16

Jack jumped into his work truck and thanked God that the keys were in the ignition.

He started the engine, put on his seat belt and drove off in pursuit. He'd seen the face of Alana's kidnapper, and he knew this would be no easy battle.

Special Agent Parker Howell knew how to fight.

And win.

The SOB had Alana. And when Parker had shot at him and tried to run him down, the agent had made it crystal clear that he wasn't a good guy. Jack figured it was only a matter of time before he tried to kill Alana.

If he hadn't tried already.

Parker's car kicked up some dust as it barreled down the narrow road that led away from the ranch. Jack needed to keep a visual on the car's taillights because once Parker reached the highway, he could go in either direction, and there'd be no dust trail to follow. Jack didn't intend to lose the man. He vowed he'd stop Parker and get Alana safely back.

Jack kept a firm grip on the steering wheel and took out his phone to call Reyes so he could request backup. But it didn't work.

No signal.

There were plenty of reception dead spots around the ranch, but this shouldn't have been one of them. Did that mean Parker had somehow jammed the phones so they couldn't be used? Probably. As an FBI agent, Parker would have had access to that type of equipment. But that wouldn't stop Jack, either. He kept the accelerator pushed to the floor, and tried not to think of what Alana was going through. She was no doubt scared out of her mind. But she would almost certainly know that he would come after her.

But then, Parker would know it, too.

That thought had no sooner formed in his head than he turned a sharp curve. The sides of the road were thick with trees on each side, and along with the darkness, it made it impossible to see what was ahead until he was already deep into the turn.

Parker's car was right in the middle of the road.

Jack slammed on his brakes, but he knew there wasn't enough distance between him and the car. He was about to crash into it, and that couldn't happen. He would hit the passenger's side, right where Alana was sitting.

Hell.

Parker had parked the car there so he could set Jack up to kill her.

Jack jerked the steering wheel to the left, praying that it would be in time to miss Parker's car. It was. Barely. His truck slammed into the back end of the car, knocking it forward but leaving it intact. Jack didn't have time to celebrate his victory, though, because his truck left the road and went flying down the steep embankment.

A tree limb smashed into his windshield, cracking the glass so that he couldn't see what was ahead. But he knew. There were more trees—big sprawling oaks—and a creek. This was the shallow side. He wouldn't drown if he hit the water, but an impact with trees and the limestone boulders in the creek bed could be fatal.

Jack braced himself for the collision. He didn't have to wait long. The truck plowed into an outcropping of rocks, and that propelled the right side of his vehicle into a tree.

The jolt snapped him forward, and the airbag slammed into him.

Jack didn't waste any time assessing if he was hurt. He elbowed the airbag aside and threw open the door. He hit the ground running toward Parker's car and kept his gun ready. He couldn't just open fire and risk hitting Alana, so he had to choose his shots carefully.

His knee throbbed as he ran up the embankment. He'd hit it during the wreck but didn't care. Nothing was going to stop him from making it to Alana.

He slowed when he got to the top and tried to keep low. He walked toward Parker's car. The road was eerily quiet, with just the sound of the summer breeze rifling through the tree branches and the soft ripple of the creek flowing over the rocks. The car sat there, surrounded by the pitchy darkness.

"This ends now," Jack shouted to Parker. "I want you to release Alana."

No answer.

That could mean Parker was sitting there, waiting to ambush him, but Jack couldn't just wait him out. The car was still in the middle of the road, and if any other fire department vehicles came racing this way, they'd plow right into it. He had to get Alana out of there.

"Parker?" Jack called out.

Still nothing.

Jack eased closer, with his gun still ready, and he looked inside the darkly tinted windows.

He cursed.

The car was empty.

Jack dropped to the ground and not a second too soon.

A bullet came right at him.

He scrambled to the back of the car so he could use it as cover. He needed to get off the road, and to Alana, and staying put wouldn't accomplish that.

Another shot fired. Then another.

The shots came from the opposite side of the road from where he'd crashed.

Jack lifted his head slightly and looked around. He didn't see any sign of Parker or Alana, but they had to be out there somewhere. What he needed was a little visual help.

Staying low, he made his way back to the passenger's-side door, reached up and grabbed the handle. The door was unlocked. That was a lucky break. He opened it and reached inside to turn on the headlights.

The high beams were aimed right at the trees where Parker was hiding.

Jack saw a flash of movement. But he had to duck back down because another bullet came his way. This one smacked into the car just above his head.

"Parker, you're only digging your own grave," Jack shouted. "Surrender now. You know I won't let you get away with this."

Jack waited for an answer for several long moments.

"Okay," Parker yelled back. "I'll trade Alana for a head start. You get her, and I get back in my car and drive away. You all right with that?"

He wasn't. Jack didn't want Parker getting away. But Alana came first. Once he had her back, then he could go after Parker.

"Let's do this," Jack agreed.

"First, put down your gun," Parker shouted.

Jack cursed under his breath. "Not without some kind of assurance that Alana is all right." Even then, he was taking a huge risk because Parker could just shoot him.

In fact, that was probably Parker's plan.

The agent wouldn't want to leave any witnesses, especially a sheriff and a former hostage. No, this was almost certainly a trap to draw Jack out so that Parker could kill him and then hightail it out of there with Alana. But that did make Jack wonder…why had Parker kept her alive?

What did he want with her?

"Alana's fine," Parker insisted. "A little woozy from the chloroform, but she doesn't have a scratch on her. Cooperate, and she'll stay that way."

Jack wasn't untouched by that threat, but if he allowed himself to be killed, then Alana would be at Parker's mercy.

"I want to see her now," Jack countered.

The silence returned. So did the fear. Not for himself... Jack was terrified for Alana.

Finally, there was some movement in the trees, and a second later, he saw Alana. Alive, thank God. And Parker was right—she didn't appear to be harmed. Well, except the look of terror on her face.

Parker had positioned her in front of him to use as a human shield. He had his left hand squeezed over her mouth, and his right hand held a gun pointed directly to her head.

"Now you've seen her," Parker said. "Put down your gun."

Jack stood there, debating. He couldn't put his gun down. But he had to do something. "Bring her closer so I can get a better look at her."

From the way Parker's mouth tightened, it was obvious he was having a debate with himself, as well. Still, the man walked closer and stopped just at the edge of the embankment. With the slope, Alana was still a good fifteen feet away. Much too far for Jack to try to lunge at the man.

"Put down your gun," Parker repeated.

"I will. Just as soon as I'm sure she's okay. Take your hand from her mouth so she can speak." Jack eased closer. Just a step.

"There's no reason for her to speak. She's fine. And you're stalling."

Jack took another step. "I want to hear from her own lips that you haven't hurt her."

"I haven't," Parker snapped. He jabbed the gun harder against her temple. "But I will if you don't stop this. Put down your gun now!"

Jack managed another step, but he figured that was as far as he could go. Parker already seemed ready to snap. He certainly wasn't the composed agent who'd visited Jack earlier. So even though he was still about ten feet away, Jack would have to risk making a dive for Parker if the man showed any indication that he was going to shoot Alana.

"Okay, I'm putting down my gun." Jack started to lean down.

But then he saw Alana.

She frantically shook her head.

That garnered her another jab from Parker's gun, and he cursed at her. As hard as it was to do, Jack ignored that latest jab and followed the direction of Alana's gaze toward the woods.

The headlights didn't illuminate that area, but Jack fastened his attention there, and saw something move.

"Get down!" Alana shouted, tearing Parker's hand from her mouth.

Jack dived to the asphalt just as someone fired a shot from the pitch-black woods.

Alana knew her warning was too late. The shots had already started.

She saw Jack hit the ground and prayed that the bullet hadn't found its intended target.

Parker took aim at Jack while he shoved his hand

back over her mouth and tried to drag her back behind the trees. Alana was still dizzy and weak from the
drug, but she couldn't let that stop her. She had to help
Jack survive or they would both die right here in these
woods.

She rammed her elbow into Parker's stomach. It
didn't pack much of a wallop, but it did cause him to
move back slightly. It was just enough for her to turn
and grab his wrist so that he, too, couldn't shoot at
Jack. One shooter was more than enough.

"Alana!" she heard Jack say.

It was a warning for her to be careful. But she didn't
have the luxury of being careful now.

The shots from the other side stopped as she hoped
they would. But Parker was still a huge threat.

She dug her fingernails into Parker's wrist and drew
blood. But it wasn't enough to stop him from hitting
her. He slapped her with his left hand and sent her staggering backward. Alana felt herself falling, and there
was nothing she could do to stop it. She crashed into
some thick underbrush, and her head smacked hard
against the rocky ground.

Jack called out her name again, and she tried to get
up. Thorns and sharp brush cut into her hands, but
still she tried.

Parker raised his gun, and aimed at Jack. Alana
struggled even harder to get up and managed to fight
her way out of the underbrush. There was no time for
her to yell for Jack to get down, to take cover.

She was too late.

Jack launched himself at Parker, and the two men

crashed into each other. She heard the sickening sounds of bone and muscle colliding.

She got to her feet, somehow, and tried to help, but the men were in a fight for their lives. Worse, they maneuvered themselves out of the line of the headlights, and in the darkness, she couldn't see who was winning.

Alana grabbed a fist-size rock from the ground and went toward the fight. It wasn't much of a weapon, considering that both men were still armed, but she might get lucky and land a blow on Parker's shooting hand.

"I can't let you do that," someone said.

Margaret.

Alana's heart went to her knees. She looked up at the top of the embankment and spotted the woman with the rifle. It had a night scope, and even though Margaret wasn't holding the weapon with much confidence, it didn't take a mountain of confidence to kill.

Just seconds before Parker had stopped his car in the middle of the road, he'd called someone and told them to "get ready." In that moment Alana had realized that he had a partner, but she hadn't thought it would be Margaret. She'd expected her brother or Dr. Bartolo to be positioned in those woods.

"Don't move," Margaret warned.

Alana shook her head. "I can't let Parker hurt Jack."

Margaret shook her head, as well. "And I can't let you and Jack escape."

Alana glanced at Jack just as he landed a hard punch to Parker's jaw. Jack was winning, but even if he managed to subdue Parker, they had to deal with Margaret.

"What's in this for you?" Alana asked. She kept her

eye on Margaret's trigger finger while she tried to inch her way to Jack.

"I won't go to jail."

"Don't be so sure about that." Alana managed another step.

"I didn't know Parker kept you at Sauder illegally. I swear, I didn't know, but a judge will never believe that."

"He will if I testify for you."

Parker shouted, "Shut up!"

But Margaret shook her head again. "Parker said I can have a fresh start in Mexico. He gave me money."

"Money he stole from me." Alana took another step toward Jack and tightened her grip on the rock. "You can testify against him, Margaret. You might not have to go to jail at all."

It was obvious that Parker was the dirty one here. She didn't know all the details of what he'd done, but Margaret could provide some answers.

But for now, Alana had to do something about Parker.

She prayed she was reading Margaret right. The woman didn't seem to have murder on her mind. Yes, she had the rifle pointed right at Alana, but she was making no moves to stop her. So Alana turned toward the men, just as Parker managed to aim his gun at Jack.

She saw Parker's hand tense, and knew that unlike Margaret, he would shoot to kill. So she did the only thing she could.

Alana dived at them.

The rock fell as she latched on to Parker's hand. But

she could only hold him for a few seconds before he shoved her aside.

But with Parker's right hand temporarily occupied fighting her off, Jack took full advantage. He bashed his fist into Parker's jaw twice. The bone-crushing blows echoed through the woods, as did the feral growl of pain that came from the man's throat.

Jack didn't let Parker regain control. Neither did Alana. She snatched away his gun and scrambled away so that Parker couldn't grab her again and use her as cover. Jack shoved his gun right against Parker's head.

"Move and you die," Jack said. It wasn't just a threat. His tone, tight jaw and fierce expression made it a promise.

Parker stared at Jack, and for one horrifying moment, Alana thought he might force Jack to kill him. But he only cursed, and his hands fell against the ground.

"Well?" Jack called out.

Not to her, Alana realized. He was speaking to Margaret. Even though he'd been embroiled in that fight with Parker, he had still realized what was going on.

"Put down the rifle," Jack insisted.

The woman stood there, her rifle still pointed at Alana. Alana had Parker's gun, but by the time she aimed it, Margaret would have plenty of time to fire.

Plenty of time to kill.

Or to allow Parker to get away.

Alana glanced at Jack. He hadn't been shot, but there was blood streaming from a gash on his head. After crashing into that tree and the fight he'd just had with Parker, he might have injuries that needed immediate attention. That wasn't going to happen until Margaret was out of the way.

"You want to die, too?" Jack asked Margaret. "Because that's what'll happen if you don't put down that rifle."

Alana held her breath and prayed. But she also got ready, just in case. She slid her finger over the trigger and tried to prepare herself for whatever might happen next.

Margaret lowered the rifle.

Jack hauled Parker to his feet, but kept his gun on him. "Get behind us," he instructed Alana.

She did. But she also kept her finger on the trigger.

"You might as well kill me," Parker grumbled. "I can't go to jail. You know what they do to former agents inside a prison? I wouldn't last a week."

Jack got him moving toward the embankment. "You should have thought of that before you shut Alana away in that institution you created so you could steal her money."

"I had to have her money. I had people to pay off. The wrong people."

"If all you wanted was my money, then why try to kill me?" Alana wanted to know.

Parker stopped at the embankment and looked over his shoulder at her. The corner of his mouth lifted in a warped half smile. There was blood on his lips and teeth, and that only added to his sinister expression. "You honestly don't know?"

"Know what?"

He laughed. "Now, this is true irony. I set up that diamond deal, and you started asking too many questions. You figured out what I'd done, that I was the seller. That I'd stolen the diamonds from evidence storage. I hired Thatcher, sent him after you and paid him well. He failed. Three times."

She shook her head. "But I didn't know you had set up the deal. I didn't remember it."

"That's the irony. But that doesn't mean you wouldn't have remembered, eventually. I couldn't take that risk."

Jack shoved Parker up the first few steps of the embankment. It was steep, and both men staggered to keep their footing.

Everything seemed to move in slow motion. Parker turned, slamming his arm into Jack's chest. Jack fell backward, while Parker reached into the back waist of his pants and pulled out a small handgun. His backup weapon.

An oily smile twisted Parker's bloody mouth as he took aim at her. Alana didn't have time to react. She could only brace herself for a fatal shot.

The sound of the shot blasted through the air.

Her heart jumped from the jolt of adrenaline, and she got a split-second glimpse of what it was like to die. Her biggest regret was that she hadn't had time to be a real mother to Joey. Her son wouldn't remember her. He wouldn't know how precious he was to her. But she also regretted that Jack hadn't heard her when she'd said "I love you."

But the impact never came.

Parker hadn't fired.

Jack had.

Parker's body jerked violently, and she saw the blank

expression in his eyes as he tumbled face-first to the ground.

Jack quickly took aim at Margaret. The woman's mouth was open in a silent scream. The rifle dropped from her hand.

Without taking his gaze off Margaret, Jack reached down and put his fingers to Parker's neck. "He's dead," he told Alana.

"Dead," she repeated.

Relief rushed through her and robbed her of any energy she had left. Jack made it to her in one step and pulled her into his arms before she collapsed.

Chapter 17

Eighteen.

That was the number of cuts and scratches Jack counted on Alana's body. The majority were on her hands and arms, the result of Parker shoving her into the thorny underbrush. There was also one on her forehead. Another on her chin.

All her injuries had been examined and were being cleaned by a med tech. The E.R. doctor had insisted that none were serious. Maybe the physical injuries weren't. But Jack wasn't so sure about the mental ones.

Alana had been shot at, drugged and taken hostage. And to top it all off, she'd had to witness him kill two men. Jack wondered how many sleepless nights that would cost her.

Wearing a badge didn't make him immune to the sickening feeling that he was responsible for two men no longer being alive. But he hadn't had an alternative. He knew that, and he would have to learn to live with any feelings of guilt.

Alana winced a little as the tech dabbed at the scrape on her knee with antiseptic, but he stayed back and let the tech do his job. Jack was afraid that if he went to Alana now and pulled her into his arms she'd fall apart. Her raw emotions were simmering right below the surface.

He heard footsteps behind him, turned and spotted Reyes walking up the E.R. corridor toward him. His deputy had gotten stuck tying up all the loose ends because Alana had insisted that Jack receive medical attention for his own cuts and scrapes. Jack had agreed because that was the only way Alana would go to the hospital. If she'd had her way, she would still be waiting at his office for Sheriff Tanner to return with Joey and Tessie.

"Margaret's in custody, and Parker's body is on the way to the morgue." Reyes let him know. "Joey's not back yet?"

"Not yet. Soon." He hoped. Jack needed to hold his son.

Reyes glanced at Alana. "Is she okay?"

Jack nodded, though he didn't know if she truly was.

"And you?" Reyes questioned. "Are you hurt?"

"No."

Reyes looked concerned. "You were just doing your job, Jack."

No, he had been doing a lot more than his job. He'd been protecting Alana and ultimately Joey. That's how he'd get through this.

The medic bandaged Alana's knee and started to work on the large scrape on her elbow.

"I found a cell phone jammer in Parker's car," Reyes continued. "You said you hadn't been able to make a call, and that explains why." He paused. "I also found some papers."

Jack looked at the man when he didn't continue. "What kind of papers?"

"I'm not a lawyer, but these were pretty easy to figure out. Parker was going to have Alana sign away her part of the family business. The money would have gone into an offshore account. My guess is that he would have moved the money around for a while to make sure it wasn't traceable to him. But in the end, he would have had a big payoff."

"That's why Parker kept me alive," Alana said.

Jack hadn't even realized she was listening, but she'd heard every word.

Yes, the money would have been motive to keep her alive. First, he'd drained her trust fund and investments. Parker had been smart to do it slowly so it hadn't raised any red flags. However, cashing in her business accounts would have alerted Sean, and that probably meant Parker intended to cash in the account as quickly as possible, hide the money and try to cover his tracks.

He nearly succeeded, too.

"Did my brother have anything to do with those papers?" she asked.

Reyes shook his head. "Doesn't look like it. Parker would have been the only one benefiting from this. But I think Parker did a darn good job convincing your brother you were crazy. That's why Sean pushed the judge so hard to have you recommitted. In his own warped way, Sean thought he was helping you and thereby helping himself and your company."

Jack saw the relief slide through her otherwise weary expression. This didn't mean her relationship with her brother was fine and dandy, but at least Sean hadn't endangered her.

"They put out the fire at your house," Reyes continued. "There's some serious damage. Everybody's already chipping in to get the repairs started. All of you can stay at my place until they're done. I can bunk with a friend to give you more room."

"Thank you." Jack meant it. He wasn't surprised by the man's generosity. Willow Ridge was home, and Reyes wasn't just his deputy but also his friend.

Alana stood the moment the medic finished, and even though she winced as she got off the examining table, she quickly made her way to them. "What about Dr. Bartolo?"

"He called me on the way over. Said it was on the news about Parker being killed. He says now that he's not in danger, he's coming back." Reyes paused. "He might have to face charges for his role in the diamond deal."

Maybe. But Jack was betting that if the doctor had any info about Parker being dirty, Bartolo could trade that for immunity or probation. Not a bad outcome considering the alternative. Parker would almost certainly have tried to kill Bartolo so he could eliminate anyone who could connect him to the diamonds.

"So we're really safe," Alana said.

"We're safe." Since she didn't look too steady on her feet, Jack eased his arm around her waist.

"I knew we were. I mean, you wouldn't have sent for

Joey if all weren't well. But it's nice to hear it aloud. To know that all the pieces are in place." She came up on her toes and kissed him.

Jack was pleased with the response, but he was sure that little display of affection surprised his deputy. Reyes fought back a smile. "I guess I should be going—"

"I'm in love with you, Jack," Alana said.

Now it was Jack's turn to be surprised. He stared at her.

She wasn't shaking. Her eyes were clear and focused. "When I was in that car with Parker and thought I was going to die, I regretted not telling you that I loved you. So I'm telling you now." She glanced at Reyes. "Sorry. I should have waited until Jack and I were alone, but I didn't want to waste another second."

Reyes continued to fight that smile. Jack didn't have a clue what to say or do. And Alana just stood there, waiting for a response.

From the other end of the hall, Jack heard familiar voices. He glanced over his shoulder and confirmed that Sheriff Tanner, Tessie and Joey had arrived. Alana stepped away to hurry to them, but Jack caught her arm.

He didn't want to waste any more time.

"I'm in love with you, too," he told her.

That stopped Alana. And it had Reyes moving quickly away.

Alana smiled. "You mean that?"

"With all my heart."

Her smile widened. "That's a lot." She hooked her arm around his neck and pulled him to her for a long, lingering kiss.

"Da-Da," Joey called out.

Jack wanted to hold his son, but he had to do something else first. Even if meant doing it in front of an audience.

"Will you marry me?" he asked Alana.

Despite Joey's chatter and the fact that Reyes, Sheriff Tanner and Tessie were only inches away, Alana didn't take her eyes off Jack. In her eyes, he could see her love for him.

He could also see their future.

"Yes, I'll marry you."

Jack hadn't realized he was holding his breath, waiting for that answer. This time, he was the one to initiate the kiss. He pulled her back into his arms and reminded her of just how much he loved her.

"Da-Da," Joey insisted. The little boy reached out, and both Alana and Jack took him, each of them cuddling an arm around Joey.

"I'll have to teach him how to say *Mama*," Tessie volunteered.

"Ma-Ma," Joey blurted out, and then clapped as if very proud of himself.

Jack was certainly proud of him. His son had more than enough room in his heart for both a mom and a dad. He didn't feel threatened that he was losing Joey. He felt…complete.

Tears started to shimmer in Alana's eyes, but Jack knew they were tears of pure happiness.

Joey had been the one to bring them together, but it was the love that Alana and he felt for each other that made them more than just Joey's parents. That love had made them something Jack had always longed for.

A family.

* * * * *

We hope you enjoyed reading

Stranger on the Island

by *New York Times* bestselling author

LISA JACKSON

and

Secret Delivery

by *USA TODAY* bestselling author

DELORES FOSSEN.

Both were originally Harlequin® series stories!

From passionate, suspenseful and dramatic
love stories to inspirational or historical,
Harlequin offers different lines to
satisfy every romance reader.

New books in each line are available every month.

The whole desperate plan began simply as a last-ditch attempt to save his life. He never intended for anyone to get hurt. That day, not long after Thanksgiving, he walked into the bank full of hope. It was the first time he'd ever asked for a loan. It was also the first time he'd ever seen executive loan officer Carla Richmond.

When he tapped at her open doorway, she looked up from that big desk of hers. He thought she was too young and pretty with her big blue eyes and all that curly chestnut-brown hair to make the decision as to whether he lived or died.

She had a great smile as she got to her feet to offer him a seat.

He felt so out of place in her plush office that he stood in the doorway nervously kneading the brim of his worn baseball cap for a moment before stepping in. As he did, her blue-eyed gaze took in his ill-fitting clothing hanging on his rangy body, his bad haircut, his large, weathered hands.

He told himself that she'd already made up her mind before he even sat down. She didn't give men like him a second look—let alone money. Like his father always said, bankers never gave dough to poor people who actually needed it. They just helped their rich friends.

Right away Carla Richmond made him feel small with her questions about his employment record, what he had for collateral, why he needed the money and how he planned to repay it. He'd recently lost one crappy job and was in the process of starting another temporary one, and all he had to show for the years he'd worked hard labor since high school was an old pickup and a pile of bills.

He took the forms she handed him and thanked her, knowing he wasn't going to bother filling them in. On the way out of her office, he balled them up and dropped them in the trash. All the way to his pickup, he mentally kicked himself for being such a fool. What had he expected?

No one was going to give him money, even to save his life—especially some woman in a suit behind a big desk in an air-conditioned office. It didn't matter that she didn't have a clue how desperate he really was. All she'd seen when she'd looked at him was a loser. To think that he'd bought a new pair of jeans with the last of his cash and borrowed a too-large button-up shirt from a former coworker for this meeting.

After climbing into his truck, he sat for a moment, too scared and sick at heart to start the engine. The worst part was the thought of going home and telling Jesse. The way his luck was going, she would walk out on him. Not that he could blame her, since his gambling had gotten them into this mess.

He thought about blowing off work, since his new job was only temporary anyway, and going straight to the bar. Then he reminded himself that he'd spent the last of his money on the jeans. He couldn't even afford a beer. His own fault, he reminded himself. He'd only made things worse when he'd gone to a loan shark for cash and then stupidly gambled the money, thinking he could make back what he owed and then some when he won. He'd been so sure his luck had changed for the better when he'd met Jesse.

Last time the two thugs had come to collect the interest on the loan, they'd left him bleeding in the dirt outside his rented house. They would be back any day.

With a curse, he started the pickup. A cloud of exhaust blew out the back as he headed home to face Jesse with the bad news. Asking for a loan had been a long shot, but still he couldn't help thinking about the disappointment he'd see in her eyes when he told her. They'd planned to go out tonight for an expensive dinner with the loan money to celebrate.

As he drove home, his humiliation began to fester like a sore that just wouldn't heal. Had he known even then how this was going to end? Or was he still telling himself he was just a nice guy who'd made some mistakes, had some bad luck and gotten involved with the wrong people?

Don't miss
Christmas Ransom *by B.J. Daniels,*
available December 2022 wherever
Harlequin books and ebooks are sold.

Harlequin.com

SPECIAL EXCERPT FROM

(H)HARLEQUIN
SPECIAL EDITION

*By the book success story Alexandra Herrera's got it
all mapped out. But when her birth father leaves her
an unexpected inheritance, she impulsively walks away
from her entire life! And now that she's snowed in with
West Wright, she learns that lightning really can strike
twice. So much, in fact, that the sparks between them
could melt any ice storm...if only they'd let them!*

Read on for a sneak peek at
The Christmas Cottage,
*the latest in the Wild Rose Sisters series
by* New York Times *bestselling author Christine Rimmer!*

So that was an option, just to say that she needed her alone
time and West would intrude on that. Everyone would
understand. But then he would stay at the Heartwood Inn
and that really wasn't right...

And what about just telling everyone that it would be
awkward because she and West had shared a one-night
stand? There was nothing unacceptable about what she
and West had done. No one here would judge her. Alex
and West were both adults, both single. It was nobody's
business that they'd had sex on a cold winter night when
he'd needed a friend and she was the only one around
to hold out a hand. It was one of those things that just
happen sometimes.

It would be weird, though, to share that information
with the family. Weird and awkward. And Alex still
hoped she would never have to go there.

"Alex?" Weston spoke again, his voice so smooth and deep and way too sexy.

"Hmm?"

"You ever plan on answering my question?"

"Absolutely." It came out sounding aggressive, almost angry. She made herself speak more cordially. "Yes. Honestly. There's plenty of room here. You're staying in the cottage. It's settled."

"You're so bossy…" He said that kind of slowly—slowly and also naughtily—and she sincerely hoped her cheeks weren't cherry red.

"Weston." She said his name sternly as a rebuke.

"Alexandra," he mocked.

"That's a yes, right?" Now she made her voice pleasant, even a little too sweet. "You'll take the second bedroom."

"Yes, I will. And it's good to talk to you, Alex. At last." Did he really have to be so…ironic? It wasn't like she hadn't thought more than once of reaching out to him, checking in with him to see how he was holding up. But back in January, when they'd said goodbye, he'd seemed totally on board with cutting it clean. "Alex? You still there?"

"Uh, yes. Great."

"See you day after tomorrow. I'll be flying down with Easton."

"Perfect. See you then." She heard the click as he disconnected the call.

Don't miss
The Christmas Cottage *by Christine Rimmer,*
available November 2022 wherever
Harlequin Special Edition books and ebooks are sold.

Harlequin.com

Love Harlequin romance?

DISCOVER.

Be the first to find out about promotions, news and exclusive content!

 Facebook.com/HarlequinBooks

 Twitter.com/HarlequinBooks

 Instagram.com/HarlequinBooks

 Pinterest.com/HarlequinBooks

You Tube YouTube.com/HarlequinBooks

ReaderService.com

EXPLORE.

Sign up for the Harlequin e-newsletter and download a free book from any series at **TryHarlequin.com**

CONNECT.

Join our Harlequin community to share your thoughts and connect with other romance readers!
Facebook.com/groups/HarlequinConnection

HARLEQUIN

Heartfelt or thrilling, passionate or uplifting—Harlequin is more than just happily-ever-after.

With twelve different series to choose from and new books available every month, you are sure to find stories that will move you, uplift you, inspire and delight you.

SIGN UP FOR THE HARLEQUIN NEWSLETTER

Be the first to hear about great new reads and exciting offers!

Harlequin.com/newsletters

Get 4 FREE REWARDS!

We'll send you 2 FREE Books plus 2 FREE Mystery Gifts.

FREE
Value Over
$20

Both the **Harlequin® Special Edition** and **Harlequin® Heartwarming™** series feature compelling novels filled with stories of love and strength where the bonds of friendship, family and community unite.